...nties...

...and Leigh Vaughn have
...o raise mo... ...r friend's
...utting a basket full of spicy date ideas
... auction. But who will bid? And what, *exactly*,
will the highest bidder be getting?

Margot is hoping her college crush buys her basket.
Too bad her arch-enemy, Clint Barrows, beats
him to it...

Leigh doesn't have a buyer in mind when she creates
her auction offering. Good thing—because even
after sharing her basket, she still has no idea who
her admirer really is...

Who knew being in a wedding party came
with *these* kinds of perks?

Don't miss

MYSTERY DATE
by Crystal Green
(September 2013)

LEAD ME ON

BY
CRYSTAL GREEN

MILLS &
BOON

First published in Great Britain 2013
by Mills & Boon, an imprint of Harlequin (UK) Limited,
Eton House, 18-24 Paradise Road, Richmond, Surrey TW9 1SR

© Chris Marie Green 2013

ISBN: 978 0 263 90315 7
ebook ISBN: 978 1 408 99686 7

14-0713

Harlequin (UK) policy is to use papers that are natural, renewable and recyclable products and made from wood grown in sustainable forests. The logging and manufacturing processes conform to the legal environmental regulations of the country of origin.

Printed and bound in Spain
by Blackprint CPI, Barcelona

Crystal Green lives near Las Vegas, where she writes for the Mills & Boon® Cherish™ and Blaze® lines. She loves to read, overanalyze movies and TV programs, practice yoga, and travel when she can. You can read more about her at www.crystal-green.com, where she has a blog and contests. Also, you can follow her on Twitter @CrystalGreenMe.

To Jolie—your expertise of storytelling
and passion for knowledge inspire me!

1

THE VIDEO HAD been posted on YouTube that morning, and Margot Walker was determined to prove that it hadn't bothered her one bit.

So as she sat in a booth in the Avila Grande Suites' bar with her two best friends, she calmly sipped her Midori Sour, leaning back against the leather seat. Around them, conversation buzzed from a few other happy-hour hotel guests—none of whom were a part of the Phi Rho Mu fraternity and Tau Epsilon Gamma sorority ten-year reunion that was taking place in the hotel this weekend.

"Margot," Leigh said, leaning her elbows on the table, her blond braid hanging over a shoulder. "Are you sure you're up for this? Nobody would blame you if you decided to bug out and go home."

Margot carefully set her drink down on the polished table. Dani, with her curly red hair, porcelain skin to die for and a peach-hued shirt, was nodding in agreement beside Leigh.

"Why put yourself through this?"

"Because I'm not going to let a ridiculous prank chase me away," Margot said. "Yes, some bored moron posted that video late last night, hoping to get my goat. Yes, everyone is probably going to laugh at me because of what's on it. But I don't care. No one's keeping me away from meeting up with my friends after all these years."

"You're talking like it's just any old video." Leigh picked up her beer bottle and reclined in her seat, a sexy, laid-back cowgirl in her tight pink-plaid Western shirt. "It was bad enough when it was circulated in college. Now, to have it show up again…?"

"It reflects worse on whoever did this than it does on me," Margot said. And it almost sounded like she believed it.

After all, it *was* humiliating. A dimly lit fraternity room. A couch. Heavy breathing. Her giving in to the one guy she should've never said yes to.

The jerk Clint Barrows.

As Margot pushed a rush of heat back—she was angry, which was why she was blushing and flushing—Dani laughed in amazement.

"That video embarrassed the hell out of you the first time and you never forgave Clint Barrows for it. And don't lie to us, Marg, because we know that's the truth."

"As I said, I got over it." But, when a group of white-collar men wandered into the bar, she momentarily stiffened, waiting to see if she knew them. Waiting to see if they would laugh their asses off at her.

But…no. Just some random guys here on business or whatever.

She forced herself not to hang back in the booth. She was here to show whoever had put up that video that she was an adult, impervious to the slings and arrows of juvenile jokes.

And what a joke it had been. A prank. A camera hidden in a fraternity house during a party one night—the night she'd finally dropped all her hard-to-get flirting with Clint Barrows and given in to his cowboy Romeo charm, going to his room to "watch movies." But movies were the last thing on their minds, and she'd told him that she would kill him if he let anyone know that they were doing anything more than hanging out and eating popcorn.

She hadn't expected to be filmed while saying that and getting hot and heavy with the campus lothario.

Very hot and heavy, although not all-the-way hot and heavy, thank God.

To think, she'd actually liked Clint before she'd gone off with him, had been attracted to him even if he'd had a heck of a lot of women on that secondhand couch and had watched quite a few "movies."

But there was just something about him that had drawn Margot in, even though she'd known he was bad news. Something in his eyes that sparkled dangerously, daring her, inviting her to come on a big adventure she'd never regret. And no guy had ever made her skin tingle with just a look, made her belly flip just at the sound of his voice....

She'd been taken in, though, made sport of. Hunted and caught in the lens of a camera. She'd known it when she'd seen the red eye of the device in the near-dark just as he'd been undoing the buttons on her shirt.

She'd smacked the ever-lovin' charm out of him and left the room, too shocked to even think to destroy the tape. Too... Well, she would've said *hurt* if she'd cared enough.

And she didn't. Really. Because, even when he'd sent an email to her the next morning, telling her that he hadn't known about any camera, that it was his roommate who'd set it up, and that the tape had been demolished, she hadn't answered. Her humiliation had only flared when she'd heard that the video was making the rounds around campus.

Sure, some good sources had backed up Clint's story that he wasn't the one who'd set up or circulated that tape, but when she really thought about it, that wasn't the true reason she couldn't stand him. She'd been caught with him, the conquest king, on film, telling him that their night should be kept a secret. What a laugh riot that must've been for the video's audience before seeing the fireworks that had begun between them.

First off, Margot didn't like being the butt of any joke. Second, she could imagine Clint basking in the glory of the video—proof that he had finally gotten her to bend her will to him. Third, she never wanted to be just a number for *any* guy.

She'd spent college playing hard-to-get for a lot of boys, and her reputation and pride had sure taken a hit after the scandal. And *his* reputation had only grown, his college nickname, "Stud," reaching epic proportions in their social circles for the rest of their senior year.

Her dislike of him had grown with every knowing glance she'd received at every social event after that.

But then summer had come and life had really started. A decade had passed since, and the video had become just one of those ridiculous college mistakes that no one mentioned anymore. It'd been all but forgotten.

Until last night.

Just as she'd been checking her email this morning, all packed and ready to hit the road for this reunion between her sorority and its fraternity counterpart, she'd found messages from her sorority sisters about the video. No one knew who'd posted it, but Margot's first thought went to Clint.

Had he lied about destroying the tape way back then because he thought he could get into her good graces… or her pants…so he could close the deal? And had he aired it now, just because he thought it'd be funny for the reunion?

She wished he'd walk into the bar so she could face him down and tell him to grow up. She was so far beyond him and that night.

As she rested her hand on her glass of Midori Sour, she smiled at her friends. "Why bring that crap up again when we have more important things to talk about? As in, auction baskets for this weekend?"

Leigh caught her cue and shot a glance to Dani. They'd all met in the lobby about fifteen minutes ago and had just sat and started chatting when the scandal had reared its ugly head again. Margot had already told them she was over it on the phone during her drive there, but leave it to Dani and Leigh to question her.

Anyway, when they'd first seen each other, hugging and laughing, she and Leigh had sprung their own surprise on Dani, telling her about the charity auction the two of them were throwing tomorrow night because they wanted her to have the big wedding she'd always yearned for. It'd be an All-American college-reunion good time that wasn't going to be ruined just because some ass—*had* it been Clint?—had decided to pep up the event with a memory Margot would've rather forgotten.

Once again, she thought of the cowboy, with his denim-blue eyes, his lackadaisical way of watching her walk through one of the many parties their fraternity and sorority had thrown together. Then, just as quickly, she tamped down that spark in her belly.

Jerk.

"Guess what I'm going to call my auction basket," she said, ignoring thoughts of him.

Dani was strangely quiet, just as she'd been when Leigh and Margot had launched the surprise on her, come to think of it.

But Leigh was already talking, leaving the video behind, although Margot suspected it'd come up again.

"Lord knows what you conjured up, Marg."

Her smile grew. "'Around the Girl in Eighty Ways.'"

She waited for them to give her that "come again?" look that she'd gotten so used to back in college when she'd whipped up similar harebrained ideas.

And, yep, there it was.

Come again?

Leigh took the bait first. "How does going around the girl in eighty ways fit in an auction basket?"

"I'm betting it'll fit very nicely on auction night. Hopefully even more than once." Margot shot Leigh a saucy grin, while Dani just lifted an eyebrow at Margot.

Then Dani said, "I'm not sure about all this...."

Leigh nudged Dani good-naturedly. "You've got to hear Margot out. She came down here, even in the midst of a pride-spankin', just for you, Dan."

"Thanks," Margot said, narrowing her eyes at Leigh. She spoke to Dani. "This is just the first of many gifts for our bride-to-be."

"But I don't need—"

"It's not a matter of need or not need," Margot said, on a roll. See—it wasn't so hard to forget about that video. Sort of. "You used to talk about the perfect wedding all the time. *Everyone* wants it to happen for you at the end of this year in the huge, grand way you used to describe to us."

"You were our Wedding Girl," Leigh added, giving Dani's arm a friendly, light squeeze.

Dani said nothing, and Margot caught Leigh's gaze. Sure, they'd talked about whether or not they were being too intrusive, assuming Dani would want their help, since her funds were too low to afford that dream wedding. But, my God, this was *Dani*. And this was their chance to help her achieve the fantasies she'd collected in her wedding scrapbook—pictures of frothy white dresses and creamy cakes, blooming flowers and a bride and groom who couldn't take their eyes off each other.

If someone good like Dani didn't deserve it all, then who did?

"You've already talked about this auction to everyone?" Dani finally asked.

Across the table, Leigh looked a little sheepish as she put down her beer. "We might've secretly suggested it to the sisters on our email loop."

Dani was flushing, and Margot wasn't sure if she was embarrassed or angry with them. But Dani never got angry.

When she spoke, she made Margot rethink that.

"So everyone knows that poor me, the lowly caterer and not the Paula Deen she aimed to be back when she majored in home ec, can't afford a decent wedding? And her fiancé is only a small-estate manager, not the business mogul he wanted to become, so that means they can't possibly afford even fancy flower arrangements?" She laughed. "I suppose that's not too embarrassing."

Margot glanced at Leigh again. *Whoops.*

Leigh seemed just as helpless as Margot as she peeled away the label of her beer. "Can I just put things in perspective and volunteer that Margot's video is going to take all the 'embarrassing' out of the reunion for you, Dan? That's what everyone'll be talking about."

To Leigh's credit, she was merely doing her best. Margot followed suit.

"Once again, Leigh, thanks so much." She smiled at Dani. "No one thinks you're destitute. It's only that your wedding plans were legendary in the sorority. Hell, your nickname during pledging was 'Hearts.' We'd talk about getting together for the ceremony someday and how it'd be a time when we could all celebrate together."

"It was going to be a milestone," Leigh added.

Margot went on, and it was just like the old days, when she would get a lightbulb idea going and Leigh would join in, eventually followed by Dani.

"The wedding is as much for us as it is for you," she said. "It means everything because you're marrying the guy from our counterpart fraternity, and everyone knew you were going to get together with him even before the two of you knew it. It's a big deal for all of us Rhos and Taus."

Dani finally smiled, probably because of the memories.

Times like the spring-break trip to Cabo—a Bacchanalia that had sworn Margot, Leigh and Dani off booze for…well, weeks. It had been just one of many adventures they'd shared as sorority sisters and Margot would never forget them. The three of them had grown up together during some very pivotal years, then tossed their graduation caps in the air as one, letting them rain down with the joy of exploring all the roads ahead.

Back then, Margot had nursed so many ambitions— to travel the world, to write books—and she'd done *all* of it in the time from there to here.

But dreams could last only so long.

She ate the maraschino cherry in her Midori Sour, yet it didn't taste as good as it used to—not after the bad news she'd gotten last month about how her latest "single girl on the go" travel book had done.

Or, more to the point, *hadn't* done.

As usual, Margot tried not to show how upset she was. She'd been keeping the news to herself that her publishing company hadn't wanted to go to contract after she closed out this most recent book. Surely something else was bound to come along.

Wouldn't it?

Dani was talking. "But…I still don't know about raising money for my wedding."

Leigh said, "Don't they have money dances at receptions? We'd just be doing the asking *before* the wedding."

"Besides, it's not any old auction," Margot was quick to add, dangling the cherry stem between her fingers. "This is something everyone will love. A basket auction, just like they used to do in the old days at picnics. You know, when the girls packed a lunch in a basket and tied a telltale ribbon around the handle so the boy she was crushing on would know it was hers and take her out?"

"Days of innocence," Leigh said in her ranch-girl drawl. Country-singer cool, she rested her free arm over the top of the booth. She seemed as down-to-earth as they came—if you didn't know her very well. Leigh was the type to come off as earthy, even though she was a rising star at The Food Network with a new show that Margot could describe only as "sensuous farmhouse cooking"—like putting Faith Hill in Martha Stewart's kitchen.

For a second, Margot could almost see her friends as they used to be: Leigh, forty pounds heavier, laughing at the nickname—"Cushions"—that everyone had given her, even while inside, Margot knew, Leigh hadn't found it so hilarious. And Dani, a home ec major like Leigh, known as the romantic "Hearts," who used to love matchmaking at the dinner parties she put together.

But Margot had them beat. She'd been an endangered species on their rural San Joaquin Valley campus—an English major among all the agricultural business majors and local cowboys and cowgirls. She'd never minded standing out, though. Leigh, who'd been her dorm roomie, and Dani, who'd lived down the hall, had talked Margot into joining Tau Epsilon Gamma, and she'd never regretted a day of it.

Even if her parents hadn't been quite as excited.

Sororities are for girls who'll never find a day of independence in their lives, her dad had said. *Don't you want to have a mind of your own?*

Of course she did, but joining the Taus hadn't quashed the free spirit her hippy-minded parents had raised her to be as they'd moved from town to town, "experiencing all life has to offer." They'd take temporary jobs and then one day jerk her out of school before she could find a best friend. Sometimes she'd wondered if they cared about how she fit into their whole "see the world!" philosophy…or if she'd just been one more item on their bucket lists.

But she'd found a whole lot of friends all on her own, thank you very much.

And *that's* what mattered.

Margot searched Dani's gray-hued gaze. Was her friend about to come around to the idea of the auction? She and Leigh hadn't meant to mortify her; when

Dani had told them during their own private yearly get-together a few months ago that she and Riley couldn't afford the wedding she'd been planning since she was a little girl, it'd looked as if her heart was about to break.

Or was Dani going to tell them to go to hell?

"Dani," Margot said, reaching across the table to enclose her hand, which rested by her untouched wine spritzer. "We can call off the auction if you want. Really."

Leigh looked as if she was holding her breath, clearly just as torn about this. Since she'd lost weight last year, she'd made a pact with Margot to be more adventurous than ever. Hence, this basket thing. Even though she'd always seemed confident, she hadn't been anywhere near it. Now, though, Leigh was different, and she was going to take her new attitude into the bedroom for the very first time in her life with this auction. She'd vowed to do things like making love with the lights on and playing all the bedroom games she'd never allowed herself to play.

And Margot… Well, *she* was pretty much already one of those girls, never settling into a relationship, since there was so much to do out in the world, so much to see and experience. Putting together a sinful basket would be one more adventure for the adventuress— and it'd be a way to say "See? That damned YouTube video isn't going to cow me" to whoever had posted it.

Clint?

Truthfully, there was a bonus in the basket auction. This weekend would also be a chance to reconnect with her old boyfriend, Brad, maybe relive some good old times.…

Margot stopped herself. These days, *she* wasn't as

confident as everyone thought. She felt like a real fail-ure at the moment, with her less-than-bestselling books.

Most Likely to Succeed?

Not so much anymore. But she was damned if she was going to let anyone see the self-doubt. Nope—she had taken the lead in putting together this auction, and she wanted it to go off without a hitch, video or no. She would do it for Dani's sake and…

Well, to let everyone know that nothing was going to get her down.

"Dani?" Leigh asked. "Do you want us to cancel the auction?"

A second passed, and Margot maintained her poker face, even as her heart beat against her ribs.

But then Dani smiled. "I'd hate to ruin anyone's fun…."

"I knew you'd be on board," Leigh said, beaming.

Margot raised her drink, even though she thought she still detected some reluctance in Dani. "To a hell of an auction, then?"

"I'll drink to that." Leigh toasted, too. "Then again, I've got the feeling we'll be drinking to a lot of *thats* this weekend."

Dani brought her spritzer glass up as well, and they all clinked, then threw their drinks down the hatch.

When they finished, Margot noticed that the room was filling up. Businessmen cluttered the mahogany bar, loosening their ties and glancing around.

When the waitress stopped by to check on the three women, Leigh ordered another round of drinks. Then the server went to the next booth, the occupant obscured by the strip of stained glass edging the top of the seats.

Obviously, someone had slipped in, unnoticed, during their conversation, because the waitress took that order, too. Couldn't be anyone they knew, Margot thought, or they would've said hi.

"So, Margot," Leigh began, "how about that Around the Girl in Eighty Ways basket?"

"What, are you going to steal ideas from me?" Margot asked playfully.

"Like I'd need to."

They'd always tried to top each other in grades and at social events, and they'd made each other challenge themselves, too, Margot thought. Too bad she didn't have Leigh around more these days.

She brushed off the pessimism. There wasn't room for it this weekend. "The title pretty much says it all, doesn't it? I have little pieces of paper with different... scenarios...on them. Whoever bids the highest can enact one or more of them during our date."

"Whoa," Leigh said. "Brassy. I thought I'd make mine a little vaguer, you know? Just in case it goes to someone who doesn't really appeal."

"Oh, I'm going to make sure it goes to someone who appeals to me. But not to worry—the scenarios I've chosen can be interpreted in various ways. They can be as naughty as I want...or as nice."

"You devil," Leigh said.

"Or angel." Margot winked and took another drink.

"Just exactly what kind of scenarios are they?" Dani asked.

Behind them, in the other booth, someone cleared his throat.

Margot barely heard, because she was concentrating on Dani. She loved to see that her friend was warming to this basket idea. "*Scenarios.* You know me. My books were all about seeking fun for the well-traveled girl, so I've got several adventures already researched and tested."

She hesitated. Her books *were* all about seeking fun? Had she really just used the past tense?

Leigh's olive-colored eyes lit up. "I can see where this is going."

"Can you?"

"Please, Marg," Dani said. "Even a few months ago, you were talking about seeing Brad here at the reunion. I think we can figure out that you're going to make sure *he's* the one who bids the highest, so you can rekindle that flame you had in junior summer break."

"Did you tell him about your basket yet?" Leigh asked.

Margot thought that she could finally taste a hint of the thick, decadent juice that had come with the maraschino cherry. "I had no idea that Brad was going to be here," she said, all sweetness and cluelessness.

"Right," Dani said.

"As if you didn't know he got divorced recently," Leigh added.

He was the only guy Margot had connected with in a half-serious way. Okay, the relationship had lasted only about three months, during a summer when he'd taken off from Cal-U and interned on a local dairy near Chico, where she'd been staying with a cousin during break. But he'd lit her teenage fire on more than one occasion.

What she'd give for a little of that fire now.

She glanced around to see if any of her classmates had noticed she was here yet.

Dani cleared her throat. "Riley told me he heard Brad's going to break away from work this weekend. He'll be here, all right."

Leigh waggled her eyebrows. "You plan to have a special mark on your basket so he can bid on it?"

"A burst of gold and silver stars." Margot smiled at the waitress as she brought the new round of drinks.

Leigh murmured, "A burst of stars, just like he'll see after Margot—"

She cut Leigh off. "When did Riley say Brad was coming, Dan?"

"I think he's here already, playing golf with Riley and some of the guys before things really get started."

Everyone would be here by tomorrow for the homecoming football game, then a casual meal and the auction, followed on Sunday by a more formal dinner before they all headed off in their different directions again.

Leigh leaned back in the booth, surveying Margot. "Honestly, I never really saw Brad's appeal. He always reminded me of the type of guy who checks himself out in windows when he walks by them. He was kind of self-involved, if you ask me."

"He was not." He was smart and ambitious, going places. Margot had related to that. Plus, he'd been in the area, and they'd gotten to know each other without all their Greek brothers and sisters around.

Dani was leaning her elbows on the table, looking at Leigh. "I never thought Brad was that hot, either."

Hot?

The word conjured up a maddening image of Clint Barrows. That damn video had shoved him into her mind and was making him stay there beyond a decent hello. God, she hoped he wouldn't be at the reunion.

Margot took another drink, as if she could wash him away.

Dani started to slide out of the booth. "Don't hate

me, but I'm really bushed, you all. I catered a big fortieth birthday party last night. Can we meet up later?"

When Margot started to protest, Leigh stood to leave, too. "Don't hate *me,* but I've got a script to look over and approve tonight so we can hit the ground running at the studio on Monday."

"Lightweights," Margot muttered. She wasn't nearly ready to hole up in her room yet, even if her classmates would soon be here to tease her about the video.

Bring them on.

Leigh seemed impressed. "You're actually staying here?"

"To face the lions when they arrive? You'd better believe it. I want to get this over with. Besides, if Brad's already in town, he might drop in for a post-golf drink."

"Okay, Braveheart." Leigh smiled. "How about dinner with us later?"

"No doubt."

Dani just grinned again, swinging her small, patchwork purse over her shoulder. They both waved as they walked away, and it wasn't four seconds later that Margot started rethinking this Braveheart stuff.

Did she really want to suffer through the ribbing all alone?

But it wasn't in her nature to wimp out, so she took another drink.

A deep voice behind her made her almost spray the Midori out of her mouth.

"I've always wondered what'd be in your basket."

She knew that voice, even years later.

Clint Freakin' Barrows.

2

INEXPLICABLY, A DELICIOUS shiver danced up Margot's back, just like fingers running over bare skin then stopping at her neck, stroking until the fine hairs stood on heated end. And that wasn't the only part of her body that responded; she went tight nearly everywhere, from her sensitized nipples to the clenching of her belly.

She also felt a sharp ache between her legs, but she chased it away.

She blew out a breath, wishing her stomach wasn't all scrambled. Then she turned around to find the one and only Clint Barrows leaning off the edge of the bench seat, his arms resting on his thighs, his cowboy hat tipped back on his head.

A slow melt started inside her as she took in his grin. This wasn't the college kid she remembered. Not exactly. The Clint Barrows who'd lured her to his room that one night had been cute—no doubts there—but now?

Now he had shoulders *this* wide under his white T-shirt. And his thighs hadn't been so muscular under faded jeans. And there was some age to him—smile lines around his light blue eyes and hair that seemed to be an even thicker golden mess under his hat.

Like a fine bourbon, he'd aged well.

Damn him for looking so good. Damn her for feeling a little dizzy just from standing near him.

How…after all these years…?

And, after what he'd done?

"You've got some gall," she said.

He laughed. "Because I'm saying hi?"

She just stared at him. Talk about thickheaded.

"Darlin'," he said, clearly knowing that she was talking about the video. "Don't go accusing me of anything. First off, I don't have the time to be digging through old videos and sharing them with the world. Second, I destroyed that tape."

"Well, then, I guess it magically came to life again and found itself a cozy home on YouTube. You're in the clear, *Stud*."

He laughed once more, smooth and low, and her clit gave a vicious little twist.

Oh, come on—she hadn't gone without a man *that* long. Or maybe she had. Now that she thought about it, it'd been months. She'd been locked away, pounding out a draft of her most recent book, which had given her more trouble than most. The wildness and joy just didn't come as easily as it used to. Maybe that's why her book sale numbers were going down….

She lifted a finger at him. "If you're not here to rub that video in, then why did you show up? I didn't think reunions would be your scene."

"Just call it a last-minute decision."

Cryptic, and so Clint Barrows. And with that grin of his, she wanted to solve whatever mystery he was putting out there.

Or did she?

"Come on," he said. "Why don't you just sit down and talk about this."

"Are you kidding? *First,* I don't believe your story. *Second,* I think we'll get along much better if I'm on one side of the room and you're on the other."

He sighed. "Have it your way, then. For now."

For now?

Shaking her head, she grabbed her Fendi purse and got out the hand-worked leather wallet she'd bought in Florence once upon a time. Earlier, she'd told the girls she would be taking care of the bar tab, even though she wasn't sure she could afford many flights of generosity like this in the future.

"So about those baskets…" Clint said.

Once a tease, always a tease.

"Don't even start."

"Start what? If you recall, there're things I start that you have a problem ending."

"See? Rubbing it in. I knew you wouldn't be able to resist."

"Give me a chance here, Shakespeare."

Her libido gave another hot jerk. She'd liked how he used to call her English author names the few times they'd actually talked during parties. He'd amused her—and she'd been turned on that a cowboy had known his literature, to tell the truth.

But that was before she'd found out he'd only wanted to set her up for an adolescent joke.

"You think this is all so funny," she said.

He sobered and, for a second, she thought he was actually being sincere.

"I don't think it's a bit funny. But—"

She slapped her cash on the table and left, even while

every cell in her body was pulling her toward his booth, vibrating with the curiosity she hadn't been able to fully appease on that long-ago night.

But if there was one thing Margot would guard until the end, it was pride.

Luckily, that's when she heard her name being called from the other side of the bar.

A group of fraternity brothers, including Dani's fiancé, Riley, had just walked in, and she recognized her ex-boyfriend Brad among them.

Or, at least, she thought she did.

He looked like one of the businessmen at the bar—creased khakis and a crisp, long-sleeved shirt. His dark hair was neatly trimmed, unlike a certain cowboy's that looked as if he turned tail and ran every time a barber came near.

Brad lifted a hand in greeting to her, giving her a friendly smile. He didn't seem to care about the video. None of them did, maybe because Riley had told them to back off during their golf game.

Margot waved back, then waited for the rush of heat to swamp her horny body, just as it had with Clint.

Waiting…

Waiting…

It only happened again when she heard Clint's voice behind her.

"You'd best go to Brad," he said. "Good ol' dependable Brad…."

She felt Brad watching her from across the room, and she didn't want to give him the impression that she was taking up where she'd left off in that video with Clint Barrows.

"You can walk away now," Clint said. "But I'll be seeing you later."

"Dare to dream," she said over her shoulder.

And she left him with that, his laughter skimming across her skin, heating her to blazing for no good reason she could think of.

Except for the million and one tongues of flame licking at her, daring her to turn around and scratch the itch that'd never quite gone away.

CLINT WATCHED HER leave, enjoying the sway of her hips beneath her tight pants, which were tucked into high boots, giving her the kind of flair you'd normally see with a hoity-toity princess out for a ride on an English saddle.

He'd always been a legs and ass man and, thanks to those clothes, both were on cock-teasing display with Margot Walker.

She got to him in a lot of ways, with her long, layered dark brown hair that was somehow classy and gypsylike at the same time. With pale sea-hued eyes that always seemed to be shining with a sense of humor that also came out in her carefree laugh. Her delicate features—a slightly turned-up nose, high cheekbones, a heart-shaped face—reminded him of one of the wood fairy figurines that his mom used to keep on the top shelf in the family room. Statues that had stayed there even years after she'd died, when Clint was just learning to break in horses.

Dignified, delicate, yet slightly wild. That was Margot Walker to a T.

Something fisted in his gut, reminding him of how much he'd wanted her ten years ago. The smart girl who knew how to put down the books and have fun. The life of every party, who lit up a room just by walking into it.

And that was the exact reason he'd been over the

moon when she'd come up to his room with him that
night.

The thing of it was, he'd genuinely been aiming to
watch a movie with her, since they'd been chatting about
The Untouchables down at the party and he'd owned
a copy.

Her willingness to be alone with him had stunned
him, because Margot had always seemed untouchable
herself, the only girl who never gave him the time of
day…until she'd let down her guard in his room.

At first, he'd sat a decent distance from her on that
Naugahyde couch. But, slowly, they'd gotten closer, as
if attraction had pulled them together like magnets. And
by the time Kevin Costner and Andy Garcia went to the
train station to intercept a witness for their case against
Al Capone, his gaze was on Margot, not the screen.

And she had been watching him, too, with a softness
in her eyes he'd never seen before.

"God help you if you tell anyone about this," she said
before they'd come together.

He'd never been swept away by a girl before, but
this one night, it'd happened. And as they kissed—
her breath in his ear as she whispered his name—he'd
thought that this was it. Margot Walker was the one
woman who could make him think there was no one
else, just as his dad had thought the same about his mom
when they were both alive.

Then, unbeknownst to him, she'd seen the camera,
and before he could ask what had gotten her so upset,
she'd slapped him, pulled her shirt together, angry as
hell, and bolted out of the room without telling him
what was wrong.

As confused as he was, he hadn't gone after her.

And he hadn't noticed the camera hidden in the corner.

Soon afterward, he'd gone back down to the party to see if she was still there, but she'd left him in the dust, wondering what he'd done.

It wasn't until the next morning, when his roommate, Jay Halverson, the fraternity historian, couldn't hold it in any longer, that he found out what'd happened: Jay had seen Clint downstairs, making inroads with the one girl who'd always eluded him. He'd bet that Clint would pull through and bring her back to his room and that the moment should be recorded for the brother-hood's posterity.

Clint's blood had been boiling, but when Jay had cued up the video and shown it to him, they'd come to blows. As collateral damage, the video was decimated, smashed to pieces.

But it didn't matter, because Jay had already made a copy and had given it to some of his friends to watch.

Of course, Margot had sent Clint an email about it that night but he hadn't seen the message until after the fight with Jay. The content was curt and crisp, barely hiding the hurt that he knew she must've felt. He'd writ-ten back that he'd destroyed the tape, leaving out the part where Jay had actually been the one who'd filmed her. But she never answered.

Especially after the video made its way from the TV of one fraternity member to the next.

The copy was never found and, for more reasons than the video, Jay was eventually blackballed. But that didn't give Clint another chance with Margot. It didn't make him forget her, either, as he ran the cutting horse ranch he loved just a half hour away from Avila Grande, California, and their alma mater.

As he sat in that booth now, watching her walk to Brad, he thought how sad it was that he'd actually come to understand why Margot had reacted the way she did: she didn't intend to be just an item on a list, or a person a man would forget when he moved on to the next girl. She'd never been merely one of the crowd, and she'd gone out and proved it to the world with that sophisticated career of hers.

And she hadn't wanted to be the fool, caught on tape as Clint "conquered" her.

Who would?

Seeing her today, a disturbingly hot woman who grabbed him and twisted him inside out, Clint was fascinated all over again. Not that she'd given him the chance to explain, but he'd come to this reunion for one reason and one reason only.

To set matters straight and make it up to her.

He hadn't planned on coming, not when there was so much going on with his younger twin brothers and the ranch. But when he'd been told the video had found new life on YouTube, he'd blown a gasket, immediately sending an email to his fraternity brothers saying that if they razzed Margot about it this weekend, they'd answer to him.

So far, it looked like they were respecting his requests. Margot stood at the bar with Brad Harrington, laughing and pushing a hank of that stylish gypsy hair away from her face. She was saying hi to the group that had just walked into the dark-wooded room. From this distance, it was pretty obvious that Brad was being amiable enough, but...

Could it be that he wasn't really in to her?

Nah. Clint couldn't imagine a red-blooded male

anywhere within the boundaries of the U.S. of A. who wouldn't be eating up her charms.

As Clint toyed with his shot glass, one man broke away from the crowd and moved toward the booth. Clint nodded in greeting to Riley Donahue, then stood to shake his hand just as the waitress came with the other whiskies he'd ordered.

"Took you long enough to get here," Clint said.

"We were having too much fun. You should've come with us."

"Golf's not my game." Again, he stole a glance at Margot, who'd taken a seat on a bar stool and was leaning toward Brad. From here, he could see her sweater gaping open, revealing a gut-punching hint of black bra. Her breasts were round and full, pressed into smooth globes by the tight lace.

He could feel himself getting hard, and he pulled his gaze away. "How's the life of a happy bachelor?" he asked Riley instead.

Riley, who'd also pledged with Clint and become a good friend, ran a hand through his short black hair. "Happy? I guess you must not have heard the news."

He wasn't talking about getting married, seeing as Riley and Dani had been engaged for about a year. They'd been friends until they'd "awakened," or some such greeting-card crap, one day and really "seen" each other.

Fairy tales, Clint thought. His parents had had a lot of great years together, but it'd just never happened for him. Then again, it wasn't as if he'd ever wanted to settle down. He'd grown up as a lone wolf while his brothers had depended on each other, forming their own inner circle and keeping him out, and he'd been the same way with everyone else, especially women.

The true love of his life had always been the ranch—a paradise invaded by twin snakes, aka his own flesh-and-blood siblings. Funny how he'd found much better brothers, like Riley, away at college.

Clint made himself comfortable in the booth. "Oh, I've certainly heard the news. I've already heard more than I bargained for about the auction."

Margot telling Dani and Leigh about her basket… The sparkly stars that would be a sure sign that it was hers…

But she meant the damn thing for someone else, so why was he even dwelling on it?

Because there are definitely at least eighty ways you could get around her, he thought. And he could guarantee that she enjoyed every one of them, making up lost time with her.

Saying sorry about that tape in every way he could.

Riley spoke, his voice edged with mild frustration. "The guys were all over me about this auction when we were playing golf. I guess the girls' email loop got everyone talking before we got here and Dani didn't know it. Nothing like finding out that everyone is swimming in your personal business. I damn well hope Dani put an end to it this afternoon."

"From what I hear, the girls just want Dani to have that wedding she always planned for. No harm, no foul."

"I already feel like shit that I can't give that wedding to Dani myself, and to have us turn into some kind of charity case…?" He shook his head.

From what Clint had overheard, Dani hadn't asked Margot and Leigh to call off the auction. But—

Sparkling stars… Around the Girl in Eighty Ways…

Riley interrupted. "Ever since I heard about that auction, I've wanted to tell Dani that I'd rather elope to a

Vegas chapel. But then I think about how much she's always talked about the dress with one of those long trains or whatever they call it, and how she wants things to happen in a big church with a big reception, and…I just lose the words."

Clint signaled for yet another round. Riley sure looked like he needed it. Honestly, Clint could use some more drinks, too, because every time he glanced at Margot across the room canoodling with Brad, he felt a keen urge to water down.

"What're you going to tell Dani, then?" Clint asked. "I think the sisters who keep in touch on email are looking forward to this auction."

And he was, too?

But that was idiotic, because that basket of Margot's was aimed at Brad. Plus, she wanted Clint on one side of the room and her on another.

He was damned sure going to change her mind about that.

Riley blew out a breath. "I know Margot and Leigh went to a lot of work. *Everyone* who brought a basket did, and their intentions are good."

"Then let everyone play. You can tell the sisters that you're not taking a dime and the proceeds can go to a charity."

Riley's head jerked up, and he looked at Clint as if he were a genius. Yeah, well, he would be about the only one to think that.

But Clint wasn't here to dwell on the troubles back on the ranch, not when he was among people who'd been even closer to him for a time than his own family. He hadn't ever thought that his relationship with the twins could get worse, except it had, a couple years ago, when Dad had passed on and split up his estate, giving Clint

60 percent of the cutting horse ranch and Jeremiah and Jason each 20 percent. It made all the sense in the world to Clint, who'd come back home after getting his agriculture business degree and developed the Circle BBB, while the twins had opted for the city and an agriculture development firm they'd built from the ground up.

Things never changed, and the twins still stuck together like glue. According to them, Clint didn't know what he was doing with the ranch, even though he ran a solid and profitable operation. But, with their business experience "out in the world," they thought they knew better.

"Why don't you just drink on this auction business," he said to Riley, raising his shot glass.

They slammed back their whisky, then bolted their glasses to the table.

As the waitress slid another round to them and left, Clint's gaze inevitably fixed on Margot again. By now, she was resting her hand on Brad's arm as they shared another joke.

Clint threw back the newest shot. He kept telling himself Brad was his fraternity brother. Brad was making her laugh when she needed it, which was more than Clint had accomplished earlier.

Riley was rolling up his sleeves, as if acknowledging it was going to be a long-ass reunion weekend. Then he noticed the direction of Clint's gaze, and he followed it out the booth and over his shoulder, spying Margot.

He turned back to Clint, holding back a grin. "Got your email about the video this morning. Still have some feelings for her?"

"Not even a speck." He was pissed that it was so obvious. "I just figured it'd be proper to do some damage control for her sake."

"Right." Riley fiddled with his glass. "Was Jay the one who posted that video?"

"It appears so. He runs his family's farm now, so I got a hold of him there. He took the video down already."

"Did you threaten to cuff him again?"

"No. I just did what my brothers do and I threw a few legal words around. That did the trick."

"Why'd he even post it?"

"He said it was his contribution to the reunion, but you remember Jay well enough. He was bitter after we blackballed him for not paying dues and—"

"In general being a douche bag."

"That, too." Clint pushed his glass away. "Him posting the video was nothing against Margot, but it sure feels personal."

Riley paused, making Clint shift in his seat. No use lying about how interested he still was in Margot.

"Just a warning," Riley said. "Dani will even tell you that Margot is still as hard to get as ever."

Now Clint's pride was poked, and dammit, it'd been happening too much lately for him to tolerate it.

"She may be hard to get," he said, "but not impossible."

"Good luck, after what happened last night with the video."

"She'll put it behind her."

"Whoa. Is that a challenge I hear?"

Clint smiled, then jerked his chin toward the bar. Margot sat right next to Brad, arm to arm.

God.

He glanced away, not wanting to watch, but clearly unable to help himself.

"Not that I want to encourage you," Riley said, "because I think she's a lost cause, but Brad doesn't seem all that interested in her. I remember way back when he dated Margot that summer and it didn't work out."

Clint's smile was back. "Why do you think that was?"

"You know Brad. His parents were conservative as hell and raised him to marry a girl who'd be a good wife. Margot was just a fling while he was interning far from home and both of them probably knew it wouldn't go anywhere. Besides, he got divorced a few months ago, and he's a long way from dating anyone again." Riley picked up his next glass. "But if your mind is set on Margot, I'll be your wingman. Dani knows that you're not really the guy with the bad reputation you got because of some college joke. I don't know why you never stressed to Margot that Jay was behind it all."

"Wouldn't have done any good. She'd already written me off."

"So why do you think things will change now?"

"Just a hunch."

Clint glanced at the ill-fated couple. Brad leaned his elbow on the bar instead of canting toward Margot, his disinterest clearer than shiny glass.

Maybe things would work out, he thought.

Maybe he *would* get to make everything up to her.

3

So far, everyone had treated the subject of the video as if it was no big deal, and that gave Margot quite the shot of joy. Why had she even been worried? They were all way past college mischief.

But she couldn't ignore how some of the brothers, as well as Brad, kept glancing over at Clint. Even if they weren't teasing her about that video, it was on everyone's mind.

Just one more reason to avoid him.

She'd actually been working up to telling Brad about her basket for the past hour, but things were still a little haven't-seen-you-in-a-long-time tense between them. Still, he hadn't dropped any hints about having a girlfriend or anything.

So why not go forward?

She ran a gaze from his wavy dark brown hair to his smile. He'd always reminded her of Ben Affleck but much less cocksure…unlike another person she could name.

But she wasn't going to think of Kid Quick-Trigger on the other side of the room, in his booth, drinking whiskey. Mr. I'm-So-Cool-in-a-Cowboy-Hat. Señor Slick. She'd been telling herself to ignore Clint Barrows over and over, but this time she meant it.

Brad set his beer down on the bar. It was still half-full. "It really is good to see you, Margot."

Did she hear a "but…" in there somewhere?

"I liked seeing you, too," she said. "Catching up has been nice."

Was *nice* the word for the conversation they'd been having about running a dairy farm?

Then again, was her auction basket all about the art of conversation?

He fiddled with his beer mug for a moment, then said, "Some of us are getting up early tomorrow to go fishing. Don't ask me why we torture ourselves like this."

"Why do you?" She smiled, hoping to get past this semi-awkward stage and right to the basket.

"Because that's what we used to do," he said. "Fish. Golf. Be sportsmen." He checked his silver watch, then got out his wallet to pay the bar tab. "I'll see you tomorrow at the homecoming pregame kegger?"

He was…leaving?

Margot's Girl Survival Mode kicked into gear, telling her this was a bad time to blurt out that, hey, she'd really like to spend some private, quality sex time with him, and by the way, here's what her basket would look like tomorrow evening at the auction, because she really, truly thought they could have quite the reunion all by themselves.

One more adventure, right?

But, ever since she'd gotten the news from her publisher, she'd started to wonder if, after college, she had set out to have adventures on her own only because experiences filled a hole that'd been put there by never having a true home. Had she been trying to find one by going from place to place, person to person, just as her parents had before they'd passed on eight years ago?

And…her parents. It's not like they'd taught her about a whole lot besides "loving life" and "smelling the roses along the primrose path." Sometimes, she even wondered if they'd loved her half as much as all their pleasure-seeking activities. One time, they had even turned a room in the two-bedroom house they'd been renting into an art studio for their projects, and she'd had to sleep on the couch. She'd been eight.

The thoughts dogged her, even as she started to get the vibe that things weren't gelling with Brad.

He rested a companionable hand on her shoulder and squeezed it, then started to leave the bar. "See you later, Marg."

As he left, she tried not to let hurt set in. She was usually much better at this, distancing herself before anyone could do it to her first.

She just sat there as he disappeared, wondering why Brad's attitude didn't hurt more.

She decided to go, too, and she thought she felt Clint's gaze tracking her out the door. Then it occurred to her… Even though Brad hadn't teased her about the video, had it made him look at her differently?

As used goods, viewed by hundreds of people sitting in front of a computer?

It didn't matter anyway, because she'd blown her chance to tell Brad about her basket so he could bid on it.

On her way into the lobby, she came to a dead stop. What was with her? She'd always taken charge. It was what a single girl did.

At least, the type she used to be.

Full of determination, she went to the reception desk, asked for paper and an envelope, then scribbled a note, since the clerk wouldn't release a room number that she could call.

Brad,
I didn't get the chance to broach the subject, but I'd love to get together before the weekend's over. If you're interested, you could always bid on the basket with the silver and gold stars attached to the handle. It might bring back a few adventurous memories…or make a few new ones.

It wasn't like her to hesitate, but she definitely did when she reread that last part.

Ah, screw it. Adventure!

She signed her name, stuffed the note into the hotel envelope, then generously tipped the concierge and asked him to deliver it to Brad. She liked this much more mysterious way to approach him rather than just calling him up. It was part of the basket's seduction.

Feeling much better, she took a detour outside to the parking lot, to her Prius, where her bags were still in the trunk. She had arrived before her room was ready and met Leigh and Dani right after checking in.

The night was mid-October-crisp, with the scent of wood smoke in the air. Avila Grande, home of Cal-U, was near Route 99, and she could hear the faint swish of cars traveling along it. In high school, she'd loved John Steinbeck's work—what could she say about the streak of Americana in her?—and when Cal-U had offered her a scholarship for their fledgling English program, she'd snapped it up.

But being here now felt a little lonely, and she tried not to sink into the mire of her thoughts again—the voice of her literary agent telling her that it didn't look likely that she would be picked up by her publishing house anytime in the near future. She fought back the looming question of where her paychecks would be coming from after her royalties dried up and her savings had been gutted.

This weekend was supposed to be about Dani, but maybe also about thinking of a new direction for herself, right? So why wasn't she feeling brave?

When she heard boot steps on the pavement, she slammed down her trunk and set her bags on the blacktop. She'd taken Krav Maga, and she was always ready to use it.

"Whoa," said a familiar male voice that made shivers sweep up and down her skin.

She went tight all over again—in her belly, then lower, until she got a little wet at the sight of a lamp-lit Clint Barrows in that cowboy hat, snug T-shirt and jeans.

Wonderful, faded, leg-hugging jeans....

"I saw you go out of the hotel by yourself," he said. "It's not exactly a concrete jungle out here, but it's dark."

He'd taken off his hat, the illumination making his hair look golden and so thick that it conjured naughty thoughts about that night all those years ago. Hot, dizzy, breath-stealing thoughts. Her mind went even further, and she pictured him kissing his way down her neck, her chest…lower, until he made his way across her stomach and then…

Her pulse was thudding in all the places she'd just pictured, as if his mouth was actually on her, driving her wild.

"Why're you really out here?" she asked, cooling herself off, making a show of corralling her luggage— which she did quite easily all on her own. A girl never traveled with more than she could handle.

As she headed back to the hotel, pulling her suitcase behind her, she walked closer to him. He was leaning back against what had to be his truck—a comfortable, beat-up blue Dodge—and he'd rested his hat on top of the cab, his thumbs hooked into his belt loops.

"I'm going to tell you my side of the story," he said. "Maybe not out here, maybe not at the kegger tomorrow, but you'll know it before the weekend comes to a close. And you'll know how much I regret what happened."

The soft rumble of her suitcase wheels went silent as she stopped just past him. "How could you regret it? You're the one who came off looking like a stud. I came off looking like something…rented."

She hadn't meant to say that much, but it'd come out, anyway.

His voice was low and, again, seemingly genuine. "I'm truly sorry about that, Margot."

She didn't like the way he said her name. Or, more to the point, she *did* like it. Way too much.

She turned to him, chin a notch higher than usual. "So what do you want to tell me? That Jay Halverson was behind all the camera stuff back in college? Because I've heard it all from Riley over the years."

"And you didn't believe him."

She only shrugged. She didn't owe him the truth.

Had she started to enjoy thinking he was the bad guy? Did it give her some kind of excuse to stay away?

His peace-offering grin stroked over her, and her heart lost a beat.

She girded herself. "Next thing you know, you'll be telling me that Jay posted that video last night."

"He did."

Okay, then. Mystery solved. "I guess that settles the score."

She started to leave.

"Not so fast." He'd lowered his voice to a sexy timbre, making her wonder why the hell she had her sights set on Brad, who was already in his room.

But she knew the answer. Brad was a known quantity, and maybe she needed someone safe this weekend, even as she imagined him part of some big adventure with her basket. Mild-mannered Brad had never broken her trust or given grist to the gossip mill with a video.

It'd bothered her more that her privacy had been violated, and especially that she'd been filmed with the playboy who'd had every other girl except her, it seemed.

Before she knew it, Clint had reached out, gently taking hold of her sweater, near the bottom. It gaped away from her body, the air like a caress, tickling her belly.

No, make that tickling her *everywhere,* especially in the last place she wanted Clint Barrows to be.

But she ached there, too, between her legs. Ached so badly.

He must've sensed that, because he tugged her closer. As the night breathed under the cashmere, she let go of her suitcase and stumbled toward him, close enough to smell the hay and clover on his clothing and skin.

The pure masculinity of him—the clean scent, the knowledge that there was muscle under his own shirt, so close, just a touch away—spiked desire through her.

"I'm going to make it all up to you," he said. "That's why I'm here."

She swallowed at his bold comment. A melting, lazy pull of sensation stretched in her, creating friction until there were sparks flaring in her stomach.

"You can't make up for what's been done," she said breathlessly.

He laughed, soft and low. "Sure I can. And in eighty ways, too."

Great—he must've overheard what the tag would be on her auction offering.

She grabbed his hand and tried to pull it away from her sweater. "That basket's not for you."

She realized her mistake right away, because beneath her palm and fingers, his skin was well worked, manly, strong. The feel of it fired a need through her that she hadn't realized was there, and it made her go even wetter for him.

"So you're saving yourself for another man," he said, twining his fingers through hers.

Oh, God, even such a simple connection sent the adrenaline racing through her, awakening her completely.

"Margot," he said softly. "You're being real difficult about this when it should be so easy."

But it wasn't. Not even close. Giving in to Clint Barrows was unthinkable at a reunion where everyone was just waiting for him to finally nail the one girl who'd slipped through his fingers.

Still, when he slid his other hand to her hip, massaging it with his thumb, she almost gave in.

She'd had too much to drink, she told herself. And she'd been lonely for the first time in her life because she was facing things she'd never faced before. All of that added up to a vulnerable Margot, and when he moved his hand to her backside, cupping her derriere, she sucked in a harsh breath.

"Just hear me out," he said.

Yes. It was on the tip of her tongue. It was screaming in her head, pulling her toward him even as she tried to stay away.

But it wasn't going to happen, because she still had a little something called pride.

"I've listened enough," she said.

She stepped away and grabbed her suitcase handle again, the wheels reverberating over the blacktop just as loudly as an unexpected, almost overwhelming hunger rumbled through her.

BY THE NEXT morning, Margot hadn't heard from Brad, and she told herself that it was still early—they had plenty of time before the auction.

And it wasn't as if she was depending on him for *the* best good time ever, anyway. She'd had pretty decent fun last night after she'd unpacked her suitcase, then met Leigh and Dani again in the café, where they'd caught up with other sisters who had offered solace about the video. That hadn't surprised Margot, because everyone but the biggest prudes had backed her up years ago when the first one had gone public.

Naturally, Margot had done her best to avoid the questions about future books and how well her sales were doing, all the while wondering if the concierge had gotten ahold of Brad yet with the "this is what my basket looks like" note and its less-than-subtle invitation to bid on it.

But there'd been some moments last night—a lot of them, actually—when she'd found her mind on someone else.

The cowboy with the cocky grin.

The man who'd used his sexy voice in the parking lot as if he were fully confident she was going to succumb to his supposedly irresistible charm.

Right.

She rolled out of bed, the digital clock on the nightstand blazing 9:00 a.m. in the dim room, darkened by the pulled heavy curtains. And when she glanced at the phone, the message light was dark, too, staring back at her blankly.

No calls.

But dammit all if she was going to bug the concierge by asking him if he'd even delivered the note to Brad.

Jeez, now she was wondering if it'd been such a good idea in the first place....

At least Leigh had told her last night that her note was a perfect prologue to her basket. Very old-school. And, hey, what guy wouldn't be interested in that kind of message?

Margot cracked the curtains, squinting at the sunlight. She smiled when she saw the wide tomato fields and the pine trees lining the nearby open road.

Unfortunately, her gaze then went to the parking lot, where she saw Clint Barrows's faded blue Dodge truck lounging next to her little Prius.

Why did it seem as if even his pickup was ready to devour her car?

Rubbing her arms, she wandered to the bathroom, turning on the shower, stripping off her long nightshirt. The second the heated mist whispered over her skin, she tightened with goose bumps, imagining that she heard a voice, soft and low, whispering quiet apologies to her.

Clint Barrows's apologies.

Just hear me out, he'd said last night in the parking lot, when she'd known he meant so much more.

She stepped into the shower, hoping the water would wash her into a sane place. But as it sluiced over her, she imagined his hand on her hip, just like last night when he'd been bold enough to touch her.

Yet, now, there were no clothes between them, and as she closed her eyes, the uninterrupted flutter of water against her became his fingers, and she felt them ease to her belly, a fleeting butterfly touch.

You're being real difficult about this when it should be so easy....

She leaned forward, bracing her hands against the tile wall. The water gently ran down her body, slipping over her thighs, in between her legs.

Wantonly, she opened them a little, loving the sensation as it skimmed over her clit.

The water became his fingers again, finding just the right spot, her breath quickening right along with her heartbeat.

You used to be a risk taker, she heard him tell her, as if they were talking again. The butterfly wings on her body traveled inward, beating in her belly, electric and tickling, making her bite her lip.

So why're you set on safe, boring Brad?

Why not go for this new direction?

She took her hand from the wall, trailed it between her breasts, down her stomach to her pulsing center. Sliding her fingers through her cleft, she massaged herself, thinking of Clint.

At least, with Brad, they'd had a summer together. And when they'd returned to college, after the bloom had faded off their little affair, they had floated away from each other, going different ways.

It'd all been perfectly safe with Brad, just as it could be this weekend. No deception, no videos.

But, as she touched herself, the water caressing her, the mere thought of that unpredictability sent a jolt through her, making her breath catch.

Wet. Excited. And every time she circled her clit with her thumb, imagining that it was Clint touching her, her temperature rose. The heat pushed her up, up, tighter and tighter, until a tiny series of impending explosions quivered in her.

She fought the first one, pressing herself forward against the wall....

Then the second, as it rolled through her, shake by contained shake....

But the third—

She started to give in to it for the first time in months, slipping down the wall as blasts of sensation seized her, making her gasp just before she let go with one long, hard inhale...then...

As the water ran over her—just water now—she groaned, aching.

Still aching.

And hardly knowing just what it was anymore that she really wanted.

4

AFTER THE PREGAME party and the homecoming football match itself, the reunion moved to Main Street, to the back room of Dani's favorite hangout in Avila Grande.

Desperado's was one of those country joints that was marked by the smell of hops and fried food every time you walked through its swinging doors and hit the planked floor. On the walls above the bar were deer antlers, a buffalo head and a menu that showcased Rocky Mountain Oysters—a dish that Dani didn't have the stomach for once Leigh and Margot had told her that the name was actually a euphemism for bull-calf testicles.

Ah, yes, good old Desperado's, where the Valley's farm and ranch kids had hung out, where music had always been 100 percent country, the beer cheap and the food rugged and, as it turned out, disgusting.

But the moment Dani had strolled in with Riley tonight, greeted by the thud of hip-hop and the sight of undergrads doing everything but the two-step on the small dance floor, it was obvious things had changed.

"So it's come to this," Dani said as she and Riley left the main room and made their way through the slim lantern-lit corridor toward the back, where the auction was scheduled to start in an hour. "Desperado's is now pure evil."

"Evil?" Riley rested a hand on the back of her neck, cupping it. "Strong word, Dan."

"Okay, maybe not *evil,* then. It's just..." She motioned toward the dance floor and almost flinched at the loud music, which was making them raise their voices. "I miss how it used to be."

He guided her to the side of the corridor. No one else was there right now—they were early. And when he leaned back against the wall, putting his hands on her jeaned hips, pulling her to him, her heart jittered. But it was always that way when she looked into Riley's deep blue eyes.

"I don't like it, either," he said. "But things never stay the same. Not anywhere."

"I guess I'm just getting old and cranky." She'd also felt that way before the game, while walking around campus. Dressed in her old Cal-U sweatshirt against the fall chill in the air, she'd felt like a grandma next to all the students running around, their lives ahead of them as they dreamed of success. "Everything just seems so...corporate. Cal-U used to be small, homier. Now it's—"

"Trendier than hell. I noticed."

He bent forward, kissing her forehead, and they stayed like that for a few seconds, his breath stirring her hair, infiltrating her, just as it had ever since she'd glanced up one day on a sorority/fraternity reunion cruise five years ago that neither Leigh nor Margot had signed up for. That's when she'd seen Riley giving her that look—one she'd never noticed before. It was the look of a friend who had apparently been thinking some extremely more-than-buddies thoughts without her even knowing it until that moment.

It had changed her world, changed her mind.

But it hadn't changed either of *them*.

Or so she'd believed. It hadn't occurred to her that change was everywhere except in her until last night, when Margot and Leigh had sprung this auction on her.

She held on to Riley, her hands wrapped in the bottom of his long, untucked shirt, cocooned there. After last night, she'd started wondering just how people perceived her—had *always* perceived her.

Was she someone in need of rescuing? A pitiful dreamy princess who'd been defined all her life by one goal and one goal only?

To be the ultimate bridezilla?

Just…wow. And, the thing was, Dani feared that her friends were right. What had she done with herself all these years besides get a job as lead caterer for someone else's company? What true ambitions had she possessed?

She'd always looked up to Margot—and who hadn't? Margot led the pack, getting them into trouble while watching over them at the same time. Dani loved her friend's independence, her go-get-'em approach to life. And the same went for Leigh, who had overcome a tragic childhood filled with sadness after the accidental drowning of her sister. Leigh had also struggled with her weight when she was younger, but now she was as svelte as Margot and just as successful a businesswoman. And what was Dani?

Down the corridor, she heard a door close, and she caught a peek of Margot, dressed as stunningly as ever in what looked to be an Ann Taylor leather jacket, a pencil skirt and high boots as she made a beeline for the back room. She was carrying an iPad, probably to keep track of the baskets that had already been dropped off, and she didn't see Dani and Riley as she disappeared.

Riley's voice rumbled through his chest as he spoke. Dani could feel it while she pressed against him.

"Do you think Margot's pissed after what you told her at the game?" he asked.

"Not pissed. Disappointed, I'd say." After Dani and Riley had talked this whole auction thing over last night, they'd decided that Margot and Leigh could still hold the event—it just wouldn't be for their wedding. Instead, he had suggested a charity that fed the homeless in Avila Grande.

"She'll get over it," Riley said.

"I'm sure she's already knee-deep in the excitement of tonight." But, still, Dani *had* seen disappointment in both Margot's and Leigh's eyes this afternoon. They clearly hadn't believed her when she'd told them that it didn't matter *how* she and Riley got married—a small ceremony, an elopement. Whatever. She and Riley had been together for long enough that marriage was only a piece of paper to them.

Or maybe Dani had just been saying this so often that she believed it. And Riley, being Riley, hadn't pushed her on the subject too hard. He'd heard enough stories about the curveball her parents had thrown her just before she and Riley had gotten together. Married thirty-seven years, obviously just pretending to be happy, then *boom*.

Divorce. Because of a cheating dad.

As if knowing what had entered her thoughts again, Riley stroked her curls away from her face. Patient, wonderful Riley, who'd waited around long enough for

her to finally start planning a wedding after the fallout
from her mom and dad.

"Is Margot excited because she thinks Brad is going
to bid on her basket?" he asked, knowing just how to
change a subject.

Dani smiled up at him. "No doubt. It's strange,
though, because never in a million years would I think
that a woman of experience like Margot would be in to
a garden-variety type like Brad these days."

"Clint's in to her."

"What? When did you find this out?"

"Last night. You went out with the girls, and I was
asleep when you got back, and then we had breakfast
with the others and the game…"

Little time for talking. Or much else. "Margot told
me and Leigh that she had an 'incident' with Clint in
the parking lot last night. She stiff-armed him, though.
Doesn't trust him as far as she can throw him, even
though he's told her that Jay was the culprit who posted
the video."

"It doesn't matter to Margot, does it?"

"Nope. I think that, if she gives Clint the time of day,
it'll be like she's surrendering or something. Like there's
this battle of wills going on, and it started way back
when she didn't want to be one of his many women."

"Until she *was*."

Dani gave him a light push. "Hey, they didn't have
sex. She didn't give in to him at all."

They laughed. It was always so easy to do with each
other.

Then Dani said, "Margot has this idea that she's
going to re-create her golden summer with Brad or
something."

"We'll see. He wasn't at the game, and I thought he said this morning during fishing that he would be."

"You think he's going to ditch the auction, then?"

Riley shrugged. "If he does that, he should've let Margot know. She sent him that note."

"And don't you dare let her know I told you. She'd kill me if she heard I was letting you in on everything."

"Hey—we're about to get married. People expect us to share."

The intimate comment made her shoulders tense ever so slightly. Just because people got married, it didn't guarantee that they'd be some eternal, single entity. Or maybe, for a time at the beginning, it *did* mean just that, and when things went wrong and you had to rip yourself away from your other, the wound would never heal.

She'd seen proof of it in her mom and dad, who still didn't speak to each other unless they had to.

Riley's arms tightened around her, and she locked gazes with him. Somewhere along the way, the wind had ruffled his dark hair enough so that he had bedhead, and it gave him a boyish look that nicked her heart. And his smile… It was sexy and youthful, both at the same time.

They wouldn't turn out the way her parents had. She told herself that every day.

"I've heard enough about Brad," she said softly, losing herself in his eyes as deeply as she had ever allowed herself to be lost.

Then she put her arms around him and hugged him even closer, shutting her eyes out of pure instinct so she wouldn't get *too* lost.

AN HOUR AND a half later, Clint reclined in a chair at the rear of the back room in Desperado's, his hat tipped back on his head, his boots propped on the table in front of him. He'd stayed distant from the crowd as they joked and jested and gathered near the front, where the baskets were set out in an anonymous parade of color and ruffles.

But it was Margot who had his full attention. Margot Walker, with her fancy, big-city, spike-heeled boots, short straight brown skirt and creamy top that clung to her curves.

And, boy, had he felt a few of those curves last night when he'd impulsively met her in the parking lot, intending to help with her luggage, only to decide on the turn of a dime to try a little bit of something else.

Maybe he'd been too aggressive though, because, once again, he'd been shot down in flames.

Clint grinned to himself. Yep, he'd been put in his place, but there'd been one moment—a hesitation, a heartbeat—when he'd seen something in her eyes.

Something that told him she was wondering what it'd be like with him. Something that hinted she enjoyed being touched the way he was touching her.

And that was all Clint had needed to come here tonight, to this basket auction.

The president of his pledge class, Walt Tolliver, who'd been on the student body and had gone on to run successfully for his local town council, had volunteered to lead the charity auction since Margot and Leigh were the ones who'd turned tonight into a charity event.

Margot stood by, handing out the baskets as the bidders won them. By now, they'd gotten to the last few. And, wouldn't you know it, hers hadn't come up for auction just yet.

But Clint could wait.

He'd been setting aside "fun money" for years, never using it for vacations or the like. On the interest alone, he could afford to spend a pretty penny tonight, especially because he'd also been saving for possible legal fees with his brothers.

But this was as much fun as any money could buy. He also wanted to make this auction a major success for Margot.

And the time was getting near.

Margot picked up a "basket" that was actually a large pot with the word "honey" painted on the outside, and she set it on the podium where Walt waited.

"Who's looking for a taste of honey?" he asked, weaving the title of the basket into his question, just as he'd been doing all night.

Clint's fraternity brothers laughed and catcalled about honey-this and honey-that, but he refrained. The basket with the gold and silver stars would come up soon enough, and as Margot swept another surreptitious glance around the room, Clint wondered if she had put off bringing her basket up for auction because her dear Brad was MIA.

Looked as if she had no idea that ol' Bradley Harrington had been called home on business. Wasn't that a bummer?

"Bidding starts at a hundred bucks," Walt said, looking for takers.

"*Two* hundred," shouted Ed Kendrick. "I could use some sweetening."

Before everyone stopped laughing, another brother, Mark Heinbeck, yelled, "Three hundred."

As the bidding continued, Dani and Riley sat down at Clint's table. The two of them got cozy in their chairs, leaning back and surveying the controlled chaos. Riley was holding a red, white and blue basket with curly streamers, which Dani had put together at the last minute. He'd won it, no problem, because of course no one would dare step on Riley's toes.

"Just think," Clint said, leaning toward Riley so his voice wouldn't carry over Walt's calls. "You could've had some real cash thrown at that wedding of yours tonight. They're raking it in."

"I'm glad it's going where it's going," Riley said, exchanging a grin with Dani.

Clint noticed a shadow in Dani's eyes, but then something happened at the front of the room that pulled his focus there.

A woman had stepped forward to bid on the honey basket, and Clint recognized her as Beth Dahrling, a sorority sister who was a couple years older than he was. She was wearing a conservative skirt set, her long dark hair held back by an expensive-looking shell barrette.

"Five thousand," she said smoothly.

Everyone in the room froze, even Clint. Then someone whispered to another person, and a gossipy hum filled the place.

Up in front, Margot was staring wide-eyed at Leigh, who was sedately lounging in her chair in a corner, a cowboy-booted foot propped over her knee. The only thing besides Margot's expression that confirmed this basket was Leigh's was the too-cool way she didn't move a muscle.

The room went quiet as everyone else glanced at Leigh, too. Hell, nobody had expected a woman to bid on another woman's basket, and Clint wasn't sure Leigh swung that way.

Dani shifted in her chair, and Riley stifled a grin just before his fiancée smacked his leg.

Walt cleared his throat. "Five thousand going once?" he asked, obviously testing Leigh.

She smiled, then laughed, making a bring-it-on motion with her hands.

Margot smiled at her, then at Beth Dahrling, who gave Leigh a little friendly wave, then said, "I'm here for someone else, Leigh. Don't panic."

A buzz rose in the room as people started to ask just what Beth was up to. But the woman remained silent, shrugging and calmly grinning.

Riley leaned toward Clint. "Glad I didn't put the kibosh on this auction, after all."

President Walt was calling for order, and when he got a semblance of it, he yelled, "Is there anyone here who can beat five thou? It's for charity."

When he didn't get any takers, he held up his gavel. "Okay. Going once…twice…" *Bang.* "Sold!"

The applause was louder than usual as Margot took the basket to Beth, and Leigh, with her typical sense of humor, stood and went to her fellow sorority sister, linking arms with her and walking out of the room with an exaggerated sashay of her Wrangler-clad rump.

"Nothing's gonna top that," Riley muttered as the noise died down and Margot picked up another basket.

I can think of at least eighty things that very well could, Clint thought, barely keeping track of the last few auction items before they finally came to Margot's offering.

Almost time…

Just before Margot went to the table, slowly picking up her basket, Clint noticed Leigh slipping into the room and leaning against a wall, a furrow to her brow as she stood alone, without Beth.

President Walt rubbed his hands together. "Wonder whose *this* could be...."

Every guy who hadn't won a basket tonight hooted and whistled; it was obvious that Margot hadn't walked out of the room with anyone yet, and the basket had to be hers. She gave a sassy, narrowed glance to the room in general, but Clint could tell that she was indulging in one last scan for Brad.

For a moment, Clint swore that Walt was about to make a joke about the video, but then he only grinned. Clint nodded slightly to him.

"Let's start with a hundred for what promises to be a very exotic offering," Walt said. "Around the Girl in—"

Margot cut him off. "It's a travel basket. That's all."

Clint laughed. She was playing down the spicy title, wasn't she? Those cards in the basket would be worded so vaguely that she could give the winner a hot date or a cool one, depending on whoever won.

He'd take his chances.

Since he didn't want to seem too eager, he waited out the initial bidders. It was only when he snagged Margot's gaze as she surveyed the room again that he finally rose to his feet, lethargically sweeping off his hat.

"Six hundred," he said with great relish as he met Margot's gaze.

There was a sizzling connection between them as she glared right back.

He thought he heard a few *oohs* in the room. If they couldn't talk about the video, they'd certainly *ooh* about it.

One of the sorority sisters said, "Don't get slapped this time, Clint," and that caused somewhat of a minor kerfuffle. It also caused Margot's laserlike glare to intensify.

"I bid seven hundred," she said.

That got a rise out of the room. And, truth be told, it did the same to Clint, too.

Riley punched Clint's side and gave him a challenging look. *Yeah, don't get slapped.*

Clint propped his booted foot on his chair and leaned his elbow on his thigh. He could do this all night.

"Eight hundred," he said.

"Nine," she shot back.

Walt laughed right along with everyone else before saying, "Hate to tell you, Margot, but you can't bid. It's against the rules."

"Hey," she said, clutching her basket to her. "I organized this auction."

"Oooh," went the crowd again.

But then Leigh drawled from her side of the room. "You're not the only one who put this thing together, Marg, and I say you're breaking the rules."

A bigger *"Oooh."*

If looks could kill, Leigh would be in a million pieces. It was pretty obvious that the friendly one-upmanship between her and Margot hadn't died since college had ended, but Leigh obviously thought this whole thing was hilarious.

Margot? Not so much.

"I'll tell you what," Clint said, after holding up his hand for silence. "Let's just make it an even thousand and call it a night. There're people who have baskets to open."

"But—" Margot said.

Walt hit the gavel on the podium before Margot could get too far, and Riley stood, pushing Clint forward. His brothers patted him on the back as he made his way to the front, his gaze never leaving Margot's.

A thousand bucks was going to put a real dent in his fun money for the year, but he didn't have any vacations planned.

Except for the ones Margot's basket had arranged.

He planted himself in front of her, nodding at the basket that she was hugging for the life of her, just as Walt yelled, "Sold!"

But from the looks of his date, Clint was pretty sure that she was anything but.

5

EARLY SUNDAY AFTERNOONS were usually Margot's favorite. They were a time for sleeping in, then lounging on the balcony of her condo with a cup of tea while taking in the view of the fruit trees and bricked walkways that decorated her complex. They were full of sunny moments reading the paper, savoring the scones she liked to pick up at the local bakery the night before.

But *this* Sunday?

Was the polar opposite. And Dani seemed to sense it, too, as she took a seat across from Margot at the hotel's café, where only a few other customers were talking quietly over late breakfasts.

Luckily, none of them had been at the auction last night, so Margot had been enjoying a little peace while waiting for both Leigh and Dani before they wiled away the hours before the final event—a formal dinner at the hotel.

"Morning, sunshine," Dani said, plopping into her seat with an impish grin. She looked just as fresh as a rose, her red curls pulled back into a ponytail and a white blouse tied at the waist. A high flush colored her smooth, pale cheeks.

Nice to know that *someone* in the hotel had enjoyed a good night. "Peppy, aren't you?"

"I had a great time last night. Why shouldn't I be full of smiles when I was so highly entertained? If you hadn't taken off like a shot after the auction—and if you'd returned my calls—we could've had a good laugh about things over drinks."

"I texted you back." Margot had wanted to be by herself, where she couldn't see everyone's amusement as the reunion continued.

Didn't Dani get it? Clint Barrows had been instrumental in embarrassing her publicly once before and here he was again, bidding on her basket, making sure everyone knew that he was still the fraternity stud and that being slapped back in college wasn't going to stop him.

The waiter interrupted, and Dani asked for orange juice and fried eggs. Margot, who already had her Earl Grey tea, ordered a fruit bowl. Leigh had asked her to get black-as-night coffee and waffles topped with lots of fresh strawberries.

After the server had left, Margot took up where their conversation stopped. "So last night tickled your funny bone."

"I wouldn't put it that way."

"Good. Because there wasn't much that was funny about it."

"Margot." Dani smiled gently. "It's not every night that someone pays a thousand smackaroos for one of my best friends. Can't you see what a compliment that was? As far as I'm concerned, Clint was showing that he values you. It would've been more embarrassing if your basket had gone for peanuts."

Right. A thousand-dollar bid. Margot didn't want to even consider what kind of indecent proposals Clint Barrows was no doubt thinking he would discover inside her basket.

Perv.

"It wasn't a compliment," Margot said, cupping both hands around her mug. "Clint just wanted to show everyone that he's out to close the deal on that video."

"But that was years ago." Dani cleared her throat as the waiter brought her juice. An elderly couple passed their table, and she lowered her voice. "Riley says that Clint doesn't have anything up his sleeve."

"Fraternity brothers. They look out for each other… unless they're Jay Halverson."

"Who got blackballed, by the way. And Riley wouldn't lie to me about Clint."

Dani just sat there for a moment, long enough so that Margot stopped fiddling with her mug and settled back into her seat.

"He says Clint's changed, and he's got some very real adult problems to deal with now. For one thing, his two brothers are trying to force him into doing business on his ranch their way."

A surprising pang hit Margot. Maybe it was because she'd always had a soft spot for underdogs. But…Clint? She'd never seen such an arrogant one, so she doubted her instincts.

"How can his brothers do that if it's not their ranch?" she asked.

A small smile lit Dani's face. She obviously thought Margot was interested or something.

"Clint's father left him the majority percentage of

the ranch after he passed away, but they've been hinting that, since they own a part of it, they might get legal about the way the ranch is being run." Dani shrugged. "But I don't do business, so what do I know?"

Margot hated when Dani got like this—lacking in confidence. "You could've had your own business, Dan. Still could."

Dani didn't say anything, but she had a faraway look in her eyes.... A hint of something that Margot had never seen there before, as if she was really thinking about what Margot had said for the first time since they'd known each other.

But it disappeared when Leigh arrived, dressed in a fancy, silver-threaded cowgirl shirt that nipped in at the waist, plus jeans and a pair of hand-worked boots. She'd fixed her blond hair into a low braid that hung down her back.

She sat, resting a booted ankle on her knee, stretching her arms as if she'd just rolled out of bed.

"Finally," Margot said, signaling to the waiter to bring Leigh's coffee. "Someone who can take the heat off me about last night."

"Oh, goody," Leigh said, putting her hands behind her head and closing her eyes. "We have to launch into *this* first thing."

Dani brightened up. "No matter how many drinks we plied you with last night, we couldn't get the truth out of you about your bidder."

"And why should I start pouring out my soul this morning?" Leigh asked, accepting a mug from the waiter and blowing on her steaming coffee.

As Margot and Dani darted expectant looks at her, Leigh finally rolled her eyes in surrender.

"There's nothing to report, girls. I don't know any

more information about who won my basket than I did twelve hours ago."

"Nothing?" Margot asked.

"Nothing. Beth Dahrling said she'd been instructed not to tell me much—just that a secret admirer had asked her to represent him at the auction. Apparently, he's out of town on business for a while, and that's why he sent a representative."

"Aren't you wary of the situation?" Dani asked, but the rush of excitement in her voice made her a liar.

Margot waggled her eyebrows. "So he's got to be one of the brothers. I'm going to get on the computer and do some research, narrow it down, come up with an answer."

"I already did a search," Dani said. "I haven't come up with any candidates who can afford to spend five thou on a basket."

Leigh shrugged. "Don't bother trying anymore."

"Is there anyone you're hoping it is?" Margot asked.

She anticipated what came next: Leigh getting that "who cares?" posture, one arm resting on the back of her chair, the rest of her body just as languid.

"You all know me," she drawled. "Chubby girls don't get a lot of action in college, so I didn't bother with crushes. I didn't pay much attention to the brothers in that way, and I can't believe any of them paid much mind to me."

She was half-right. Leigh had been just as focused as Margot on her studies, doing a lot of side projects like creating campus cookbooks and working on the Cal-U Rodeo Days as one of the student board members each year. But now, after the weight loss and a whole lot of career success, things had to be different for Leigh.

Right?

Margot surveyed her for a second, and Leigh squirmed in her chair.

"Just say it," she muttered.

"Well, clearly someone paid attention to you," Margot said.

"Or," Leigh shot back, "they saw my show on TV and they suddenly got interested. Let's not make this into some epic love story."

"I don't know." Margot leaned back again. "It's all so very mysterious and hot. A secret admirer for our Lee-Lee."

She chuffed. "Don't you sit there all smug, just like you're not caught up in as much fallout from the auction."

Dani interrupted. "You two brought it on yourselves."

Margot pointed at her. "And who's the smug one now?"

"I'm not the girl who's going to be going eighty ways to Ha-cha-cha-ville with my college enemy," Dani said. "So I do feel pretty smug about my stress-free fiancé at the moment."

Margot made a point of calmly refreshing her tea with the hot water pot. "I'm not going anywhere with Clint Barrows."

Leigh stopped drinking her coffee. "Maybe you need a refresher course on what happened last night."

Ha-ha. "I'm going to get out of this. Just watch me."

Dani laughed. "How's that?"

"I'll just give him back his money."

Both of her friends sighed, but not before Margot caught them glancing at each other.

"What?" she asked.

Leigh punched her in the arm, kind of hard, too, and Margot pressed a hand to her skin.

"Ouch," she said. Cowgirl Leigh had always been strong.

"If I'm going through with this basket thing," she said, "you'd better do it, too."

"Or what?"

"Or you'll regret it."

"Why? Because you'll call me a chicken for the rest of my life?"

"No," Leigh said. "Because you'll be calling yourself a chicken. I know you, Margot—when you were sparring with Clint at that auction, you lit up. You liked it."

"I was pissed that he would come after me like he did."

"You were excited."

Margot opened her mouth to retort, but she didn't have anything to counter.

Because Leigh was 100 percent on target. Margot *had* been excited, and she'd been praying for all she was worth that no one would notice.

Especially him.

But it wasn't as if she was going to let Leigh know that she'd scored a direct hit. Hell, no.

She reached down to her Gucci tote bag and pulled out her iPad, turning it on and changing the subject so thoroughly that both Dani and Leigh laughed under their breaths.

"I'm not going to waste my time talking about him," Margot said, accessing a file on the screen. "Not when I spent most of the night being gainfully occupied."

She didn't add that she hadn't been able to get to sleep, anyway. Not with Clint Barrows on her mind… and under her skin.

When she showed Dani the wedding-dress pictures that she'd stored in an e-file, her friend went quiet, just as she had the other day after the news about the auction.

"I have a friend," Margot said, treading lightly now, wondering if Dani would be offended by her wedding-planning initiative once again. "She designs gowns, and she doesn't cost an arm and a leg because I'm sure I can work a deal with her. I thought you might want to take a peek at her designs."

Dani didn't take the iPad. "You know someone who offers discounted wedding venues, too? And cakes? How about massage oils and sex toys, Margot?"

She laughed a little, and Margot took the iPad back. Yep, she'd overstepped, just as she and Leigh had done when they'd set up the auction without Dani's knowledge in the first place.

As if she realized that she'd caused Margot discomfort, Dani smiled that sunny smile and held out her hand.

"Let's see what you've got," she said.

As Margot handed over the computer, she caught Leigh's eye. She winked at her, and Margot returned the gesture.

Wedding dress viewing soon turned into an online search for venues as they ate breakfast, and soon the late-morning crowd had turned into an early-lunch one.

They paid up, then exited the café, catching an elevator to their rooms.

"See you at the dinner tonight?" Leigh asked as the panel dinged at Margot's floor.

The door opened, and over her shoulder, she said, "Sure. I'll be the one hiding in the corner."

"As if," Dani said, before the doors closed on her and Leigh.

Margot smiled while she walked down the hall toward her room. Yeah, they all knew damned well that she wouldn't be hiding from anyone, especially Clint. After Margot returned his money, she was planning to dance the night away and show him just who had come out on top in this little power game they were playing.

She rounded a corner, so intent on finding her key card in her tote bag that she didn't notice that someone was waiting for her.

When that someone took her by the waist and scooped her into the ice-machine alcove, her breath was already halfway out of her lungs.

And when that someone turned out to be Clint Barrows grinning down at her, his light blue eyes full of amusement, Margot lost her breath—and her will—altogether.

CLINT'S HAND RESTED on her waist while the other tipped up his cowboy hat.

"You sure took your sweet time at breakfast," he said. "I couldn't help seeing you and the girls in that café and wondering just when you'd be done."

Even though he had her cornered near the ice machine, a pulsating wisp of space between their bodies, she didn't take the escape route.

But maybe that was only because she couldn't resist the opportunity to sass him.

"Just to be clear," she said tightly, "I was planning on writing you a check for every cent you spent on that basket."

"A refund?" He ran his gaze over the dark, long layers of her hair, then up to her face, with those startling pale eyes fringed with sweeping lashes, those red lips…

The words almost snagged in his throat. "I'm not interested in getting my money back."

Her pupils had gone wide, as if, with every look he smoothed over her, she was forgetting how much she couldn't stand him. His gut tightened with heat and yearning.

That night, so long ago… Their kisses…

No, he didn't want a refund. He wanted a replay.

And this time he wanted it all to turn out right, without her burning rubber after she thought he'd humiliated her.

"What makes you think you run the show here?" she asked, her voice softer now. "What makes you think you have any sort of choice about what I do?"

"Darlin'," he said, "letting me have your basket could be the best choice you've ever made."

He grinned down at her and, for an expanding second, he thought she might close her eyes, invite him to kiss her, tell him that bygones were bygones and…

What?

It wouldn't go beyond that, but at least he'd go home happy before getting real unhappy with his brothers again.

Before being isolated from what was left of his family.

But she seemed to snap out of it, nudging away from him, taking off just as quickly as she had done all those years ago, except without the slap and the door slamming.

"Margot," he said, following her out of the small room and into the hallway.

"Don't 'Margot' me when we've got nothing to 'Margot' about. I forgot my checkbook in my room, but I'm going to write you the fastest check I've ever written in my life."

His steps were twice the length of hers, and in no time, he'd come to the front of his own room, deftly slipping his key card into the reader, then opening his door.

She started to pass him, then paused, obviously unable to stop herself from peering inside.

And why not, when he'd raided that fancy-schmancy store in the downtown village of Avila Grande bright and early, just to create his own version of a basket?

Step one, win her over.

Step two, win *her*.

He'd been waiting for Margot to finish breakfast to set his intentions into motion. And, after slipping one of the desk clerks a hefty tip, he'd even made sure that he transferred to a room on her floor.

He opened the door a little wider, so she could get a better view of the bamboo stand he'd set up near the entrance. The faux candle in it cast a dim, sultry light over the sheer scarves he'd draped over the small dressing screen he'd found in the same shop.

"What the hell is this?" she asked.

He only shrugged. Her question had an edge, but Clint knew an intrigued woman when he heard one, and he stepped aside to let the adventuress see more.

She was the woman who'd taken off to Europe after college to "experience life," according to her bio in the back of the books he'd also purchased today. The woman who'd pushed her travels further when she'd gone on to write about sexy swims in hidden pools on the paradise roads of Maui and about the most enticing foods to be found in exotic places like Shanghai.

The smart, seductive woman he'd seen in her that

night, one who had taken her fantasies and made them realities.

He left the door open as she crossed his threshold and looked around at the dressing screen, then the items he'd arranged near it.

A tray full of truffles and chocolate-drizzled croissants from the bakery downtown.

A basket of bubble bath, lotion and sinuously carved soaps.

A beautiful white slip of a negligee that was as innocent as it was suggestive.

She slid him a look out of the corner of her eye. "Did you go to The Boudoir?"

"I made a stop." The boutique had been around since their college days, a Cal-U institution. "But I also hit a few other places."

"Why?"

"Because I went through all those slips of paper you have in that basket." He pulled one of the scenarios from his back pocket and read it. "'The Grand Palace in Thailand, home of a king.' I couldn't get too fancy at such short notice, though I figured you'd like the truffles at the very least."

Did she look…touched?

But he wasn't sure, because her expression went back to normal—amused, cool. Margot.

He said, "You really did word those scenarios carefully, didn't you?"

She narrowed her gaze at him, but she didn't go anywhere. He took that as a good sign and allowed the door to ease shut behind him. The soft click of the lock was the only sound besides the thud of his heartbeat.

Any minute now, she was going to tell him to go to hell.

Any minute now, he would feel just as confused as he'd been that night when she'd acted as if their kisses hadn't affected her as much as they had him. If she'd been as turned inside out as he was, she would've believed him about Jay and the camera. Or at least she would've come back to him after accepting his explanations.

But Margot surprised him, reaching out to touch one of the scarves hanging from the dressing screen.

Could keeping her in this room really be that easy?

"You went to a lot of work," she said.

"I take my investments seriously."

Holding his breath, he stepped toward her, daring to touch her hair.

Soft. Just as silky as one of those scarves. His blood screamed through him.

As he skimmed his hand downward, over her shoulder blade, he heard her inhale.

Was she going to run?

Or would she stay and let him make every fantasy he'd had over the past ten years come true?

EVEN WITH THE silk of her shirt as a barrier between his fingers and her skin, Margot could feel the heat of him seeping into her, flowing downward, flooding her with jagged pinpoints of need.

Her pride told her to get out of there, but her body…

Her body wasn't moving, just like the other night when he'd waylaid her in the parking lot, touching her, flirting with her until she'd almost melted into his arms.

She was pounding all over, craving him in a way that only a memory could bring on—a memory of that night the camera had recorded them.

Part of her wanted to show him that he would never

have her. Show him that she wasn't going to lose this contest of wills between them.

The other part of her knew it was a bad, bad idea to be here at all, because he was Clint Barrows, bane of her existence.

But it was another, steamier part that was winning yet again. Hands down.

Shivers spilled through her as his fingertips traced down her back, over her spine. Shivers that speared her, tingling, destroying every resisting thought.

His voice was low, hot.

"Your basket promised eighty ways around a girl," he said, his breath stirring the hair by her ear. "But I'll bet I could find eighty other ways all on my own, without your help."

He skimmed his fingertips to the base of her spine, slipped under her blouse, touched her with the lightest of strokes.

She flinched at the bare contact.

"Seems I've found number one," he said.

God, he sounded so arrogant. And why shouldn't he be when he was reducing her to a pool of thick honey and making her stay when she knew she should go?

He found the zipper at the back of her suede skirt, and when he started to pull it down, the sound ripped through her.

Stay? Go?

Her mind was a mess, reeling with desire.

As he tucked a finger between her and the skirt, skimming just over the line of her panties, she bit her lip, keeping herself from responding. Even so, a little moan escaped her.

"Way number two," he said.

He left her zipper partly open, resting his other hand

on her hip, then tugging lightly at the waistline. Air hushed against her exposed skin, and she turned her face away from him.

It'd be a good time to tell him to stop.

A real good time.

When he coaxed a finger into her skirt, exploring her hipbone, then wandering over to whisk over her belly, her stomach muscles jumped, and she leaned forward, one hand seeking the low dresser for balance.

"Three," he said.

As he ran that finger down toward her panty line, she canted forward a bit more, both hands on the dresser now, her breath sharp, hard to come by.

He coasted his finger beneath the front elastic of her panties, back and forth, stirring her up until she was stiff and achy and oh-so drenched.

Four, she thought.

He didn't have to count anymore as he went lower, more aggressive now, sliding that finger between her folds, making her take a step forward and gasp, then part her legs for him.

What was she doing?

It didn't matter, because she'd already given him all the permission he needed to do whatever it was he'd planned. And she didn't care.

Didn't care one damned bit now.

As he caressed her, up, down, around her clit, she didn't try to stay cool with him anymore. A moan escaped her, and she pressed back against him, feeling his erection.

He cupped a breast with his other hand, his mouth at her ear. "You were already wet for me, Margot."

She ignored the taunt, moving with every motion he made, instead.

Hadn't she imagined something like this in the shower yesterday? His hands, his fingers, then his mouth, all over her, building up a fire in her, pressure, pushing down, up, out, all over the place until—

He thrust two fingers up and into her, and she cried out, mostly because his thumb was working her clit with masterful care, just as if he'd already gone eighty times around her and wasn't about to stop there.

In, out… She wasn't going to last much longer, not with this need to explode. Not with the stiffness of his cock pressed against the back of her.

She wanted him to rip off her skirt, her panties, then pound all the way into her…

Bringing her higher…

Pushing her faster, harder—

An orgasm ripped through her with such force that she sucked in a breath that nearly cut her in two. Once. Then again. And he kept massaging her clit until she couldn't stand anymore and she was suddenly on the floor, boneless, clutching at the dresser. He'd come down to the ground with her, his hand still in her panties as if he owned that part of her.

Now she really couldn't move. Too weak. Too…

She had to admit it. She'd never reacted this way with any man in any country, whether he was a seductive stranger she'd built up in her mind to *ooo-la-la* levels or if he was a short-term fling she'd lost interest in after they'd gotten what they'd needed from each other.

As he pulled out of her, she almost told him not to. He felt too right in her, and she wondered just how right more of him than his fingers would feel. But she also wondered what the college girl who had been humiliated by a joke—and, truthfully, crushed by the realization that Clint really was just a Casanova—would've thought if she could see adult Margot now.

She was slumped back against him, and when she realized that his arm was cradled over her—his possessive, muscled arm—a shock of warmth tumbled through her.

It felt like…affection. But that was impossible when she and Clint Barrows didn't know each other from Eve and Adam.

He was straightening her skirt, tugging it to cover her modestly, and that struck her, too. It struck her so hard that she straightened up and got to her knees, pushing his arm away from her as she took up the job of fixing her own clothes.

"Well," she said. "I guess you got a good return on your investment."

He didn't answer, and without thinking, she peered over her shoulder to see why.

His knees were up, his arms resting on them. Somewhere along the way, his cowboy hat had fallen off, and his golden hair was mussed.

Her heart jerked in her chest, the dumb thing.

"Believe it or not," he said, "I wanted to take this step by step with you."

"Take what?"

He laughed. "Whatever was going to happen with us."

Now she laughed, but it wasn't out of gaiety. "You're sure full of yourself, aren't you? Bringing me in here and thinking…"

"That something *would* happen?" He glanced at her waistline, where her blouse was still untucked. "Call me crazy."

She didn't know whether to hate him or hop on him.

Truthfully, though, she knew it wasn't Clint she hated—
it was the fact that she'd given in without much of a
fight, and she wanted to do a lot more of it, too.

Clint sighed, running a hand through his hair
roughly. "Margot, if you're thinking that you're going
to come out of this room looking like a fool because
you got together with me, don't. What happened in the
past is water under the bridge."

"Not when everyone was served up a memory the
other night, after that video rose from the dead." She
had already gotten to her feet.

His chest constricted. "No one cares. Let it go."

"Why? Why is it so important?"

He raised both hands, then let them fall back down.
"I told you—I feel bad for everything that happened."

He said it as if there was more.

But she didn't want to press him. Once she got back
home, real life would take over. No more baskets, no
more of the animating spark that Clint seemed to bring
to her life.

A blush roared up to her face at the realization that
he was more than just an enemy. Wait until everyone
heard about *this*. Wait until they were all laughing over
their beers, acting like college kids again, gossiping
about how Clint Barrows had finally closed the deal.

He seemed to read her thoughts. "They wouldn't
have to know."

She stared at him as his meaning sank in. She'd told
him that once, before kissing him on his college couch.

He grinned that Romeo grin. "If you want to show
me the rest of what's in that basket tonight—and just
tonight—no one would ever be the wiser. And I mean
that."

Her sense of adventure flared up, but there was more to it than that.

Her body wouldn't forget what he had done to it, and she was already hungering for more. Damn her crazy libido, she was already jonesing for something that had been absolutely unthinkable just a night before, and she didn't know how it'd happened or even when she'd made the choice for it to happen.

Slowly, she tucked in her blouse. And, in spite of everything, when she was done, she decided to tell Clint Barrows just what he could do with that basket.

6

DAMN, MARGOT WAS a tease.

After their encounter, Clint had retreated to familiar ground, going with Riley to the Phi Rho Mu house just off the Cal-U campus. The fall leaves colored the trees and, in the distance, the hills rolled off beyond the brick dorms, academic buildings and the ranchland and orchards that were used to teach hands-on classes to the majority of agriculture students.

He'd thought that getting away from the hotel and sitting here by the pool with some of his brothers at his old fraternity would clear his head, but nope.

He just kept thinking about earlier in the day, after Margot had tucked in her shirt and straightened out her clothes and hair.

She'd sauntered around the room, and he'd known that she was checking for a camera. Satisfied there was none, she'd gone over to her basket on the dresser and almost defiantly brought it over to him. He'd just stared at her while she'd let out an exasperated breath.

"You already know how this works," she said. "You just reach in and pick out a slip of paper."

Was she messing with him? Just a few minutes ago, she'd seemed ready to kick him to the curb for going too far with her.

Not knowing exactly what she was up to, he'd drawn a folded piece of paper from the basket. He barely even read the words before handing it back to her.

She'd taken one look at it, put the basket on the dresser again, grabbed a truffle and a croissant from the tray he'd put together and left the room.

But not before she'd flung one last comment over her shoulder.

"Nine o'clock, my room."

And that was it.

Had she just agreed to experience one of those eighty ways with him tonight?

As Clint mulled over the possibility, he was brought back to the present by an object hitting him in the shoulder. It didn't take him long to see what it was—a wet, spongy ball that some Phi Rho Mu pledges had been zinging at each other in the whirlpool in a game of close-quarter dodgeball.

Clint threw it right back at them, hitting a redheaded pledge in the chest.

All the older guys sitting in lounge chairs around the pool were entertained, including Riley. He was right next to Clint, wearing a baseball cap over his dark hair, protecting his Irish skin from the mild central California sun.

"Rise and shine, Barrows," he muttered.

So Riley had noticed he was a little out of it. Before Clint could explain why, all the brothers who were lounging at the side of the pool, whether they were part of the ten-year reunion or active, started barking orders at the pledges.

Clint hadn't been the only one who'd come to his college stomping grounds to relive old times during the reunion.

"Out of the cushy spa, scrubs!"

"Recite those stud numbers!"

"Into the big pool—*now!*"

Clint took a drink of his beer. It was as flat as his enthusiasm for joining in.

"Was that all we did back then?" he asked Riley as the other brothers surrounded the pledges. "Haze our underlings, drink beer all the time and generally act like idiots?"

"Pretty much." Riley set his bottle down on the concrete as he watched the pledges swim as many laps as the brothers told them to.

Clint glanced at Riley. Something wasn't sitting right with his friend today, either.

"Did the girls take Dani out this afternoon?" Clint asked, thinking that Riley's "something" probably had to do with his fiancée.

He shifted in his chair. "Dani's in the room, resting. I think she's looking at wedding stuff on our laptop. Margot and Leigh's enthusiasm seems to have gotten to her."

Clint recalled what Riley had told him the other day about not being able to give Dani the perfect wedding. Clearly, it was still eating away at him.

Now that Riley had started, he was on a roll. "There're times I wonder if Dani just isn't telling me how disappointed she is in how things have turned out with us. Margot and Leigh are helping her find reasonable alternatives to that grand wedding she always wanted, but…"

"But those alternatives aren't what you would give her if you could. You told me all about it."

Riley took a drink. He didn't have to answer.

Clint watched his brothers hazing those pledges, making them cling to the sides of the pool and kick their legs in a contest to see who lasted the longest. A thought hit him, just as that sponge ball had bopped into his shoulder earlier.

"You have a place for that wedding?" he asked Riley.

"Not so far."

Clint smiled. "Maybe I can at least help you out with that part."

He mentioned his ranch—the wide-open spaces, the grassy lawn, the guest cottages and the gazebo where his own parents had gotten hitched once upon a time.

When Clint was done, Riley was leaning forward in his chair, a big smile on his face.

Clint went back to his beer. Riley couldn't have missed how much he loved that ranch, and Clint didn't want to make a big deal out of it.

Mostly, though, he didn't want to think about how much it'd hurt to lose it.

"You'd go through all the trouble of having a major ruckus like a wedding on your spread?" Riley asked, instead of commenting on Clint's emotional slip.

"Of course. The twins are talking legal threats right now, but they won't be able to take the ranch away by the end of the year, when you were planning to get hitched, so why not?" He shrugged. "You know it's not a big deal. Besides, you've been there and you know it'd work for you."

They grinned at each other, friend to friend. Then Riley's smile got a little devilish. "Okay, I'll ask Dani about it. But let me know if there're any favors I can do for you—getting you some nice wine from my boss's vineyard, putting in a good word for you with Margot…"

No one will ever know, he'd told Margot about tonight.

No one. Not even their friends.

So he kept his end of the bargain. "Didn't you hear that she's planning to give me my money back on that basket?"

"She can't do that."

"I won't force her to do something she doesn't want to."

Riley looked disappointed for him. And, for all Clint knew, maybe tonight wouldn't be worth lying to his friend about, anyway. Was Margot going to pull the rug out from under him by leaving him stranded outside her door, horny and expectant? Would she initiate an even bigger joke if he got inside her room, set on revenge for the embarrassment she'd suffered all those years ago?

Hell, he'd take his chances after what'd happened with her earlier today. Thinking about it made his cock threaten to go stiff again.

Riley said, "Just so you know, there's been a lot of talk in this house from some of the visiting brothers. You sure have tongues wagging."

"Because of the basket."

"Because of you and Margot, together again. 'The fraternity stud and the unfortunate girl who got her pride dented by a camera.'"

Clint pushed back the brim of his hat. "Is it bad of me to wish that it was more than just her pride that was dented?"

"What do you mean?"

Maybe this would be a good time to shut up. But it wasn't as if Clint could go home and bounce this off his twin brothers. "I mean that I've always wondered if she got angry just about the camera…or if there was something more to it."

His friend waited, and when Clint didn't offer anything else, Riley said, "You can't say it, can you?"

What? That he thought Margot had nursed some hopes about what might've happened after finally admitting she was attracted to him? That she'd had a flicker of a deeper emotion, as he did, and wondered if their obvious attraction might turn into something more lasting?

Hell, no. Romantic what-ifs weren't his style. Had never been.

But today, after holding her, feeling her… It'd all come rushing back.

Maybe he really had pinned his hopes on something that had never materialized back then, thanks to that practical joke. Whatever potential there was between them had been destroyed.

And he'd been nicked good, too.

One of the fraternity brothers by the pool, Tyler Hague, had overheard their conversation.

"Is our studliest stud in love?" he called out, while hovering over a pool-bound pledge doing a series of jumping jacks. "Hate to tell you, Barrows, but Margot wasn't so thrilled about you buying her basket last night."

Laughter ensued around the pool. Hilarious.

But they hadn't seen her today with him.

His ego told him to crow about his earlier encounter with her, just as he might've bragged back in college about all the other women he'd kissed and dismissed. Yet somewhere along the line, he'd lost his taste for conquests, and it'd happened after Margot and the video.

They were all staring at Clint, waiting for him to come back with a confident retort.

He kicked back into his chair instead and said, "Margot and I have agreed to forget about the basket. There's nothing between us. Never has been, never will be."

His brothers good-naturedly offered some off-color remarks about Clint's manhood that he ignored, and they soon refocused their attention on the pledges, ordering them out of the pool and telling them to drink from some full red beer cups that a brother had brought over.

Clint looked away. It'd been good to visit the old house where he'd lived throughout most of his college career. It'd been nice to gaze at the wall of pictures—of brothers come and gone—and to give a heartfelt hug to Mother, a paid house mom who'd watched over them and still watched over a new generation of beer-guzzling kids.

But during this particular visit back to his old stomping grounds, Clint realized that there had to be something more than drinking and floating along from day to empty day.

He just wasn't sure what that something more was yet.

"If you wanted to win some brownie points with Margot," Riley said, getting to his feet, "I think you just scored."

Clint stayed silent. Riley didn't know it, but he intended to score a whole hell of a lot more tonight.

LATER THAT DAY, Margot was running on all cylinders, almost as if she'd eaten an entire bowl of raw sugar and she needed to burn it off.

Antsy. *Nervous.* Almost regretting that she had told

Clint to report to her at nine o'clock, after the reunion-closing dinner had been served downstairs.

If she were smart, she would just call off this fiasco-in-the-making, distancing herself from Clint altogether. How hard could it be, anyway, when tonight was the last official event of the reunion? She wouldn't ever have to see him again, wouldn't ever have to think of his cocky smile, his sure hands, his way of making her feel as if she were the only woman he'd ever touched in the way he'd touched her this afternoon.

But Margot didn't want to be smart about Clint Barrows. Not after the heights he'd taken her to with only a little foreplay.

Since Dani had opted to stay back at the hotel, Margot and Leigh had decided to get out and about, to see some of their college downtown haunts while they still could. Margot didn't mention that she actually had another agenda, and it had everything to do with the piece of paper Clint had pulled out of her basket.

Le Crazy Horse, Paris...

She told herself that she was in this merely for the fun as she and Leigh combed the tree-lined downtown streets, meandering in and out of the shops, some of which had survived the years, while others had been taken over by corporate chains.

When they came to The Boudoir, the lingerie shop that every Cal-U girl had visited at least once in her college career, it was just as kitschy and tempting as it had been when Margot was young. Back then every sex toy had made her and the girls giggle and every see-through nightie had been a romantic dream.

Margot managed to slyly purchase a couple of erotic items while Leigh perused the massage-lotion area. Back outside, they passed a new tavern that advertised

Red Bull drinks and Rave Night, a far cry from the country bar that used to thrive here.

"Were those booby tassels I saw you buy?" Leigh asked out of nowhere, her boot heels clicking on the concrete as they walked.

So much for secrecy. "Why would I need tassels?"

"Exactly my question. Because I'd think they wouldn't be so comfortable to wear. They seem too... jiggly."

"I know." Margot scoffed. "*I* don't wear tassels."

At least, she hadn't in the past. But she was rather looking forward to it tonight.

Too much, actually.

Leigh narrowed a glance at her. "And I saw some sexy bubble bath going into your bag, also."

"Do you have eyes in the back of your head or something?"

"Marg, you're just really bad at trying to be stealthy."

Nosy old biddy.

And Leigh wouldn't let up. "You told me that you canceled Clint's basket, but you didn't, did you?"

"Maybe I just want to take a nice bath tonight. Did you ever think of that?"

"Some bath. I've never used booby tassels for one of those."

Up ahead, Margot spied Alicia's Bridal Boutique, and a clear way to get out of this conversation came to her like an angelic chorus.

She grabbed Leigh's arm and steered her toward the store. "Check it out—we can do some reconnaissance work for Dani here."

"I don't know," Leigh said as she was pulled along. "She wasn't too happy about us butting in with the auction."

"But she warmed up to those wedding-gown pictures during breakfast."

Unwilling to take no for an answer—and to hear any more of Leigh's all-too-on-the-nose suspicions about Clint—Margot hauled her into the shop. A bell dinged at the door and a white puffy lace heaven of bridal finery welcomed them.

The clerk wasn't around, so Margot left Leigh and headed straight for the veils, choosing a flowered crown with a fall of tulle.

"Here we go," she said, pretending to wear it while showing Leigh. "Elegant and very Princess Grace-y."

Leigh grinned as she chose her own veil—a simple white flower with netting. She poised it on top of her head and to the side, making sure the netting came over one eye. "Do I look like Miranda Lambert at her wedding to Blake Shelton?"

"Better. There isn't a country singer in the world who could carry that off the way you do."

For a second, Leigh got a look on her face that was very un-Leigh. In fact, it was downright dreamy.

Margot put her veil back. Neither she nor Leigh had ever possessed illusions about getting married. But as she saw Leigh go to a mirror and look at herself with a starry-eyed gaze, she wondered if, somewhere along the way, Leigh had deserted her in the Single Girl Forever Sisterhood.

And... Well, it was lonely being abandoned like that, especially in the middle of a bridal store. But Margot had learned to be independent a long time ago, moving from place to place, never setting down roots or getting to know anyone—especially boys—on a deep level. Yes, she'd kissed her share of them, but there was always a distance that she felt, because she knew she would be leaving.

And things hadn't changed, even in college. She'd been comfortable being on her own, doing what she wanted to do, never being attached at the hip to a guy like some of her sorority sisters tended to be.

But now…

No, she wouldn't think of Clint. Why had he even popped into her head when she was just going to have a secret no-strings, this-one's-for-my-libido fling with him tonight? She'd scratch the itch that had been burning in her ever since that night in college, appeasing the curiosity of what his mouth would feel like on all the throbbing places on her body. She'd fill herself up with him as she'd filled herself with adventures her entire life, then go home, closing that chapter for good.

Wandering toward the gowns, Margot focused on Leigh as her friend checked herself out in the mirror, flushed.

"Are you thinking about the guy who bought your basket?" she asked.

That seemed to wake Leigh up, and she let out a belly laugh as she put her veil back on its rack. The laugh sounded a little hollow.

"I told you I don't ever get my hopes up about men," she said, her hand lingering on the veil one extra moment before she walked away. "I'm still just like you in that way, Marg."

Just like her.

Margot didn't like the sound of that, even if she'd made a career and a brand out of "independent woman adventures" with her books.

But it was as if something had dropped inside of her now—a little stone that fell and fell through the emptiness until it hit bottom, making a pinging splash that reverberated through her.

Leigh ambled around until she came to a tea-length gown. She tilted her head, as if picturing herself in it.

"Leigh," Margot said, without even realizing that she'd intended to talk. "Maybe I'm not the best example for anything."

It was on the tip of her tongue to tell Leigh how her glamorous life wasn't so glamorous these days. Without steady work or success, she wasn't sure how happy she could be or would be.

Leigh looked baffled. "Don't say that, Margot. You live under a lucky star, whether it comes to men or anything else, and I always thought how damned nice it'd be if I didn't have to work twice as hard to do everything you did so easily."

Margot swallowed. A confession was there, in her throat, but it had balled up, burning, waiting for her voice to utter the words.

But they never came.

CLINT DIDN'T BOTHER to go down to the final dinner in the Golden Coast Ballroom. He was hungry for something else entirely, and he had no stomach for mere food.

He took a long, cold shower, then forced himself to sit in front of the TV, watching ESPN until five after nine.

He didn't want Margot to think he was too excited.

Still, before he left, he brushed his teeth one more time, put his Stetson on and went to his door. Then he backtracked, cursing under his breath, and grabbed that white negligee he'd bought earlier today for Margot, gathering all the soaps and lotions, too. He left the dressing screen, scarves and bamboo candle stand alone.

As he approached her room, he had a flashback to the night he'd brought Margot to his college room, never imagining that there was a camera set to record them. His veins tangled, just as they had back then.

Before he knew it, he was knocking on her door, waiting, thinking after a long second that, yeah, this was going to be a joke she'd created to exact her revenge, not only for all those years ago, but for today, too, when he'd been less than a gentleman with her.

Not that she hadn't enjoyed it.

Finally, the lock clicked and the door cracked open. It seemed to take forever.

He couldn't see her, but it was dim inside the room and music was playing, maybe from that computer he'd seen her using at breakfast with the girls.

The tune was slow and sultry, with an accordion and a woman's red-light voice.

Le Crazy Horse, Paris, he thought, the words from the note he'd drawn from Margot's basket flashing in his head like neon.

He pushed the door open slowly, and when he stepped into the room, the bathroom door was just closing.

Flickering candlelight showed through the open slit just before the door shut tight.

"I'll be ready in a minute." She was talking in a candlelit tone, as if she was waiting for him in the shadows.

As he went to put down the negligee and bath products on the dresser, he pictured what she might be wearing, what she was planning. Something tugged at him inside his belly, tightening him up.

So far this was no joke.

He heard the sound of water splashing against the tub inside the bathroom, and his knees nearly buckled.

Yet she kept him waiting.

And waiting.

He was just about ready to knock down the door when he heard the sound of the shower curtain being drawn, then her voice again.

"You can come in now…without your phone."

She was cautious about him filming this. "I don't have it on me."

"Good."

Playing it cool, he entered the bathroom. Candlelight flickered orange against the walls and, from behind the shower curtain, he saw light, too.

And a silhouette.

His mouth went dry.

Margot, every curve of her in smoky black shadow. Her hair was down around her shoulders, one hand resting on the back of her head as she stood in profile, accentuating her breasts.

Was she wearing a piece of lingerie that clung to her? He couldn't tell, but he leaned against the wall to keep himself from ripping the curtain aside and ruining the sensuous image.

Just enjoy, he thought. *It's the only night you'll be able to do it.*

"What's going on, Hemingway?" he asked, his voice thick as he teased her about being an English major, just as he used to. The scent of peaches wafted to him, making him dizzy.

"This is your first and only stop of eighty," she said, sassy as could be. "That's what's going on."

"What's this stop?"

He would play along. For now. Let her feel the power

that had been taken away from her with that camera a decade ago.

She touched the curtain, and he sucked in a breath.

"Don't you remember what that slip of paper said?" she asked. "You drew it from the basket only a few hours ago."

"Humor me."

She laughed again, shifting so that her silhouetted hips swayed to the other side. "Le Crazy Horse, Paris. Do you know anything about it?"

"I think I know everything I need to." *Let's get on with it,* his body screamed.

"That's not how we play this," she said, swaying again, her hips so ripe, so in need of touching and caressing.

He settled in for her brand of verbal foreplay. "Then tell me."

She sounded satisfied. "The club was started up in 1951 by Alain Bernardin in Paris. He was an artist with avant-garde tastes and an appreciation for women. Le Crazy Horse is known mainly for its burlesque—racy acts with musical numbers and humor thrown in for relief."

"Relief from what?"

She pulled on the far side of the shower curtain just enough that it offered a peek of the wall tile, and that was all.

Why did it seem that she was always offering a tiny glimpse of herself, and not just in a physical sense?

Why, dammit, did he want more?

But she was already speaking.

"What kind of relief do you think I'm talking about?" she asked. "If you get a rise out of every female act they perform, wouldn't you need a break?"

Speaking of which… His jeans were getting awful tight.

The water swished against the sides of the tub again as she began to move to the music—an enticing blend of the singer's come-hither voice and the lazy pull of that accordion.

Clint watched her for a while, imagining what she might do if he reached behind the curtain and touched her. He hadn't seen her face this afternoon when he'd brought her to orgasm, and the more he watched her dance for him in silhouette, the more he wanted to know if she had closed her eyes when she came, what her mouth had looked like shaped around a cry of ecstasy.

What she felt when he got close like this.

When the song ended, another one began.

"Do you know who Gypsy Rose Lee is?" she asked. "Or Lili St. Cyr?"

He was dying here. "No."

"They were famous in the striptease world and a big influence on Dita Von Teese. She's one of the biggest names in the business, and she played Le Crazy Horse not too long ago."

He was just about to destroy that curtain when she finally pulled at it, wrapping it over her body so it molded every curve of her figure.

Her face… God, he hadn't realized it, but he'd wanted to see her face so badly, and the sight of those pale eyes and dark lashes and red lips didn't disappoint. It gutted him, pierced him through with a lust so strong that he could barely stand it.

"Ms. Von Teese," Margot said, "does a little number called '*Le Bain.*'"

Clint had barely squeaked by the foreign-language requirement in college—he'd taken a semester of French just because he knew a lot of romantic-minded girls would be in the class—and he remembered what *le bain* meant.

The bath.

Margot's gaze locked to his as she pushed the curtain all the way to the side.

His lungs cut off his air supply when he saw her standing in front of a candle in the corner. She was wearing a pink chiffon slip that was so tight it left very little to the imagination. Her arms were slim, toned, her legs going on forever. Under the material, he could've sworn that she was wearing tassels over her breasts.

She bent to the bubble-laced water, still looking at him, then splashed a handful over her chest.

As it drizzled down into her cleavage and dampened the material over her breasts, he laughed softly, taking off his hat and tossing it outside the bathroom.

"Don't do this to me," he said, half kidding. Because he liked what she was doing, even though it was one long tease that was making his balls blue.

But, being Margot, she did it again.

Two scoops this time, one over each breast.

He couldn't see the tips of them through the more padded parts, but the water plastered the rest of the sheer lingerie to her stomach, her belly, hinting at the lace panties she was wearing.

Those were getting wet, too, droplets clinging to the thighs exposed by her short gown.

"Dammit, Margot," he murmured.

As if driven on by those words, she turned her back to him, once again swaying to the slow music. She reached to the front of her slip, undoing the buttons there. Then, inch by inch, she lowered the material from her shoulders, exposing her bare back.

He leaned against the wall, gritting his teeth.

Smiling—maddeningly, teasingly, totally knowing that she was in control of him—she allowed the slip to drop to her waist.

The slope of her back drove him wild, but he didn't show it.

"What comes next?" he asked.

She turned toward him, revealing her breasts. They were tipped with silver tassels that she touched, stroked.

He wiped a hand down his face. So close to seeing more of her, yet so far. The mounds of her breasts were beautiful to him, perfect, begging for his hands and fingers and mouth. And as she wiggled out of the rest of her gown, tossing it to the tiled floor, he yearned to relieve her of those lace panties, too.

She palmed more water, but now she slid her hands up her legs, wetting them, allowing the liquid to roll down her skin.

"I think," she said, still leaning over, giving him a good view of her breasts, "you like this trip so far."

"I've always liked," he said. "I've always wanted."

He just wouldn't tell her how much.

He took a step forward without even thinking, but she held up a hand and shook a finger at him playfully.

"We've got a long way to go, Stud."

She reached for the handheld showerhead and turned on the water, her smile all-knowing.

So seductive that he didn't know if he could last as long as this trip would take.

7

THEY SAID THE first rule of striptease was that you can touch him, but he can't touch you.

At least, that was what Margot had seen and heard in the clubs she'd been in, like Le Crazy Horse. She'd written about the girls there and everywhere—women who seduced men with long looks and suggestive dances.

And now, as Clint Barrows watched her, she became one of those girls—someone who was wanted by a man more than anything else in the world. She could see it in his eyes, the wanting. Could practically feel it rising above the bath-steeped humidity in the room as the candles flickered.

She recognized the same yearning look from that night so long ago. Naked need in his gaze and... Now that she was in the moment, she remembered there'd been something else she'd seen in him that had scared her, even while making her heart beat with the same stilted, unfamiliar rhythm that it was right now.

But, at this moment, she wasn't that Margot, was she? She wasn't the girl from college who'd had an awkward incident with him that had sent her bursting out of a dim room, leaving him behind and darkening his name in her personal history. And even though the thought of becoming someone else for the night—someone who had no worries about her future and lived for the day—appealed to Margot, it was actually the only way she was going to be able to get through this seduction.

The only way her pride was going to stay intact while her body had a holiday.

As the water sprayed from the showerhead she held, the peach-scented bubbles from the bath clung to her calves, water beading on her skin. She ran her fingers down her soaked panties, up over her belly, then between her legs.

His gaze followed, a muscle in his jaw pulsing as he kept leaning against the wall, otherwise as casual as you please.

But that ticking muscle told her that he was steamed up inside, no matter how cool he looked.

"Imagine," she said as the music kept playing. "My hands are your hands, touching me, making me hot."

She slipped the showerhead inside her panties, dousing herself with water, leaving the lace clinging to her. Pressing back against the wall, she kept showering herself, stroking herself.

Hungry. He looked hungry enough to stop this show altogether and have his way with her. His gaze was burning with it.

But so was she. Her juices were swamping her, her breath coming faster and faster, especially when she pulled her panties away from her so he could see a bit more—but not much more—while she aimed the stream of water at her most sensitive parts.

She hauled in a hard breath, arching into the spray as it tickled her clit.

Then she whispered, "Your hands and fingers feel so good on me."

She closed her eyes, maybe because she didn't want to look at him, to see the reality of what she was doing. She and Clint Barrows—a scenario she would have fought tooth and nail before today. Her pride wouldn't let her forget it.

But here she was.

And it *was* good.

She opened her eyes to see him grinning now, starting to unbutton his shirt.

"Uh-uh," she said, shaking her head while still massaging herself, building herself up to a point where she wouldn't be able to even talk or make intelligible sounds much longer, just like yesterday, when she'd pleasured herself to thoughts of him.

A fantasy.

Not real. Never real with him.

"There's been enough teasing," he said. The candlelight laved the tanned skin of his muscled chest, the bunched abs.

As he shrugged off his shirt, a pierce of desire made her stifle a moan.

Her nipples went hard, sensitive as hell, aching to feel his chest against hers.

And he noticed, his gaze eating her up.

He laughed, low and wicked, as he undid the top button of his fly, where a bulge strained against his jeans.

Something like panic shot threw her. *She* was the one who would set the pace today. She flicked the showerhead in his direction, spraying some water at him.

"You need to cool off," she said.

He only laughed again, leaving his fly slightly open at the top, where a thin trail of golden hair disappeared.

The sight of it excited her even more.

As he removed his boots and socks, she took her hand out of her panties.

"I think you need to be reminded," she said, gesturing to her entire body, "that this isn't for you. You can look, but you can't touch."

"You sure about that, Tolstoy?"

Before she could be mildly impressed with his continued recall of Literature 101—how many authors' names would he call her before this was over?—he undid another button on his fly.

"When you were touching yourself," he asked, "were you thinking of how much better it'd be if I was doing it? If I was inside you, making you want to cry out like you did earlier today?"

She would never admit any of that to him. Hell, she'd spent the beginning of the night laughing downstairs at the dinner and acting like nothing was bothering her—surely she could do that with Clint, too.

"You think a lot of yourself," she said. "Don't you, Stud?"

"You know what I think a lot about?"

Another button, undone.

Another part of her, undone, as he took a step toward the tub.

He lowered his voice. "I think a lot about you. I haven't been able to stop since I laid eyes on you again."

She could barely find the oxygen to speak. "That's because you want what you can't have."

When he got close enough, he reached out, hooking a finger in her panties, tugging at them, and it was as if she had turned to hot water herself, near boiling.

"You want me to have it," he said, slipping her panties down an inch, so that her hip was exposed.

She was pulsing for him, between her legs, in her chest. Was she going to let him have it?

Yes, she thought. *Hell, yes.*

But only when she said so.

As he pulled down her panties more, she covered herself with a hand. Another rule of striptease—hide your bits.

Keep teasing.

He worked the material down her legs, and she allowed him to do it. She even stepped out of the lace without being urged, watching him throw it carelessly behind him.

He glanced up at her with those light blue eyes— eyes that could talk her into anything. A gaze that had probably talked any number of girls into more than they should've given him.

For a long time, she'd been determined never to be one of those girls—not with any man. She was better than that.

But as she saw how much he wanted her, she knew that it would be fine if it were on her terms.

When he stood, she reached for his fly, undoing the last button. Then she took him into her hand—hard, long, stiff. Everything she'd never gotten ten years ago.

All for her.

She caressed him, up, down, so slowly that he shut his eyes, clenching his jaw.

"Maybe *you're* the one who wants to be inside me more than anything," she said. "You're thinking about it right now, feeling how you'd slip into me, coming inside me over and over again."

She circled a thumb over his tip, and he groaned low in his throat.

"Just how long do you think you're going to last?" she asked, ruthless.

"All night if I have to."

Oh, really? Now who was wielding the power?

Ramped up, she decided to tease him even more, skimming her fingertips underneath his shaft until she got to his balls. She toyed with him, watching how his nipples went hard, how a vein in his throat strained.

"You're not going to last another second," she whispered.

It was a challenge the adventurous side of her wanted him to accept.

And he did.

Everything happened at once—his eyes opened, his fingers locked around her wrist, and before she knew it, he was in the tub with her, splashing water with such force that he doused the candle in the corner.

Her pulse was nearly deafening as he lifted her, bringing her against the wall, gently yet firmly removing one tassel from her breast before latching on to her with his mouth, sucking at her until the pleasant throb between her legs became unbearably painful.

In a good way, she thought as she wound her fingers through his thick hair. In one of eighty good ways....

As he worked at a nipple, his fingers sought the other, taking off the tassel, then playing with her as mercilessly as she'd played with him, bringing her to a peak so quickly that her mind couldn't catch up.

But he had to know that he was driving her crazy, and he looked up at her with those hungry eyes and a cruel grin.

Who's not gonna last? that grin seemed to ask.

She heard the answer echoing in the back of her mind. *Me. I can't stop myself with you, damn you.*

She yanked down his jeans, bringing them around his hips as she slid down the tiled wall to the bath. He stopped her, reaching into one of his pockets for a condom, then worked off his jeans the rest of the way, discarding them with a wet thud on the floor.

Once she was sitting in the water, warm, frothy bubbles popped over her everywhere as she watched him sheathe himself, then kneel in front of her in the bath, lifting one of her legs over his arm.

Open to him. She was so damned open, the water lapping at her, once again making her want to scream.

He only made it worse when he teased her with his tip, running it down between her folds.

"Is this what you want?" he asked. "Are you still playing a game?"

It would always be a game with them, nothing more.

But even as she thought it, that inner sinking sensation—the stone hitting water and causing ripples—hit her.

She ignored it, wiggling under him, giving as good as she was getting from him.

"You want it more," she said.

Another laugh, gritty and amused. "I want it a hell of a lot."

And he drove into her, as if to show her that he wasn't going to deny anything—not his lust, not the lengths to which she'd driven him.

Not her.

She gasped, digging her nails into his arm, water slick over his skin and muscle as he rammed into her again.

Bathwater sloshed over the sides of the tub as she moved with him at every thrust, her other hand planted in his hair while she insisted on dictating the pace.

He didn't seem to mind—not even when she demanded that she be on top, forcing him beneath her, riding him, causing frenetic waves to slap the tile floor.

She braced a hand on the wall, working him, feeling him go deep inside her, closing her eyes again as patterns of light ricocheted wildly across her field of vision.

At first she didn't know what she saw in them, all of the shapes unfamiliar, just as foreign as what she'd seen in his eyes back in college, just as confusing as the strange emotions that had nipped at her as he'd kissed her, caressed her.

And now, they were back, but intensified.

Flashes of heat. Swirls. Jags of lightning…

The rumble of oncoming thunder in her body.

It started in her clit, gathered in her belly, pushing out with such energy that the orgasm came like a bolt out of the blue, hitting her, rattling her, making her take such a needle-sharp breath that she didn't think she'd ever be able to breathe again.

He wasn't far behind, though, and when he came, he said her name.

"Margot…"

Not an English-major nickname, not the name of a famous author, just…her.

The sound of it melted off the walls like beaded steam, slipping down like drops.

Slipping into her as if finding someplace it truly belonged.

AFTERWARD, CLINT watched her just as longingly as when he'd watched her perform the striptease.

Watched her push back a hank of hair that had come to cover her face while she climaxed. Watched her watch him, then catch a breath, looking away.

After that, he wasn't sure what happened. He just knew for certain that she was piecing herself together while she climbed out of the tub, water sluicing down every angle of her beautiful, long body before she grabbed a towel from the rack and started to dry off. He watched her as she wrapped that towel around herself, hiding everything from his gaze, before she walked out of the bathroom without another word.

He'd stayed in the tub a little longer, reveling in the aftermath, satiated.

That's what he was, right? Satiated? Sure, the pit of his belly ached for more. And, yeah, he hadn't been lying when he'd told her that he could last all night, because he was ready to go again.

And again.

But he was feeling something else, and he was afraid to look at it too closely, because this was it. One night only. A last hurrah at a reunion.

Obviously, she wouldn't let this go any further. She'd made her point to him already—that she'd won some kind of contest between them—and that was good enough for her.

The longer he sat in that bath, the more her attitude bothered him.

He got out of the tub. The water had gotten cold, anyway.

After he wound a towel around his hips, he found Margot by the window, the curtains shut. She'd turned off the music and turned on a light, but if she thought that the glare would wipe away the fantasy of what had gone on in the tub, she was dead wrong.

She was just as desirable in reality, with that towel wrapped around her and the ends of her lustrous hair plastered to her skin. And even with her back to him as she went through her suitcase, he couldn't deny that he'd seen that all-consuming light in her eyes when he'd been inside her.

"I haven't gone on a lot of trips in my lifetime," he said, "but I doubt there's one that would top where I just went."

Her shoulders stiffened as she held up a nightshirt for her inspection. Was she about to shoo him out so she could go to bed, dismissing him?

Well, it wasn't as if he hadn't gracefully put an end to more than a few nights like that himself.

"You must not take many vacations." She sounded so cool and collected.

Something about her tone made him angry. Okay, maybe not angry, but it tweaked that part of him that Margot always seemed to rile up.

The part of him that no one else ever got to.

He rested his hip against a dresser, crossing his arms over his chest. "You're the traveler. I'm the small-towner who likes where he's at."

"Then this should be enough excitement to last you." Burn.

"You know," he said, not taking her words to heart, "there are way more slips of paper in that basket of yours. I'd hate for all your hard work to go to waste." He jerked his chin toward the soaps and lotions he'd brought over. The pretty white negligee. "And all these things I bought this morning? They can't just sit here."

"Use them on the next girl who comes along."

Could there be more to her attitude than he'd first thought?

"You're not pissed at me because you finally gave in, are you?" he asked.

In immediate hindsight, maybe this hadn't been the right subject to broach at the moment.

She turned around, her posture ramrod-straight. She held that nightshirt in front of her like a shield. "*I* gave in? As you might recall, you were pretty easy."

"I can't say you're wrong about that."

His carefree comment seemed to take the steam out of her argument—and Lord knew it looked as if she was ready for one. It didn't take a college graduate to know that this was her way of distancing herself.

She let the nightshirt fall to the bed. "I don't know. I'm just… It was fun, okay? It was a nice night. Let's not ruin it by analyzing it."

"Nice and fun. I guess that's one way of putting it." *Mind-blowing, earth-moving…* Those were other ways.

"You're no stranger to fun," she said.

"No, I'm not." He moved away from the dresser, his body drawn toward her. "I'm just wondering why it'd be a bad idea for us to have fun all night. After all, I didn't see any limitations on how many trips I'd get when I bought the basket."

"It was a one-time thing."

He decided to play this from a different angle. "You're right. It was nice and fun. I'm sure we can be adults about this and we won't get awkward when we see each other again."

She frowned. "We're seeing each other again?"

"You didn't think I'd skip Dani and Riley's wedding, did you?"

"It's entirely possible to avoid people at weddings."

"Well, I hear you're pretty involved with the planning, and since Dani and Riley are thinking about getting married on my ranch…"

Her eyes widened. "What're you talking about?"

He didn't need to tell her that it was only an idea that he'd floated by Riley this afternoon. "I offered up my ranch for the wedding. It's something that might put us in some amount of proximity, Margot."

Even when she doubled her frown, she was the most gorgeous woman he'd ever seen.

"Oh, come on," he said. "Don't tell me you'll be able to resist checking my place out with Dani and hanging around to offer decorating tips. I know she'll ask you and Leigh to do that, since you're the Three Musketeers."

"You did this on purpose, didn't you?"

"Strategized to have the wedding on my property just so I could see you again?" He shrugged. "I only made a kind gesture to one of *my* good friends."

"Don't twist my words."

"Okay." He comfortably crossed his arms over his chest. "I take it back—you *didn't* mean that I wanted to somehow lure you to my ranch so we could have more fun times together. But now that I think about it, that *is* a real good plan."

"You're impossible."

"I thought you said I was easy." He grinned.

Clearly, there wouldn't be any more going around the girl tonight—not with the mood she was in. But, even if Clint had to wear bath-soaked jeans back to his room, he'd gotten what he'd wanted from her, wasn't that right?

So why did he feel so…empty?

Before she could launch into a real argument, he sauntered back to the bathroom, managed to get into his wet clothes, picked up his boots and went to the door.

"Night, Margot," he said, tipping his hat to her. "I'll be seeing you."

"Don't count your weddings before they hatch."

Although it didn't sound like an endearment, he took it as one as he opened the door and risked a glance behind him, finding her watching him with a glimmer in her eye that told him she just might be looking forward to seeing him again, no matter what she said.

THE ROAD AHEAD of Dani and Riley stretched well into the darkness, illuminated by the headlights of his truck.

Dani, who was full from the subpar hotel banquet food, as well as all the socializing from the reunion, was just drifting off to sleep with Riley at the wheel when her phone played an ancient song from the '80s.

"Girls Like Me." Margot's ringtone.

Dani hopped on it, automatically pressing the speakerphone button. "You still back at the hotel?"

"I told you at the dinner that I decided to stay an extra night."

Funny thing. Riley had said that Clint was staying over, too.

She exchanged a glance with him, and he cracked a grin, his hand resting comfortably on the steering wheel as they zoomed along.

"Am I on speakerphone?" Margot asked.

"Nope."

Dani made a face at Riley, who put a finger to his lips. She shook her head, telling him that she was going to take this one in private.

After she pressed the button and put the phone to her ear, she asked, "So…anything going on in the hotel?"

"Nothing major."

Dani had known Margot a long time, and she could pinpoint when her friend was dancing around something.

"Did you and anyone…?" she started to ask.

"*Hell,* no."

Dani smiled, because Margot was protesting too much. Riley grinned as he guessed Margot's answer.

Maybe someday she would spill the beans about Clint, but it wouldn't be tonight.

"What I'm calling about," Margot said, "is a rumor I heard. Are you and Riley thinking about having your wedding on Clint Barrows's ranch?"

Dani mouthed to Riley, *"Ranch,"* then answered. "He mentioned it to me today, and I think it's a fantastic idea."

She thought she heard Margot mutter, "Crap."

"Riley's seen Clint's spread," Dani said, "but I'd like it if you and Leigh would check his place out with me. I need people who can look at it with wedding bells in mind."

Truthfully, Dani liked Clint. He put a light in Margot's eyes. He'd *always* made Margot act a little differently when he was in the room, not that she would ever cop to that.

"Are you sure about having Leigh and me out there with you for a look-see?" Margot asked. "We don't want to interfere…."

"Haven't you been doing that all along?"

Margot laughed. "All right. You've got me."

"I've got you for a visit to the ranch? If you're not busy, Riley and I were talking about this weekend."

Dani could just picture Margot softly banging her head against a wall.

"There's really no other place on earth you can have a wedding?" Margot asked.

"The price is right, baby. Plus, it sounds beautiful at

Clint's place, and there's enough room to accommodate everyone we want to invite."

A pause crackled over the connection, and if that wasn't enough to convince Dani that something had gone on with Margot and Clint this weekend, nothing ever would.

"Dani," Margot said. "You know I'd do anything for you."

"Even this?"

"Even this. I mean, what's the big deal, anyway, right? I had to see Clint Barrows *this* weekend and I got through it. I can do it again."

If that's how you want it, Margot. "I'm sure you can."

Margot blew out a breath. It was the closest she would ever come to an admission.

After they said their goodbyes and hung up, Dani rested her head against the seat.

"So?" Riley asked.

So what should she say? She'd just been thinking about all Margot's adventures, and how she and Clint might've had a real good one tonight.

Why hadn't *she* ever been able to have an adventure?

Because I'm too boring, Dani thought. *Too...me.* Always needing someone else—sorority sisters, a perpetual fiancé—and never a woman who sought out excitement on her own. Even sex with Riley was tender, sweet. But there'd never been *adventures.*

Maybe that was because Dani had always been afraid of feeling too much, like her mom had felt for her dad before he'd stepped out on her and they'd split up, becoming shells of their old selves.

She finally answered Riley's question. "I definitely think they had a moment."

"Clint and Margot?"

"It had to happen sometime this weekend."

She thought of what Margot might do if she were in a car with Clint, how they probably wouldn't be able to keep their hands off each other.

Adventures.

Why *not* her?

Slowly, she reached over to Riley, traced a finger over the side of his leg.

He smiled down at her, apparently expecting nothing more than a simple touch that said "I love you."

Something bent inside of her, like it was turning around, and she slid her hand up to the top of his thigh, toward his penis.

No. His *cock*.

The car jerked toward the side of the road.

"Jeez, Dani," he said, chuckling and righting the wheel.

She liked his shock, so she did it again, running her fingers over the bulge in his jeans, squeezing gently.

This time, he took her hand in one of his, brought it up to his mouth, kissed the back of it.

Her heart contracted, even though she knew that he hadn't exactly rejected her. He was just Riley and she was just Dani, and they had been best friends who'd turned to lovers.

That was the only time they'd surprised each other.

As Riley held her hand to his heart, his eyes on the straight road ahead, Dani thought about how Margot and Leigh had tried to raise money for her wedding, how everyone still saw her as that steady, dependable, romantic sorority sister nicknamed "Hearts."

Maybe it was high time for some surprises.

8

A WEEK HAD never passed more slowly for Clint, but when Margot's trendy Prius finally pulled into the long graveled driveway that led to his ranch house near Visalia, about a half hour away from Cal-U, he somehow stayed cool.

Dani, who'd been sitting next to him on the living room's cowhide sofa, popped out of her seat when she saw Margot through the window. She touched her hair self-consciously, probably because she'd gotten most of it chopped off this week in what she'd called a "modern bob," which basically meant that one side of her red curls now came to her chin while the other was a little longer.

"Finally!" she said, taking off in the direction of the front door.

From the chair next to Clint, Riley got up, too. As he watched Dani disappear from the room, he wore a look that was part affection, part puzzlement.

"Still getting used to the new fiancée?" Clint asked.

Riley sighed, then shrugged while ambling in the

direction of the entryway. "Even if she got a haircut on a whim, she's still my Dani."

When Clint glanced out the window again, he saw Margot getting out of her car and embracing Dani. His heartbeat did a strange jig in his chest, and he wondered why he was feeling something there when it should've been limited to his nethers.

He'd sincerely missed her, he thought. And in spite of all the work he'd been faced with after leaving the cutting horse operation during the reunion, he'd actually felt kind of bored without her around.

But it was just because of the sex.

Only the sex.

He walked to his foyer, then exited onto the porch with its hickory-wood chairs and tables and gliding swing, then down the few steps to the stone-lined entry path that led to the parked vehicles.

"Let me take a look at you," Margot was saying, holding Dani away from her as Riley lingered nearby.

Lightheartedly, Dani primped for her, showing off that stylish new hairdo.

Margot's smile was a million watts. "You look amazing!"

Clint couldn't stop gazing at her as something in his chest flared. Rays of energy beamed everywhere in him.

Weird.

As Margot linked arms with Dani, she sent a subtle wink at Riley, who ran a hand through his dark hair and returned the grin.

Finally, Margot glanced at Clint, and he casually nodded in greeting, as if his world wasn't being shaken.

"Good to see you, Margot," he said. How about that. He didn't sound affected by her at all.

But from the way she gave him a too-polite smile, he suspected that she was still in argument-mode from last weekend, when she'd pretty much told him that the sex had been good, but *bye-bye*.

"Good to see you, too," she said. "Thanks for having us here."

Riley cleared his throat, snagging everyone's attention. "Looks like it's just the four of us, then."

Margot seemed relieved to break gazes with Clint. "Leigh told you she has reshoots for one of her cooking episodes?"

Riley and Dani nodded as Clint said, "Did she ever hear anything about the secret admirer who won her basket?"

Margot's gaze widened ever so slightly, as if baskets were the last thing she wanted to be talking about with him around.

Dani answered for her. "The only thing Leigh found out was that he should be back in the country by the end of the month, and he'll be contacting her then."

"Out of the country?" Clint wondered which fraternity brother did all that traveling, plus had a lot of play money. He couldn't come up with a name offhand. "I guess he's a jet-setter, just like Margot."

It was as if, once again, he'd said something that didn't sit right with her, because her smile didn't reach her eyes.

"I'm just a writer who likes doing what she does. That's all."

Why did she seem a little...sad?

Dani started pulling her away from the car. "Clint promised us a beautiful sunset, so you're just in time to see it at the gazebo where Riley and I could take our vows. You ready for a tour?"

"Show me the way."

The women took off, leaving Riley and Clint to walk after them. Clint didn't object, because it gave him ample opportunity to enjoy the way Margot's rear filled the back of her dark knit dress.

What kind of panties was she wearing today? Lace? Nothing at all?

As they passed the cottages where the original owners had lived before the main house was built, Dani pointed to the west. The tops of the ranch hands' bunkhouses met the horizon off in the distance.

"The working part of the ranch is over that way," Clint said. "Near enough so that your wedding guests could go for a horseback ride if they want, but far enough so this living area doesn't have too much of that ranch…"

"Aroma?" Margot asked.

"Exactly."

Dani was a small-town girl, but she hadn't grown up on a farm or ranch like most Phi Rho Mu members had. She was a bit of an outsider, and that's probably why she got along with the biggest outsider of them all—Margot.

And that's why Clint had been so attracted to her, he thought. Because she'd always been different. Challenging.

His blood pumped as he watched the breeze toy with the layers of Margot's long hair, but then, when he thought about how she'd just about vowed they'd never get together again, his pulse mellowed.

Strangest of all, his heart actually felt heavy.

It didn't take long to get to the gazebo, which was surrounded by autumn-hued bushes with anemic leaves. Margot immediately went to them.

Dani said, "Clint told us we could plant flowers for

the late spring. Since we're having a bigger wedding now, we decided to move the date back."

"That'll be gorgeous." While Margot surveyed the rectangular pine gazebo, that sad smile Clint had noticed earlier tipped the corners of her mouth. "This is absolutely perfect, Dani."

"I think so, too."

As they stood there, still linking arms, Clint had another rogue thought: yes, this was somehow near to perfect, seeing Margot on his property, in front of the gazebo where his parents had gotten married.

While he tried to figure himself out, Margot climbed the steps to the gazebo's spacious floor.

"Are you going to use the catering company you work for?" she asked. "Aren't they too far away to be convenient?"

Dani glanced at the group, seeming anxious about what she was going to say next. She walked over to Riley, touching his arm. "So…about the catering. I won't be using my company because… Well, I've actually been thinking…" Now she looked up at Riley. "I'm not sure how much longer I'll be working with them."

When Riley glanced down at her, it was obvious this was the first time he was hearing this.

Margot piped up. "Come again?"

Dani tucked a strand of her new, bobbed hair behind an ear and smiled at Riley. "I've been thinking about quitting." She added in a lowered voice to Riley, "It's been on my mind, hon."

Silence flapped in the air until Riley turned around, shaking his head as he walked away. Dani offered an apologetic glance to Margot and Clint before she went after him.

That left the two of them standing there, awkward as hell.

Clint spoke. "Who knew those two were capable of a disagreement?"

"The hard feelings won't last long. Riley and Dani are one of those couples who don't really have problems."

Not problems you can see clearly, anyway.

That part of it went unspoken between them.

As they waited, all but shuffling their boots, Margot got that sad distance in her eyes again, as if she couldn't help keeping her mind off what was troubling her.

Then she sighed. "I suppose I should get settled."

"Right." It wasn't as if they were friends and he could ask her what was wrong.

So he led her back to the ranch house, a canyon of tension between them.

IT'D BEEN A semi-awkward dinner, with Riley as unreadable as a closed book and Dani filling the silence by chatting away about her future plans for her own catering company.

Lord knew what had gotten into her, Margot thought, but she could just imagine the private conversation that'd gone on between Dani and Riley after that mini-bombshell at the gazebo.

"You're going to quit?" he probably would've said once they were alone. *"Where did this come from, Dani?"*

Fortunately, Margot had gotten the opportunity to ask Dani the same question while Clint and Riley had bonded over grilling steaks outside and Margot had helped Dani in the kitchen with twice-baked potatoes,

Caesar salad, plus mushrooms stuffed with spinach and topped by a béchamel sauce.

She hadn't gotten much out of Dani, though.

"Everyone and everything changes," she had said simply. "Remember last weekend when you told me that I was capable of running my own business, and I just hadn't taken the opportunity to try it? Well, that stuck with me, Margot. It made me rethink where I'm going and where I've been."

Margot ran her gaze over Dani's saucy haircut, but didn't say anything more. Quitting a job and pursuing a new business was a serious turn of events for anyone, but the issue was between Dani and Riley. And, until her friend wanted advice or feedback, Margot would let them work it out.

AFTER DINNER, DANI shooed everyone out of the kitchen, preferring to clean up "like the totally efficient home ec machine" she said she was, so Margot wasn't sure what to do with herself. She was hardly tired, though, so she retreated to the porch, where night had already fallen across the clear California country sky, stars winking down.

She chose to sit in a gliding herringbone swing and leaned back, finally breathing for the first time that day. It'd been a rough one. Yesterday, she'd gotten news from her agent that her publishing house hadn't merely decided to refuse any future contracts with her, but they had actually told her to forget about fulfilling the final book on her present agreement. She couldn't stop worrying about it.

I'm an official, utter failure, she thought. And where was there for a failure to go now? She heard the door open, and she straightened up.

It was Clint, holding two crystal shot glasses with golden liquid, backlit by the warm illumination from the foyer.

His boot steps thudded on the planks as he walked toward her, and her heart imitated the sound with tiny booms.

The two of us alone...Le Crazy Horse...a bubble bath...

"Nightcap?" he asked, handing her a glass.

"What did you bring me?" It'd been asinine to think that she wouldn't find herself alone with him again. But this time, she would stay strong.

Even if she was already going weak, just from smelling the clover and hay on his skin.

Something in her chest seemed to expand because he was near, and she shooed the sensation away.

"It's a liqueur," he said. "St. Germain. They say it's really rich, made from elderflowers."

"You've never had it before?"

"First time for everything, even for a fellow like me."

She couldn't help laughing at that and took the glass in hand.

He said, "I figured you all might like it."

"I've had it before, and it's wonderful. Thank you." She almost tacked on a "stud" at the end of the sentence but bit her tongue before old, flirting habits could take over.

No need to flirt with him when they'd finally gotten each other out of their systems.

He sat next to her in a rustic chair. Couldn't he leave her alone to wallow in her misery with a fine libation, just as if she were a poet with her absinthe?

He'd doffed his hat earlier, and his hair was a mess.

Damn him for that, too, because she found it adorable in a dumb, schoolgirl-crush way.

"So," he said.

"So." She searched for words. "How about the drama you've got on your ranch? And we haven't even come to a wedding yet."

"Are you talking about the girl with the new haircut?" He jerked his chin toward the door, indicating Dani. "I'm leaving her and Riley to work everything out."

"I can't blame her for flailing around a little. She's getting married and making a huge life change. I think this is her version of cold feet."

Why was she talking so much?

Clint only nodded as he took a sip of the St. Germain. When she caught herself aping his movements, she paused. Then she thought, *Screw it,* and drank away, letting the thick warmth of the liqueur travel down her throat and through her limbs.

What to talk about now? It wasn't as if they'd ever had a normal conversation. But here, under the stars, at his home, normal seemed…well, normal. It was nice to be someplace comfy like this. She'd never really sat on a porch with someone before and felt like she didn't want to rush off anywhere.

"You've got a great place here," she finally said. "It'll be a fabulous location for the wedding. You were right about that."

"Thanks."

"Your brothers don't care that you offered it to Dani and Riley?"

He took his shot glass and held it up, absently looking through it, as if to inspect the golden nectar. Offhandedly, he said, "I'm going to assume Riley told you much more about Jeremiah and Jason than I thought."

She was skating on thin ice here, and she wasn't sure if it would hold. Why had she even mentioned his brothers?

Out of anxiety, she thought. Out of the pure, scary adrenaline freeze of trying to have a regular conversation with Clint Barrows.

"I heard something about the notorious Jeremiah and Jason," she said. "They're giving you trouble."

"*Trouble* is such a kind word." He kept considering his drink until he took another swig, then let out a deep breath, lowering the glass. "See, my grandparents bought this place, turned it into a working ranch, left it to Dad, and he took it from there with Mom. I always had a deep interest in it. They said I was more a cowboy than either of my brothers. Jeremiah and Jason were interested in the money side, and I wasn't. That's the last part I ever cared about."

"You were all about the cutting horses."

"And cattle and ranch hands and everything that goes with the operation. All of us work together to care for, train and breed the cutters."

He seemed proud of what he accomplished on a daily basis. She'd never noticed that about him.

"We've got one hundred and eighty acres of roads and trails, pastures, horse barns, cattle pens, an arena… and all my brothers want to do is start selling off the land to some ag business that will pay top dollar, in spite of the economy. I say that sounds a mite suspicious, if you ask me."

"You don't trust your brothers to have your best interests in mind?"

He seemed to process that. "I'd like to think so. But

brothers don't threaten each other with lawsuits and strong-arming. At least, not the brothers I know."

He was talking about Phi Rho Mu, but she wanted to know more about his blood brothers—whether they were true family or not. "It sounds like Jeremiah and Jason don't care about what you've always done here."

"You're right. When my parents sent them off to college, they became 'businessmen,' and they only see bottom lines. They've always been of one mind, though. Twins."

"I see." She paused. "It almost sounds like they've left you out of their plans."

"That's not the only thing."

She almost asked what he meant, but the moment passed. It almost seemed he got no support around here.... He was on his own.

Margot crossed one booted leg over the other, barely recognizing that she'd turned her body toward him. "From the way you talk, it sounds like your brothers came out of school with a different philosophy than your parents had. What about you?"

He chuckled. "To this day I maintain that I didn't need schooling, but Dad insisted. Mom, though? She said I was a natural for the ranch, no matter how many courses in ag business I took."

"Your brothers disagree, I take it."

"True."

As he leaned his arms on his thighs, he moved into a patch of light. She hadn't ever thought Clint Barrows was capable of a conversation, much less one about business. She wouldn't have guessed he could be serious about anything.

"You've got some brains, stud," she said, lightening the moment. "Who knew?"

He grinned.

"You're the one with the brains," he said. "What with all your books. That's impressive stuff, Dostoyevsky."

In spite of his kidding, she almost cringed. Yeah, being an out-of-work author was truly an achievement.

For some reason, she found herself talking when, with everyone else, she had shut down. It had to be the St. Germain.

"To tell you the truth," she said, "I don't know about my future books."

"You're getting tired of writing them?"

Wouldn't that be an easy excuse to use? *Yes, the reason I'm not publishing more girl-around-the-world books is because I've gotten over the whole scene.*

She hedged. "I'd just love to go a different direction." With her travelogues. With life.

"Which direction do you want to go?" he asked.

So many questions, so few answers.

He gestured toward the night, with its near silence—so quiet she could actually hear herself think for once.

"Know what you should write a book about?" he said. "The *Sex in the City* girl goes country. It'd be one of those… What do you call it?"

"Fish-out-of-water stories?"

"Exactly. You could do one of those blogs, too. Like a journal."

He'd been teasing her, but…

She liked the idea. If only she liked it more than the books she was already writing.

Still, the more she thought about it…

Nah. "That's actually a marketable idea. For someone else."

"But not you." He put his glass on the armrest and placed his hands behind his head, so nonchalantly that she wondered if she'd said something that had rankled him and he was proving that she couldn't affect him at all. "I don't know why I was thinking that you'd want to stay more than a night out in the boonies."

"I'm staying two nights. Give me some credit."

As she tried to get over the fact that he'd been the first person she'd given any hint to about her career predicament, he got out of his chair, took her shot glass, then his and headed for the door.

"One more before the night ends," he said.

While she waited for him to return, she absorbed the sounds around her: a breeze combing through oak leaves, an owl off in the distance, the beautiful quiet she'd noticed before. So peaceful. So much more comfortable than anything she'd heard in all the out-of-the-ordinary places she'd sought.

He came back with her drink, but instead of sitting, he leaned against a porch pillar, staring into the night.

A fist seemed to be squeezing her heart, stopping it for a moment as she ran a gaze down him. If he'd been any other man, she might've…

Done what? Asked him to come back to her room with her?

She squashed her thoughts by talking. "The most country *I* get is going back to my condo. And it's more suburb than country."

"Chico, right? It's a nice area."

"It's a good place to hang my hat after a trip." But as she said it, she realized that the condo was basically a pit stop, just like all the other houses she'd flitted through in her life. Hell, she'd even switched rooms when she'd stayed in the sorority house, telling everyone that she always went for the best upgrade possible.

And, really, had she ever felt as if she'd been at home

while she traveled to places as far away as the cluttered streets of Bangkok? Or had she always just been a visitor, searching for a place where she belonged?

She was getting warm from her drink…or maybe for another reason altogether as she sat there watching Clint under the porch light, his hair thick enough to make her fingers itch to touch it.

And, damn, she really wanted to touch it right now.

He downed the rest of his liqueur, as if he'd needed one last shot before bed, and went toward the door.

"Sweet dreams," he said, and it wasn't even followed by one of his patented, suggestive stud winks.

All alone now, Margot stayed out in the darkness, wishing he was still here and not having a clue why that was.

AFTER SHE TUMBLED out of bed the next morning, Margot made a beeline for the bathroom down the hall, hoping no one would see her with "morning face." She was an expert at saying goodbye to men before the sun lit the sky and they could clearly see the bags she always got under her eyes when she didn't get a good night's sleep.

It wasn't that the guest room bed hadn't been comfortable or the room cozy. Her mind had just been busy, despite sleeping on a feather mattress among the soothing Southwestern décor that Clint's mom must have introduced and he'd never bothered to change.

If she was right about that, she figured she'd probably have liked his mom. Mrs. Barrows would've been a heck of a lot more comfort-minded than Margot's own mother or dad. They hadn't believed in weighing themselves down with furniture, so they'd always lived with the least amount possible.

After Margot emerged from the bathroom, she went

downstairs to find Dani at the long wooden dining room table with a buffet of eggs, cereal, bacon, English muffins, juice and a coffeepot laid out.

"Did you do all this?" Margot asked.

Dani, who looked almost like a stranger with that new hair and a new sweater-and-skirt outfit, put down her newspaper and beamed up at Margot.

"This is all Clint's doing," she said. "Wouldn't he make a good wife?"

"To someone who needs one." Margot took a cactus-patterned plate and began to load it with food. "Where're the guys?"

"Riley was keen to get to the horse barn and hang out with Clint while he put in his work for the day."

"And how're things with Riley?"

"Fine."

Don't interfere, Margot thought. *Don't...*

But Riley was her friend, too, and she couldn't bite her tongue. "He seemed pretty put out with you yesterday. Or did you not notice?"

"I noticed."

Margot ate standing up. "You sure about that? Because you were doing everything you could to avoid talking with him—barely looking at him during dinner and cleaning up afterward in the kitchen while he went to your room."

"Obviously he wasn't bothered by anything, because he was sleeping like a baby when I got to bed."

Margot paused with an English muffin halfway to her mouth. This didn't sound like Dani, who would've never let Riley go to bed angry.

"Is everything okay?" Margot asked.

"Perfect."

"I'm asking because... Frankly, Dani, yesterday was like a day on Mars with you."

Dani neatly folded the newspaper.

"What I mean," Margot said, "is that it seemed like Riley didn't even have a hint that you wanted to quit your job before you announced it. You don't spring things on him like that."

"You're right. He didn't know." Finally, Dani came back to her old self. It was as if she'd never gotten her hair cut or wasn't wearing a sleek sweater that seemed as if it could've been pulled from Margot's closet.

Now Margot did sit. "I understand about cold feet. Your parents weren't exactly good role models for a long-lasting marriage."

Dani sighed. "This has nothing to do with them or with cold feet."

"Okay. But I have to say that it's like something's exploded in you." She motioned toward Dani's bob. "You never, ever changed your hair this drastically before, not in all the years I've known you."

"And that's why I did it." Dani casually stood. "I never have adventures or impulsive moments like you, and I don't have a fabulous new cooking show like Leigh, even though we were both in home ec and we're both just as good in the kitchen. If you want me to be completely honest, seeing where you guys are and where I am really made me reevaluate myself last weekend."

Margot wanted to smack herself. She didn't say it, but she had the feeling that this had a lot to do with her and Leigh and the auction. They'd treated Dani like she couldn't fend for herself.

Worse yet, Margot wondered if this *did* have anything to do with Dani's parents. She didn't know much about psychology, but Dani had always been the wounded bird of the group, torn apart by her mom and dad's separation.

Was it all playing out now?

"Dan," Margot said, going to her, taking her hands in her own. "Do you know that I was wildly envious of your hair, especially back in college when I didn't know what to do with my own mop? Did you know that you always created a menu on dinner nights that made me wish I had even an iota of the talent you have?"

"Please," she said. "You don't have to make me feel better."

"I'm just telling you the truth."

"And I'm telling *you* the truth when I say that…"

She trailed off.

"What, Dani?"

She took her hands from Margot's. "I watch you and Clint. There's chemistry—don't deny it. And I wonder why the room doesn't catch on fire with me and Riley like it does with the two of you."

Margot flinched. "Clint and I don't even like each other."

"Yes, you do. God, you two are hilarious, barely even acknowledging each other when anyone else is around. I mean, really, Margot, nipple tassels and bubble bath?"

She was going to kill Leigh for blabbing.

Dani rolled her eyes. "Just for the record, you guys don't have to stay away from each other's rooms this weekend just because you think Riley and I are idiots."

Well, there it was. Called out.

Margot waited for the world to fall down around her, now that someone had announced the very idea that she'd given in to Clint. But…

The world was still there.

It was everything *inside* her that was crumbling, and that sensation didn't necessarily involve Clint, just book contracts and sales and… Oh, a little thing Margot liked to call an ego.

Dani's gray gaze sparkled now that she'd been successful in changing the subject from her to Margot. "There isn't any chance that you and Clint can…"

"No."

"I wasn't about to say that you should jump all over each other in a bubble bath again. I meant—"

"Definitely no."

Just the thought of trying to wrangle a stud like Clint into what Dani was referring to—a relationship, of all things—was laugh-inducing.

Yet, oddly, Margot didn't feel like laughing.

Taken aback by that, she focused on Dani again. "I hope you and Riley work this out. You're my favorite couple ever, you know."

"Of course we will."

"Because," Margot said, "if anyone in this world would make me want to settle down, it would be a guy like him."

Damn, that sounded pathetic. Not wanting to settle down. She'd been indepen— *No.* It went beyond independence. She'd been lonely for most of her life, and she'd started to lose hope, sticking to the patterns that'd been ingrained in her, moving on, moving on, never planting herself in one spot.

And she was tired. Suddenly so tired of it.

Dani was looking at her as if she knew this conversation was about more than her and Riley.

"I know Riley's a keeper," she said, "and I'm never letting him go."

They hugged, but Margot's own words were the ones

that kept ringing through her mind as an image of Clint Barrows floated over her gaze.

If anyone in this world would make me want to settle down...

As she hugged Dani tighter, Margot told herself that there were more appropriate men to settle down with, even if Clint was the one on her mind and in every cell of her body every second, every minute of the day.

9

THAT EVENING, LONG after Clint and Riley had finished putting in a day's work with the horses and the women had wandered the property to inspect every wedding nook and cranny, Clint settled into the kitchen.

He'd decided to whip up a simple dinner, since Riley had been determined to sit Dani down and have a long talk about what was really going on with her.

He was just putting the main dish in the oven when he heard someone come in the front door.

Margot. It was the way her fashionable boots hit the floor with that easy, swaying stride. Or it could've been wishful thinking.

But he was right, and when she strolled into the kitchen, she greeted him while setting her computer pad down on the table.

"Whatever it is you're cooking smells amazing," she said.

"Lemon-garlic chicken."

"Oh." She laughed. "Good thing Riley is having that up-close-and-personal chat with Dani now and not later."

The garlic. He got it.

"Where did they end up?" he asked.

"The gazebo, I think. Who knows how long they'll be, though."

"Dinner won't be ready for about forty-five minutes, but they can grab some when they're ready."

"You should've asked for help." Margot hovered by his side at the stove, all summer-wind shampoo and skin-fresh heat. "I'm not the world's greatest cook, but I can be of some use."

"It's all under control." He was talking about the food, because *he* sure wasn't anywhere near control. His body felt as if it had a legion of pistons pumping inside him, even though he had nowhere to zoom off to.

Margot gathered some used bowls, transferring them to the sink. She had pulled her dark hair back in a barrette today, and it made the beauty of her face stand out that much more—the high cheekbones, the pale eyes, the feeling that, in spite of her steel spine, she was still a porcelain figurine, delicate and off-limits in so many ways.

As lust—because it was lust, wasn't it?—swirled inside him, she seemed totally unaware of how she threw him into utter inner chaos.

Not knowing what else to do with himself, Clint got out two wineglasses, then a bottle of chilled chardonnay from the fridge. He poured them each a dose.

"Here's to your crazy cooking skills, then," she said as they clinked glasses.

They remained standing by the stove, drinking.

Why was this feeling like a date of sorts?

He could answer that more easily than anything else about them. Dinner was heating up in the oven and they were alone in a house that was silent except for the beat of the grandfather clock in the hallway and the night sounds outside the windows.

Maybe the same date question had entered her mind, too, because she took another belt of wine, as if she needed a buzz to be around him on a personal level.

Click, click, went the clock, chipping away at him.

Finally, he couldn't stand the tension anymore.

They both started to talk at once, then laughed, and he gestured toward her.

"You first." *Please.*

She traced a finger over the ceramic tile of the counter. "I was just going to say that you're full of surprises. Handy with dinner, a house that's way neater and cozier than I anticipated…"

"What did you expect—a cave with a fire for roasting the meat I hunt down every day?"

"That's not too far off the mark."

"Thanks."

"No, I didn't mean for my initial compliment to come out that way." She set her wine on the counter. "It's just that I thought your house would be…"

"The ultimate bachelor pad? Nah. Believe it or not, my dad was a neat freak, an army man before my grandpa passed away and left him this ranch. My brothers and I grew up doing hospital corners on the beds and passing muster every Sunday night to get allowance. Dad was fun-loving, though. He and Mom brought that out in each other."

Margot was watching him closely, a warmth in her gaze, and she seemed to realize it just as he did.

Or had he been mistaken?

Did he even *want* a warmth to be there?

Clint gazed around the kitchen. "Anyway, it just feels

downright disrespectful to not look after what Mom left here after she passed on."

"I'm sorry to hear that—about losing her, I mean."

"It happened a long time ago. I was only old enough to remember that she was here one day and not here the next. She was driving and they say her tire blew out."

"Oh, God, that's awful."

It really had been and, as he looked over the pine-cone clock, the hutch with the desert-patterned plates and the cookie jar with two ceramic bear cubs climbing up the side, he wished she could've been here to see how everything had turned out. How *he* had turned out, loving the home she had loved.

"Dad was the one who kept things as she'd had them," he said. "And when he willed me the house and the ranch, it didn't feel right or necessary to change much. Just a few things here and there."

Even if life had been changing outside the ranch, he'd retained what was familiar and comfortable.

"She had nice taste," Margot said.

"I hate to think of what my brothers might've done with the house. They're both married, so their wives would've probably redecorated." Clint set down his glass. Wine wasn't really his thing, anyway. "Dad invested in a lot of property out of state, and that's where they live, because that's mostly what he left them. But if you look at my share of the ranch, compared with what my brothers inherited, you'd think I came out on the short end."

"You didn't."

"Not by a long shot."

She tilted her head, considering him. "If I didn't know better, I'd say that you've got a nest that you don't care to venture from."

It could be that he did, and hearing Margot say it made him wonder just what her place in Chico looked like.

"I read a couple of your books, you know," he said.

"You did?"

She flushed, and he quelled the sudden, emphatic blip of pleasure in his chest.

"Yeah," he said. "And that's saying something, since I'm not really a bookworm. But I got the impression that you're a restless traveler, not so much someone who feels at home in all the places you visit. You might rather just stay home."

Now she looked pissed. *Well done, stud.*

"That's not true," she said. "Home is nice, but it doesn't…" She swallowed, shrugged. "Challenge me."

Did she believe what she was saying? It didn't seem like it.

It seemed that maybe Margot had been looking for a home for a long time, and she hadn't had one since her sorority days.

"You need a challenge," he said, testing her.

"Don't we all?"

It was like a dare that dangled right in front of him. Why was it that she was the only one who made him want to step out of his comfort zone, even for an hour or two?

But the mere thought of going out into Margot's world discomfited him. He wouldn't ever fit, just like she would never fit into his.

And that's why what they'd had last weekend had suited him fine.

He gave her a challenging look right back, and she raised her chin a bit.

"How did you get to be such a traveler, anyway?" he asked.

"It's in my blood." She got quiet a moment before going on. "I was the only child of parents who had raging cases of wanderlust. I think I've lived in every state of the union. We'd travel out of country, too, when they got the bug."

"Where are they now?"

She smiled a little, sadly. "Long gone. When I was away at Cal-U, they moved into this crummy casita in a bad part of San Diego. But it was exotic, you know? In a colorful, arty section of town. One night, the place had a gas leak."

"Wow. I'm sorry."

"You'd understand how awful it was, as a fellow orphan."

She'd tried to make the conversation lighter, but when the mood didn't lift, she wandered away from the oven, out of the kitchen. He followed, leaving his wine behind.

"So what do you do for excitement around here, anyway?" she asked, pausing at the entrance to the family room. "Watch TV? Tip cows?"

It was an obvious change of subject, and he went with it. "Some nights I'll hang around the hands who stay on the ranch and shoot the breeze with them. Some nights, there's a bar we like to go to, but it's the same people all the time."

"Don't tell me… You get bored of the same chicks over and over again."

"What, you think I've gone through every single woman in the area?"

"I didn't say that."

He leaned against the wall on the opposite side of the door frame. "Ouch. You're hard on me, Dickens."

"That's the price you pay when you're a stud."

Silence. Tension.

Awkward.

He was sick of walking on eggshells, though, so he came right out with what they'd been tiptoeing over all weekend.

"There's one thing I want to know before you go home," he said, "and that's why you didn't just lie to me about what was in your basket. When I overheard you in the bar at the start of the reunion, you said that if someone you didn't like bought it, you were going to adjust the sexy scenarios you'd made up. You were going to make the dates innocent."

She did a slow blink, as if he'd crossed some social boundary. But then she smiled, almost to herself.

"I could've lied to you," she said. "I could've told you that you were mistaken in what you overheard and that there was nothing sexual in that basket at all. But you wouldn't have let me get away with that."

Getting her to admit that she was attracted to him was a real bitch. But, again, it was a challenge.

And challenges always seemed to work with them.

He lifted an eyebrow. "Le Crazy Horse, Paris. How would you have spun that for someone who didn't know any better?"

"Easy. I would've taken him for a horse ride and fixed a French-food picnic for him while regaling him with tales about my time in the City of Light."

"Not bad. I guess that's why you write for a living."

She got the same sad expression on her face that he'd noticed yesterday, and he wanted to ask her why.

But she had already banished the sentiment, as if by pure will alone.

"Just think," he said, wanting to see her get fired up again. "Brad could've had all eighty ways."

"How about we never bring him up again? From what I heard through the grapevine after the reunion, my ex-boyfriend's back home, chasing around the wife who left him. If I'd known…"

"You didn't. Don't beat yourself up about it."

So no more Brad. He didn't like to think about Margot's initial basket date of choice, anyway.

Clint went into the family room, where he'd stored her basket in a cabinet. He'd thought about displaying it on the fireplace mantel, just to get her goat, but he'd decided against it after they'd somewhat called this truce or whatever it was between them.

But, now, he couldn't resist.

When he took it out of the cabinet, she groaned.

"Don't get uppity," he said, pulling out a slip of paper. "I just want to hear you in action. Besides, I didn't get to claim more than one scenario."

"We just had one night, remember? Besides, I wasn't in the mood." She swirled her wine in its glass. "But then again, why not? It's better than TV."

Somewhat surprised that she'd agreed to go forward, he read the destination.

"This one says *'Kama Sutra.'* How would you have explained that?"

She sat on the cowhide sofa. "It would've been trickier than Le Crazy Horse."

"The *Kama Sutra* is a sex book, right?"

"Yes, but it's also a guide to gracious and virtuous living. It talks about family and love, too, and how to take delight out of all aspects of life. I would've prepared some Indian food, talked about deep philosophical stuff with my date and maybe have given him a chaste, yet soulful kiss at the end of the evening."

He chose another slip of paper. "'Lupanar, Pompeii.'"

She sank back into the cushions. "That's one of my favorites. Italy's the best, especially the Roman ruins."

"Pompeii is where that volcano erupted. But I have no idea what a lupanar is."

"Well, I could've spun that one as the literal translation for lupanar—a 'den of she-wolves.' I could've centered that basket date on an evening in the woods with a dinner that had lots of sloppy meat and finger foods."

"But what's the real definition of the term?"

Margot flashed him a sassy grin. "A brothel. The most famous one in Pompeii. You can still view the erotic paintings on the walls."

He tucked the paper into his jeans pocket. He could already imagine what Margot would've done with this one if he had picked it last weekend.

"The Lupanar isn't a terribly romantic place," she said. "It had about ten rooms because it was a bigger brothel than most in Pompeii. Wealthy people didn't really visit those places, either, because they had mistresses or slave concubines. And the beds? They were mattresses on brick platforms. It was the paintings that interested me."

She smoothed a stray, dark lock of hair back over her shoulder, a sensual move that dug deep into Clint. Then she set her wine on an end table, relaxing back into the cushions.

Talking about the basket had done something to her, and Clint realized that everything she had written down was as much a fantasy for her as it was for him.

She watched him, and he watched her.

"What're we going to do about this?" he finally asked.

"I really have no idea."

But he had one, and it involved turning off the oven in the kitchen and turning on Margot in the bedroom while Riley and Dani were still out of the house.

WHY AM I DOING THIS? Margot kept asking herself. She'd assuaged her curiosity about Clint already, but here she was, following him out of the living room.

This would never go anywhere. Forget the video incident—that was in the past. But the closer he got to her, the more she realized that she had no idea how to relate to anyone on a profound level. Her parents sure hadn't given her much insight into being loved, and they had made her feel that it was necessary to never get deep, to always keep a buffer between her and someone else because she wouldn't be around for much longer, moving on, moving on...

Just the old, tried-and-true sex. That's what she needed.

That's what she wanted.

And she was about to get it here in Clint's room, she thought, as he shut and locked the door behind them.

"Tell me about one of those paintings in the Lupanar, Margot," he said softly, and even from across the room, his voice had the power to send goose bumps over her flesh.

She went to his large bed, running a hand over the iron footboard. Was this really her, in a lion's den instead of one that belonged to she-wolves?

Yep. And she was going to enjoy this for what it was, nothing more.

"There are a lot of paintings that feature the phallus,"

she said to start off. "*Huge* ones. You wouldn't believe the size of those penises."

Behind her, she heard the rustle of clothing, and her body flashed with heat.

Lust. It was just lust.

She didn't turn around yet. Allowing her pleasure to also be pain, she reveled in the craving to see him in the flesh again, without that shirt, without those jeans, tanned and bare and rippling with hard-labor muscles.

She kept talking. "There's also graffiti on the walls. *Hic ego puellas multas futui.* I remember that one. The loose translation of the Latin is 'Here I screwed many girls.'"

Had she meant that to be a dig at Clint's college lifestyle?

"Sounds charming," he said.

He was closer now, but she didn't turn around. Not when there were a thousand delicious tingles running down her spine.

"There's another painting that I remember well," she murmured. "Two naked people on a bed. The man has the woman's legs over his lap, but there's a space between them."

He was right behind her now, and she kept remembering the day he had touched her from behind, massaging her into a climax that had rolled through her with a ferocious growl.

"Take off your clothes, Margot."

Her name sounded just as bare as he probably was, but she found herself obeying him. It would be the last time, though.

Just one more time.

She peeled off her sweater, skirt, boots…everything.

Then she went to the bed on her own before he could demand anything else of her.

Bold as you please, she slid onto the quilt, her back against the pillows that bunched at the headboard. She kept her knees together, refusing to show him more than she wanted to right now.

But the sight of *him* rocked her—broad shoulders, chest. Those abs.

And his cock.

It was ready for her as he climbed onto the bed and brought her legs over his lap.

"Did that painting look something like this?" he asked.

"Yes."

He swept his fingertips up her leg, coming down the side of it. Her nipples went stiff, her center dampening.

Such an intimate touch, she thought, her heartbeat quickening, telling her it was time to run.

But she was staying for some reason.

Her body, she thought. This was what she needed from him tonight.

As he circled his fingers over her belly, making her shift, butterflies clustered inside of her, swiping her with light flutters that winged up to her chest, around her heart.

She chased them off. "There's another picture I remember. On a bed again, a woman riding a man."

His smile was tight, as if he knew that she couldn't take the intimacy. Maybe he couldn't, either.

He guided her into position—her on top, him on the bottom, his hands braced on her hips.

Giving him a look, lashes lowered, she imitated the painting further, putting her hand on his head.

"The woman in the painting was doing this. I think

it was because she wanted to show him that she was in charge."

"She wouldn't have it any other way."

His words went beyond a comment on the painting, straight to a reflection of her, but he didn't elaborate, instead reaching toward a nightstand into a drawer. He came out with a condom and tore into the packaging.

She took it from him, then slowly covered his cock.

"Was the man's 'phallus' inside the woman in that painting?" Clint asked, teasing, referencing those penis pictures she had mentioned while a pulse throbbed in his neck.

"You can't really tell, but I'm assuming so."

With that, she impaled herself on him, already slick with desire.

He went so deeply into her that she moaned, then began moving her hips, making him go in, out.

She'd already removed her hand from his head, but just so he wouldn't forget that this was still a painted fantasy and nothing more, she started to put it back in position.

He intercepted her before she could recreate the picture, instead placing her hand over his chest.

His heart.

A tiny explosion went off inside her, and it wasn't centered in her belly this time. It was higher, in a place that was usually so still.

Even so, she didn't take her hand away from him. She left it there, feeling the beat of his heart—*bang, bang, bang*. Feeling him inside her, a part of her, thick and long and perfect.

That last thought jarred her.

Perfect?

It was too much for her, and she switched position, turning around so he couldn't see her face.

He made a throttled sound as she rode him backward while he held her hips, pulling her back to him, pushing her forward.

She bent so that her hands were on his legs, so that she could get to an orgasm before…

Before what? Before she lost part of herself to a man who would probably only end up hurting her even worse than he'd done years ago?

He came with a curse-laden blast, then another, but she still labored, strained, a fierce and brutal pressure clicking inside of her like the clock downstairs, counting down.

One click—almost there…

Two—coming…

Three…four…*five*…

A pounding climax struck, making her vibrate in every cell until she lost all strength, slumping down on him.

But instead of leaving her like that, he pulled her back to him, tugging the covers around them and possessing her within the cradle of his arms.

Warm.

Intimate.

As she lay against his chest, she let herself become a part of him, her skin against his, melding together. She pictured nights when she wouldn't want to go anywhere, when she would only want to listen to the sounds outside, or the creaks of this old house speaking to her with reassuring welcome.

And, for a moment, it seemed so real. So possible.

But then the adrenaline started to thread through

her as she pictured him, going to another woman…or another place, leaving her behind for something better.

She pushed the images away until they faded to almost nothing, just like an old painting.

HE PLAYED WITH her hair, just as he'd always wanted to do. Margot wasn't even objecting, and that shocked the hell out of him.

What'd just happened?

In the midst of his afterglow fog, Clint wasn't sure, but he'd never experienced anything like it in his life. There'd been a closeness he hadn't expected, though now, in the aftermath, he could admit that he'd wanted it more than anything.

Too bad it'd happened with a woman who didn't want anything more from him than re-creations of brothel paintings.

"You awake?" he asked. Through the window, he could see it was dark. Bedtime.

"Yeah," she said.

He didn't know what he wanted from *her* exactly— the sense that she felt more for him than she should? The hope that she might stick around a little longer?

After blowing out a here-goes-nothing breath, he said, "That night in college…I didn't bring you up to my room just to make out with you, you know."

She waited for him to continue, almost as if she didn't want him to.

He rushed ahead. "I actually wanted to…" God, this wasn't easy. "I guess I wanted to see what you really thought of that movie."

She stirred, her hair brushing against his skin.

He said, "So that's why I brought you there."

"What I'm hearing in man-speak," she said, "is that

you wanted to get to know me, and the making-out part was incidental?"

Why had he even brought this up? The things a man said after he'd come. Jeez.

She seemed to realize his sudden discomfort, and tentatively draped an arm over his torso.

"I'm glad you told me that."

"Why?"

She swallowed. "Because it makes me feel… Just thank you. And, by the way, Riley told me that you made sure no one bothered me about the video when we were at the reunion. Thank you for that, too. It was thoughtful."

There was more to what she was saying. He knew it.

She smoothed her fingers down his ribs. "I had a little crush on you back then. There was good reason you attracted so many women."

"And you were curious about more than just my charm?"

"Very. But I was also wary, and it took everything I had to go up to that room. And when I saw that camera…"

"You still blame me for that?" He caressed her arm.

"No. But at that point, I thought you just wanted to nail me for bragging rights, especially afterward, when that tape popped up everywhere." She slid her hand under him, her breasts crushed to his chest. "Before I saw the camera, though, I thought there was something…"

Sounded like the truth bug had her tongue, too.

"What if there was something?" he asked.

She looked up at him, her hair falling over half her face, and he could feel the bad news coming.

"Clint," she whispered. "I really do like being with you."

Although she had completely avoided answering him, she couldn't have been any clearer if she'd hit him over the head with a rock.

But when she drew her leg on top of his thighs, nestling against his hip, nuzzling him beneath his jaw, he wondered if what they had together was clear to *her*.

10

OUTSIDE, THE NIGHT was mild, but the distance between Dani and Riley as they sat face-to-face on the benches in the gazebo was as chilly as it could get.

Moonlight filtered in through the open walls, shading Riley slightly. Over his shoulder, Dani could see the outline of bunkhouses in the near distance, and even the tip of the horse barn farther down the hill. Country music was playing, probably coming from a ranch hand's room.

Actually, Merle Haggard had been the only sound between Dani and Riley for the past few minutes, and she was just about ready to burst.

"You're still mad at me," she finally said.

"Not mad." Riley was staring off into the distance, his hair darker in the moonlight. "I'm just confused. Lately, it's like I don't recognize you at all."

She knew he wasn't talking about the new hairstyle or clothing, either. They were stuck on this whole thing about her wanting to quit her job.

"I've told you why I want to try something on my own," she said. "We're going to have a lot more money

in our savings account since Clint is letting us have the
ranch for the wedding. And I found a reasonably priced
gown all on my own. It's vintage. Someone's selling it
on eBay, and that'll save us money, too—"

"I'm not talking about our wedding." He exhaled.
"Do you remember everything we've worked for during the past few years? We've planned and plotted how
to get ourselves out of that rental house, for starters."

"We can still do that." Eventually. "I like where we're
living, Riley. You're the one who wants to move out,
right?"

"That's because I thought we'd be further along than
we are these days." His posture was stiff, as if his pride
was the one thing holding him upright. "I never wanted
to run small estates, and someday, there's going to be a
bigger one with bigger perks."

"You already give me what I need," she said. "Those
dreams of a big wedding were just girlish fantasies. I'm
happier with you than I could ever dream of being with
anyone else. Can't you see that?"

So was that why she was cutting her hair and quitting her job and having an early-life crisis?

Her heart reached out to Riley, the best man she
would ever find. He was her one, her only, and she was
making a mess of what they had.

She didn't mean to, though.

So why was it happening?

Scooting over on the bench, closer to him, she tugged
on his shirtsleeve, toying with it. "I think I'm going
about this all wrong."

"I just wish I knew what you were going *about*."

She paused. Should she lay it all out in front of him?
What if he didn't understand?

The words barely got out of her, then they began

tumbling like an avalanche she'd been trying to keep back. "I've been asking myself so many questions.... But, well, the biggest ones have to do with making all the right choices. How do I know that I'm not losing opportunities left and right because I haven't opened myself to them?" She inched even nearer to Riley, smelling his barely there, clean cologne. It filled her in so many ways. "But there is one thing I know for sure, and it's that you're the right decision. That's never going to change."

He held her hand, their fingers entwining.

In the near distance, Merle Haggard sang his outlaw country songs. Riley seemed content just to touch Dani, so she enjoyed the feel of his fingers wrapping around hers, safe, warm, like a cocoon.

But even cocoons needed to open at some point and reveal the changes that had taken place inside. And that was the true issue here, wasn't it?

It didn't necessarily make sense to her, but there it was.

Why did she feel so restless these days? And why was it happening even now, as the music infiltrated her, making her heartbeat speed up as she ran her thumb along Riley's?

Did he have any idea what was underneath the layers she wore? And she meant that literally, because she had hoped that they would be talking tonight, alone. She had hoped that, at some point, they would be stripping the layers off, one by one.

She moved closer to him. "Is everything good with us?"

"Everything's good."

He was looking down at their joined hands, his heart in every word he said.

Her Riley. Her good guy in a figurative white hat.

"Time to make up, then?" she asked on a whisper.

"We always do."

She didn't know what got into her exactly, but she crossed one leg over the other flirtatiously. He caught the gesture and lifted an eyebrow.

"Do you realize," she asked, "that we've never had make-up sex before?"

"That's because this was our first real fight, even after all these years."

Yeah, two even-keeled, levelheaded people. That was them. The first time they'd been together, he had pulled out all the romantic stops—the roses, the champagne, the *I Love Yous*. Nothing had gone wrong that night.

And nothing had since then, except for lately.

She subtly unbuttoned the tight sweater she'd purchased just this week—something that made her feel sexier than usual.

Even in the low light, she saw Riley's gaze go steamy. "Dani…"

She smiled, feeling like a little devil. Reveling in the urgency that had been creeping up on her this past week.

"This is our first time really fighting," she said. "I like that you care enough for me to get angry."

Again, he looked at her as if he'd never seen her before, but there was also an unknown quality in his eyes that drove her on, making her undo her sweater even more.

She couldn't wait to show him what she had under the layers, what she'd planned for their make-up time.

"We should go back to the room," he said.

"No."

He had started to get to his feet, but she pulled him

back down and began to work at her sweater buttons again.

When she was done, Riley's eyes were wide.

She had parted her sweater to show him the bra she'd purchased on the sly at The Boudoir before they'd left Avila Grande last weekend. It was a creation she'd *never* thought of buying before, and doing so had been an act of freedom.

Bras like this were for other girls.

But not anymore.

Dani could feel him running his gaze over her breasts, which were exposed, thanks to the nonexistent cups and black half-corset underneath.

As he stared, her nipples went hard. "You should see my undies and the garter belt with stockings."

Crotchless. She'd bought a set.

"Out here?" His voice was gritty. "What if one of the ranch hands walks by? What if Clint does?"

"We'll be really quiet. And it's dark enough in this gazebo so that we can just hold our breath and wait for them to pass by." She leaned toward him. "Come on, Riley. Make up with me."

This time, he stood all the way before she could pull him back down.

He began to scoop her into his arms. "We're going to the room."

"No," she said, pulling her sweater down her shoulders to her arms so he could see that she wasn't backing down, then gaining her feet and stepping away from him.

If he'd been bewildered by her before, he looked totally dumbfounded now.

Dani reached for his belt buckle. "Let's do it out here."

"On a bench?"

Wow. She wasn't sure they were ever going to have make-up sex at this rate.

"Yes, on a bench," she said. "Other people have done it in stranger places. The most exotic we've ever gotten was in your truck once."

"Maybe I'll order up some kinky equipment for a dungeon when we get back home," he said, sarcasm lacing his voice.

She'd stung him, had basically called their sex vanilla.

But making love with him had always been fulfilling. She just wanted...

More?

But what *kind* of more?

A thought sliced into her: was she pushing him away before it could happen years on down the road?

No. That wasn't it at all.

Shoving aside those thoughts, she sought out physical answers, guiding Riley firmly to that bench, bowling him over.

He grumbled her name, giving in as her breasts spilled out of that half-corset.

As he kissed her fervently, cupping her, circling her nipples and making her squirm on his lap, she thought she heard the music from the bunkhouses cut off, leaving only the memory of notes in her head.

But it was the present that mattered, because this was what she wanted from Riley—recklessness, passion, the wildness of doing it anywhere they wanted just because they could.

Did good girls like the old Dani have sex in the open like this? Nope. Did goody-goody home ec majors who had a perfect home life wear wicked bras and undies with slits in the crotch?

Now they did.

Just as Riley was unzipping her skirt, she heard a shout from near the bunkhouses, and he abruptly stopped kissing her, closing her sweater.

Was it a ranch hand who'd come out for a ramble around the property and a smoke?

"Dammit," he said. "No arguments now, Dani. I'm getting you out of here."

"Riley." She put all her weight on him, emphasizing that she didn't want to go anywhere.

Her pulse was running too hard, her belly too knotted with desire. She wanted Riley to want it as much as she did.

As another shout in the distance turned into laughter, she realized that some of the ranch hands were probably yipping it up outside their quarters, drinking beer, socializing. Their laughter floated on the night, making it seem as if they were closer than they really were.

"Let's do it," she said, pulling at his shirt. "Who cares if someone sees?"

He looked at her as if he *really* didn't recognize her now, and she knew what he had to be asking himself.

Despite what she'd told him, *did* she want more from this relationship than they had?

Carefully, he began to button her sweater, his mouth set in a grim line.

He was angry with her again.

"The girl I used to know," Riley said, "would've had more pride in herself than that."

He took her by the hips, setting her on her feet.

Her body still thudding with need, she turned on her

heel, leaving the gazebo. She wasn't sure if it was because she was mad at him, or if she was just mortified.

"Dani!" he shouted.

But *she* wasn't even sure she recognized herself by name.

MARGOT WAS UP much earlier than usual the next morning.

She'd crept out of Clint's bed just as soon as the sun had eased through his curtains. Thinking that she ought to be in her room before Riley and Dani discovered otherwise, she'd made her way over the floorboards to her discarded clothing. Then, after she was dressed, she was out his door.

Just her luck, though—Riley was already up.

And he was coming out of what she thought had been an unused guest room.

She froze when he saw her, then decided that there was no way out of this one.

"You got me," she whispered in an oh-well tone.

Riley grinned at her, but there was a melancholy slant to it.

She'd joined him downstairs in the kitchen, and while they waited for their coffee to brew, Riley spilled his heart out to her about Dani.

Now, an hour later, Margot had just gone into the bathroom to take a shower when a light knock sounded on the door. It was Dani. "We're leaving," she said, obviously having showered in another bathroom.

Her hair was neatly styled and she wore a trace of lightly applied makeup, but Dani was out of sorts, with bags under her eyes.

"Oh, Dani." Margot hugged her friend. Riley had

made it sound as if he didn't know what to do with her, but she wished she knew Dani's side of the story.

"Will you call me if you need to talk?" she asked, holding Dani at arm's length so she could meet her gaze. "Anytime, anywhere. Okay?"

"You know I will. But Riley and I will be fine." Dani swallowed. "We always are."

They said goodbye, and Margot watched her go down the stairs, wondering what the ride home for them would be like.

As she shut the door again, she plugged in the hairdryer, drowning out everything else. Worry weighed on her, and not just because of Dani.

She'd been trying not to think about Clint, too.

Things had gone so far beyond a basket-bound thing that she wasn't sure where she stood with him.

Maybe it didn't even matter, because she was leaving soon, anyway. No more Stud Barrows. No more...

She shut off the dryer. No more whatever it was that had turned her into a mental case.

Reaching for her makeup bag, she heard the floor creak outside the bathroom.

"Dani?"

Was she back, putting off the ride home in favor of having a heartfelt talk with a girlfriend?

But when Margot opened the door, it wasn't Dani standing there.

"Crap," she muttered, thinking of closing the door so he couldn't see her bare morning face.

But then she thought better of that. Oddly, he didn't seem to notice her lack of makeup.

"You disappeared early," he said, leaning against the door frame. She wondered if that was his position of choice, just like Robert Redford would've done in that cowboy movie he was in back when he was young and golden.

She dabbed some creamy foundation on her face, pretending that Clint had seen her primp a thousand times before.

This was just another show for him. Le Crazy Au Natural.

"I wasn't tired anymore," she said. "Besides, getting up at the crack of dawn gave me the chance to talk with Riley."

"Yeah. Before he left, he mentioned what's going on with Dani."

"Do you think their truck will freeze over before they get home?"

"I think they'll be okay. They're Dani and Riley."

She slid him a glance. They *had* been Dani and Riley before the reunion.

With purposeful efficiency, Margot uncapped her mineral powder and extracted the large powder brush from her bag. He was watching her every move, as if fascinated.

"I've been thinking," he said.

"Danger ahead."

"Seriously, Margot." He reached toward the counter, grabbing a tube of crimson lipstick, opening the top and spinning it until the red emerged. "What if you stayed here in the country for a couple more days, just to see if there really is a book in this for you?"

"The *Sex in the City* fish-out-of-water idea?" She finished dusting powder over her face, then took her lipstick from him. "I told you that I didn't think it was for me."

"How can you be sure about that?"

He had a question for everything.

But she made him wait for her answer as she applied the red to her lips.

When she was done, he looked at her mouth as if he had been having a few lipstick fantasies.

Desire cascaded over her, but she continued with her makeup application, fetching her blush.

Was he proposing that she stay here for a short time because he was interested in the well-being of her career? Or was it because he wanted more basket time?

A few days ago, she would've guessed the latter. But he'd shown a genuine curiosity in her writing. He'd read some of her books, which still stunned the tar out of her.

And they'd had that intimacy last night, complete with a conversation that neither one of them had been able to fully articulate their way through.

"I was going to go home and start research for my next project," she said. But she recognized the pattern.

Distance.

Time to go?

"Just do your research here," he said.

Well, it wasn't as if she was doing anything else since her contracted book had been canceled. Besides, he really did have a pretty good idea.

Should she do it?

Yes.

She answered before her instincts could overwhelm her, trap her just as they'd always done.

"Okay." She put down her blusher and went for her eye shadow. "Why the hell not?"

There were a million reasons.

"Good," Clint said, not going anywhere. "I already have plans for tonight."

"You do?"

"I'm going to ease you back into small-town life. You

might have gone to a college with a lot of cowboys in it, but Avila Grande's bars aren't real country."

He reached into the bathroom again, taking hold of her makeup bag and bringing out her mascara. With one of those arrogant grins, he handed the tube to her, as if he'd become a part of her daily routine.

But Margot made herself a promise: even if she was staying here a little longer, it didn't mean he was a part of a daily or nightly anything for her.

Or ever would be.

CLINT'S FAVORITE LOCAL bar was called The 76, named after the old, abandoned Phillips 76 gas station garage that it had taken up residence in.

He parked among the other trucks in front of the closed, rusted pumps, then went around to Margot's side to open her door.

A loud Kenny Chesney tune boomed through the open metal doors of the large converted garage.

Clint reached for Margot, taking her by the hand to help her down. She needed the help, too, since she was wearing a pair of black, high-heeled, city-street boots that came up to her knees. And he knew he was going to have to keep an eye out for her when the cowboys inside got a load of her in that tight burgundy, long-sleeved dress.

She'd also pinned her hair away from her face, leaving it to fall in a tumble of dark layers down her back, exposing a pair of dangling bronze earrings that she said were lotus blossoms.

"Thank you," she said as he helped her down.

He kept hold of her hand for a moment longer, smelling her flowery perfume. But then she was off like a shot, heading toward the building.

Research, he thought.

Shaking his head, he watched her go, swaying hips, cosmopolitan-girl attitude and all.

Did she have any idea that he was a storm of hormones, just from being around her? Worse yet, did she realize that he couldn't get his mind off her, day or night?

A temporary addiction, he kept repeating to himself as he followed her inside. *That's all this is.*

The place was hopping, even on a Monday night. It was happy hour, after all, and the beers were cheap.

She had stopped just inside, surveying the place: the plank floorboards sprinkled with sawdust, the dance floor, the tire racks on the walls, the air-hockey and foosball tables near the back, manned by a bunch of local ranch hands and farmers in tractor baseball caps.

"Country enough for you?" he asked.

She ran a hand down the side of her dress, as if second-guessing her wardrobe choice. A fish out of water, all right.

"Actually," she said over the music, close to his ear, "it's exhilarating after a day of being holed up in my room with the computer."

Her words had warmed his skin, and it tingled, bathed with her breath.

Off she went to a table near the dance floor, where cowboys and cowgirls were line-dancing.

She took a seat, but not before he noticed that just about every shitkicker in the joint was eyeing her. He gave them a back-off look—even the fellows who worked with him on the ranch.

They laughed, and went back to their beers, knowing that they needed to keep their paws off Clint's "guest."

A few small TVs flashed with the Monday-night

football game, and one of the waitresses, Lula, came to their table.

Big-haired, blonde Lula, with her baby blues and her cut-off mechanic's uniform.

"What can I do you for?" she asked in a thick drawl.

He wished she didn't have such a "Helloo, Clint," look in her eyes. Then again, a few of the waitresses here would be glancing at him that way, seeing as he'd given them something to go *hellooo* about a time or two.

What could he say? It was a small town.

"The usual for me," he said. Then he ordered for Margot. "And a Midori Sour."

When Lula had departed, Margot assessed him with those seen-it-all eyes.

"How did you know about the Midori?" she asked.

"You were drinking one the first night of the reunion," he said. "And it was your favorite in college. It's a pretty standout cocktail, being all green and everything."

"Has anyone ever told you that you've got quite a memory on you?"

The music switched to a slow Collin Raye song, and the people on the floor transitioned into a two-step. Clint focused on them.

"My memory's the last thing I depend on," he said. "Trivia doesn't have much use in my business."

Margot leaned forward, and he tried not to fix his attention on her cleavage. He wasn't even sure she meant to seduce him with it right now.

"You know what you should do with your business and your brothers?"

"Should I ask?"

She ignored that. "Get a kick-ass, top-notch lawyer

who'll make them pee their pants when they toss their next threat at you. Or have you already consulted one?"

He hesitated to tell her that he'd merely talked to a local attorney, but he was no bulldog. And Clint had been too proud to give details to any of the Phi Rho Mu brothers who had gone into law, even though rumors about his troubles had been making the rounds.

It was as if Margot read him. "I know someone who could help."

He didn't know what to say. He wasn't used to offers of support.

"You can recommend someone from your travels?" he asked.

"Sort of. But if you're thinking that there's a conflict of interest because I slept with him, you're wrong. He's married to my agent in Los Angeles. He's good, Clint, and if he can't do it, he'll know someone else who deals with ag business."

His emotions turned quickly. It'd been one thing to give Margot details about his brothers, but this was another.

Too personal.

Too much of a slap to that pride of his.

"First you meddled in Dani's wedding," he said in mild retaliation, "and now you're arranging my business? You're a real orchestrator." The fact that he'd arranged for her to stay on at the ranch to do all that research didn't escape him, but he didn't mention it.

She pressed her lips together and sat back in her chair, taking a silverware set rolled in a paper napkin from a small aluminum pail.

Once again you've done it, stud. "Sorry. It's just that this is the last thing I want to talk about right now."

"I understand." She smiled. "It's true that I meddle. I own that about myself."

As she let his comment roll off her like springwater, he decided that she wasn't fibbing. She did own it, and he liked that about her.

But did he have the guts to tell her that her idea had actually been a sound one? That, if circumstances were different, the two of them might have made a good team—him giving her ideas, while she gave him advice?

Lula returned with their drinks, setting them on the table. "Buffalo wings will be up in a jiff, plus those American fries you like."

"Thanks, Lula."

Before she left, she gave Margot the once-over, then strode away.

Margot watched after her, then turned back to Clint.

He shook his head. "Before you say something, the answer's no. I didn't bring you here so you could see Lula using her wiles on me."

"What makes you think I was going to ask that?"

God, he didn't know *why* he'd brought her here, or even why he'd asked her to stay a couple more days. The book idea had been a flimsy excuse, and he knew that she knew it.

He thought of the last time they'd been together, in his bed, him holding her, smelling her hair, trying to absorb every part of her.

It had taken all of his courage to admit that, years ago, he'd gone up to that dim room to meet her because he thought something real could happen between them.

And she'd been forced to admit she'd done the same.

But what was he doing with her now?

Trying, he thought. *Hoping.*

That last realization shook him.

He really did want something more with Margot. Deep inside, he'd always thought about the one who'd gotten away, and when he'd had a chance with her again, he'd taken it, not just because of sex, either.

It was because he was tired of floating along, cooking dinner for himself most nights, coming to this bar and seeing the same people over and over and never getting anywhere.

So why was he just sitting here hoping when he could do a hell of a lot more?

He got out of his chair and went over to her side of the table. She was drinking her Midori Sour, and as he stood by her, she put down her cocktail and looked up at him.

Was there something in her gaze?

Something to hope for?

He held out his hand as the two-step kept playing over the sound system.

Biting her lip, she looked at her drink, as if the taste of it was lingering in her mouth, helping her to remember what it'd been like to drink Midori in college, go to the small country bars, dance to the down-home music.

She took his hand, and he smiled.

"I don't remember how to do this," she said as he led her to the dance floor.

"Just let me lead, Margot."

"I…" She stumbled in those high boots. "I don't know how to let anyone lead. I never have."

"Trust me."

He had her dancing in no time, keeping her in a firm grip that was gentle at the same time. He loved the feel of his palm on her waist, her hand in his.

Skin to skin, heartbeat to heartbeat—that "something" he'd been hoping for pounded in the slight space between them.

Since they'd joined in the dance late, the music didn't last long. It trailed off as the DJ invited people to participate in a foosball contest.

Meanwhile, the two of them stayed on the floor, still holding on to each other, even without a song to join them.

Suddenly, they were back in college, on *that* night. But it was as if this were a do-over.

A chance to make things right.

He wanted to kiss her now, needed to, because in spite of all the sex, they hadn't had a moment like this yet. They hadn't had a heart-to-heart kiss full of real emotion and innocence.

They were close, so very close, and they got even closer with every breath.

Two inches apart. One and a half.

A quarter of an inch.

Their lips could've touched if he moved only a fraction more.

But then he heard the crowd around them, and he realized that this was not the place for the intimacy he hungered for.

"Later, Margot," he whispered in her ear. "We're going to take this up with each other later."

He drew away from her, and she looked at him a second longer, as if figuring out what he was all about. Then she laughed softly and headed back to their table.

Did she think he'd been teasing her again, setting her up for another sexual game?

As he returned to the table, too, he told himself that he definitely would find out later, after they got back home.

11

As THE NIGHT went on, Margot just sat there in her seat, tapping her foot to the pumping music and thinking that, sometime, Clint was going to stop nursing the damn beer he'd been working on the entire time and ask her to dance again.

Why did she have the feeling he knew that she was waiting?

And waiting.

Eventually, she decided that she would gainfully occupy herself and show him that she had other things to do.

When the Monday-night football game ended and a band came on stage, encouraging a bunch of cowboys to swing their partners around the floor, Margot got out her phone and began texting with Dani.

How's everything with you and Riley?

A few minutes passed. Then, an answer.

A-OK. Still some things to work out, but hard feelings put aside.

That news lifted Margot's spirits, and by the time the band launched into a song that brought out the line-steppers, she was done with being on the fringes.

"Let's go," she yelled to Clint over the gyrating guitar riff in "Footloose."

He shrugged and sent her one of his cocky grins, as if he'd known all along that she would be the one asking him to dance.

"I'm doing fine right here," he said.

Jerk. But he'd see that two could play at this.

Glancing around the bar, she caught the eye of a tanned, tall cowpoke—a guy she'd seen speaking to Clint earlier when he'd gone to the bar to get Margot another Midori Sour after Lula had inexplicably decided to give them the worst service imaginable.

She smiled at Mr. Tall and Tanned, but after a beat in which she actually thought he might ask her to dance, he looked at Clint, then away from her.

She got the hint loud and clear.

"Did you spread the word that I wasn't available?" she asked.

He finished his beer. "I might've mentioned it."

Oh, really?

Well, screw this. She went to the floor, to a spot not far from their table, and joined a line of dancing cowboys and girls. All night long, she'd been studying how they moved, as well as the different steps, and those college nights when she used to Electric Slide and Tush Push til closing time came back to her with a vengeance.

As she stepped and slid and wiggled her butt more than the dance really called for, she locked gazes with Clint, giving him the same cocky smile he'd sent her earlier.

But now, the expression on his face wasn't so self-satisfied. His mouth was set in a firm line while his hand gripped his empty beer bottle.

Ha! A taste of his own teasing medicine. She hoped he liked it. And she hoped he was regretting that moment earlier in the night when he'd almost kissed her.

She swore that he had come *this* close to doing it, his lips nearing hers until... Well, until the jerk had pulled away from her, playing her for a fool for real this time.

She'd hidden her mortifying frustration well, nonchalantly walking back to their table, but damn him, she'd somehow been anticipating—and worrying about—more than the games they'd been engaging in tonight.

As the song ended, the cowboys around the area applauded her hip-shaking performance. She made a playful show of turning to each and every one of them, thanking them, then facing the table again to gift Clint with a right-back-at-you grin.

But he wasn't there.

And she knew just where he'd gone when she felt a hand on her arm from behind, firmly guiding her through the appreciative crowd and toward the exit.

"Nice show," he said tightly.

"I try my best to entertain."

They were in the parking lot in record time, and he opened the passenger door with such a pull that she thought he might tear it right off.

"Is Alpha Male angry?" she asked.

"Just get in."

A thrill spun inside of her, but after a second, it didn't feel right. A week ago it certainly would have, but now?

Now she wanted to ask him what was wrong, just to see if he would answer truthfully. She wanted him to admit that he might've been a teeny-weenie bit jealous while hearing those other men applaud her line dance.

They drove back to the ranch with the radio on full volume, the tires roaring over the country road until finally they passed under the iron arch that announced the Circle BBB. When they reached the ranch house, Clint snapped off the radio and wasted no time in alighting from the truck.

She opened her own door, thank you, shutting it and following him up the steps.

"I'd call the night a major success," she said. "*Very* good research for that fish-out-of-water book. I might have to go back there tomorrow and drag some of those cowboys onto the dance floor, just to gather more anecdotal color for a possible story."

God help her, but she'd meant to goad Clint—it was a part of that "push them away" deal she had going on. And as he came to the door, he paused.

Goaded, indeed.

Why did she have the feeling that he was about to get serious?

Did she want him to?

A spark of that familiar panic that she got only when she was around Clint popped inside her. No way. She absolutely didn't want him to get serious on her.

Thank goodness he didn't do anything else but open the door, then stand aside to let her in while sweeping off his hat.

"After you, Fitzgerald," he said.

She brushed right by him. "Would you stop calling me those names?"

"They're compliments."

She opened her mouth to retort, but closed it. How could she tell him that every nickname he'd been calling her since last week was an author who'd eventually become famous and respected?

The names were a slam to her pride when her own chances of even staying employed were looking slim.

She marched the rest of the way into the house, tossing her purse on a velvet-upholstered chair in the foyer, just as if this was her own home.

Thinking twice, she backed up and retrieved it.

"Going to bed already?" he asked.

"I'm tired."

"You're pissy."

She stopped in her tracks and glanced behind her. "Excuse me?"

He was hanging his hat on a rack as if he had all the kick-around time in the world to poke at her.

"I'm just saying that you're in a mood, Margot."

"Do you maybe think it's because you acted like a possessive troglodyte back at the bar?"

His eyebrows shot up as he sauntered nearer to her. "You do have a way with words."

Why wouldn't he outright engage in a sparring battle? It was the only comfortable way she knew to communicate with him.

He walked right by her, out of the foyer and into the family room, where he grabbed a remote for the big-screen TV, dropped down onto the sofa and turned on the device. A drop-down menu revealed shows that he had recorded, and he chose one.

Of all the programs in existence, Leigh's "Come-On Down Kitchen" appeared on the screen.

"You don't really watch this," Margot said, wandering to the room's entry and lingering there. Maybe she could start a fight with him yet.

"I recorded Leigh's show because I thought you and Dani might want to see the newest episode." He glanced at her. "Do you wanna?"

Even though his question was tipped with innuendo, she thought that he might be offering an olive branch of sorts, inviting her to relax with him.

Heck. She wasn't really that tired, anyway, so she found a good spot in the corner of the cozy sofa, far enough away from him to make a point.

Clint clearly thought it was amusing.

"Get over it, Margot," he said, reaching over, wrapping an arm around her and pulling her closer to him until her thigh was flush against his.

It took her a second to get her breath back. Took her a moment to get over how sexier-than-hell that move had been.

"This is way better," he said, sounding content.

Margot couldn't think of a thing to say. She merely attempted to control her heartbeat while they watched Leigh on the screen in her softly lit country kitchen, which boasted gingham curtains, evening-shaded trees peeking through the windows and the ingredients for a sensual Southern version of red velvet cake—emphasis on the velvet part—spread out before her on the counter. She was wearing a flannel shirt with one more button undone than she would've had in real life, flashing some cleavage and a little bit of tight tummy, since she had her shirt knotted at the bottom.

Being this close to Clint had Margot's adrenaline pumping, running hot and cold. Sitting next to him with his leg against hers was...different. Especially since she kept expecting him to make a bigger move.

She tried to breathe. *In, out. Don't be too loud about it. Just breathe.*

And she was doing okay until he did make a bigger move—if you could call it that.

He slipped an arm on the back of the sofa behind

her, and she could feel the vibration from his skin on the back of her neck.

A first date, she thought. That's what this felt like.

The date they'd never had before skipping to all the other parts.

They'd seen each other naked, felt each other come to orgasm and, suddenly, she realized that she wanted something else.

A quiet date moment like this, on a sofa, just sitting around with a person who made something come alive in your chest.

Not allowing herself to think too much about that buzzing sensation—if she did, she would only run—she sank back into the sofa a little bit, against his muscle-bunched arm.

Relax, she thought.

But, naturally, she couldn't.

Hell, she couldn't even follow Leigh's show, as her friend spread the red velvet batter in a cake pan with smooth strokes.

All Margot could do was think over and over again that Clint had his arm around her, and that she felt just like a teenager, anxious about the end of the night.

But then she started getting restless.

Time to go.

Time to run before it's too late.

By the time Leigh was making a batch of sinful cake frosting on the TV, Margot was a complete bundle of nerves, wondering if Clint was going to kiss her...and wondering if he wasn't.

Finally, she couldn't deal anymore.

"Mind if I watch the rest of this later?" she asked, standing up and away from him.

Far, far away.

If he was surprised, he didn't show it. "Be my guest."

"Thanks." She started to leave, but more words wanted to trip off her tongue.

She let them. "I mean, thanks for everything. It really was a good night."

And she made herself leave before she tripped herself, falling right into his arms.

MARGOT DIDN'T ACTUALLY sleep until dawn, when she heard the door shut downstairs, indicating that Clint had left for the working part of the ranch.

Finally, she thought, her eyes closing. No more wondering if he would come to her room to finish off all the building sexual tension from last night.

She went to sleep so quickly that she didn't even have time to feel disappointed.

A few hours later, when her smartphone alarm went off, she sprang up in bed, automatically bending down and dragging her purse by the straps across the floor, then plunging her hand inside to turn off the wake-up-lazy-bones chimes.

Right away, she dialed a number.

After the pick-up, Margot blurted out, "Dani?"

"Hey."

"He's got some nerve."

Dani paused on her end of the line, obviously trying to put two and two together. Then she laughed. "I know what you're saying really isn't funny, but it just sounds like you're a character from *Bye Bye Birdie.* You know, at the beginning when all the screwy teenagers are blabbing on the phones about all the romantic gossip and—"

"Dani."

"Okay, what did Clint do this time?" Then she halted.

"Wait. How could he be getting on your nerves if you're at home and not on his ranch?"

Time to come out with it. "I'm, uh, still here."

"What?"

She'd gotten called out yet again. "I didn't want to bother you with my issues when you and Riley were having worse ones."

"I *like* your issues, Marg. Believe me, they've been the highlight of my week." She didn't go into detail but instead asked, "Why did you decide to stay there?"

Here came the grilling, but it was a relief to get everything off her chest. "Clint had this idea for a new book."

"Oh, a book. How could I not have guessed that? I'm sure you and Clint have had a lot of literary discussions."

"I kid you not, Dani." And she described his idea.

Dani seemed to chew on it for a second. Then, "I would totally read that."

"You read everything I write, anyway."

"That's because your life has always been a vicarious pleasure."

Why did she sound so wistful?

Margot didn't have time to analyze the remark before Dani went on, in a much cheerier tone.

"You must be working very hard on that book, Marg. How late did you stay up last night *working?*"

"You're mocking me about this?" Margot swung her legs over her mattress, her toes skimming the floor. "I called to tell you how much he's driving me up a wall. I need a friendly ear."

"Then talk away."

So she related everything about her and Clint's time in the bar—the near kiss, the territorial way he'd kept the other cowboys from dancing with her, even the end of the night when it'd felt so much like a date.

Dani sighed. "Like this is all a surprise. Riley said…"

She dropped the sentence midway, and Margot wasn't about to let that go.

"What did Riley say?"

Dani made an I'm-shutting-up-now sound. "Ignore me. I really shouldn't have brought it up."

"Well, you did."

"Why do you even care when you're just going to take off from the ranch soon? Unless…"

Oh, God. Even Dani suspected that Margot was much more interested than she should be.

"Listen," Dani said. "I like Clint, and I know you, Margot. And as long as I've known you, you freak out at the first sign that a guy wants to get serious."

Margot lowered her voice. "Riley told you that Clint wants to get serious?"

"I didn't say that."

"Say *something*." Anything.

Dani was definitely serious herself now. "I shouldn't be the one saying something here. *You* say something. *You* tell me why Clint has enough power to make you call me in the morning bitching about him."

If Margot didn't know any better, she would've said that the new Dani had done more than have a slight physical makeover. She had a new way of dealing with everyone, too.

Drawing her knees up and pulling them toward her as she sat on the mattress, Margot knew that the time for hemming and hawing was over with Dani.

And with herself, too.

"I have no clue what's going on," she said. "Last week, I was this fabulous single girl on the go. This week…" She closed her eyes, opened them. "This week I'm starting to think about what it'd be like to stay."

"With Clint?"

"Jeez, I can't believe I said that." Could she take it back?

Dani's tone gentled. "You're scared to death, aren't you? It's okay, Margot. Love's darn scary. It's hard to figure out."

You should know, Margot thought, wondering just how far Dani and Riley had mended the small tears in the seams of their relationship.

Her heart had started to palpitate way back at the mere mention of love. "Maybe we shouldn't say the *L* word. I can't even…"

"All right. Can I say *like* instead? Because you do like Clint, don't you?"

Margot hugged her knees even tighter. "I wish I didn't."

"But you do." There was some hope in her tone.

"Don't you dare tell Riley, because guys gossip just as much as girls. They just do it in far fewer words."

"I'll be mum about it. But what're you going to do?"

She shook her head. "I don't know." Then, after a hesitation, she slumped. "Nothing. I know I'm not going to do a damned thing, because this is a good fling, but otherwise…"

"Ah." Dani sounded disappointed.

But why shouldn't she be when Margot had no idea what it was like to be with someone in a normal relationship and would most likely blow an opportunity for one, anyway?

She shouldn't have called Dani. She shouldn't have even opened this can of worms, because what else did she have to give besides seventy-plus more slips of paper in a basket?

Nothing, she realized, thinking of her dead-end job, her restless, noncommittal spirit.

But maybe there was something after all, she thought, before saying goodbye to Dani.

She hadn't driven away from the ranch yet, and at least she could have one more night's worth of good times before she went back to whatever she had left.

AFTER A DAY full of training a quarter paint that he had bought last month, Clint returned to the house exhausted, headed for the shower.

The water's spray massaged his muscles and, of course, his mind went into fantasy mode, imagining that Margot wasn't in her room being a study bug and working on her project. Instead, she was here in the shower with him, running her hands over his body, soaping him up, easing him down from hours of labor.

It wasn't enough, though, and afterward, he went downstairs, thinking he would just throw a couple frozen dinners into the stove and see how much fight Margot had left in her when she came down to eat.

Would it be war?

Or would it be time to make up?

He found her waiting for him, sitting on a kitchen chair, her dark hair cascading over her shoulders as she wore that long white innocent-but-not-so-innocent negligee that he'd given her last weekend as a part of *his* basket.

As she smiled mysteriously at him, he nearly blew up.

Maybe she didn't notice, because she merely pushed a plate of meatloaf and vegetables across the table in his direction. She had food in front of her, too.

"I heard you come in," she said, "so I went ahead and warmed this up. I found some ground beef in the fridge earlier. Hope you don't mind."

"I don't," he said. "Thanks."

He wasn't sure what he was supposed to be doing with her sitting there in a sexy boudoir gown with meatloaf on the table. Was he supposed to choose one or the other?

Was there a piece of paper he'd missed in her basket that had some kind of Hotsville, U.S.A., scenario written on it?

The only thing he knew for sure was that she was setting up another destination—their finale.

Let it play out, he thought. *Nothing earth-shattering is ever going to happen with her, anyway.* He shouldn't have even entertained the idea last night. Or ever.

Just imagine—successful city-girl Margot and him, the simple lone cowboy.

Sitting, he took a long drink of the water she also had waiting for him. The glass clinked with ice, and a slice of lemon decorated the top.

She slid a piece of paper over to him.

And there it was—a scenario from the basket.

He didn't read it yet, only looked at her for a moment as she gave him another cryptic smile.

A second or two ticked past, and he thought, *Why not?*

What did he have to lose?

As a small voice within answered, *Your heart?* he ignored it and read the paper.

Reykjavik ice bar, Iceland.

He glanced at her in that white negligee again. An ice princess. And, unfortunately, the image was more than just a role she was playing for the basket.

She was as cool as they came.

"It's a freezing place, this ice bar," she said. "When I went there, they gave me an actual ice cup for the cocktails. They also gave us parkas, so we wouldn't chill our butts off on the ice seats." She smiled, tracing a finger over the rim of her glass, which curiously didn't have water, just ice cubes. "The bar was a great place to find someone who could warm a girl up afterward."

He tightened his hand around his glass and spoke before he could think straight. "I don't want to hear about how you got warmed up."

A pause.

A heavy thud of time during which she was probably thinking that she had him wrapped around her little finger.

For a second, he believed that she might drop the basket game altogether, but then she reached into her glass, taking out some ice.

She stood and started walking out of the room, though not before saying, "Dinner can get cold for all I care, but you might want to come and warm *me* up."

Then she left.

Clint told himself to stay put. To not give in this time, because if he did, it'd be for real.

He didn't know if he could take another night with her, pretending it didn't matter anymore.

But then he found himself standing, walking out of the kitchen and into the hallway, drawn to her.

Always drawn to her.

He saw her in the hall, disappearing into the study, the lights doused inside. She looked like a ghost or…

Or a bride in that long negligee.

But he wouldn't dare tell her that, because he suspected it would ruin the last night they had together.

And he wanted it to be special, to be different.

Dammit, how had he gotten to this point? And why did it feel like he should've arrived much sooner?

He went to the dark room where he knew she was waiting, and the summer scent of her led him deep inside, even though he couldn't see anything but the faint white outline of her gown. He knew the reason she wanted darkness—it would make him wonder where the ice would touch his skin.

"Come here," she said.

She didn't call him "stud" now. Was that a good sign?

Telling himself that it was, he walked forward.

"Take off your shirt." Her voice cracked a little, or maybe he was just imagining that.

As he went along with her, he said, "Where's this going, Margot?"

"You'll see."

He hadn't been talking about this scenario. He'd meant something much bigger and, if she knew that he'd just laid himself on the line, she didn't acknowledge it. Instead, he felt her ice-dampened fingertips on his chest, and he started, shocked by the wet charge of the contact.

He caught her hand. "What happens after tonight?"

"I go back to my place." She tried to pull away.

But he wasn't letting go. "Why do I get the feeling that you don't want to go?"

"Are you going to talk all night long?"

His heart kicked at his chest. "Maybe I should. Maybe this is the best time to tell you that I don't want you to go, even though that's how you apparently operate."

"Just be quiet."

This time, when she touched him with an ice cube,

it was more aggressive. She slid it around his nipple, and he sucked in a breath.

Is she really all ice? he thought.

And he wondered if he would ever be able to melt her all the way.

She was doing a hell of a job of melting *him*. His blood was turning into blasts of steam as she kept tracing patterns on him with the slick cube.

Water ran down his chest, over his stomach, cool and tingling.

"Thatta boy," she whispered, easing her fingers into the waistline of his jeans.

Gripping her around the wrist again, he stopped her from going further with the ice. Then he released her and backed away.

"No more games, Margot. No more bubble baths or paintings or ice."

She laughed carelessly, just as she always had during their basket time together.

He forged ahead, still in the dark, wishing he could see her face. "Last night at the bar, I didn't want another man even looking at you. You know why? Because when I think of you being with anyone else, it drives me insane. Even after one damned week, all I want to do is be around you, smell your perfume, have you next to me in bed or on the sofa or wherever it is, just so you're there. You've already become a part of my home. Don't you realize that?"

She'd gone quiet, but he was going to make this night part of their history, erasing the one that had started everything off so badly in college.

Deliberately, he stepped forward until he felt just where she was, his skin singing at the proximity of her. Then he reached out with both hands, instinctively knowing where to cup her face.

He brushed his thumbs over her cheekbones, bending down so that he was nose to nose with her.

Her breath came quick against his lips.

"You belong *here,* with me," he whispered before kissing her softly, a touch of his mouth to hers.

A hint of the tenderness from him that had always been hiding just below the surface.

She made a protesting sound in her throat, dropping the ice and circling her fingers around his wrists as he palmed her face. But when he deepened the kiss, parting his lips just slightly, she seemed to lose form beneath him, her knees giving out.

He wrapped an arm around her, keeping her steady while pressing her to him at the same time, his other hand going to the back of her head.

When she sighed against his mouth—this sound one of pleasure—he restrained himself.

A real first kiss.

A gentle one that wasn't about sex or animal instinct.

This was about showing her how he felt without having to tell her and scare her off completely.

They kissed for what felt like hours, her mouth opening under his as they drew at each other, seeking, necking like two desperate kids who couldn't stand the thought of ever being apart.

She clung to him, her hands roaming his back as she kept making those urgent yet sweet sounds low in her throat.

When he finally lost the ability to breathe, he came up for air, still pressed against her, still holding her.

"No games," he said against her mouth. "This is

more real than what I've ever felt for anyone, Margot."

He waited for her to answer, every second like a drumbeat that would announce his fate.

12

THIS WAS MORE real than anything she'd ever felt.

And it frightened Margot to her very core.

As a pulse beat rapidly in her temples, speeding up her thoughts until she couldn't latch on to a single one of them, she realized that she'd been gripping Clint's waist.

She should say something. But what? Because telling him that she felt the same way about him would be a commitment, and she didn't do those. She'd made a career of hopping from one place to another, never staying, never wanting to.

Until he'd come along, offering her the first true home she'd ever had.

Making her realize that this…and him…were all she'd ever been looking for.

But he didn't understand that homes never lasted. They were way stations, just like people were way relationships. Homes broke down, sometimes with fatal consequences, and she was fine all by herself.

Always had been, always would be.

She wanted to flee now, even as he held her, warm, strong.

"Margot," he whispered, touching her cheek. "Don't leave me hanging."

Finally, she snatched a thought out of the spinning cycle of her mind. "I don't mean to."

"Good. Because I don't regret telling you how I feel. What I would regret is seeing you drive off, knowing that there was a chance things could've been different."

"Is there a chance?" she asked quietly. It hardly sounded like her.

"Why wouldn't there be?"

She thought of the stripped-down words he'd bared to her, words about how she belonged here. Even if they were in the dark right now, he had lit her up temporarily.

She wished she were capable of doing the same for him. He needed someone who'd be there when he faced his brothers the next time, someone who wanted to see him win at everything he did in life.

She didn't want to let him down when he realized that she was just good at temporary, and that was all.

He was still stroking her cheek, conjuring those butterflies in her chest, the fluttering sensation she'd never felt before when someone cared about you.

But those wings also felt like fear, because what would happen when the butterflies got tired and stopped trying to fly? What if those butterflies weren't even real in the first place?

She yearned to touch his face in the dark, just as he was doing to her. She wanted to show him without those hard-to-say words that she was going to take this risk, put her heart out there, give it to him.

Yet she couldn't.

She was the joke this time, and she probably always would be.

When she pulled back slightly from him, his fingers stiffened, and he took them away from her cheek.

He knew she couldn't do this, didn't he?

"This is happening too fast," she said, avoiding the issue altogether. She wasn't going to let this go anywhere.

His laugh barely disguised what she thought might be an injury—one she'd inflicted.

"Is there a certain amount of time that we *should* be taking to—"

She wouldn't let him say "fall in love" or anything even close.

"I just need to think," she said, moving toward the crack of light at the doorway. "My head's scrambled. I just need…time."

You're what's scrambled, she thought. *And you have no idea how to fix yourself.*

"All right, Margot." He sounded…confident? Or was that another mask to hide his resignation? "You take your time."

He was letting her off the hook, and she wondered whether he had never meant all the things he'd said in the first place. If this was really all about getting her to fall for him, it would be the ultimate joke.

But something inside of her told her that wasn't the case at all.

Still, even if she were to go running back to him, jumping into his arms, it wouldn't last. It never did for either of them, so why should they think that the odds were in their favor this time?

She left the room, telling herself not to look back.

Only forward, just as she'd always done.

CLINT LET HER go, because keeping her in the dark with him wasn't going to solve anything. It wasn't going to make her feel something for him when she obviously didn't.

She had merely been letting him down easy, Clint thought, waiting until he heard her climb the stairs so he could finally get out of that study.

Afterward, he shut the door behind him, as if he could box away what had just happened in there. A dark stain was growing in him, heavy and lonely.

Why had he even said anything to her when he knew damned well how Margot was going to react?

Going to bed, he tried to sleep on it, but that didn't work. He ended up watching TV until he couldn't keep his eyelids open anymore.

In the morning, the TV was still on, sounding tinny and loud at a time when the dawn usually came on soft waves of color through his window.

But even the sunrise was lackluster today.

He pulled on a pair of jeans, then went to his door. When he opened it, he almost stepped on a piece of paper.

He picked it up, his heart already sinking.

Clint,
I couldn't sleep, and since I was going to leave early in the morning, anyway, I thought I would just get out of your hair sooner rather than later.

   I owe you a big thanks, not only for your hospitality, but because you do know how to show a girl a good time. I'm never going to forget this past week, and I mean that.

Here, it was as if she'd stopped writing and started again. The penmanship was a little shakier.

Dani and Riley kept telling me that you'd changed since college, and they were right. You can do anything, Clint, and I'm not just blowing smoke at you. Some girl is going to be damned lucky to have you someday. She's going to be the type who doesn't have neurotic issues. She's going to be country through and through, and she's not going to be a fish out of water in your life. She's truly going to be perfect for you, and I wish you all the happiness in the world with her. She'll be the luckiest woman.

His gaze couldn't focus on the rest, which looked like platitudes and thank-yous for having her as a guest.

The writer, he thought. The woman who couldn't tell him all this in person last night.

His gut churned as he crumpled up the letter and tossed it behind him while he went into the hallway, toward her room, throwing open the door.

All he saw was a neatly made bed, just as if no one had stayed there.

Just as if she had never come into his life and then left it in pieces.

But this was how it had always been meant to go, Clint thought. How could it have turned out any other way with two people who'd only been trying to find closure with a decade-old fantasy?

Blanking out his mind—and everything else—Clint went to work on the ranch, driving to the horse barn, walking through it, feeling like an empty page.

His employees stared, but he barely felt it. And when

he got an email later in the day while he worked in the barn's office, all he could do was laugh.

It was from his brothers. They had stopped their threats and hired an attorney.

He leaned back in his chair, remembering what Margot had said to him at The 76 as they'd talked at the table by the dance floor.

I know someone who could help.

She'd been referring to a lawyer, but she'd had no way of knowing that the only person Clint longed to have at his side, fighting every battle with him, was her.

THE DAYS PLODDED by for Margot that week.

She tried to make them go faster by "filling her creative well," seeing as many movies as she could, reading like a freak and sorting through magazines to find some inspiration for a new project.

But she kept going back to daydreams about country bars, starlit nights, comfortable cowhide couches and a gazebo on a ranch.

And a cowboy who had messy golden hair, roguish blue eyes and a cocksure grin.

Even an early Sunday afternoon on her condo balcony with the newspaper and a plate of blueberry scones under the October sun couldn't cheer her up and out of this funk.

So she called the only two people who even had a chance of making her feel better.

First, she got Dani on the line for the conference call, then Leigh, who was shooting on location at a dairy, where she was going to make homemade ice cream in passion-laced flavors.

"Still hating myself," Margot said as soon as Leigh got on the line.

The Queen of Cream answered first. "Stop beating yourself up about Clint."

"Yeah," Dani said, a good friend until the end, although Margot knew she was frustrated with this romantic outcome. "You thought things weren't going to work out with him, so you nipped it in the bud."

And she'd nipped it with a letter. Margot heard it in every syllable her friends uttered.

She hadn't even been able to tell him what she really felt in person.

She rested her head on the back of the lounge chair. "I was afraid of what would happen if I tried to say those things to him face-to-face and not in a letter. There's a reason I'm a writer."

Or *was* a writer.

She still hadn't told Dani and Leigh about the canceled book or her bleak career outlook. Leigh was riding high, Dani was going to open her own business one day and Margot was deadweight.

Why did it seem as if Clint was the only person she could've confided in? He'd given her ideas, not commiseration.

He had made it seem as if they could find their way out of a dark room together, and with every day that passed, she wanted to believe that they might've made it if she'd decided she could break out of her patterns and change.

Too late, though, she thought. She'd already written the end to that story.

Leigh's sympathetic voice came back on. "What would you have said to him that you didn't write in the letter?"

She bit her bottom lip. "I have no idea how to put

what I feel into the words that come out of my mouth. And usually *those* words are the wrong ones, anyway."

"You know exactly what you should've said to him," Dani said.

Margot sat up. "What? That I'm all of a sudden so sure that I'm not going to get bored, just like my parents always did, or that he's not going to want to move on, either, like he always did?"

Dani piped in again. "That's what the Margot who won't get out of her rut would say. This Margot is scared to death."

"No, I'm..."

Yes, she was.

Leigh said, "When you love, you have to do it with everything you've got, right, Dani?"

"Right."

Dani sounded so sad that Margot's problems disappeared, and she seized the chance to get the spotlight off her. But she also did want to know what was going on with one of her very best friends.

"Is everything okay with you, Dan?"

On the other end of the line, she could hear her friend sigh.

"I mean it," Margot said. "We can go back to working my crap out later."

"Yeah," Dani finally said. "Of course we're okay. Don't change the subject."

A clump of silence passed before Dani said, "Okay, so it hasn't been such a smooth road. But Riley's been out of town on business, looking at some real estate for his boss, and he's coming back tonight. I'm going to give him a big welcome home. You should see the stuff I bought."

Margot got a bad feeling about this. "Stuff?"

"Uh-huh. We've got a cheeky little Boudoir-type place within driving range—tasteful but tempting. It would've been perfect for my auction basket if I'd had any imagination at the time."

Both Leigh and Margot went quiet until Margot said, "I'll be the first to tell you that fun and games in a bedroom aren't going to help anything."

"It'll put us both back in a good mood."

Dani's words echoed something Margot had said to Clint the night when things had first started spiraling out of control with Le Crazy Horse.

It was fun, okay?

But that had just been the half of it. It had been the first time she had been flailing with her feelings in the aftermath of sex. The first time she had done anything to avoid examining how she really felt about him.

She wasn't sure it was love. Not yet. But love started somewhere, and if this wasn't the beginning of it, she didn't know what else it could be.

Love. Her, Margot Walker, single girl on the go.

Now a true fish out of water.

Margot picked at a nylon lacing on her lounge chair. "Whatever you do, Dan, good luck."

"Tonight will be a great night for us. I'm sure of it. And, after his welcome home, I'll show him the wedding dress I finally ordered. I sent you all a picture of it this morning, so check your email."

Margot reached for her iPad on the glass-topped table next to her, accessing her account.

When the picture appeared, her heart seized up.

"It's beautiful, Dani."

Margot wasn't just saying that. The gown was simple, with a one-shoulder bodice, chiffon ruching and beaded flower appliqués. So Dani.

But, much to Margot's surprise, it could've been so her, too. Dressed in white, just as she'd been that last night with Clint in the negligee he'd given her. She sighed, and Leigh must've thought it was just because of the gown.

"Dammit, my phone's taking forever to download my email. Reception out here is terrible."

Dani laughed. "Don't worry—you'll see it later, crabby."

"I'm not crabby."

"But you are." Dani was in teasing mode now because the heat was off her. "I would be, too, if I still hadn't heard from my secret admirer."

"On that note," Leigh said, "I need to go. Everything's set for me to shoot."

They said their goodbyes, leaving Dani and Margot alone on the phone.

Margot said, "You did good, finding that dress."

"Believe it or not, sometimes I actually know what I'm doing." She had a wink in her voice. "You take care of yourself, okay? No maudlin nights, drinking wine, pining away for Clint."

Was that how Dani saw her these days? As a helpless thing who pined away?

She thought of Clint as waves of need—and the start of something bigger—rushed over her.

A single girl on the go. That's truly not who she was anymore, and maybe the readers who had been buying her books had seen that way before Margot had.

Clint had known it, too.

Getting up from her lounge chair, she went to the railing of her balcony, looking over the wide-open spaces that just didn't seem wide enough anymore—not after being on Clint's ranch.

It was time to travel someplace she'd never gone before, wasn't it? And even if she crashed and burned, at least she wouldn't have this hollow pit in the very center of her where Clint should be.

And that's when Margot decided that she hadn't been moving forward this past week—she'd been going nowhere.

Margot finally said to Dani, "No maudlin nights. I promise."

And after they hung up, she headed straight for her room, where her suitcases and travel gear were stored. She got one of her bags out of the closet and threw it on her bed.

She'd had enough of this. If she was going to travel, it needed to be in the direction she should've been heading all along.

By THE TIME the headlights from Riley's truck flared over the family room windows of their rented suburban house, Dani was ready for him.

She took a deep breath, smoothing her hands down the negligee she'd purchased this week.

Egypt, she thought, feeling the sheer material beneath her hands. The beige gown didn't hide much, parting down the middle to show a flash of skin and belly button above the barely-there undies.

As she adjusted her headpiece—a chain of coins that dipped onto her forehead—she rushed to the hallway. But when she passed the mirror, she checked her makeup one last time.

Heavy eyeliner—check.

Red lipstick—check.

The front door opened, and she turned off the hall light, dashed to the bedroom, then lit a single candle on an end table. As the door closed, she took her place on the bed, her blood flowing hot as she made like Cleopatra and rested on her side, one hand propping up her head.

She heard a jangle of keys as Riley spilled them into the glazed ceramic bowl by the front door, then the sound of his footsteps on the wooden floor. Then...

The TV switching on?

She sprang up in bed, her headdress clinking. "Riley?"

A pause, then the TV volume going down. Footsteps into the hallway.

She got back into position.

"Dani? You home?"

"Yes, I am."

"The lights were off, so I—"

Then he stood in the doorway, the candlelight flickering over him. His eyebrows were knitted as he scanned the scene.

"Welcome to Egypt," she said, crooking a finger at him.

Her nightie covered one breast, but only with a teasing sheerness. The other breast was exposed as the material gaped away from her.

Passion clouded Riley's eyes, but she could see the sexual haze lift from them as the seconds passed.

She thought about how she'd lied to Margot and Leigh this morning. Things hadn't been so okay between her and Riley. He'd been on this business trip for most of the week, and before he'd gone, he'd spent a lot of time in the yard, mowing, cutting, weeding. She'd let him blow off steam out there, too, knowing they would sit and have another talk when he was ready.

But he hadn't been ready before he'd left town, so

she thought a little nudge might be in order. Plus, she'd missed him. Terribly.

She rolled to her belly. "I've been counting down the minutes until you got back."

"You know I have, too."

Why did he make it sound as if he'd been waiting until *she* got back from somewhere after leaving him behind?

"That's some getup," he said.

"I thought you might like a trip to an intriguing destination."

"Sounds like Margot and that basket of hers."

Another comment laden with deeper meaning. He was obviously referring to the way things between Margot and Clint hadn't turned out so well.

He came to sit on the bed, and her pulse darted up and almost out of her as she crawled over to him and started to unbutton his shirt.

"I did a lot of thinking while I was gone," he said.

She stopped with the buttons. Riley had always been a thinker—a stalwart man who never did something until he'd worked every angle out in his mind.

Why did she get the feeling that she'd been his main subject?

"You're about to say something bad," she said.

"No, Dani." He touched her headdress. "We were best friends before we were anything else, and I don't know if that set the tone for the rest of our lives. I should've expected change after being together for years."

"What do you mean?"

"I mean that what we felt for each other was always very straightforward and innocent. There were never wild nights like Margot had with Clint, where things

were stormy and crazy. I think that seeing them together did something to you, and I can't blame you for
that. You're only human." He ran a hand down her hair.
"But there're deeper things going on with you, too, and
that's what we have to work through before we set foot
in front of any wedding altar."

But we're Dani and Riley, she wanted to say. *Things
never go wrong.*

She took off the stupid headdress. "I don't want to
talk about my parents again and how they've warped
me."

He didn't say anything for a moment, but he finally
nodded. He wouldn't talk about it now, she thought,
even though it was clearly on his mind.

He took her headdress, handing it back to her. She
refused it.

"You think I'm rejecting you or something?" he
asked.

"Aren't you?"

"God, Dani. When I saw you lying here, I wanted to
tear off what little you have on."

"So why didn't you?"

He smiled. "Because I didn't choose you just for sex.
I'm going to spend the rest of my life with you, and
we're not going to work things out by going to Egypt."

He was right. Margot and Clint had found that out
the hard way, so why had she started down the same
path with Riley?

"You know what we need to do?" he asked.

She motioned to her costume. "Ask for a refund?"

With great tenderness, he kissed her, just a touch of
his lips on hers.

Just a world of exploding hearts and a shower of need
that twirled through Dani.

"We need to get to know each other all over again," he said, his fingers at her nape, his thumb caressing the sensitive spot near the center of her throat.

She made a small sound of pleasure. "I'd say you already know a lot about me."

"I think I know enough to realize that you want some excitement. And before we get married, I want you to get it all out of your system so you can't say we never tried this and we never tried that before we settled down."

It took her a moment to realize that this was Riley speaking. Her Riley.

"We're going to experiment?" she asked.

"You can put it however you want. I look at it as courting—getting to know you all over again."

"Courting." She laughed. "It's so…"

"Old-fashioned? Probably. But I can put old-fashioned behind if that's what you want."

Now she gaped at him. "What are you saying?"

There was a hint of something she'd never seen in Riley's gaze before, and it excited the heck out of her.

No—the *hell* out of her.

"I want you to show me everything about yourself, Dani, no matter what it is," he said. "Court me in whatever way you want."

Her imagination started to go berserk, as if Riley had opened a door to a room that she'd always kept locked, especially from him.

But he'd found a key.

He put the headdress back on her, that dark and sparkling gleam still in his gaze.

Dani smiled, feeling reborn.

And tonight, she was an Egyptian goddess with a servant who would do anything for her.

Anything and more.

13

THAT NIGHT, CLINT slammed the old-model push-button phone in his barn office into its cradle, letting the curses fly.

Luckily, nothing but the whicker of his stabled cutting horses answered him.

He'd just been trying to get a hold of his brothers, who'd left a message a few days ago while Clint was working, saying that their lawyer would finally be contacting Clint's own attorney this coming week for a meeting about Dad's will and the ranch.

Neither of them had answered any of his calls, so Clint hadn't even gotten the opportunity to talk some sense into them—not that they had ever listened to sense before. Hell, he didn't even have a lawyer yet. Good God, deep down, he had believed that his brothers would never go that far.

His own blood.

Yet they had, and the betrayal made Clint feel as if he'd been sideswiped by a car while sitting at a stop sign. He'd seen it coming in the rearview mirror, but he hadn't thought it would hit him.

Then...*CRASH.*

He shoved out of his chair, walking out of the sparse office and into the barn itself, his boots crunching over straw. The horses peered at him out of their stalls, and one, a favorite broodmare he called Calamity Jane, neighed at him.

It was as if she knew that he was upset about more than just his brothers. They were simply the topping on the mountain of hurt that was mostly Margot, who had also sideswiped him. And she had kept right on going down the road without ever looking back to see what kind of damage she'd inflicted.

He thought he'd be okay, but the injury had run deeper than he'd first realized. And it had only grown, day by day. Truthfully, he'd hung up the phone about a hundred times when he'd been about to call her, to ask her why she'd left that letter and nothing else.

He went to Calamity Jane, resting his hand on her muzzle as she canted her ears forward.

"I knew it all along," he said softly to her. "They all break your heart at some point. I just didn't believe it'd happen to me."

Jane sympathetically blinked her big brown eyes, as if telling him, "You can't lose hope."

God, he didn't want to let hope go. In his dreams, he kept imagining that Margot would appear one night in his room with her basket in hand, smiling, offering it to him so he could choose another destination. And when he read the slip of paper, it would say "Right here on this ranch, just outside Visalia, California."

But he would go anywhere for her, really.

Clint patted Calamity Jane. "She has no idea that I'd hop on a plane to the far corners for her. I never got the chance to tell her that."

She rubbed against him in solidarity just before he walked away, down the barn's aisle, where one of the ranch hands, a guy they called Blume, was mucking out a stall.

They said good-night, and Clint walked through the unseasonably warm evening, hopping into his truck and driving home.

His silent home with the dimly lit windows.

In the shower, he occupied himself with thoughts of what he would have for dinner, or if he should go out with the boys tonight, but he couldn't get excited about either one.

Still, he had to eat, so he put on a pair of sweats and a T-shirt, heading for the second-story hallway.

But then...

He thought he heard a voice outside the window that he'd cracked to let in some of the Indian summer night air.

Stunned into stillness, he listened again. It'd sounded like Margot.

But didn't he hear her voice and see her face in his thoughts all the time?

Just as he was about to write off the sound, he heard a pounding knock on his front door, then his doorbell rang.

"Clint! I know you're in there!"

He had to be hearing things.

He was almost afraid to go to his window and look down below, because if he was wrong—if he was just imagining this—he'd officially be crazy.

But he was pulled to that window, anyway, and he held his breath, his blood tapping as he opened the window all the way and leaned out.

And there she was, coming out from under the porch

eaves as if she'd heard the window creaking open, her hands on her hips.

Just as knee-weakening as ever under the porch light.

Her hair was piled at the nape of her neck, as if she'd haphazardly shoved it there, and she was wearing a long summer dress, as if she'd been lounging and had suddenly roused herself for a road trip.

He still couldn't believe it, but she seemed just as flabbergasted at the sight of him, her hands slipping down off her hips.

"Margot?" he asked, his voice raw.

It was obvious that she was trying to gather herself. "I...I just drove, and I ended up here for some reason."

For some reason. Had he been right to keep hoping...?

Pride and that all-too-present hurt came to his rescue, and it was as if a wall went up around his heart. He wasn't going to let her do this to him again.

"Did you forget something in the house?" he asked. "Your toothbrush? A pair of boots? Maybe a letter?"

She hung her head for a moment, then looked back up at him. "I didn't know what else to do, Clint."

"About what?"

"Are you going to make me yell everything up at you?"

He could either give her a hard time or he could hear her out.

But once she was inside his home, he wasn't sure he could ever let her out again.

Then she tilted her head. "I have a lot to say, Clint. Please."

And that was all it took to get him to fold. Dammit.

"Door's open," he said.

She glanced up at him for a few seconds longer,

and he could see that it had taken all her bravery to be here—just as it had for him when he'd put himself on a limb the last time they'd seen each other.

After she disappeared under the eaves, he heard his front door open. Then close.

Raking back his hair with his hand, he couldn't get his feet to move.

What if everything between them collapsed tonight? What if it'd never been there in the first place?

He couldn't stand more heartbreak—not after Margot's letter. Not after his brothers.

As he heard her footsteps, he finally got himself going, coming to stand by the top of the stairs.

She was at the bottom, gripping the polished rail.

And there they waited, so close but so far.

"You had a long trip," he finally said.

"I drove most of the day." She tightened her hold on the rail. "I would've driven a lot longer, though."

"For what, Margot?"

She hauled in a deep breath, blew it out. During that short space of time, he swore his heart banged at least fifty times.

"I couldn't stay away from you," she said. "I kept waking up at night, with the condo so quiet. I wished I could hear you breathing next to me, just like that one night we spent together." She laughed sadly. "I kept wondering what might have happened if I'd stayed another day with you. Then another, until they all just ran into each other in one long, happy time. Because, just like you said, this is more home than I've ever had, Clint, and it had everything to do with you."

Her emotion struck him, and he could barely get the words out. "And why didn't you just tell me that face-to-face?"

"Because I thought that if I had to say goodbye in front of you, I wouldn't have done it."

Shaking his head, he almost gave up. Sometimes she made no sense.

But, God help him, most of the time he actually understood her nonsensical thoughts—just like now.

"I was so wrong," she said. "That's why I'm here, to tell you everything that was written between every line in that letter." She took the first stair, pausing on it. "I told you that you'd find another girl who was perfect for you, when all along I knew that she might be me. I've always done the leaving, and I couldn't stand the thought of what might happen if I got in too deep with you and you someday left me."

As he watched, she climbed up two more steps, and his blood gave a push in his veins.

"Why would you think I'd leave?" he asked.

She clutched the rail. "Mainly because you seem to think I'm this successful woman, and in the near future, when you inevitably found out that I'm not anymore, you were going to change your mind about me."

"What are you talking about?"

"My writing career is going down the tubes." She tensed up, as if anticipating his make-or-break reaction.

"Are you kidding?" he said.

She gave him a puzzled glance.

"Margot," he said, coming down one stair, "you're the last person in the world who'd ever be a failure."

It was as if the air had cracked between them, tumbling down.

She lowered her head, her voice thick. "You're the only one I've told about this. And that has to say something, doesn't it? That you're the one I trusted to hear it when, not too long ago, I didn't trust you at all?"

He walked the rest of the way to meet her on the stairway, and when he did, he slipped his hand under her chin to make her look up at him. Her eyes were shiny from unshed tears.

"You don't know," he said, "just how gratified I am to be the one you told."

She bit her lip, then nodded, holding on to his arm instead of the railing now.

He touched her jaw with his fingertips, hardly believing this was happening.

"I came back to offer more than an apology and explanations, though," she said. "First, I want to be here when you have to deal with your brothers."

At this, his throat tightened up. He could give her a home, but she gave him the support he'd always wanted, though he'd never realized it until now.

They'd been drawn to each other in college, but it'd taken years of living to make their connection come alive, giving each other what they really needed.

She wasn't done. "I want to be that fish-out-of-water, true country girl who lives where your parents lived so happily. And, well, this next one proves just how superficial I am, but I want to show everyone that the joke's on them."

When he took her into his arms, she fit against him as if she was made to be there and nowhere else in this world.

"Just imagine," he murmured into her hair. "Two butts of a joke who ended up together."

Then he brushed his lips over hers, more gently than any touch they'd ever shared. But it was enough to zing a sizzling thrill over and through every inch of him.

Without having to say anything, they sank to the

stairs, him taking her weight on his body as he cradled her against him.

He worked his fingers at her nape, undoing that bundle of hair until it tumbled down, thick and fragrant. He kept kissing her—little pecks at the corner of her mouth, on her cheek, under her jaw, making her take in tiny breaths.

The first time they'd been together at the reunion, he'd told her he would find eighty ways to pleasure her, but he hadn't known about these innocent, erotic places before. Now, each one was a discovery in itself.

A kiss to the neck, and she gasped.

A nip at the skin between her collarbone and shoulder, and she clutched at his T-shirt.

Then back to her mouth—lush, devouring, slow and easy.

They made out on the stairway, her body stretched over his, for what seemed like hours. Just kissing like famished kids and nothing else.

Until she slid her hand under his shirt, her palm on his ribs.

He cupped her face, looking into her pale, clear eyes. "You don't want to take it a little slower this time?"

Because now, it wouldn't be a basket game.

She looked at him, *into* him. "I want all of you, all the time, Clint."

And she kissed him again, taking them into their own world.

MARGOT MEANT EVERY word. She'd driven for miles and miles to say them, stopping only once for gas and taking off again, and the entire time, her heart had been in her throat.

What was she going to say?

Was he going to kick her out, tell her she'd had her chance and she'd blown it?

But he'd accepted everything about her, even the parts she'd been so afraid to expose to anyone.

The *Cosmo* girl and the cowboy. Who would've ever called it?

He rolled her to the side, keeping her in his strong arms, until she grasped the bottom of his T-shirt, yanking it up and over his head. Unable to wait a moment more, she pulled down the top of her dress, where the basic white bra she'd put on this morning pressed against her breasts, making them swell.

"I didn't have time to change clothes," she said, as if in apology for the least exotic wardrobe possible.

She drew in a breath as he kissed the tops of her breasts.

This was no basket-inspired costume, but he didn't seem to mind.

"I'll change your clothes for you," he said, reaching around her back to unhook her.

Her breasts spilled out, and he smiled, positioning her above him so that he could take her into his mouth, suck on her until she wiggled on top of him, plumped and damp between her legs.

He slipped a hand under her dress, pressing against her achiest spot.

"You have way too many clothes on, anyway," he murmured.

Then he tugged her dress up, over her head, just as she'd done with his T-shirt.

"And these?" he said, pulling at her panties. "No need for them, either."

She braced herself on the steps as he worked the material down her legs and off her body.

Then he placed his hands on her ribs, guiding her so that her most vulnerable area was above him, her hands braced on the steps, her legs open for him.

Being this exposed caused her pulse to hammer, and he made her wait, no doubt teasing her, just as he'd always done.

And always would, if she had her way about it.

"Here's a place I haven't kissed today," he said, using his fingers to part her.

She held back a delighted sound, and he laughed, knowing what he did to her.

But instead of taking that as a devilish move in one of their games, she accepted it, took it wholeheartedly, then lowered her hips to him.

He kissed her thoroughly, with mouth and tongue. Slow laves, maddening sucks, licks and pulls. All the while, heat gathered in her belly, wisps curling up and up until she almost felt carried away.

"Don't come yet," he said, guiding her down his body so that she could rub herself against the bulge in his sweats, feeling his tip.

"I'm not sure I can wait," she whispered.

"Now who's the one who's not going to last?"

Le Bain. She'd taunted him about coming too soon when they'd been in that bubble bath together.

Her cowboy. Her Clint.

He took off the sweats, revealing his erection.

"Don't worry about what comes next." She touched him. "I'm on the pill, and—"

He assured her that he was fine, too. He'd barely even gotten the words out before he eased into her, so gently that she could feel every sliding inch.

They didn't move for a moment, just looked into each other's eyes.

She saw something so profound there that pressure built in her chest this time, not only in her belly.

A future. Their future.

He moved inside her, tender thrusts, the sweat of their bodies making them slip against each other. When he turned her over, his arms under her as a cushion, he pounded into her, pushing her up the stairs.

Up…up…

She was ascending in more than one way, climbing to a spot that made everything so clear, so new, so—

Her climax buffeted her, a million wet splashes, like a storm that had thrashed out of her and into him, because he came right after her.

And then, when they both had calmed a little, instead of trying to think of a way to escape him before he could look into her eyes again, she stared into his gaze.

She allowed him to see all the way into her for the very first time.

Epilogue

WITH HALLOWEEN JUST around the corner, Clint and Margot had decorated the ranch house with carved pumpkins and ghoulies like paper ghosts that hung from the corners of the family and living rooms.

He stood next to a life-size skeleton that Margot had unearthed from the storage room after she'd moved her stuff into the house.

"Is this really suitable for a housewarming?" he asked her as she fluffed the hair of a broomstick-bound witch near the fireplace.

"I think our guests have seen scarier things," she said, coming over to him and cuddling into his side.

He wrapped an arm around her—his fledgling cowgirl in jeans and a fashionable rodeo shirt. It wasn't a costume, either. It was just Margot, stripped down to her fish-who-found-water self.

He kissed her, long and easy. No rush, because they had all the time in the world.

But there was something beating at him nonetheless. Something he'd wanted to say to her for the past couple of weeks.

Nuzzling her ear, he went for it, whispering, "Margot…"

"I love you so much, Clint."

Warmth flooded him, here, there, everywhere. "You do?"

"I do." Her eyes were wide, as if this were the most momentous thing that had ever happened to her.

He must've taken too long to return the sentiment, because she gave him a little push on the chest.

"Well, do *you?*" she asked.

"Hell. Yeah." He laughed, drawing her back into his arms. "You just beat me to saying it."

As they laughed together and Clint swung her around, the front door opened.

They didn't bother to pull apart, not these days, when the secret was out about them.

"Barbecue's ready." Riley's voice.

"Be right there." Clint picked Margot up, resting her like a sack of grain on his hip until she laughed even harder.

"This is how we wrangle women on a ranch," he said, carrying her until she wiggled so much that he had to put her down.

She pushed the hair out of her face. "Try that tonight, and I just might…"

"Do what?"

She shrugged, walking away from him toward the front door, giving her hips an extra shimmy.

"I just might rope *you* up."

"Promises, promises."

He chased her out the door to the back patio, where Dani was helping Riley at the grill and Leigh was walking around on the far lawn, holding a beer in one hand and a phone in the other.

As Clint sat next to Margot at the long table, in front of a selection of salads, brown-sugar franks and beans and honey-corn-bread muffins, Dani and Riley brought over the sauce-covered grilled ribs.

When Dani reached to the vegetable plate for a piece of celery, feeding it to Riley, Margot gave Clint a knowing glance.

The other couple was "courting" all over again. They still seemed on edge with each other sometimes, as if so much had happened since the beginning of the month that they couldn't quite get over it, but this was a start.

After all, they were Dani and Riley. They would find a way.

"Eat up," Riley said to Clint as Dani finished the rest of the celery. He put the ribs on the table. "You're gonna need strength for tomorrow."

Margot was already slicing her meat, with much gusto, Clint thought.

"Clint's brothers are the ones who need the protein," she said. "Our lawyer's going to put them through the wringer."

His brothers hadn't backed off from their strong-arming. But as Clint looked around the table, he realized that he'd found a far better family.

And someone even more special than that.

He kissed Margot again, and she sent him a saucy, confident grin. Being out in the country, starting her blog about a city-girl-goes-rustic lifestyle, had put color in her cheeks.

When Leigh came wandering back to the patio, all attention rested on her, especially because she had gone a little pale.

"What's wrong?" Dani and Margot asked at the same time.

"That was Beth Dahrling," she said, sitting in a chair at the end of the table. "The man who bought my basket is arriving back in the country next week. He's wondering when we can arrange our…"

Clint cleared his throat, saving Leigh from saying the rest of it.

Margot put down her knife. "Are you going to blow him off?"

Leigh took one good look at Margot sitting so closely to Clint, and she got a yearning glint in her gaze.

Was she wondering what a basket might bring her, too?

She reached for the asparagus with lemon pasta salad. "I'm going to tell him I'm available, and we're going to see what happens."

"Even though you have no idea who he is?" Margot asked.

Leigh hesitated, then nodded.

"Go, Leigh!" Dani said.

They all lifted their drinks in a toast.

"Go, Leigh!"

She still seemed wary at the prospect of this date as she toasted right back at them, but that longing remained in her gaze—something that disappeared only when she closed her eyes while taking a deep draught of beer.

Under the table, Margot squeezed Clint's knee. She'd seen Leigh's expression, too.

As he took her hand in his, entwining fingers, he thought about all the trips left in Margot's own basket.

And the many that they would be making up on their own as they went along.

* * * * *

Is there anything sexier than a hot cowboy?

How about four of them!

New York Times bestselling author
Vicki Lewis Thompson is back in the Blaze® lineup for
2013, and this year she's offering her readers
even more…

Sons of Chance

Chance isn't just the last name of these rugged
Wyoming cowboys—it's their motto, too!

Saddle up with

I CROSS MY HEART
(June)

WILD AT HEART
(July)

THE HEART WON'T LIE
(August)

And the first full-length
Sons of Chance Christmas story

COWBOYS & ANGELS
(December)

Take a chance…on a Chance!

WILD AT HEART

BY
VICKI LEWIS THOMPSON

MILLS &
BOON

First published in Great Britain 2013
by Mills & Boon, an imprint of Harlequin (UK) Limited,
Eton House, 18-24 Paradise Road, Richmond, Surrey TW9 1SR

© Vicki Lewis Thompson 2013

ISBN: 978 0 263 90315 7
ebook ISBN: 978 1 408 99687 4

14-0713

Harlequin (UK) policy is to use papers that are natural, renewable and recyclable products and made from wood grown in sustainable forests. The logging and manufacturing processes conform to the legal environmental regulations of the country of origin.

Printed and bound in Spain
by Blackprint CPI, Barcelona

To the dedicated folks who devote endless hours and
abandon creature comforts so that
our precious wildlife is protected. Thank you!

20% OFF*

with code
THANKSJUL

Visit www.millsandboon.co.uk today to get this exclusive offer!

Ordering online is easy:

- 1000s of stories converted to eBook
- Big savings on titles you may have missed in store

Visit today and enter the code **THANKSJUL** at the checkout today to receive **20% OFF** your next purchase of books and eBooks*. You could be settling down with your favourite authors in no time!

MILLS & BOON

JUL13

Prologue

July 3, 1984, Last Chance Ranch

ON PRINCIPLE, ARCHIBALD CHANCE approved of getting the ranch house gussied up for the Independence Day festivities. He was as patriotic as the next man. But the excitement of an impending party had transformed his usually well-behaved grandsons into wild things. From his position on a ladder at the far end of the porch, he could hear all three of them tearing around inside. He hoped to get the red, white and blue streamers tacked up before any of them came out.

That hope died as the screen door banged open and a bundle of two-year-old energy with a fistful of small flags raced down the porch toward him. The kid was more interested in who was coming after him than looking where he was going. A tornado in tiny cowboy boots.

"Nicky!" The screen door banged again as Sarah, Archie's daughter-in-law, dashed after him.

Giggling, Nicky put his head down and ran as fast as

his little legs would carry him. With no time to climb down, Archie dropped the bunting, tossed the nails into the coffee can and braced himself against the ladder as he shouted a warning.

Fortunately Sarah was quick. She scooped up both boy and flags a split second before he smashed into the ladder. "Those are for the table, young man."

"I gots flags, Mommy!" the little boy crowed.

"Yes, and they have pointy ends. Don't run with them, Nicholas." Sarah glanced up at Archie. "Sorry about that."

"Gabe gots flags, too!" Nicky announced.

Sarah wheeled around, and sure enough, there was little Gabe, not yet two, motoring toward them with a flag in each hand.

"I wager somebody's supplying them with those," Archie said.

"Yes, I wager you're right. And his name is Jack. Excuse me, Archie. I have a five-year-old who needs a reminder about the dangers of giving pointy objects to little boys." Confiscating the flags from both toddlers amid wails of distress, she herded them back inside.

"You're doing a great job, Sarah!" Archie called after her. He never missed an opportunity to tell her that. She'd given birth to only one of those kids, baby Gabriel, and she'd inherited the other two as part of the deal for being willing to marry Jonathan Chance. She loved all three kids equally, and she loved their father with the kind of devotion that made Archie's heart swell with gratitude.

As he turned back to his bunting chore, the screen

door squeaked again, signaling another interruption. He'd oil those hinges today. He hadn't realized how bad they were.

Glancing toward the door, he smiled. This was the kind of interruption he appreciated.

Nelsie approached with two glasses of iced tea. "Time for a break, Arch."

"Don't mind if I do." Hooking the hammer in his belt, he carried the coffee can full of nails in the crook of his arm as he descended the ladder to join his wife. "How're things going in there?"

"Not too bad, considering. I'm glad we decided to host the after-parade barbecue this year, but we didn't factor in the dynamics of having both babies able to walk and Jack putting them up to all manner of things. They'll do anything he tells them, especially Nicky."

Archie put down the hammer and nails before accepting a glass of tea and settling into the rocking chair next to her. They'd bought several rockers to line the porch, which would come in mighty handy during the barbecue. "Those boys are a handful, all right." He took a sip of tea. "Wouldn't trade 'em for all the tea in China, though."

"Me, either, the little devils." Nelsie chuckled. "Oh, you know what? I saw a bald eagle fly over early this morning. Forgot to tell you that."

"Huh. Wonder if there's a nest somewhere."

"Could be. Anyway, I thought it was appropriate, a bald eagle showing up so close to the Fourth. Maybe he, or she, will do a flyover tomorrow for our guests."

"I'll see if I can arrange it for you."

She smiled at him in that special way that only Nelsie could smile. "If you could, I believe you'd do it, Archie."

"Yep, that's a fact." They'd celebrated their forty-seventh anniversary last month, and he loved this woman more every day. He would do anything for her. And to his amazement, she would do anything for him, too.

He was one lucky cuss, and he knew it. His father used to say that Chance men were lucky when it counted. In Archie's view, finding a woman like Nelsie counted for a whole hell of a lot.

1

Present Day

FROM A PLATFORM twenty feet in the air, Naomi Perkins focused her binoculars on a pair of fuzzy heads sticking out of a gigantic nest across the clearing. Those baby eagles sure had the cuteness factor going on. If they lived to adulthood, they'd grow into majestic birds of prey, but at this stage they were achingly vulnerable.

Blake Scranton, the university professor who'd hired her to study the nestlings, was an infirm old guy who was writing a paper on Jackson Hole bald-eagle nesting behavior. He expected her firsthand observations to be the centerpiece of his paper, which would bring more attention to the eagle population in the area and should also give a boost to ecotourism.

Lowering her binoculars, she crouched down to check the battery reading of the webcam mounted on the observation-platform railing. Still plenty of juice.

As she glanced up, a movement caught her eye. A rider had appeared at the edge of the clearing.

In the week she'd spent monitoring this nest on the far boundary of the Last Chance Ranch, she'd seen plenty of four-legged animals, but none of the two-legged variety until now. Standing, she trained her binoculars on the rider and adjusted the focus. Then she sucked in a breath of pure feminine appreciation. A superhot cowboy was headed in her direction.

She didn't recognize him. He wasn't one of the Chance brothers or any of their longtime ranch hands. Her eight-by-eight platform, tucked firmly into the branches of a tall pine, allowed her to watch him unobserved.

If he looked up, he might notice the platform even though it was semicamouflaged. But he was too far away to see her. Her tan shirt and khaki shorts would blend into the shadows.

Still, she'd be less visible if she sat down. Easing slowly to the deck, she propped her elbows on the two-foot railing designed to keep her from falling off. Then she refocused her binoculars and began a top-to-bottom inventory.

He wore his hair, which was mostly covered by his hat, on the longish side. From here it looked dark but not quite black. She liked the retro effect of collar-length hair, which hinted at the possibility that the guy was a little less civilized than your average male.

The brim of his hat blocked her view of his eyes. She decided to think of them as brown, because she had a preference for dark-haired men with brown eyes.

He had a strong jaw and a mouth bracketed by smile lines. So maybe he had a sense of humor.

Moving on, she took note of broad shoulders that gave him a solid, commanding presence. He sat tall in the saddle but without any tension, as if he took a relaxed approach to life.

Thanking the German makers of her binoculars for their precision, she gazed at the steady rise and fall of his powerful chest. He'd left a couple of snaps undone in deference to the heat, and that was enough to reveal a soft swirl of dark chest hair. Vaguely she realized she'd crossed the line from observing to ogling, but no one would ever have to know.

Next she focused on his slim hips and the easy way his denim-clad thighs gripped the Western saddle. While she was in the vicinity, she checked out his package. She had to own that impulse. If she ever caught some guy giving her such a thorough inspection, she'd be insulted.

But she didn't intend to get caught, or even be seen. After a solid week of camping, she was far too bedraggled to chat with a guy, especially a guy who looked like this one. He was the sort of cowboy she'd want to meet at the Spirits and Spurs when she looked smokin' hot in a tight pair of jeans, a low-cut blouse and her red dancing boots.

He could be a visitor out for a trail ride, but if he was a ranch hand, he might come into town for a beer on Saturday nights. She'd ask around—subtly, of course. He'd be well worth the effort of climbing out of this tree and sprucing up a bit.

She was due for some fun of the male variety, come to think of it. She'd been celibate since… Had it really been almost a year since Arnold? And that hadn't been a particularly exciting relationship, now that she had some distance and could look at it objectively.

She had a bad tendency to set her sights too low, which was how she'd ended up in bed with Arnold, a fellow researcher in a Florida wildlife program. If she should by some twist of fate end up in bed with this cowboy, she could never say her sights were set too low. He was breathtaking.

He was also getting too close for her to continue ogling. She regretfully lowered her binoculars and eased back from the edge of the platform. If she scooted up against the tree trunk, he'd never know she was there.

Emmett Sterling, the ranch foreman, and Jack, the oldest of the Chance brothers, had built the platform for her. They'd also mentioned her presence to the cowhands so they'd be aware in case they rode out this way. But even if the rider had noticed the structure, he'd have no idea whether it was currently occupied.

She could be doing any number of things. She might be hiking back to town for supplies or taking a nap in the dome tent she'd pitched down near the stream that ran along the Last Chance's northern boundary. Leaning against the tree, she listened to the steady clop-clop of hooves approaching.

She needed to sneeze. Of course. People always needed to sneeze when they were trying to hide. She pressed her finger against the base of her nose.

Finally the urge to sneeze went away, but she felt a tickle in her throat. *Clop, clop, clop, clop.* The horse and rider sounded as if they were only a few yards from her tree. She needed to cough. She really did. Maybe if she was extremely careful and exceptionally quiet, she could pick up her energy drink and take a sip.

Usually while she was up here, the songbirds chirped merrily in the branches around her and the breeze made a nice sighing sound. That kind of ambient noise would be welcome so she could take a drink of her favorite bright green beverage without danger of detection. But the air was completely still and even the birds seemed to have taken an intermission.

The horse snorted. They were *very* close. If only the horse would snort again, she could coordinate her swallow with that. She raised the bottle to her mouth but was greeted by absolute silence.

That means he's stopped right under your tree, idiot. Adrenaline pumped through her as she held her breath and fought the urge to cough.

"Anybody up there?"

His unexpected question made her jump. She lost her grip on the bottle, which rolled to the edge of the platform and toppled off.

The horse spooked and the man cursed. So did Naomi. So much for going unnoticed.

The horse settled down, but the man continued to swear. "What *is* this damned sticky crap, anyway?"

Filled with foreboding, she crawled to the edge of the platform and peered down. Her gorgeous cowboy had taken a direct hit from her energy drink. He yanked off his hat, causing green liquid that had been caught in the brim to run down the front of his shirt. "Oh, *God.* I've been slimed!"

"Sorry."

He glanced up at her. "You must be Naomi Perkins."

"I am." Even from twenty feet away, or more like ten or twelve since he was still on his horse, she could see that he was royally pissed. "And you are?"

"Luke Griffin."

"Sorry about dousing you, Luke."

"I'll wash, and my clothes will wash, but the hat... And it's my best hat, too."

"I'll have it cleaned for you." She wondered why he'd worn his best hat out on the trail. Usually cowboys saved their best for special occasions.

Blowing out a breath, he surveyed the damage. "That's okay. Maybe Sarah can work some magic on it."

"Sarah Chance?"

"Right. The boss lady."

So he was a ranch hand. "She might be able to clean it." Naomi, who'd grown up in this area, had great respect for Sarah, widow of Jonathan and co-owner of the ranch along with her three sons. If anybody could salvage a hat covered with energy drink, Sarah could.

"What's in that stuff, so I can tell her what to use on it?"

"Oh, you know. Glucose, electrolytes, vegetable juice. I think it's the broccoli that turns it green. Or maybe it's the liquefied spinach."

He grimaced. "That sounds nasty."

"I don't always eat three squares while I'm working, so the energy drink helps me stay nourished and hydrated."

"You must be really dedicated if you can stomach that on a regular basis."

She shrugged. "You get used to it."

"You might. I wouldn't."

"So are you out here checking the fence?"

He hooked his damaged hat on the saddle horn and gazed up at her. "Actually, I rode out to see how you were getting along."

"You did?" That surprised her. "Did Emmett send you?"

"Not exactly. But he told us what you were trying to accomplish—documenting nesting behavior for a professor who plans to write up a paper on it. I thought that sounded like interesting work. I had a little spare time, so I decided to find out if you're okay."

"That's thoughtful." Especially when he didn't know her from Adam. Nor did she know him, although under different circumstances, she'd be happy to get acquainted. "I'm doing fine, thanks."

"How about the eagle babies? Are they all right?"

"So far." Apparently he was curious about the eagles. She could understand that. They were fascinating creatures.

"Good. That's good." A fly started buzzing around him, followed by a couple of bees. He waved them away. "They're after the sweet smell, I guess."

"I'm sure." He'd probably hoped to visit her platform and get a bird's-eye view of the eagles. Time to stop being vain and let him do that. "Listen, did you want to come up and take a look at the nest?"

"I'd love to, but I'm all sticky and attracting bugs."

"So maybe you could wash some of it off in the stream."

"Yeah, that might work."

"I'll come down. I know the best spot along the bank for washing up."

He smiled. "I'd like that. Thanks."

"Be right there." Wow, that was some smile he had going on. It almost made her forget that she looked like something the cat dragged in. She'd read that first impressions carried a tremendous amount of weight. As she started down the rope ladder, she hoped he'd make allowances.

DESPITE HAVING BEEN drenched in sticky, sweet green stuff, Luke wanted a look at Naomi Perkins. He hoped she'd be worth the possibility that he'd ruined his best hat. Had he known she possessed a hair-trigger startle response, he would have called out to her long before he'd reached her tree.

But as he'd approached, he'd assumed the platform was deserted. That was the only explanation for the total silence that had greeted him. If she'd been there, he'd reasoned, *she* would have greeted *him*.

That was the accepted way out here in the West. When a person laid claim to a portion of the great outdoors, be it with a campfire or a platform in a tree, they welcomed incoming riders. He was an incoming rider. She had to have noticed him. Yet for some reason she'd played possum.

So it was with great interest that he watched her climb down the rope ladder. First appeared a serviceable pair of hiking boots. He might have figured that.

Then came… Sweet Lord, she had an ass worthy of an exotic dancer. A man could forgive a whole bucket of that green glop landing on him for a chance to watch Naomi Perkins descend a ladder. He no longer cared about the sad condition of his hat, even though that Stetson had set him back a considerable amount of money.

She wore her tan T-shirt pulled out, not tucked in, but even so, he could tell that her slender waist did credit to the rest of her. Her breasts shifted invitingly as she descended, and by the time she'd reached the ground, he was glad he'd ridden out here.

Besides looking good coming down the ladder, she'd accomplished the climb with dexterity. She seemed perfectly at home out here by herself. He admired that kind of self-sufficiency. He'd guessed she might be that type of woman from the moment Emmett had described the job she was doing.

She'd put her honey-blond hair up in a careless ponytail. He could hardly expect some elaborate style from someone who'd been camping for days. Then she turned around, and he was lost.

Eyes bluer than morning glories, a heart-shaped face and pink lips that formed a perfect Cupid's bow. He'd never thought about his ideal woman, but from the fierce pounding of his heart, he suspected he was looking at her.

Before coming to the Jackson Hole area to work at the Last Chance eight months ago, he'd spent a couple of years in Sacramento. Although that city wasn't Hollywood by any means, he'd met plenty of women, young and old, who subscribed to plastic surgery and Botox beauty regimes. And the makeup—they wouldn't walk out the door without it. Some slept in it.

Standing before him was someone who wore not an ounce of makeup. She had an expressive face that obviously hadn't been nipped and tucked. In her khaki shorts and tan shirt, she seemed ready for adventure, like a sidekick for Indiana Jones. He didn't run across women like Naomi all that often. He felt like hoisting this treasure up onto his saddle and riding off with her into the sunset.

Not literally, of course. Sunset wasn't for several hours. Besides, that dramatic gesture sounded good in theory, but in reality he wasn't a good candidate for riding into the sunset with a woman on his horse. That implied that he'd made some pretty big promises to her.

He was a rolling stone who didn't make those kinds of promises. He traveled light. Even so, he wouldn't mind spending some time with the luscious Miss Perkins when she wasn't busy watching eagles.

Now that she was on the ground, he dismounted. "I'd shake your hand, but I'm afraid we'd be stuck together for eternity. My hands are covered with that green stuff."

"Understood."

He waved away more flies. "Time to get it off. Thanks for coming down to keep me company." Leading his horse, he started toward the stream a few yards away.

"It's the least I could do." She fell into step beside him. Their boots crunched the pine needles underfoot and sent up a sharp, clean scent that helped counteract the sweetness of the energy drink.

"Your folks own the Shoshone Diner, right?" he asked.

"Yes."

"I like the food there."

"Me, too. Now you're making me hungry for my mom's meat loaf."

"I would be, too, if I'd been trying to survive on that green junk. Listen, I didn't mean to scare you by calling to you just now. I thought nobody was up there, but I wanted to make sure." He glanced over at her to see what she might have to say for herself on that score.

Her cheeks turned pink. "I didn't realize you'd come out here because of the eagles. I assumed you'd ride on by."

"You didn't think someone riding by would stop and say howdy?"

"Sure, if they knew I was up there."

"So you were hiding from me?"

She nodded.

"Why?" He had a terrible thought. "Did you think I might hurt you?"

"No. I'm used to taking care of myself. I have bear spray and I know karate."

"I'm glad to hear it." It was the way he'd imagined she would be, resourceful and ready for anything. Very attractive traits. "But it doesn't explain why you were hiding."

She gestured to her herself and laughed. "Because I'm a hot mess!"

"You are?" He stared at her in confusion, unable to figure out what she meant.

"Okay, now you're just being nice, and I appreciate it, but I've been out here for a week. I've slept in a tent, washed up in the stream and put on clothes that were stuffed in a backpack. And then there's my hair."

"Okay, your hair might be sort of supercasual." He reached over, pulled a twig out of her ponytail and dropped it to the ground. "But the rest of you is just fine." He didn't know her well enough to tell her she looked sexy as hell. Her rumpled, accessible presentation worked for him way better than a slinky outfit. He related to someone who could survive without modern conveniences.

"Supercasual." She chuckled. "That's a great euphemism for *trashed*."

"I've seen celebrities whose hair looked way worse than yours, and it was fixed like that on purpose."

"What a gentlemanly thing to say." She pointed through the trees. "Right over there is a nice sandy spot. It's where I go in."

"Perfect." When he reached the bank of the creek, he let Smudge, the Last Chance gelding he usually rode, have a drink.

She came to stand beside him. "You're right, Luke. I overreacted to the idea of having company."

"I'm surprised you'd be so embarrassed." He finished watering the horse, backed him up and dropped the reins to ground-tie him. Then he turned toward Naomi. "Like I said, you look fine to me."

"I wouldn't have been embarrassed if Emmett had come out, or Jack. But I'd never met you." She shrugged. "I guess the vanity thing kicked in."

He gazed at her. "How did you know I wasn't Emmett or Jack?" Then he realized she must have binoculars. "Oh. You were spying on me."

Her blush deepened, giving her away.

Gradually he began to understand the issue. She'd used her binoculars to identify the person riding toward her lookout spot, which was natural. But when she'd discovered he was a stranger, she'd worried about making a bad impression. That was flattering.

"If it makes you feel any better," he said, "I wore my best hat out here on purpose. I wanted to make a good impression on you."

"You did? Why?"

"Well…" He started unsnapping his sticky shirt, starting with the cuffs on his sleeves. "I've been hearing a lot about you."

"Like what?"

"Oh, that you were this cute blonde who'd just moved back home after doing wildlife research for the state of Florida. They said you wrestled alligators and captured pythons and such." He unfastened the snaps running down the front of his shirt and pulled the tail out of his jeans. He felt her gaze on him. Well, that was okay. He wasn't ashamed of his body.

She seemed to get a kick out of the talk about her, though. "You'll have to forgive people for exaggerating," she said with a smile. "I didn't wrestle alligators. Sometimes I had to snare them and move them away from populated areas. But I never dealt with a python by myself."

"Even so, here you are out in the wilderness studying a nest of eagles. In my book, that makes you unusual."

"Sorry to disappoint you, but I'm not that exciting."

"I'm not disappointed at all. I'd have been disappointed to come out here and find you using a battery-powered hair dryer and painting your nails." If she was paying attention, she'd figure out he was attracted to her outdoor lifestyle.

"Thank you. I appreciate your saying that."

"On the other hand, I'm sure I failed to make a good impression on you, swearing and carrying on like I did. Sorry about that." He stripped off his shirt and wadded it up in preparation for dunking it in the water.

"No need to be sorry. I would've reacted the same way if I'd been showered with sticky green stuff."

Something in her voice made him pause and glance at her. To his delight, she was looking at him with a definite gleam in her eye. When he caught her at it, she blushed and turned away.

All righty, then. It appeared that taking off his shirt had been a very good idea.

2

IF NAOMI HAD realized that spilling her energy drink would make Luke take off his shirt, she would have done it on purpose. Pecs and abs like his belonged in a calendar. And unlike the shaved versions featured in muscle-building magazines, Luke had manly chest hair that highlighted his flat nipples and traced a path to the metal edge of his belt buckle.

But he'd caught her looking. He hadn't seemed to mind. In fact, she'd spotted a flicker of amusement in his eyes, which were, thank you, God, velvet brown.

"I'll go rinse this out."

"Good idea." Now, there was an idiotic response. Rinsing out his shirt wasn't merely a *good* idea. It was the *whole* idea, the reason they'd walked to the stream in the first place.

She watched him kneel on the embankment and dunk his shirt in the water. The stream wasn't large, no more than fifteen feet across at its widest point, but it ran deep enough in spots for fish to thrive, which was why the eagles were nesting here.

But she wasn't thinking about eagles now. Instead she gazed at the broad, muscled back of Luke Griffin and wondered what it would be like to feel those muscles move under her palms. Having such thoughts about a virtual stranger wasn't like her.

Except he didn't feel like a stranger. He'd come out here because of an interest in the eagles and curiosity about the woman studying them. Instead of being turned off by her rumpled appearance, he seemed to prefer it. That made him the sort of man she'd like to get to know.

At first he'd been understandably upset about getting doused with the energy drink, but apparently he was a good-natured sort of guy who rolled with the punches. Anyone would think he'd had to wash out his clothes in a stream numerous times from the efficiency with which he swirled the shirt in the water and wrung it out.

Then he set it on a nearby rock. Reaching into his back pocket, he pulled out a blue bandanna and plunged it into the water before rubbing his face, chest and shoulders with it.

Naomi felt like a voyeur standing there while he washed up. She could offer to help, but she wasn't sure that was appropriate, either. What could she do, wash his back?

At last he stood, his dripping shirt in one hand and his soaked bandanna in the other. "I'm considering whether I should put my hat in the water or not."

"I can't advise you." Wow, he was beautiful. She had a tough time remembering her name while he faced her, his chest glistening with droplets of water. Evaluating the best procedure for cleaning his hat was beyond her mental capabilities at the moment.

"I'm doing it. It can't get any worse." He walked toward her with the shirt and the bandanna. "Maybe you could find a tree branch for these."

"Sure." She took them, although she wondered what his plan might be. Hanging something to dry implied sticking around awhile. Was that what he had in mind?

Maybe he only wanted his shirt to get dry enough that it wouldn't feel clammy when he put it on, but that would take more than ten minutes. Fine with her. She wouldn't mind spending more time with this sexy cowboy. She found a fairly level branch for both the shirt and the bandanna. As a veteran camper, she was used to such maneuvers.

As she finished hanging up his stuff, he came back holding his saturated hat. "At least it won't attract flies on the way home." He looked around, found a convenient twig sticking out of a tree trunk and hung his hat on it. "I need the bandanna back. One more chore." Grabbing it, he returned to the stream and soaked the bandanna.

Naomi wasn't sure what his goal was until he walked over to his horse and started wiping its neck. Apparently the energy drink had anointed the brown-and-white paint, too. She gave Luke points for wanting to get the stuff off to keep the animal from being pestered by flies, as well.

His considerate gesture also provided her with quite a show. She wondered if he had any idea how his muscles rippled in the dappled sunlight while he worked on that horse. If she could have taken a video, it would be an instant hit on YouTube—gorgeous guy demonstrates his love of animals. What could be sweeter?

Finally he rinsed out the bandanna again and returned it to the branch where his shirt hung. "I think that takes care of the worst of it."

"You're causing me to rethink my consumption of energy drinks. I never dreamed one little bottle could create such a disaster."

He smiled at her. "Ah, it wasn't so bad. The cold water feels good."

"I know it does. That stream was a lifesaver this week when the temperatures kicked up."

"I'll bet. Now that you mention it, you look a little flushed. You can use my bandanna if you—" He paused and chuckled. "Never mind. You probably don't want to rinse your face with the bandanna I just used on my horse."

"I wouldn't care about that. But don't worry about me. I'm used to being hot."

His sudden laughter made the brown-and-white paint lift his head and stare at them. "I'm not touching that line."

"Oh, dear God." She felt a new blush coming on. "I didn't mean it like that." But he'd taken it like that. To her surprise, this beautiful shirtless cowboy was flirting with her. What a rush.

"Now you really look as if you could use a splash of cold water."

"It's my blond coloring. I blush at the drop of a hat." Or the drop of a shirt.

"It looks good on you." He gazed at her with warmth in his brown eyes.

She felt that warmth in every cell of her body, causing her to think of truly crazy things, like what it would be like to kiss him. She'd actually moved a step closer when the piercing cry of an eagle grabbed her attention.

Breaking eye contact, she looked up through the trees and saw the female sail overhead, a fish in her talons.

"Wow." Luke stared after the departing eagle. "He's huge."

"She."

He glanced at Naomi. "She? You mean her mate is even bigger than that?"

"No, her mate is smaller. Female eagles are bigger than the males." After a week of observation, Naomi could distinguish the female's eight-foot wingspan from that of her smaller mate.

"Well, blow me down with a feather. I didn't know that."

"Many people don't. They think any male creature is automatically bigger than the female, but that's not universally true."

He grinned at her. "You said that with a certain amount of relish."

"Maybe." She returned his smile. "It's fun to smash

stereotypes. By the way, did you happen to notice what kind of fish she had?"

"Looked like a trout to me."

"I thought so, too. I have to go back up and document the feeding time and the type of food on my computer. As I said, you're welcome to come up and check out the nest."

"I'd love to." He sounded eager. "But not if I'll get in your way. Or break the platform."

"You won't. Emmett and Jack were both up there together, testing its strength. They made sure it was sturdy."

"In that case, lead the way."

She walked quickly back to the tree. "This ladder will hold you, too. But we can't be on it at the same time." She started up.

"I'll wait until you give me the okay."

Climbing the dangling ladder was much easier than going down, and she made the trip in no time. "All clear. Come on up." She stood, glanced around her little research area and wondered what he'd think of it.

He hoisted himself up on the platform with another display of muscle. "What a view! Makes me want to be an eagle."

Funny, but she could almost imagine that. He had the alert gaze and restrained power she associated with eagles and hawks. "Not me. Flying would be cool, but I wouldn't like living without a roof over my head."

"I could live with that in return for the freedom of being able to fly anytime I felt like it. Yeah, the life of an eagle would suit me just fine." His glance took in the trappings of her work—the webcam mounted to the railing, the camp stool and small folding table for her laptop, her camera bag and a small cooler for her snacks and energy drinks. "Cozy setup."

"Thanks." It felt a lot cozier with him in it. At five-four, she didn't take up much room, so the area had seemed plenty large enough. Now she wondered how she'd be able to move around without bumping into him.

"Aren't you supposed to be recording stuff?"

Yes, she was, and his bare chest had distracted her from her duties. "Right." She picked up her binoculars and handed them to him. "You can help. Do you see the nest?"

"Sure do. From up here it's hard to miss." He raised the binoculars. "Big old thing, isn't it? Wow! There they are, two baby eagles getting lunch from Mom. That's impressive."

"See if you can keep track of whether one's getting more than the other." She sat down and turned on her laptop. "One of the nestlings is bigger and I suspect it's getting more food."

"That's what it looks like." Luke stood facing the clearing, booted feet spread. He looked like a captain at the helm of his ship as he studied the nest through the binoculars. "Look at that! Shoving the other one out of the way. Hey, you, you're supposed to share!"

Naomi smiled. She'd had the same thoughts, but hearing them come out of Luke's mouth made her realize how silly they were. Wildlife researchers couldn't afford to anthropomorphize their subjects. Giving them human attributes might work for Disney, but not for science.

Speaking of science, she'd better start making notes instead of watching Luke watch the eagles.

"Here comes the dad."

Yikes. She'd completely missed seeing the male eagle fly overhead. "If you'll describe what's happening, I'll just take down what you dictate."

"He came in with another fish, and that's definitely a trout. I think we're safe to say they're having trout for lunch. Now Mom's flown off and Dad's feeding the kids. Damned if that bigger baby isn't getting more of the second course, too."

"It happens. I'll bet you've seen it with puppies and kittens. They compete for the food. The most aggressive ones get the most food."

"Yeah, but when that happened with a litter my dog had, I supplemented so the runt didn't die."

She gave him points for that, too. "But these are wild creatures. If you tried to interfere, the parents might abandon both of them. I wouldn't worry too much. There are only two babies. I think they'll both make it."

"I hope so. How long before they can fly?"

"If all goes well, less than two months. They'll be on their own by fall."

"Then your job will be over?"

"It will, but this is only a stopgap until I get another full-time state job, or maybe something with the national parks."

"It's a pretty cool temp job, though. It would be exciting to see those little ones fly for the first time."

"I hope to. If I don't personally catch it with my still camera, I'm hoping the webcam will. Is the father still there?"

"Yep." Luke shifted his weight and the platform creaked. "But I think he's about done with the feeding routine. There he goes. Now the babies are huddling down."

"Unless the mother comes back, there won't be much to see for a while."

"No sign of her." Luke lowered the binoculars and crouched down next to the webcam. "So this is on 24/7?"

"Yes. Fortunately it has a zoom, so the pictures are pretty good, but quite a few researchers prefer to mount the camera on the tree where the nest is."

He glanced over his shoulder at her. "How the hell would you do something like that without freaking out the eagles?"

"You have to mount it before they start nesting and then hope they come back to that same place." She powered down the laptop to save her battery. "The professor who hired me hopes to get someone to monitor the nest next year and see if the pair returns. This year, by the time someone discovered the nest, the eggs were already laid, which meant this was the best we could do."

He stood and turned back to her. "Are you hooked up to the internet so you can broadcast it? I've seen people do that."

"So have I, but that wouldn't work here because of the location."

He glanced around. "Too remote?"

"No, too accessible. The professor doesn't want the place overrun by tourists trying to see the eagles up close and personal, which could disturb them. The Chance family isn't too eager to have that happen, either. Eventually, with proper supervision, the Chances might approve an ecotour back here, but it would be carefully planned."

"Makes sense. So this is a strictly private study."

"It is. The professor would be up here himself if he could manage it. He's the only one who gets the webcam feed, and I send him written reports."

"Am I breaking any rules by being up here?"

She smiled. "It's not *that* hush-hush. Everybody on the ranch knows about the eagles, and quite a few people in town. Fortunately, we're a protective bunch of folks around here, so the eagles should be safe."

"I think you're right about that. I've only lived here since the end of October, but I can tell it's a close community. You take care of your own."

So she was right—he was a fairly recent hire at the ranch. Getting one piece of the puzzle made her curious to find out more. "What brought you here?"

"More a *who* than a *what*. Nash Bledsoe. He was my boss when he co-owned a riding stable in Sacramento with Lindsay, his former wife. She wasn't much fun to work for after he left. Actually, she wasn't much fun to work for while he was there. I stayed because of him. Once he moved back here, I asked him to put in a good word at the Last Chance, and here I am."

"And now Nash has his own place, the Triple G. Are you headed there next?"

He shook his head. "Wouldn't be fair to Nash. I tend to move on after about a year, no matter where I am, so my time's two-thirds gone. He needs a ranch hand who'll stick around longer than a few months."

"You leave after a year?" She'd never heard anything so ridiculous in her life, unless he was trying to escape a woman or the law. "Are you on the run?"

"Nope." He smiled.

She looked into those smiling brown eyes. He didn't seem to be hiding anything. "Then I don't get it."

"Most people don't. It's just the way I like it. New scenery, new people. Keeps things interesting."

She should have known there'd be a fly in the ointment. He might be the sexiest man she'd met in ages, but if he avoided all attachments, then she literally couldn't see any future in getting to know him.

"That bothers you, doesn't it?" He sounded disappointed.

She shrugged. "Not really." At least it shouldn't. She'd leaped to some unwarranted conclusions about how this would go, and now he'd set her straight. At least he'd told her up front, so she could back off. "It's your life. You're entitled to live it the way you want to."

"Yes, I am." He sighed. "But I guess I'll pay the price where you're concerned."

"What price?"

"I...was hoping to get to know you better."

"Oh?" She wondered if this was leading where she thought it was. "In what way?"

"Well, I thought we might become friends."

"Sure, Luke. We can become friends." But from the way he'd flirted with her earlier, she didn't think he was looking for a platonic relationship. Maybe she was wrong. "You can come out here and check on the eagles from time to time, and we'll chat. Is that what you had in mind?"

"Uh…no." He rubbed the back of his neck and looked off in the distance, clearly uncomfortable with the discussion. "See, the thing is, I thought, from the way you looked at me back there at the stream, that you might be willing to go a little beyond friendship."

How embarrassing that he'd read her so accurately. "I see."

"But I can tell you don't like the idea that I don't stay around. Your attitude toward me changed."

"You act as if that's hard to understand. Do most of the women you meet like the idea of a temporary affair?"

"They do, actually." His gaze was earnest. "I tend to be attracted to women who have something going on in their lives, like you. The last thing they want is some needy guy who wants to monopolize them. So we get together, have great discussions, great sex and no strings attached."

"That must suit your lifestyle perfectly." Having this discussion while he stood there looking virile as hell wasn't helping. She didn't want to want him. He was a girl-in-every-port sort of guy. And yet…her insides quivered at the tantalizing possibilities.

"It does suit me, and it seems to suit them. I jumped

to conclusions about you, though. I thought you'd be happy to hear my exit plan, but you're not."

She cleared her throat to give herself some time to think. He was right about the signals she'd been giving off, so she couldn't blame him for putting her in the same category as his other girlfriends. Maybe she *was* in that category and hadn't realized it.

Although she'd like to settle down someday, she hadn't yet felt compelled to do that. She'd been building her career in wildlife research in Florida, but that had petered out. She hoped to get another full-time job in her field, which could be anywhere in the country. She didn't want to be either saved or tied down by a guy.

But in the meantime, she was going through a period of sexual deprivation, and he'd suggested a reprieve from that. Was it so terrible that he wasn't into making a lifelong commitment, especially when she wasn't looking for that, either?

"I need some time to think about this," she said. "After all, I just met you."

"Fair enough." He moved closer. "Just to be clear, are you saving yourself for Mr. Right? Because I'm not that guy."

She struggled to breathe normally, but she kept drawing in the intoxicating scent of Luke Griffin. "I'm not saving myself for anyone, but I…" She lost track of what she'd meant to say. This was her brain on lust, and it was fried.

"Then think about it." His lips hovered closer. "And while you're thinking, consider this." His mouth came down on hers.

She should pull away. She should give herself more time to review the situation with cold, hard logic before she allowed him to influence her by… Oh, no… he was good at this…very good. Before she realized it, he'd invaded her mouth with his tongue. No, that wasn't true. She'd invited him in. There had been no invasion at all, because she wanted…everything.

He lifted his head.

She didn't want the kiss to be over, but she wasn't going to beg him to do it again. A girl had to have some pride, which was why she wasn't about to open her eyes and let him see the turmoil he'd created.

His breath was warm on her lips. "Think about it. I'll come back for your answer." There was a movement of air and the sound of him climbing back down the ladder.

Opening her eyes, she sat down on the platform and held her hand against her pounding heart. She'd never deliberately set out to have a no-strings affair. But he'd been so sweet about it.

Still, she wasn't the type of woman he thought she was. Her answer should be no. Shouldn't it?

3

LUKE THOUGHT ABOUT Naomi all the way back to the
Last Chance Ranch. He was worried that he'd insulted
her by the way he'd acted. The thing was, her behavior toward him had been *exactly* like the women he'd
known in the past.

In those cases, instant chemistry had been followed
by a clear understanding. Sex would be purely for fun,
because the intelligent ladies he'd connected with had
other things to do besides take care of a man and his
ego. They'd considered him a gift because he required
nothing of them but multiple orgasms.

If Naomi didn't fit that category, he'd definitely insulted her, which didn't sit well with him. He knew the
guy to talk to—Emmett Sterling. Emmett had helped
her set up out there and might give him some insight
into her character.

But he'd have to be careful. He didn't want any of
the other cowhands hearing such a conversation. Luke
hoped he could find a quiet moment to speak man-to-

man with Emmett, but when he arrived back at the ranch he wondered if that would be possible.

Emmett, along with Sarah Chance's fiancé, Pete Beckett, had eight adolescent boys in the main corral for a roping clinic. The boys were all part of Pete's program to help disadvantaged youth. By living and working alongside cowboys several weeks out of the summer, they had an opportunity to learn discipline and routine.

Luke didn't see much of either going on in the corral. Ropes flew helter-skelter. They caught indiscriminately on fence posts and people. Clearly at least one more adult was needed in that arena.

The boys had been in residence for a couple of weeks, so Luke already knew them all pretty well. Wading into the confusion was no problem for him. He called out a greeting to Emmett and Pete, who seemed overjoyed to see him.

"I'll take these two." He motioned to Ace, a skinny, dark-haired, tattooed boy with attitude sticking out all over him, and his unlikely friend, a pudgy blond boy named Eddie who was always eager to please. Nash had been their favorite cowboy on the ranch, but Nash was busy with his own neighboring ranch these days, so Luke had stepped in. By pulling Ace out of the confusion, Luke knew he'd remove fifty percent of the problem. Ace resisted being told what to do, but he had no trouble telling everyone else what they should be doing.

Luke brought them next to the fence. "Roping is not only a skill," he said, "but an art." He'd figured out that beneath the tough exterior, Ace had the soul of a poet.

"Not when I do it," Ace grumbled.

"That's because you're treating it like a sport."

Eddie slapped his coiled rope against his thigh. "It *is* a sport." He peered at Luke. "Isn't it?"

"It can be both, I guess, but when it's done with style, it's more than a sport. It's an art form. Can I borrow your rope, Eddie?"

Eddie handed over his rope.

"Anybody can throw a loop and catch something," Luke said.

"Not me," Ace muttered.

"The trick is to make that loop dance." Luke had always loved the supple feel of a good rope. He'd been lucky enough to learn the skill from an expert roper on a ranch in eastern Washington. Luke roped the way he made love, with concentration, subtlety and—he hoped—finesse.

But he didn't like to show off, so he'd never demonstrated his skills to the folks at the Last Chance. Nash had known, but Nash would never have embarrassed him by making him perform on command like some trained monkey.

Ace needed a demonstration, though, because the kid wouldn't be interested unless he could see the beauty inherent in the task. Luke built his loop and proceeded to show him. Not only did he make the loop dance, but *he* danced, leaping and weaving in and out of the undulating circle he'd created.

He was so involved that he didn't realize all other activity had ceased and he'd drawn a rapt audience. He figured it out when he allowed the rope to settle at his feet and people started clapping. Glancing around, he saw that he'd brought the clinic to a halt.

"Hey, I'm sorry," he said. "I didn't mean to interrupt the proceedings."

"I'm glad you did." Pete surveyed the circle of admiring boys. "You've just become our new roping instructor. Welcome to the staff."

"Why didn't you tell us you could twirl a rope like that, son?" Emmett asked. "I had no idea."

"It never came up."

"He didn't tell you because he's too cool to brag." Ace's hero worship echoed in every syllable. Then he gazed up at Luke, his expression intense. "I want to learn how to do that."

"Good. I can teach you."

"Teach me, too!" Eddie's comment was followed by a chorus of others.

"Looks like you have a group of eager students," Pete said. "We'll be your assistants."

The rest of the afternoon passed quickly as Luke worked with the boys. He didn't remember he'd skipped lunch until his stomach started to growl.

As the boys were herded off to have dinner at the main house, Emmett came over and hooked an arm around Luke's shoulder. "I'm buying you a hamburger and a beer at the Spirits and Spurs. You rode in like the cavalry today, and I appreciate it."

"Thank you. I accept." Luke recognized a golden opportunity when it was presented, and he wasn't about to turn down the chance to talk to Emmett about Naomi. "Give me twenty minutes to shower and change."

"You got it. I need to freshen up a bit, myself. I'll bring my truck around to the side of the bunkhouse."

Within half an hour Luke was sitting in the passenger seat of Emmett's old but well-maintained pickup as they traveled the ten miles from the ranch to the little town of Shoshone and the popular bar. They rode with the windows down, and every once in a while they'd pass a stretch of road where the crickets were chirping like crazy.

It was one of those nights that wasn't too hot and wasn't too cold—the perfect night for lovers. Luke thought of Naomi, who was probably tucked into her tent right now. Before he'd ridden away, he'd made a quick survey and located that tent, a faded blue dome-style.

She was probably fine. Yet whenever he thought of her by herself, he had the urge to head on out there and make sure she was okay. That might not be particularly evolved, and an independent woman like Naomi wouldn't appreciate an overprotective attitude from anyone, let alone some cowboy she'd just met. Funny, he didn't usually have those protective feelings toward women, but with Naomi he couldn't seem to help himself.

Right now, though, he had to stop worrying about Naomi sleeping alone in her tent and grab this chance for a private discussion with Emmett. He didn't want to blow it. Once they arrived at their destination, their privacy would disappear.

Luke took a steadying breath. "I mentioned that

I was riding out to check on Naomi Perkins today, right?"

"I believe you said something like that. Did you go?"

"I did, and she's surviving great out there. It's pretty amazing to look at those baby eagles."

"So you climbed up to the platform?"

"She was nice enough to ask me, so I did. You built one hell of an observation spot for her, Emmett. She's really set up well."

"Good. I'm glad it's working out for her. I kept meaning to go out and I haven't made it, so I'm glad you did. She's a scrappy little thing, but I can't help worrying about her sometimes. Her mom and dad worry, too, but they've told me they've worked hard to give her room to be herself."

All that fit with what Luke had sensed about her from the beginning. "So I guess she's a modern woman who doesn't need a man around to protect her."

Emmett didn't answer right away. "If you mean that she doesn't need a man to physically protect her, that's probably right," he said at last. "She took karate when she was still in high school, and she could flip me onto my back if she wanted to."

Luke thought about that. "Good to know."

"And she takes other precautions. She has bear spray, and she makes sure her food is stowed. Naomi has a better chance of surviving out there by herself than some men I've known. But…"

"But?" Luke waited for the other shoe to drop.

"I could be way off base, but I don't think she's a

true loner. I think she'd love to find somebody to share her life, as long as it was the right somebody."

"Hmm." Well, that sealed his fate. He couldn't mess around with a woman like that. If Naomi yearned for someone steady in her life, he'd back off. His free-spirited father had tied himself to a job, a wife and a mortgage. He obviously regretted his choices. Luke had inherited that same free spirit, and he had no intention of repeating his dad's mistakes.

"Then again, how should I know what's in Naomi's heart?" Emmett said. "I'm the last person who should give out opinions on such things. I'm a divorced man in love with a wonderful woman, but the idea of marrying her scares me shitless."

"That's not so hard to understand, Emmett. Pam Mulholland has big bucks and you're a man of modest means. I watched my buddy Nash fall into the trap of marrying a woman who had a pile of money, and it was a disaster." Luke paused. "Then again, he's now planning to marry Bethany Grace, who also has a pile of money, and I think it'll be fine."

Emmett sighed. "So it all depends on the woman. And I know in my heart that Pam wouldn't let the money be a problem, but my damned pride is at stake. I can't seem to overcome my basic reluctance to marry a wealthy woman when I'm certainly not wealthy myself. I'm afraid I'll feel like a gigolo."

Luke dipped his head to hide a smile. The interior of the truck was dim. Still, he didn't want to take the slightest chance that Emmett would see that smile. But if Emmett Sterling, the quintessential rugged cowboy, could label himself a gigolo, the world had turned completely upside down.

NAOMI HAD MEANT to spend one more night out at the research site before hiking back to Shoshone for supplies and clean clothes. But the visit from Luke had thrown her off balance. She decided to take her break that very afternoon.

After clearing her platform of everything except the webcam and securing her campsite, she hoisted her backpack and made the trek into town. A night sleeping in her childhood bed at her parents' house would be a welcome luxury.

Her folks were thrilled to see her, as always, but business was brisk at the Shoshone Diner and they didn't have much time to chat. She'd anticipated that. At one time the diner served only breakfast and lunch, but recently they'd added a dinner menu.

Prior to that, the Spirits and Spurs had been the only place in town that served an evening meal. But as the tourist business had grown and the wait time for a table at the Spirits and Spurs had become ridiculous, Naomi's parents had decided to expand their offerings.

It had paid off for them. They'd hired extra help because Naomi wasn't there to waitress anymore, and both women were capable and had a set routine. If Naomi hung around the diner tonight, she'd only get in everybody's way.

So she ate the meat loaf her mother insisted on feeding her, went home for a quick shower and a change of clothes, and walked over to the Spirits and Spurs. On the way, she thought of Luke, who quite likely wouldn't be there on a weeknight. Ranch hands generally came into town on the weekend.

As she walked toward the intersection where the bar was located, she remembered the foolishly grand entrance she'd envisioned making in her tight jeans and revealing blouse. Instead she'd pulled on her comfort outfit—faded jeans and a soft knit top in her favorite shade of red. Nothing about her appearance tonight was calculated to turn heads.

Ah, well. She'd scrapped her plan to knock Luke back on his heels and make him her slave. Luke didn't intend to be any woman's slave. He was a love-'em-and-leave-'em kind of cowboy.

She'd never met a man who'd laid it out so clearly. At first she'd been appalled by the concept of a relationship based mostly on sex, with some interesting conversations thrown in, a relationship with an expiration date stamped plainly on the package.

She laughed to herself. And what a package it was, too. That was part of her dilemma. She wanted that package, even if she could enjoy it for only a limited time.

Music from the Spirits and Spurs beckoned her as she approached. During tourist season the bar had a live band every night, and Naomi loved to dance. She wouldn't mind kicking up her heels a little if anyone inside the bar felt like getting out on the floor. She could do with a little fun.

Maybe that was how she should view Luke's suggestion, too. She'd never seen herself as the kind of

woman who would have a casual fling, but maybe she
was needlessly limiting herself. She might be back in
her hometown, but she wasn't a kid anymore. She had
the right to make adult decisions. Very adult. A sensual zing heated her blood.

If the thought of parading her behavior in front of
her parents bothered her at all, and she admitted that
it did, they wouldn't have to know. She was living out
in the woods, away from prying eyes. Luke might have
to explain his behavior if he made regular visits to her
campsite, but she'd let him worry about that.

As she pushed open the door to the Spirits and
Spurs, the familiar scent of beer and smoke greeted
her. This bar might end up being the last place in the
entire world to ban smoking. Even if they did, the place
was supposed to be haunted by the ghosts of cowboys
and prospectors who'd tipped a few in this building a
century ago. No doubt they'd bring the aroma of to-
bacco with them.

The band started playing a recent Alan Jackson hit
she happened to like. Couples filled the small dance
floor. The place was jumping, with most of the round
wooden tables occupied and very few vacant seats at
the bar.

Coming here had been a good idea. She watched the
dancers and tapped her foot in time to the music. She'd
have a beer and dance if she found a willing partner.
Then tomorrow, or whenever Luke came back for his
answer, she'd tell him not only yes but hell, yes. Look
out, world. Naomi Perkins was ready to cut loose.

"Naomi?"

The rich baritone made her whirl in its direction. She'd last heard that voice after being kissed senseless twenty feet above the ground. She found herself staring into Luke Griffin's brown-eyed gaze. Her heart launched into overdrive.

They spoke in unison. "What are you doing here?"

"You first." Luke tilted back his hat and stared at her. "You're the big surprise. I thought you'd be curled up in your blue dome tent fast asleep."

She fought the urge to grab his shirtfront in both hands and pull him into another kiss, one even more potent than what they'd shared earlier today. "I'm staying with my folks in town. And how do you know I have a blue dome tent?"

"I checked it out before I left."

"For future reference?"

"No. In fact, that's why I hotfooted it over here. I—" He gestured toward the band. "Love that song, but I don't want to have to yell over it. Can we move outside for a minute?"

"Okay." She gulped in air and did her best to calm down. When she agreed to this affair, she wanted to appear in command of herself, even if she wasn't. He was used to sophistication, and she would exude that.

He held the door open and she walked out into the soft night air. He followed. As the door closed behind him, the music faded into background noise.

She turned to him. "Luke, I'm glad you're here tonight, because—"

"No, wait. Let me say something first. I was off base today, and I apologize with all my heart. You're not that kind of woman. I made a mistake and no doubt insulted you in the process."

Yikes, now what? Right when she'd decided to accept his outrageous proposal, he'd withdrawn it on the grounds that she wasn't *that kind of woman.*

She swallowed. "What kind of woman do you think I am?"

"The kind who needs stability. You deserve someone who wants to become a permanent part of your life, and I'm not that guy."

"Luke, I don't know what my life is going to be yet. You made me do some serious thinking today. I was shocked by your assumption that I'd want a fling, but—"

"I know you were, and I feel pretty rotten about that."

"Yes, but you see, when it comes right down to it…" She placed both hands on his chest so she could feel his heart beating and know for sure that it was racing as fast as hers. This wasn't a cold, calculated decision, after all. It was being made in the heat of the moment, and she was ready to dive headfirst into the flames.

She looked into his beautiful eyes. "I do want a fling with you, Luke." Heat sizzled through her as she plunged into the fire. "In fact, I can't think of anything I want more."

4

LUKE WAS SUDDENLY so short of breath that he was a little scared he might black out. That wouldn't be cool in front of this woman who'd said she wanted to have sex with him. But he couldn't kiss her until he stopped struggling to fill his lungs with air.

The corners of her beautiful mouth tipped up. "Apparently you didn't expect me to say that."

"No." He dragged in a breath. "That's a fact. I definitely did not."

"I've never had this kind of effect on a man before." She gazed up at him as amusement turned to concern. "Are you going to be all right?"

"I'm going to be terrific." There. That statement sounded normal. Finally trusting himself to wrap her in his arms, he nudged his hat back with his thumb and pulled her close. Damn, that felt good. "*We're* going to be terrific."

"I'll have to leave that up to you." Her eyes caught the sparkle from the bar's neon bucking bronco. "If you've spent your adult life playing the field, then I guarantee you have more experience than I do."

"Maybe." He aligned his body with hers. They fit so perfectly it was a little scary for a guy who didn't believe in perfect fits. But he'd figured that she'd be soft and pliable, warm and willing. His cock responded quickly. He'd have to remember they were standing on the corner of the town's only intersection. "But I can recognize natural talent when I see it."

Her smile widened. "You think I have a natural talent for sex?"

"I know you do, at least for kissing, which usually tells me a lot about a woman." Keeping one arm firmly around her narrow waist, he slid his free hand up through her silky blond hair. No ponytail tonight.

"We only kissed once."

"True." He cradled the back of her head. "I should gather more information before I come to any firm conclusions."

She rocked against him. "Feels like you've already come to a very firm conclusion."

"See, that's what I'm talking about." Cupping her bottom, he snuggled her in tight. "A natural talent. And, lady, sassy comments and sexy moves like that will get you anything you want from me."

"Anything?"

"Sky's the limit." He lowered his head and brushed his mouth over hers. So delicious. But he dared not get involved in the kind of kiss he wanted, the kind that would make him forget where he was.

She clutched his shoulders and joined in his little

game of butterfly kisses. "I've already told you what I want."

"In general terms, yes." The feathery touch of her lips could drive him crazy if it went on too long without some way to release the tension. "But we have to work out the details."

"We can't do anything here."

He chuckled. "No, obviously not." Although with the blood pumping hot in his veins, he'd already fantasized about coaxing her into the shadows behind the building. "We're standing in front of the most popular spot in town."

"I mean not here, as in not in Shoshone."

He nibbled her full lower lip. "You want to drive to Jackson?" He hoped not. He wouldn't be able to swing very many trips to Jackson and still handle his assigned work on the ranch. But with a hot woman in his arms, he was ready to do whatever it took to have her.

"No, nothing that drastic." She placed tiny kisses at the corners of his mouth. "I was referring to my campsite as being the most discreet choice."

"It's perfect, except you're not there." And he wanted her now, tonight. Moments ago he'd given up all hope of a relationship, but her unexpected decision and these flirty kisses had flipped the switch on his libido and destroyed his patience. He outlined her mouth with the tip of his tongue.

Her breathing had changed, signaling that she was getting as worked up as he was. "I will be there."

"When?" His fingers flexed against her bottom.

"Tomorrow."

He groaned. "That's forever."

"I can't hike out there in the dark."

"I know. But I—whoops, somebody's coming." He released her and stepped back. With luck, whoever it was would simply call a greeting and pass on by. Then he glanced over and realized that wasn't going to happen. Thank God for the shadows that should keep his aroused condition from being too obvious.

Emmett walked toward them. "Hi there, Naomi." He touched the brim of his hat. "Nice to see you."

"Hi, Emmett. It's good to see you, too. You don't usually come into town midweek."

"I wanted to treat Luke. He showed up in the nick of time and put on a roping demonstration that saved what was fast becoming a disaster."

"Ah, you would have worked it out." Luke pulled the brim of his hat back down and hoped Emmett hadn't noticed how he'd shoved it back, which was typical for a cowboy who'd been kissing a woman.

"I'm not so sure." Emmett glanced at Naomi. "Take my word for it. We had a snarled-up mess, but five minutes after Luke showed up and started twirling a rope, the kids were mesmerized. They hadn't seen the possibilities of roping until then. Pete and I aren't that fancy. This boy has hidden talents."

"Talent, singular," Luke said. "Trick roping. That's my only hidden talent."

Naomi glanced at him. "Oh, I doubt that."

"Anyway," Emmett said. "I didn't mean to break up your conversation, Luke, but your food's getting cold.

Naomi, why don't you join us? We have an extra chair. Have you had dinner?"

"Yes, thanks. I ate at the diner before I came over. But I don't want to keep you two from your meal. Let's go in."

"Excellent. You can fill me in on how the eagle project's going."

"I'd love to. That platform you and Jack built is working out beautifully."

Luke followed them in. As Emmett asked more questions about the eagles, Luke quietly ground a centimeter off his back molars. He hadn't been sure when Emmett first showed up, but he was now. The foreman was deliberately interfering in what he saw as a problem situation between Luke and Naomi.

No doubt Emmett saw Luke as the aggressor and Naomi as the sweet local girl about to be seduced by a guy who would leave her in the lurch. It wasn't like that, of course. Luke had been ready to back off and Naomi had turned the tables on him. But he couldn't very well explain that to Emmett. A gentleman wouldn't put the blame on a lady.

The foreman had every reason to misunderstand what was happening. When Luke had been hired on at the Last Chance, he'd warned both Emmett and Jack that he tended to move along after a year or so. They'd both predicted he'd change his mind, that the Last Chance had a way of getting in a person's blood.

But last month he'd turned down Nash's offer of employment and had made no secret as to why. He believed in being up front with people, so he could see why Emmett thought Naomi needed someone to step in and keep her heart from being broken.

Luke didn't want to get crossways with the foreman. He liked and admired the guy, and until now they'd had no real issues between them. But Luke would be damned if he'd allow Emmett to louse up a perfectly acceptable arrangement between two consenting adults.

He thought about his options as he ate the excellent dinner Emmett had bought him and listened to the foreman and Naomi talk about the eagles. Luke even participated in the conversation because he was interested in those birds, too. He was more interested in the woman watching the birds, but he found the eagle study fascinating. He hadn't been kidding when he'd told Naomi that an eagle's freedom of movement appealed to him.

"That nest's not as big as some." Naomi took a sip of the draft she'd ordered. "It's only about seven feet across. I've seen reports on nests that are ten feet and weigh close to two tons."

Emmett shook his head in disbelief. "That's like putting my pickup in the top branches of one of those pines. I had no idea they could be that heavy. I'd—" He stopped talking and glanced at the door. "What do you know? There's Pam. Excuse me a minute, folks. I need to go over and say hello. Maybe she can join us." He stood and walked toward the door.

Luke grabbed his chance. He kept his voice low as he looked over at Naomi. "You do realize Emmett's trying to save you from me, right?"

"I thought he might be."

"He told me earlier tonight that he thought you wanted a steady guy in your life. That's why I backed off."

Naomi sighed. "I'm not surprised he'd say something like that. He's friends with my parents, and he's a dad. He probably sees me as being like his daughter, Emily."

"Ah. Okay, I get that." Luke thought about the blonde woman who was in training to eventually take over Emmett's job when he retired. Emily and Naomi had several things in common besides their coloring. They were both only children who had been raised to be independent and fend for themselves without leaning on a man. They both enjoyed testing themselves with physical challenges.

But Emily was now married to Clay Whitaker, who ran the stud operation for the Last Chance. Emmett might figure that Naomi, having similarities to his daughter, also should find herself someone like Clay.

He glanced at her. "Maybe Emmett knows what he's talking about. Maybe I should just—"

"Don't you dare back off because Emmett thinks I'm just like his daughter. I'm not."

The defiant sparks flashing in her blue eyes gladdened his heart. She thought for herself, and that was a quality he admired. "I'm sure you're not just like anyone."

"Nobody is. We're all unique, which means we get to choose our own path. What you and I decide to do is none of Emmett's business."

The tension that had been tightening a spot between Luke's shoulder blades eased. "And you won't be upset if I tell him that?"

"No, but I think I'm the one who needs to tell him."

"I'll tell him." He started to add that it should be a man-to-man talk but decided that might not sit well with Naomi. She liked being in charge of her destiny.

"No, you work for him and I don't."

"But he built you a research platform."

"Well, one of us needs to say something. Uh-oh. Here he comes. And he doesn't look happy."

"Bet it has something to do with Pam." Luke noticed that Pam Mulholland, the woman Emmett cared for but couldn't bring himself to marry, was being helped into her chair by a guy Luke didn't recognize. The barrel-chested man dressed in flashy Western clothes and what looked like an expensive hat. "Or that guy."

Emmett returned to his seat, his expression grim. "It's my own damned fault," he muttered to no one in particular.

"What is?" Luke asked. "And who is that guy with Pam? I've never seen him before, and if that's the way he normally dresses, I doubt I've missed him."

"You haven't missed him." Emmett picked up his beer and drained the contents. "Name's Clifford Mason. Just flew in today from Denver. Booked a room at the Bunk and Grub."

Naomi looked over at the table where Pam and the newcomer sat. "Does Pam normally go out to dinner with her B and B guests?"

"No, she does not." Emmett smoothed his mustache. "Far as I know, it's never happened before."

Luke could see Emmett was seething with jealousy and was doing his best to keep a lid on his feelings. "Is he on vacation?"

"No, he's been in contact with both Pam and Tyler Keller, Josie's sister-in-law." Emmett looked over at Naomi. "I don't know if your folks told you that the town hired Tyler a while back as a special-events planner to bring in more business. She's been doing a great job."

"I think Mom and Dad said something about it. And I certainly see the results in the increased tourist trade. So this guy is connected to an event?"

Emmett nodded. "Something to do with special preparations for the Fourth of July celebration. All very hush-hush. They want to surprise the good people of Shoshone."

"Well, then." Luke sat back in his chair. "It's only a business dinner. He'll be around until everything's set up, and then he'll leave. No big deal, right?"

Emmett scowled at him. "It wouldn't be if I hadn't seen the way he looked at Pam, like she was a helping of his favorite dessert."

"That's understandable." Naomi seemed to be trying to soothe the troubled waters, too. "She's a beautiful woman. But there's no way she'd prefer a citified dandy like him to you, Emmett. She probably went to dinner with him to be polite."

"I'd be willing to believe that if she hadn't flirted with him right under my damned nose."

Naomi smiled. "Emmett, that's the oldest trick in the book. She's trying to make you jealous. Everybody knows how you feel about her. And she's made no secret about how she feels about you, too. Why not end the suspense and propose to her?"

"Can't bring myself to do it. Doesn't seem right when she has so much and I have so little."

"Love?" Naomi asked with a twinkle in her eye.

Emmett snorted. "'Course not. Money's the problem, not love."

Luke checked on Pam and Clifford's table. "Then you're leaving the door open for the likes of him. I agree with Naomi. I'm sure Pam would rather have you than that character. But she might be tired of waiting for you to get over this hang-up."

Emmett muttered something that could have been a curse.

"I have an idea." Luke tucked his napkin beside his plate. "Go over and ask Pam to dance. Stake your claim."

The light of battle lit Emmett's blue eyes as he pushed back his chair. "All right, I will. That sonofabitch probably can't dance a lick."

Luke grinned. "If he could, he wouldn't dress like a peacock."

"That was brilliant," Naomi murmured as they watched Emmett amble over to the table.

"Let's hope it works." Luke thought it might. He hadn't spent his adult life romancing women without learning a thing or two. Pam looked surprised, but she left her chair and walked to the dance floor with Emmett.

Luke pushed back his chair. "That's our cue. Dance with me, Naomi Perkins."

Laughing, she took the hand he offered and soon he had her right where he wanted her, in his arms. He'd had a hunch that she'd be a good dancer. He thanked the series of coincidences that had given him the opportunity to dance with Naomi. What a joy.

Her breath was warm in his ear as she twirled with him on the polished floor. "Did you talk Emmett into dancing for his sake or yours?"

"I figured it would help us both out." He spun her around. "I couldn't leave here tonight without at least one dance."

She brushed a quick kiss on his cheek. "I knew you had more hidden talents."

"Anything I have is yours for the taking." He moved her smoothly across the floor in a spirited two-step.

"I'm taking it."

"When?"

"I'll be up on my platform by ten in the morning. After that, it's up to you."

He twirled her under his arm. "Are you sure we can't manage something tonight?"

"Positive. You're going home with Emmett and I'm sleeping in my parents' house."

He brought her in close for one precious second. His heart hammered so loudly he could barely hear the music. "I want you so much."

"I want you, too." Her cheeks were flushed. "And I will have you. And you'll have me. Tomorrow."

The music ended, and he held her close. "Promise you'll think about me when you're lying alone tonight."

She gazed up at him, her lips parted as she breathed quickly, recovering from the exertion of the dance. "Only if you'll promise to think about me."

"That's an easy promise."

"I think I should leave now." She eased out of his arms. "See you tomorrow."

He watched her go and fought the urge to follow her outside for one last kiss.

"That was a good idea you had." Emmett came over and clapped him on the shoulder. "We dance great together, and I don't think she'll be flirting with that Clifford guy so much now. Thanks, son."

"You're welcome. Ready to go home?"

"Yeah. I made my statement." He reached for his wallet and tossed some bills on the table. "Let's leave."

Back in Emmett's truck, they rode in silence for a couple of miles. But finally Luke decided he needed to clear the air. "I know you're worried about me getting involved with Naomi."

Emmett blew out a breath. "I wouldn't be, except you keep talking about leaving. I wish you'd rethink that, Luke. Frankly, I've never quite understood it."

"I have more things to see and do. Too long in one place and I get restless, wondering what's on the other side of the hill. When you start getting attached is when you're reluctant to leave, and then you slowly settle into your rut."

"I suppose you think I'm in a rut, then."

"From my vantage point, yes, but if you're happy, that's all that matters. I was born a wanderer, just like my dad."

Emmett slowed down so that a family of raccoons could cross the road. "So he travels all over the place, too?"

"Nope. He got mired in a mortgage, car payments, a lawn that has to be mowed, a fence that has to be painted, a garage that has to be cleaned. My mother wanted all that, and he became trapped by those things in order to please her, or at least keep the peace. He never went anywhere. He warned me that he was a cautionary tale."

"Hmm. So your father is miserable?"

Luke nodded. "Not completely miserable, but he has regrets. He sighs when he glances through the travel section of the newspaper and he watches every travel documentary he can find. He even clips out coupons for discount travel adventures that he can't follow up on."

"Excuse me for saying so, Luke, but unless he's an invalid, he could still travel. What's stopping him from going?"

"Like I said, the responsibilities at home, and my mother, who has no interest in traveling." But as Luke laid it out for Emmett, he had to admit that his father was an adult with free will. If this was his passion, he could find a way to make it happen. Maybe it was easier to stay home and complain.

"You know, son, could be he's using your mother as an excuse not to go."

"Maybe. He might be scared to actually go now. I see your point, but that only emphasizes mine. I don't want to tie myself to the same things that weigh him down, whether he's allowing that or not. I'd rather avoid being in that mess in the first place. I wouldn't be good at settling down, and I know it."

"I suppose, with an example like that, you don't think so."

Luke had the feeling that Emmett had more he could say, but he was refraining from saying it. That was okay with Luke, because they'd strayed from the topic, which was his intentions toward Naomi and hers toward him.

So he tackled the subject again. "Naomi knows all about my wanderlust. She and I are attracted to each other, and I've told her I'm not a forever kind of guy."

"Yes, but she might think she can change you."

"I don't think she wants to."

"All women want to get a man to settle down. It's the way of the world." Emmett spoke with certainty.

"It used to be, Emmett, but not so much anymore. Naomi's like a lot of women—not sure where she's going, what her next job will be. She wants to stay flexible. She's no more ready for a husband than I'm ready for a wife."

"She told you that?"

"She did. And she's not the only woman who's said the same kind of thing. I don't want to go behind your back, Emmett, but I intend to spend time with Naomi, and she's heading into it with her eyes wide open. In fact, she likes the idea that I won't be begging for her hand in marriage."

Emmett was quiet for at least a full minute. "Her folks wouldn't appreciate knowing about this."

"I'm sure they wouldn't."

"So I won't tell them."

"Thank you."

"I won't pry into your activities during your free time, but I expect the same amount of work out of you that I've always had."

"You'll get it. But I have an afternoon off coming, and I'd like to take it tomorrow."

"Guess I don't have to ask where you'll be going."

"No. And…I'd like to borrow a horse. If you can't lend me one, I understand, but I—"

"You can borrow the damned horse." Emmett sounded gruff. "Smudge can always use the exercise."

"Thanks, Emmett."

"You're welcome. And if you have any more bright ideas regarding Pam, don't keep them to yourself."

Luke smiled. "I won't."

5

NAOMI HAD EXPECTED to toss and turn, but she slept
great. She loved camping, but there was something to
be said for a good innerspring. As she packed up for
the hike back to the campsite, she thought about what
likely would be happening there in the next few days
and searched around for items she wouldn't normally
take camping.

Lacy underwear topped the list. Then she threw in
a see-through nightgown that she'd never considered
wearing while sleeping in a tent. She had a perfume
bottle in her hand, ready to pack it, when she came to
her senses.

Good grief, had she completely lost her mind? Fragrance of any kind was a no-no. She was in bear country, for God's sake, not at a beach resort.

For that matter, she might want to forget the see-
through nightgown, too. It was the sort of thing a
woman wore when she emerged from the bathroom
of a luxury suite and sashayed over to the king-size

bed where her lover waited, his gaze hot. When two people were crammed into a small dome tent, transparent lingerie lost most of its impact.

With reality smacking her in the face, she pulled out her lacy underwear, too. She was doing field research on a nesting pair of eagles, not arranging a romantic tryst with the man of her dreams. Luke had suggested this arrangement after catching her at her rumpled worst. If she got all fancy on him, he might laugh.

Or worse yet, he might wonder if she was trying to snare him with her feminine wiles. Then he'd turn tail and run. He'd proposed a straightforward liaison where they both understood the parameters. Seductive clothing could easily send the wrong message.

Because she could cut cross-country to the campsite, her hike was only about five miles. Hiking always helped her think. As she walked, she examined her knee-jerk response to this situation with Luke.

She'd automatically reached for the accepted female lures—fragrance and suggestive clothing. She'd reacted as if she needed to make herself more desirable to him. Oh, yeah, Luke would have been suspicious of her motivation for doing that.

She was suspicious of her motivation. Before this affair started, she might want to search her conscience to make absolutely sure no hidden agenda existed. This relationship couldn't be a bait and switch where she accepted his invitation to a no-strings affair and then subtly tried to bind him to her.

Hiking across a sunny meadow filled with sage and wildflowers, butterflies and songbirds, was perfect for soul-searching. She did a mental practice run through the scenario. For a few weeks, she would enjoy Luke's company and his gorgeous body. They'd have great sex and watch the eagles together. She'd become used to having him around.

But the eagles would leave the nest. Luke had already said that was about the time he planned to head for parts unknown. She'd have to bid him goodbye without making a big deal out of it. Could she?

Well, of course she could. After she'd graduated from college and before starting her first job, she and some friends had spent the summer backpacking through Europe. They'd had an amazing time, but that trip had ended and the friends had scattered. They kept up through emails, but their summer of bonding was only a memory now.

Had she been sad when the trip had ended? Of course. Would she like the chance to do it again? Definitely. But that wasn't possible. Everyone's lives had taken different turns.

She vowed to think of this time with Luke that same way, minus the continued email connection. She doubted he'd want that. For the next few weeks, she'd pretend to be on vacation with Luke Griffin, her traveling companion on the road to sexual adventure.

Satisfied with her conclusions, she hurried toward the campsite. Fortunately it was as she'd left it. The tent was secure. After stowing her food supplies in a canvas sack attached to a pulley, she hoisted it out of bear reach. Then she opened the outside tent flaps to air it out and tucked her clean clothes in another canvas sack inside the tent.

At last she was ready to check on the eagles. With her computer, her camera and her binoculars in a smaller backpack, she climbed the ladder to her platform. Like an absent mother coming home to her children, she was eager to see what had happened to her charges while she'd been gone.

And like that same mother, when she looked through her binoculars and spotted the two nestlings, she was sure they appeared bigger than they had the day before. Her scientific self knew that one day wouldn't have made much of a difference. Yet they seemed to be moving around more. The larger of the two lifted its fuzzy head and looked in her direction.

"Hi there," she murmured with a smile. "Miss me?"

The nestling turned, giving her a profile view, and blinked.

"Someday you're going to be a magnificent eagle with a snowy head and talons strong enough to grip a small deer. I won't recognize you."

She wouldn't have any artificial means of tracking them, either. She agreed with the professor's decision not to use telemetry to keep tabs on these birds after they left the nest. Radio tracking could help researchers learn about the eagles' habits, but Naomi disliked anything that might interfere with their normal behavior.

Yet at times like these, when she felt a kinship with the creatures she'd been studying, she longed for a way to trace their journey after they left this meadow. She thought she'd be able to recognize the parents if they returned next spring. The male had a scar above his right eye, and the female was missing one toe on her left claw. But even if the babies came back here, too, they would have changed drastically by then.

Lowering the binoculars, she set up her folding table and camp stool. Then she turned on her computer and checked the webcam feed. She hadn't updated Professor Scranton recently, so she sent him a report and received an immediate and grateful response.

The guy could easily be in his nineties, and he had done his share of fieldwork in his day, but now health issues prevented him from doing the research for his paper. He'd told Naomi that her information provided the energy boost he needed to keep writing.

Even so, he'd urged her to take breaks and not neglect her normal life while observing the eagles. She'd assured him that at the moment, she didn't have a particularly exciting life and would be happy to spend most of her time focused on the nest and its occupants. Of course, that had been before Luke Griffin had ridden under her tree.

But Luke didn't want her to drop everything for him, even if she'd been so inclined. He actively *wanted* her to be involved in her career, because that guaranteed she wouldn't become needy. She began to see the sense in what he'd been trying to tell her. He was a man for the new breed of independent women, of which she was definitely one.

An eagle's shrill cry caught her attention. Raising her binoculars, she watched the female glide into the nest with another fish in her talons. Feeding time.

Naomi grabbed her digital camera and took several shots. Then, using the webcam image, she sat at her computer and made rapid notes.

After the female left the nest again, Naomi scanned the area with her binoculars for no particular reason, except…a feeling. Something about the scenery had changed. The more she'd worked in the wild, the more her senses had sharpened, so maybe she'd known he was coming even before he'd appeared.

Through the powerful lens she watched Luke riding toward her, exactly as he had the day before. He had the same relaxed style, and although his shirt was a different plaid than the one he'd worn yesterday, he looked very much the same. But nothing was the same.

She lowered her binoculars, unwilling to spy on him today. He was no longer a hot stranger to ogle as a distraction from her research duties. He was Luke, the man she'd agreed to have sex with. And he was coming for her.

LUKE RODE INTO the clearing and wondered if she was watching him through her binoculars. He couldn't remember ever starting an affair this way, where they'd discussed the issue and had come to the conclusion they'd go for it a good twelve hours before anything actually happened.

Usually the decision was made during a passionate make-out session, and there wasn't much logic involved until later. After they'd had wild sex, he would gently explain his position on commitment, and because he'd chosen wisely, the woman in his arms would thank him for not expecting anything permanent.

Everything was different with Naomi, probably because they'd met out here, under the blue Wyoming sky, and he was fascinated by the nature of her work. In the past he'd hooked up with business types who'd been looking for a hot cowboy in a country-and-western bar. That had to be the source of the difference. His other lovers had come looking for someone like him.

When he'd heard about Naomi's eagle research and her wildlife background, he'd been so intrigued that he'd made a point to connect with this interesting woman. That had put him in the unfamiliar position of trying to impress *her*. He seemed to have done a decent job so far. He couldn't speak for her anticipation level, but the twelve hours since they'd decided to become lovers had ramped up his libido considerably.

Still, he might want to add some style to his entrance. Slapping his hat against Smudge's rump, he urged the gelding into a gallop and cut across the meadow, heading straight for her tree.

He didn't dare look up to see how she was taking this frontal assault, because he had to keep his attention on the terrain. Racing toward her wasn't all that bright, perhaps, but it had chutzpah. A few yards shy of the platform, he reined in his horse in a spurt of dust.

Very showy, if he did say so. He kept a tight hold on Smudge, who was prancing and blowing like a stallion. Tilting his hat back with his thumb, he glanced up. "Howdy, ma'am." He might sound casual, but his heart was pounding like crazy.

"Howdy, yourself." Grinning, Naomi leaned over the railing. She looked adorable, with her hair in a high, flirty ponytail. "That was quite—"

"Stupid?"

"I was going to say dashing."

"Dashing." He squinted up at her. The sun created a halo around her blond hair, but he knew she was no angel. Desire tightened his groin. "That's what I was going for. Dashing."

"You achieved it. You looked like a Hollywood cowboy."

"You should see me twirl my lariat."

"I'd love to."

He couldn't seem to stop staring at her. The sunshine fell on her like a spotlight, turning her into a blonde princess. If he hadn't pushed his horse into a gallop on the way over here, he could have ground-tied him and ascended to the platform as any decent Hollywood cowboy would do.

As the ache for her grew, he longed to climb that ladder and claim his prize. But Smudge needed a cooldown. And while Luke was at it, he might as well settle the horse into his temporary quarters.

"Are you coming up or do you want me to come down?"

"I'll come up. Let me get Smudge sorted out first. How are the eagles?"

"Good. All seems to be well."

"Excellent. I'll be right back." He clicked his tongue and guided Smudge around the tree and over toward her campsite. After walking the horse around the campsite awhile, Luke dismounted.

He'd come prepared for the duration, with supplies in two bulging saddlebags. Unsaddling Smudge, he put the saddle, blanket and bags over by Naomi's tent. "Welcome to your home away from home, Smudge." He replaced the horse's bridle with a halter and led him down to the stream for a drink.

His promise to "be right back" might have been overly optimistic. Returning to the campsite, he tied Smudge to a tree while he found a good grazing area near the tent. Then he pulled a ground stake out of a saddlebag, along with a mallet, and planted the stake. Finally he transferred Smudge's lead rope from the tree to the stake.

That should take care of the horse until tonight, but he understood why Naomi chose to hike out here instead of riding. A horse was one more thing to deal with. Still, he had limited time to be with her, and even with these few chores, he'd saved valuable minutes by riding instead of hiking.

After scratching Smudge's neck and giving him a handful of carrots from his pocket, Luke walked down the path Naomi's hiking boots had created during her many treks. He couldn't remember the last time he'd been this excited about being with a woman.

He could easily guess why that was. Her interest in wildlife indicated that she was as interested in adventure and exploration as he was. At least she was now. He cautioned himself not to make assumptions of how she'd be in the future.

But he didn't care about the future. At this moment he had the green light to spend quality time with a woman who studied eagles. That would make everything more exciting, including the sex. He had condoms in his saddlebags and in his pocket. Life was good.

He'd look at the eagles first, because he really was interested in them, and because if he didn't look at them first, he might never get around to it. After he'd checked out the eagles, he intended to kiss Naomi until they both couldn't see straight. That dramatic race over here had made him feel like a conquering hero.

"Coming up!" He climbed the ladder and thought of Rapunzel. Naomi was also a blonde, but he appreciated being able to use a ladder instead of her braided hair to reach her tower.

"Hurry!" she said.

"Why?" He hoped it was because she couldn't wait to feel his hands on her.

"Both parents are there for feeding time! It's like a family portrait."

Luke smiled. She really dug those eagles, and he liked that about her. Any woman who was passionate about one thing had the capacity to be passionate about other things, too. He'd sensed that about Naomi from the beginning.

Once he reached the platform, he was struck again by the spectacular view. This platform would be an awesome place to watch the sunset. He'd keep that in mind for later.

She glanced over at him, her color high. "Here." She took off her binoculars. "Take a look."

"Thanks." He accepted the binoculars, but he couldn't resist cupping the back of her head and giving her a quick kiss. "Hi."

"Hi." She sounded breathless.

That was good. She would be even more breathless before long. Adrenaline rushed through his veins. Eagles and a hot woman. What could be better than that?

"I think the nestlings have grown a little." She came to stand next to him. "Tell me what you think."

With her standing so close and radiating warmth and the tantalizing scent of arousal, he couldn't think very well at all. But he made a valiant attempt. Lifting the binoculars, he focused on the nest.

To his surprise, he did notice a difference, even if it was slight. "They're growing, especially the bully. Look at that little sucker, shoving the other one out of the way. C'mon, you. Let the little one have some food."

She chuckled. "So you root for the underdog?"

"Doesn't everybody?" Between having her right beside him and the incredible view of the eagles, he was on sensory overload.

"Humans often do. We're at the top of the food chain, so we can afford to worry about the weak link. Wild animals don't always have that luxury."

"Good point." Luke desperately wanted to slide one arm around her and pull her close, but he knew what that would lead to. Once he touched her, there would be no eagle watching going on.

"Most of the time they're focused on survival." Naomi sighed. "They're so vulnerable."

"You mean the babies?"

"And the parents."

He focused on the sharp beaks and strong talons of the male and female eagles. "They look so powerful."

"I know. But all it takes is a shortage of food, or a car windshield, or an electrical wire, or a gun. We nearly wiped them out."

"Thank God we didn't. Now people are into watching them instead of shooting them."

"Which means I'm employed. That reminds me that I need to make some notes. Can you keep track of the feeding session and report what's happening while I type?"

"Sure." He missed her warmth the second she moved away to sit at her folding table, but he couldn't forget that she had a job to do. That's why he'd planned to stay overnight. She wouldn't be watching the eagles once darkness fell.

He hoped she'd go along with the plan. Now that he thought about it, he wondered if he should have checked with her first. They'd been hot for each other last night, and he was still burning, but she might have cooled down since then.

Well, he'd find out soon enough. In the meantime, he'd act as her research assistant, which wasn't a bad deal. In fact, he considered it a privilege to be involved, even a little bit, in her work.

"After they leave the nest, will you have any way of tracking what happens to them?"

The steady click of the keys stopped for a moment. "No. I won't be banding them. It's too invasive."

"I agree." He went back to describing the movements of the eagles, and she continued to type.

Then she paused again. "I take it you got the afternoon off?"

"Yes, I did. Okay, it looks like the father is getting ready to leave the nest."

She started typing again. "When do you have to go back?" The keys clicked rhythmically.

"Tomorrow morning."

Her typing came to an abrupt halt.

Although his back was to her, he swore he could feel the intensity of her stare. Suddenly it seemed several degrees warmer on the platform. "If that's okay with you."

Behind him, the laptop closed with a soft snap.

"I won't interfere with your work." Lowering the binoculars, he turned around, hoping he hadn't misjudged, hoping he would find... *Yes.* The same emotion sizzling in his veins heated her blue gaze. His pulse hammered as he held that gaze.

Slowly she stood. When she drew in a breath, her body quivered. "Interfere with my work." She stepped out from behind the small table. "Please."

6

EVER SINCE LUKE had come charging toward her across the meadow, Naomi had felt like a shaken bottle of champagne ready to blow at any second. Intellectually she'd known that leaping from his horse and scaling the platform would be silly, but her romantic heart had wanted him to do that all the same. She'd wanted to be taken in a mad rush of passion that gave her no time to think.

But he'd taken freaking *forever* to deal with his horse, which was a good thing but didn't scream eagerness on his part. So she'd concluded he was here as much to see the eagles as to see her, especially after he'd mentioned them before he'd ridden over to the campsite.

But now...now he looked the way she felt. His throat moved in a quick swallow. "How sturdy is this platform, anyway?"

Her heart rate climbed. "Sturdy enough, but—" She

thought of the logistics. Both of them were wearing complicated clothing.

"Right. We're both way overdressed for this."

"We are." She thought longingly of her transparent nightgown and the entrance she could make if they were in a hotel room instead of on a wooden platform twenty feet above the ground. Instead she wore extremely unsexy hiking shorts, a T-shirt and, most problematic of all, hiking boots.

No man should be forced to remove his lover's lace-up hiking boots before they had sex. So that meant she needed to undress herself. Then she thought of what fun it would be to watch Luke strip down right here on her observation platform. Anybody could make a luxury suite seem seductive, but how many people could say they'd had sex in a tree?

She turned and grabbed her camp stool. "I don't know about you, but I'm going to slip into something more comfortable."

A slow smile made him look even more breathtakingly handsome. He took off his hat and laid it brimside up on the platform. "I knew we were going to get along."

"That's a different hat." She unlaced her boot and pulled it off along with her sock.

"Sarah's going to see what she can do with the other one." He unsnapped his cuffs as he watched her pull off her other boot. "But if you ask me, one ruined hat is a small price to pay."

Her body tingled from the gleam in his eyes. "You don't know that yet."

"Yes, I do." He unsnapped his shirt.

"I might be lousy at sex."

He laughed.

"Really, I might. You know that underdog syndrome we talked about?" She stood and the wood felt warm under her bare feet. "Those are the guys I tend to pick."

"So I'm an underdog? Ouch!" He pulled off his shirt and dropped it to the platform.

"Oh, no." Her gaze traveled lovingly over his broad chest. "You're no underdog."

"That's a relief." He sent her a sizzling glance as his hands went to his belt buckle. "Better get moving, Perkins. You're falling behind."

"No, I'm not." But she'd been caught standing motionless and staring. She'd admit that. "You still have your boots on."

"So I do." He paused, his fingers at the button of his jeans. "After you take off your shirt, how about tossing that stool over here?"

"I can do it now." She reached for it.

"Please pull off your shirt," he said softly. "Your boots seemed to take forever. I thought I'd go crazy."

She paused. Until now she'd been so focused on him that she'd forgotten that he might be as eager to watch her undress. "Don't expect sexy underwear," she said.

"Why would you wear sexy underwear when you're camping?"

With a smile, she echoed his earlier comment. "I knew we'd get along." Then she grabbed her T-shirt and yanked it over her head.

"Mmm."

His murmur of approval sent heat flooding through her, and moisture gathered between her thighs.

"More." His voice sounded husky. "The bra, too."

She trembled as excitement warred with her natural modesty. "I've never stripped for a man in broad daylight."

"I'm honored to be the first." His chest expanded as he dragged in a breath and let it out slowly. His glance was hungry. "Come on, Naomi. I want to see you with sunlight on your breasts."

Pulse hammering, she reached behind her back and unfastened the hooks of her white cotton bra. Then she drew it off and let it fall to the platform.

His gaze held hers for a few seconds before dipping. Then it returned to lock with hers. His voice was tight. "You're incredible. And I want to touch you more than I want to breathe."

Her nipples tightened and she quivered with longing. "Then touch me."

With a groan of surrender, he eliminated the space between them and crushed her in a fierce embrace. Bare skin met the solid wall of his chest, and she gasped at the pleasure of that first contact.

"I need you so much." His mouth found hers as he pulled her in close, letting her feel the hard ridge beneath the fly of his jeans.

The urgency of his kiss drove her wild. No man had ever wanted her like this, as if he couldn't contain the passion gripping him. Keeping her firmly wedged against his crotch, he continued kissing her as he leaned back enough to cup her breast in one large hand. His moan of need vibrated through her.

His hands were calloused from his work, and that only made his touch more erotic. She squirmed against him, aching for relief from the tension that tightened with each thrust of his tongue into her mouth and squeeze of his hand on her breast.

Desperation drove her to shove her hand between them and unfasten the button on his jeans. As she began working the zipper down, he lifted away from her, giving her access. When she slipped her hand inside his briefs and wrapped her fingers around the silky power of his cock, he began to shake.

He lifted his mouth from hers and gulped for air. "I'm going insane."

She moaned as his thumb brushed her nipple. "Me, too."

"We have to… We're not…"

"Condom. Do you…?"

"Yes, but I haven't…my boots are still…"

Her fevered brain searched for the quickest way for them to achieve their goal. "The stool."

"Oh." He let her go long enough to find the stool and grab it.

She used that time to get out of her shorts and soaked panties. When she turned back to him, he was sitting on the stool pulling off his boots, and he held the condom packet in his teeth.

"Forget the boots."

The one he'd been holding fell from his hand with a clatter as she stood before him, trembling with urges stronger than she'd ever had in her life. Those urges made her bold.

"Put on the condom." She braced her hands on his broad shoulders.

His breathing ragged, he quickly did as she asked.

"Now…" She gripped his shoulders. "Help me down."

Hands at her waist, he looked into her eyes as he supported her slow descent.

She felt the nudge of his cock.

Lightning flashed in his brown eyes. He shifted slightly, found her moist entrance. "You're drenched."

"Your fault."

"Hope so." His jaw muscles flexed as he drew her down.

Her fingers dug into his shoulders and she moaned softly.

"Too much?"

She shook her head, unable to speak as he took her deeper and touched off tiny explosions all the way down. So this was what they wrote books and songs about. Now she knew what she'd been missing.

At last she was settled on his lap, her feet on the platform, her body gearing up for what promised to be a spectacular and imminent orgasm. The advance-warning signals rippled through her, making her gulp.

He continued to hold her gaze, but his jaw muscles tensed even more, making the cords of his neck stand out. Sweat glistened on his powerful chest. "Don't move." He shuddered. "I don't want to come yet."

But she couldn't control what her body craved. An involuntary spasm rocked her.

He sucked in a breath and squeezed his eyes shut. "Don't."

"Can't...help it."

Slowly he opened his eyes again, and a wry smile touched his mouth. "You're potent."

"You, too." Another spasm hit.

He swallowed. "Okay, if that's going to keep happening, we might as well go for it."

"Yes, please."

"Oh, Naomi." Laughter and lust sparkled in his eyes. "I had no clue." He drew in a shaky breath. "Ride me, lady. Ride me."

She did, and it was a very short ride. She came almost immediately, gasping with the wonder of it, and he followed two strokes later with a groan wrenched from deep inside him. Quivering in the aftermath, she leaned her forehead against his damp shoulder and listened to the labored rasp of his breathing.

A soft breeze sighed through the pine needles and brushed against her skin. Gradually she became aware of small birds chattering and the rustle of a squirrel in the branches somewhere nearby. She'd always felt a part of nature, but never more so than at this moment.

Luke gently massaged the back of her neck. "That was quite a beginning."

"Uh-huh." She wondered if sex was always this good for him, but she wouldn't ask. "Am I too heavy?"

"Light as a feather." He ran a hand up her back. "Soft as satin."

"I suppose we'll have to move sometime."

"Definitely. Especially if we want to do this again in the near future."

She lifted her head to stare at him. "How near in the future?"

He grinned at her. "That was just a warm-up." He gazed into her eyes. "Am I shocking you, Naomi Perkins?"

She didn't want to admit that she'd never been with a guy who suggested more sex immediately after having it. Apparently she really had been choosing from the shallow end of the gene pool, picking underdogs with a low sex drive.

"We don't have to have sex in the near future," he murmured. "If you need more time, we can wait."

"I don't need more time, but I thought that you, being a guy, would."

"If I weren't starving to death, I'd be ready to go in about ten minutes, but I'm hungry. Are you?"

She hadn't given herself a chance to think about it, but she'd skipped lunch. "Yes, I'm hungry, but I'm all set with my energy drinks and a few munchies. I doubt that you—"

"You've got that right. I brought food enough for both of us, so save your energy drinks for when I'm not here. That way there's no danger of history repeating itself."

"I wouldn't spill it on you again, I promise."

"You never know." He traced the outline of her mouth with the tip of his finger. "You could be drinking one of those green concoctions, be hit with the sudden need to have sex with me and knock the bottle over in your hurry to rip my clothes off."

She laughed. "That's pretty far-fetched." In reality, it wasn't, but she had to be careful not to let him know how powerfully he affected her.

"So you say, but please humor me and don't open one of those while I'm here, okay?"

"Do they carry a bad association for you, then?"

"Actually, no. It's a good association, but even so, I don't care to repeat it. The energy drink served a purpose by bringing us together, so I'm done with it." He gave her a quick kiss. "Let's disengage and I'll head back to the campsite and fetch our lunch."

"Okay." She eased away from him and stood. "FYI, there's a little garbage bag over by the cooler."

"Thanks."

She walked to the far side of the platform to give him some privacy to deal with the condom. How odd that she wasn't embarrassed about strolling around the platform naked. At least she wasn't until she saw a rider at the far edge of the clearing. "Yikes. Someone's coming." She scrambled for her clothes.

"You're kidding." Luke zipped his pants. "Damn it. Where did I set the binoculars?"

"On the table. You'd better put on your shirt." She scurried around getting her clothes back on. Fortunately they always looked rumpled. She used the stool to balance as she put on her socks and hiking boots. That stool would always have the memory of what they'd used it for today.

Luke peered through the binoculars. "It's Jack. And he's got little Archie in the saddle with him."

"Oh." Naomi felt silly for not remembering. "That's my fault. I told him to bring Archie to see the eagles sometime."

"And he picked today. I wonder if that's pure coincidence." Luke put down the binoculars and picked up his shirt. "Emmett's supposed to be the only one who knows I'm out here with you."

"So you talked to him?" She took the elastic out of her hair and redid her ponytail.

"Last night on the way home." Luke buttoned his shirt and tucked it into his jeans. "He reluctantly accepted the idea that you and I would be hanging out together during my time off."

"Then it's probably coincidence that Jack decided to come out today." She was grateful that she hadn't been wearing makeup. She turned toward Luke. "How do I look?"

He smiled. "Like a woman who's been up to no good."

"Really? What's different about me? Is my mouth red?"

"A little, but not much." He rolled back the sleeves of his shirt instead of fastening the cuffs.

"Doggone it."

"Hey." He took her by the shoulders. "I was kidding you. You look fine. I'm probably the only one who would notice a postorgasmic gleam in your eye."

"Luke! I don't want to have a gleam in my eye!"

"Sorry. You probably can't do anything about it.

I'm pretty good at detecting that gleam, but most people aren't."

"I'll bet Jack is. Before he married Josie, he was quite the ladies' man. I wish I had a mirror."

"Trust me, you look fine. That's not what's going to get us in trouble."

She stared at him. "What's going to get us in trouble?"

"I unsaddled my horse and took the time to stake him out in a grazing area. A short visit wouldn't have required all that. I would have left Smudge ground-tied beside this tree."

Naomi groaned. "Then I guess we'll have to see what kind of reaction Jack has to that. He's not a blabbermouth, so maybe this won't get back to my folks."

"Yeah, Emmett said they wouldn't like it."

"Only because they want me to find a guy who's steady. That's not you."

"Nope. Not me."

The sound of hoofbeats grew louder. Naomi glanced at Luke. "We could sit down against the tree and pretend we're not here."

"Like you tried to do with me?"

"Right."

"Forget it. If Jack brought his son all the way out here to see the eagles, he'd haul him up on this platform even if he thought nobody was here. Then he'd find us hiding and looking guilty as hell."

"You're right. That would be embarrassing."

"And because we've stood here debating the issue

for too long, there's no time for me to climb down and disappear into the woods."

That made her laugh. "Hardly. Even if you made it down the ladder, you couldn't get away without Jack hearing you sneaking away through the trees. That would be just as bad as staying here and facing the music."

"At least we're dressed. And we're not actually in the midst of—"

"Oh, God." She put her hands to her hot cheeks. "What if he'd ridden up twenty minutes ago?"

"Little Archie would have gotten an education." Luke shrugged. "He's a ranch kid. He needs to understand the facts of life."

"He's only two," she said in an undertone. "He doesn't need to understand anything yet." She took a calming breath. "This could have been so much worse. I'm grateful that it wasn't."

"Naomi!" Jack's deep baritone drifted upward. "You there?"

She walked to the edge of the platform. "Hi, Jack! I sure am. Hi, Archie!"

The little blond toddler waved wildly. "Hi, hi! Birds! See birds!" He didn't look much like his dark-haired, dark-eyed father. Instead he'd inherited his fair coloring from his mother, Josie.

He was an adorable kid, beloved by his parents, aunts and uncles and grandparents. Naomi's heart did a little flip-flop. No matter what awkwardness the situation produced, this child deserved to see the eagles.

He was very young, but even early memories could have a lasting impression, if only in his subconscious.

"Come on up," she called. "I have a surprise for you. Luke's here."

Jack tipped back his hat and gazed up at her. "Oh, is he, now?"

Archie bounced on the saddle. "Luke! Wanna see Luke!"

Luke joined her at the edge of the platform. "Hey, buddy! How're you doing?"

"Luke!" Archie stretched his arms up. "Wanna see Luke!"

"We'll be right there," Jack said. "Make sure the eagles are ready for their close-up." He dropped his reins, gripped Archie around his chubby middle and dismounted.

"Archie seems excited to see you," Naomi said quietly.

"I've done some babysitting now and then."

She glanced over at him. The drifter babysat for little children? That didn't fit his supposed philosophy of not becoming attached to his surroundings. Little kids like Archie could grab hold of your heart and refuse to let go. "You're a man of many parts."

"I am." He gave her a cocky smile and lowered his voice. "After they leave, I'll show you some of them."

7

FROM THE MOMENT Jack arrived on the platform, Luke knew that he'd come to check out the situation brewing with Naomi. Jack was easing into the role of reigning monarch of the Last Chance, despite the fact he wasn't yet forty. But he considered everyone on the ranch, and most of the people in town, too, as his people—people who required his guidance.

Luke had found it kind of amusing until today. Yes, Jack was his boss, and technically what happened on his property was under his control, but… Okay, maybe Jack had some authority here. Luke didn't have to like it.

Archie, though, was another story. Luke couldn't resist that rosy-cheeked little boy. He dragged the stool over to a spot that would give Archie the best view of the eagles and sat with the kid on his lap and helped him look through the binoculars. It was tricky because Archie didn't quite get the concept of the binoculars.

Luke had a little trouble managing both child and

binoculars. He didn't want to drop either one, with the kid being the more important of the two.

Naomi came to his rescue. "You hold Archie, and I'll hold the binoculars."

"Wanna hold nockles!" Archie stubbornly refused to give up his right to have a hand on them, even if he didn't quite understand how they worked.

"Okay," Naomi said. "We'll all hold them. You, me and Luke."

"'Kay." Archie settled down.

Naomi crouched down next to them. "Archie, can you make your fingers do this?" She created two circles with her thumbs and forefingers and held them up to her eyes.

Archie imitated her, which meant he had to let go of the binoculars, but Luke made sure they didn't drop.

"That's how the binoculars work," Naomi said. "Like your fingers, only better."

Jack observed from the sidelines. "Brilliant."

"We'll see." Naomi had Archie practice with his fingers some more, and then she tried the binoculars again. Eventually Archie caught on.

Once he did, he was very excited. "Birds! I see birds!"

Luke held him as he bounced, but Archie kept his eyes pressed against the twin lenses. Glancing over at Naomi, Luke discovered her looking back at him. They exchanged a smile.

He had a brief flash of what it would be like to be a dad teaching his kid how to use binoculars for the first time. He'd always assumed that whenever he wanted a kid fix, he'd borrow one, like now. But being able to share this kind of moment on a regular basis had its appeal, especially if the other person in the equation happened to be a woman like Naomi.

Then he corrected himself. Not someone *like* Naomi, because he'd already determined that she was one of a kind. It would have to be Naomi herself. He was thinking crazy. He'd been over this ground and knew what he wanted out of life. Absolute and complete freedom.

Being a father came at a stiff price. His own father had made no secret of that. At a young age, Luke had asked for a baby sister or brother. Luke's dad had rolled his eyes and proclaimed that one kid was more than enough to take care of. Luke had never forgotten his father's martyred expression.

Luke could have fun on a temporary basis with other people's kids, like Archie. The little boy had a fairly long attention span for his age, but when the thrill was gone, it was totally gone. Luke handed the binoculars to Naomi and stood up, hoisting Archie into his arms.

Archie wiggled in protest. "Wanna get down!"

"That's my cue," Jack said. "Time to get this guy home. Can't have him running around on a platform twenty feet in the air."

"Great job on the platform," Luke said. "It's plenty sturdy."

"Glad to hear it." Jack continued to eye Luke with suspicion. "How about helping me get Archie down the ladder? Climbing up is much easier. I'd appreciate it if you'd go down and hold it steady at the bottom."

"Will do." It was a reasonable request, but Luke

couldn't help thinking there was an ulterior motive involved.

Sure enough, when Jack reached the bottom safely with Archie on his hip, he turned to Luke and lowered his voice. "What's going on with you and Naomi?"

Luke glanced up toward the platform. He wasn't sure how well sound carried. "We're attracted to each other, and we're both consenting adults."

"I figured something like that."

"Did Emmett say anything?"

"No, he didn't." Jack speared Luke with a glance. "Is he aware of this?"

"He is. I talked to him last night. He said I could ride Smudge over here."

"That reminds me. You were at the Spirits and Spurs with Emmett last night. What was your take on this Clifford Mason guy?"

"Dresses like a rhinestone cowboy, but other than that, I know nothing about him. Emmett's not happy that Pam went to dinner with him."

"She did that because she's the main sponsor of the town's Fourth of July spectacular. Mason is providing the fireworks, and Pam's paying for them."

"Does Emmett know that?"

"He does now, because I told him. I also told him that rumor has it the guy is interested in Pam. He didn't take that well. So FYI, he's not in the best of moods."

"Thanks for the warning. I'll watch myself. He's not totally in favor of my coming out here, so if he's upset about something else besides…" Luke sighed. "I'll just be careful."

"Do that. Look, I don't care what you do on your own time, for the most part, but Naomi is a great person, and you've made it clear you're leaving."

"She knows that. She's fine with it."

"Okay." Jack didn't sound as if he believed it.

"Wanna go home." Archie laid his head on Jack's shoulder.

"I know you have to head back, but I have a question." Luke could see Archie was fading. He needed his nap. "If Emmett didn't say anything about me coming to see Naomi, how did you figure out what was going on?"

"Mom asked me if I had any ideas about cleaning your hat. I know Naomi's big on that green glop, and when I realized that was the liquid that had ruined your hat, I put two and two together."

"My hat's ruined?"

"It's ruined, bro. You can't treat a good hat that way and expect it to survive." Jack looked rather cheerful delivering the news.

"Sorry to hear that." Luke decided not to point out that Naomi had been the one to spill the energy drink on his hat. He'd had nothing to do with the accident. Oh, well. He'd resigned himself to this loss, but that didn't make him happy to hear the hat was DOA.

"Just so you know, if you break Naomi's heart, more than your hat is in jeopardy."

"I've been completely honest with her, Jack. She knows I don't intend to settle down."

Jack gazed at him. "If you say so. But she's one of

ours. And you're not." He touched the brim of his hat. "See you back at the ranch."

As Jack walked away and mounted up, Luke ran a hand over his face. *She's one of ours. And you're not.* That was true, and it was his choice. He'd never been part of any group, and he'd liked it that way.

So why did Jack's words sting? He didn't want to be tied down to this community, or to any community, for that matter. Sure, Jack had a close family, a loving wife and a cute kid, but they all came at the price of his freedom. Jack couldn't pick up and leave whenever he wanted to. He had obligations.

Knowing that, Luke shouldn't be affected by the dire warning Jack had thrown out. The guy's threats were empty and meaningless to someone like Luke. They shouldn't have any effect on him whatsoever.

And they wouldn't. He knew who he was and what he wanted out of life. Many people didn't, and they stumbled along without a plan, allowing circumstances to dictate their future. He wasn't like that.

He waited until Jack and Archie rode away. Then he called up to the platform. "Still want some lunch?"

Naomi came to the top of the ladder. "More than ever. I'm famished." She hesitated. "Did Jack give you a talking-to?"

"Oh, yeah. He and Emmett are both worried that I'm going to break your heart. But Jack was more direct. He promised if I broke your heart, he'd break my legs. Or something to that effect."

"Good grief! Don't these guys realize I can take care of myself?"

"Apparently not."

"I find that rather patronizing...but sort of sweet, too."

Luke took note of that. She might not like being considered a fragile flower in need of protection from men like him, but she didn't mind having representatives from the community watching out for her, either. He'd be wise not to criticize either Emmett or Jack for their behavior. Naomi loved them both and was flattered that they cared enough to stick up for her, even if it wasn't required.

But she'd welcomed Luke to her hideaway, and he'd had one hell of a time with her until Jack had shown up. Despite Jack's obvious scrutiny of their arrangement, Naomi hadn't told Luke to go away. She, at least, didn't think Luke was taking unfair advantage of her. In fact, he'd be shortchanging her if he let Jack's visit cast a pall over the celebration.

He gazed up at her. "I'll be back in a flash with some food."

"Sounds great."

"If you feel like taking off your hiking boots, don't let me stop you."

She laughed, as he'd hoped she would. Then she blew him a kiss and moved away from the edge of the platform. Yeah, they would get their groove back. Jack Chance wasn't going to rain on their parade.

Within fifteen minutes, he had a feast spread out on the platform. He'd even brought a tablecloth, which impressed Naomi to no end.

"Pretty fancy for camping, Griffin." She sat on the

far side of the checkered cloth he'd spread out on the platform. And she was, happy day, barefoot.

"You're camping, but I rode in on a horse, so I can provide more luxuries." He was proud of the cheese, cold cuts and sliced bakery bread he'd brought for making sandwiches. Shoshone's little grocery store wasn't huge, but it carried quality stuff. He'd included only mustard because mayonnaise didn't keep as well.

"This is wonderful." Naomi took one of the paper plates he'd provided and made a sandwich.

Luke waited until she was finished before putting his together. "I considered bringing wine, but I didn't want to sabotage your eagle research, so I brought sparkling water instead. Which reminds me, do you need to check on the birds?"

"After we finish lunch. The webcam does the bulk of the work, but someone should be monitoring the nest on a regular basis and taking some digital still shots. The professor gets the constant webcam feed, but he makes good use of my personal notes and the stills, too."

"How did you hook up with him?"

"He put an ad in the paper, and out of all the people who answered it, he picked me."

"Of course he would." Luke was quickly becoming her biggest fan. "You have the credentials and you're extremely personable. I'm surprised you haven't landed a job with one of the national parks yet."

"Everyone has budget issues, and I'm relatively new to the profession. The parks are struggling to keep their veterans employed, and that's what they should do. I can wait it out. I don't have lots of bills, and I can stay with my folks and pay a small amount of rent. I also have some savings."

He nodded. "You're like me. I don't worry if I don't have a job right this minute, because I know I'll find something eventually. Whereas my dad got a job with an electronics company right out of college and never left. He thinks if he did, no one else would hire him."

"And you don't want to live in fear like that," she said.

"God, no. Fear makes you afraid to take risks." He bit into his sandwich. It was about a thousand times better than her energy drink.

"Have you ever been engaged?"

Now, there was a question right out of left field. She should know that he wouldn't do that. "I'm not into marriage." He glanced at her. "How about you?"

"A guy asked me once, but I couldn't see him as the father of my children. So I said no, but I did my best to be gentle about it."

"So that's your criteria? A guy has to pass muster as the future father of your children?"

"Well, I need to love him passionately, and we need a good sex life, but yeah, I'd want to be able to picture him as my future children's dad. Animals in the wild use that yardstick all the time and it's not a bad one."

She sure wouldn't consider a wanderer like him as a viable father of her kids, which was a good thing, really. "I take it you are planning to have kids, then."

She laughed. "I'm planning and my parents are

praying. I'm an only child, so if they're going to have grandchildren to spoil, I'm their only hope."

He was also an only child. His mother had made some noises about grandkids, but his dad had cautioned him to live his life for himself and not worry about providing grandchildren. Luke had heard the unspoken message—*don't make my mistakes.*

Naomi gazed at him. "Did you think I wouldn't want kids?"

"I don't see how you'd manage a family and still be so involved with wild-animal research."

"People do manage it. There's a woman who took her little boy out on the boat while she studied whales. If I could get a job at Yellowstone, then being married and having a family would be no problem at all because it's so close to Shoshone. My folks would help when they could, and I know a bunch of people around here. Child care would be a breeze because I'd have a support system."

He stared at her as a million contradictory thoughts battled in his head. "That kind of thinking is so foreign to me. I've never thought in terms of having a support system." He was both attracted and repelled by the concept.

Something that looked dangerously like pity flickered in her blue eyes. Then it was gone. "If you're a really strong person, I guess you don't need one. When I was in Florida, I had friends, and I cobbled together a loose kind of support system. But it wasn't anything like I have here."

"So does that mean you feel tied to this place?" He was still sorting it out.

"Not at all. In fact, it's the opposite. Let's say I did get a job around here, found the right guy, had a couple of kids. And then I had some fabulous research opportunity for a few weeks. Being here would mean I could consider it, because I'd have backup. Backup in addition to my husband, of course, whoever he might be. I'd have other people I could count on, too."

"I don't know." He shook his head. "It seems a little too cozy for me."

"I'm sure it does. You're a lone wolf. I shouldn't describe this as a one-way street, either. If I expect to count on others to help me, then when they need backup, I have to make myself available."

"Aha." He knew there had to be a catch. "So you could end up being tied down by them."

"For a little while. It's supposed to even out. If I ask my parents to babysit, then I have to be willing to watch their house and feed their dog if they go on vacation. It's a trade-off."

Luke shuddered. "I couldn't deal with that."

"Then it's a good thing you've created the life that you have, isn't it?"

He met her gaze across the tablecloth, littered with the remains of their lunch. "Yes. I like it." He allowed himself a slow perusal of Naomi Perkins, from her bare toes to her golden ponytail. He and Naomi might be headed down different paths, but right now, they occupied the same place and time. "I'll tell you what else I like."

Her skin had turned a sweet shade of pink as he'd studied her. "What's that?"

"The idea of you naked on this tablecloth."

Her breath hitched. "That's quite a change of subject."

"We needed one." He started moving the food off the red checkered cloth. "All this talk about family ties and obligations was playing hell with my sex drive."

"Is that why you're such a sexy guy? You don't get involved in all that cozy family stuff?"

"You tell me." He pulled off his boots.

"Could be. You're a wild guy, Luke." Rising to her knees, she stripped off her T-shirt for the second time today.

And for the second time today, he drank in the sight of her undressing for him. "That must be why you like me." He unsnapped his shirt and took it off. "You're attracted to wild things."

"That's part of it." She gave him the same sort of once-over he'd given her and smiled. "Mostly I just want your body."

Lust shot straight to his groin. "Likewise." He lost track of his own undressing when she arched her back and reached for the clasp of her bra.

Snap, it came undone, and she pulled it off by the straps before tossing it aside. The motion made her breasts quiver. He became completely absorbed in watching them as she moved. When she unfastened her shorts and slid them, along with her panties, down to her knees, he had a visual feast.

He couldn't imagine ever growing tired of this

view—her pale, full breasts tipped with wine-dark nipples, her slender waist and the gentle curve of her hips. She would put an hourglass to shame. His glance traveled lower, to those blond curls covering what was currently his favorite place in the world.

"Now who's falling behind?" She rid herself of her shorts and panties, and her breasts jiggled again, capturing both his attention and his fevered imagination.

"I can't concentrate when you're doing that."

She gave him a saucy look. "I'm only following instructions."

"Then here's another one." He stood and unfastened his jeans. "Take your hair down."

"Okay." She lifted her hands to her ponytail.

"Stop."

"But you said—"

"I know, but I just want to look at you for a minute like that, kneeling on the tablecloth, your hands in your hair. You look like a wood nymph."

"Don't they usually wear clothes?" She pulled the elastic out of her hair and laid it on her pile of clothes.

"Not in my fantasy." He shucked his jeans and briefs while she combed out her shining hair with her fingers. He'd never thought he had a preference for a woman's coloring. But surely nothing was more beautiful than blond hair filled with sunlight.

"And there's my fantasy." She focused on his jutting cock. "Come closer." She ran her tongue over her lips. "I have a taste for something wild."

The blood roared in his ears as he walked toward her. Oh, yes, this was going to be good. Very good.

8

Driven by urges she'd never had before, Naomi boldly wrapped both hands around his rigid penis. Until today, she'd never been naked with a man outdoors in broad daylight, and she'd certainly never done *this* out in the open, under a clear blue sky and a warm sun.

Holding him felt like clutching a lightning rod. Energy coursed between them, and her pulse rate skyrocketed. Glancing up, she looked into eyes filled with primitive fire. For this moment, he was truly a wild creature, and so was she.

Slowly she leaned forward. She began with her tongue, and he gasped. She wanted to make him gasp and groan and abandon himself to her questing mouth. Glorying in his salty taste, silky texture and blood-warmed strength, she accepted all he had to offer. The blunt tip brushed the back of her throat, and he trembled.

Then she began to move, applying suction here, a swirl of her tongue there, until his breathing grew labored. He slid his fingers through her hair and pressed them against her head. Another strangled moan was followed by his rapid breathing.

Her heart beat frantically as his excitement fueled hers. She sucked harder, and he cried out. His fingers pressed into her scalp and his body shook. When she was certain he was going to come, he tightened his hold and pulled back, out of reach. "No." He struggled to breathe. "No. I want—"

Quivering, he dropped to his knees. Still holding her head, he gave her an openmouthed kiss. His tongue dived into the warm recesses where his cock had been. But he didn't have the breath to kiss her for long.

He raised his head and looked into her eyes. "Let's do that…again…sometime."

"Anytime."

He smiled and massaged her scalp as his breathing grew steadier. "You may regret that."

"Never." Loving him that way, here on this open platform, had been wonderfully freeing. She vibrated with the power of it. She felt as if she could fly.

"Don't go away."

"Not a chance." She waited while he retrieved a condom from his jeans pocket. "Let me put it on."

He laughed. "Not yet." He tossed the packet next to the tablecloth and met her gaze. "First, I intend to taste the wildness in you, Naomi Perkins."

Ah. The air whooshed right out of her and liquid heat surged right in.

"Lie down," he murmured, his voice as soft and sexy as black velvet. "It's my turn to play."

She wondered if he could simply talk her into a climax with words spoken like that. The man knew his way around a seduction. She didn't care where or how he'd learned to make a woman melt like wax before a flame, as long as he kept that flame burning.

As she stretched out on the smooth cotton, she imagined herself a lioness on the African veld. Nothing covered her but the sky. And now, caressing her with his mouth and tongue, a powerful male was about to make her roar.

That roar began with a whimper as he touched her in secret places, sensitive places, erotic places. She writhed under the teasing lap of his tongue and the urgent tug of his teeth. His mouth was everywhere, exploring her with the thoroughness of a mapmaker.

And then...then came the most intimate touch of all. He tasted her with slow sips at first, but gradually his demanding tongue grew more self-assured. Spreading her thighs, he lifted her, creating the angle that he needed to take her in the most thorough, uncompromising kiss of them all.

His intent was clear, his pursuit of her orgasm relentless. She surrendered, arching against the determined thrust of his tongue and crying out as the spasms rocked her.

She was still riding the crest of that climax when he lowered her gently. Cool air touched her heated body for a moment before he was back, hovering over her, seeking, finding and driving deep.

She gasped and opened her eyes. He was there, gazing down at her, his expression fierce.

Leaning down, he bestowed a flavored kiss on her trembling lips. "You—" he eased back "—are...*magnificent*." And he shoved home once more.

She looked into his dark eyes, clutched his hips and rose to meet his next stroke. Yes, she was magnificent—magnificently alive. She was bursting with energy and willing to dare...anything, even making love on an open platform twenty feet off the ground in the middle of the day.

"You're going to come again."

Her laughter was breathless. "Is that an order?"

"A promise." He shifted his angle slightly and increased the tempo.

Oh, yes. That would do it. The sweet friction had been wonderful before, but now he'd found the key to unlock her personal treasure chest. Her muted cries grew louder the faster he pumped.

"That's it." He began to pant. "I can feel you squeezing. Let go... There!"

He'd known it a split second before she had, but when her climax arrived, she yelled as she'd never yelled and she hung on tight as the swirling, tumbling force flung her into a brilliant realm of dazzling sensations.

She lost track of where she was, but she never lost track of who was with her. Luke—a god imbued with amazing powers. He'd given her pleasures she'd only dreamed of.

He didn't stop for her, nor would she have wanted him to. His thrusts prolonged the intensity, and when he came, his bellow of satisfaction vibrated through her, too. Then she absorbed his shudders as they blended with the aftershocks of her release. It was perfect sex. She might never have it again, but at least she'd had it once in her life, thanks to Luke Griffin.

She had no idea how long they lay there before he stirred.

Moving slowly, he propped himself on his forearms to gaze at her. "Wow."

She considered making a smart remark to lighten the mood, but he truly did look blown away. "Wow is right."

He smiled. "This was better than the stool."

"Think of what we could accomplish on an actual bed."

"Boggles the mind, doesn't it? I don't know, though. Being up in this tree house gives the whole experience a certain something."

"It's not boring."

"No." He dipped his head and kissed her softly. He added more kisses to her cheeks, her eyes and her nose. "But I have trouble imagining anything being boring with you."

"Coming from a man who treasures variety, that's quite a compliment."

He looked into her eyes again. "I meant it to be. That's probably what brought me out here yesterday. I couldn't imagine how a woman who studies eagles from a platform twenty feet in the air could be boring."

"Thank goodness I didn't disappoint you." But she got a glimpse of how his restless nature might feel confined in a typical relationship. He really wasn't suited for a cottage surrounded by a white picket fence.

"You couldn't if you tried. But I don't want you disappointing that professor who hired you, either. You need to get to work."

"I do."

"And if it's okay, I want to help. I love being your spotter."

"Then you're hired. How much do you charge?"

He laughed. "I've already been paid in full. This has been a great afternoon. Possibly the best of my life. Now let's get moving."

As they dressed and settled in to observe the eagle nest, she kept thinking about that comment. This had been a great afternoon for her, too. Possibly the best afternoon of her life. But she was reluctant to say so because she didn't want him to think she was getting attached.

He was free to say it, though, because he'd already declared his independence. He could rave about their time together, knowing that she wouldn't expect him to stay. It was a lopsided situation.

Somehow she'd set the record straight without being too obvious about it. She had to let him know in no uncertain terms that she didn't *want* him to stay. Then she could relax and make any appreciative remarks she cared to. She simply had to find the right moment.

LUKE HADN'T BEEN kidding. Today had been outstanding, an afternoon he wasn't likely to forget. He had high hopes for tonight, too. Sex in a tent could be a lot of fun. They'd also sleep in that tent, though. Both of them had to work the next day, and all he needed was for Emmett or Jack to catch him dragging around tomorrow.

As the sun started its descent, Luke announced his plan to cook dinner, and Naomi seemed grateful for that. He'd tucked two frozen steaks in his saddlebags, and they would be about ready to put on the grill now. He left her to finish up her work on the platform and walked back to the campsite.

Once there, he gathered firewood and soon had a nice little blaze going in the rock fire pit that he found near the tent. He took a couple of foil-wrapped potatoes and tossed them into the flames. The corncobs, still in their husks, would go on top of the grill once the flames died down a bit.

Next he fed Smudge oats, and because Luke still had a little time, he unrolled his sleeping bag in the tent. Hers was pushed over to one side. It might be the way she normally arranged it, but he'd pretend she'd done that to make room for him in case he showed up. He liked to think she'd hoped for that.

As he smoothed out the sleeping bag and tucked a couple of condoms under it, he found himself whistling. Good sex certainly could make a guy feel like a million bucks. And it wasn't only the good sex. Being with Naomi was a real kick.

He'd already started estimating how often he could make it out here. He wouldn't have another afternoon off for several days, but that didn't mean he couldn't spend some of his nights with her, if she didn't mind sharing her tent.

Normally when he became sexually involved with a woman, they got together only a couple of times a week. That had been plenty. He realized that his thinking was different this time, but he explained it away by the novelty of the situation.

His former girlfriends had lived in apartments, so they'd either spent time at his place or hers, or at a hotel for variety's sake. For some reason he'd never thought to take any of them camping. The professional women he'd dated hadn't seemed like the camping type. Maybe he hadn't given them enough credit, but he couldn't imagine any of them going without makeup and taking a quick bath in a mountain stream.

Today he'd learned something valuable about himself. He *loved* having outdoor sex during the day. He was amazed that he'd never tried it before, but now that he had, he was a real fan. Not every woman would agree with him on that, but he'd been lucky enough to hook up with a woman who was willing to go along.

Having a platform high in a tree helped, too. They weren't as likely to be caught in the act. Actually, if they were going to continue with those episodes, they'd be wise to bring the ladder up. That way they really couldn't be caught in the act. He'd see what Naomi thought about that suggestion.

Before he left the tent, he took off his hat and laid it brim-side up on what he now considered his side. A hat only got in the way when there was a beautiful woman around, so why wear it? He wanted to be free to kiss her any old time he had a chance.

He had the corn and the steak cooking by the time she walked into camp. Even with her clothes and her hiking boots on, she still looked like a wood nymph. She matched the environment, and he liked that about her.

She sniffed appreciatively. "Smells wonderful, Luke. I haven't had steak in ages. You're hired as the camp cook, too."

"I'm happy to accept the job." He crouched down and turned the steak with the long-handled fork he'd brought with him. "I like to make myself useful."

He glanced over his shoulder and caught her eyeing his butt.

"You're *very* useful." She ogled him openly now, hamming it up. "There's something really sexy about a guy slaving over a hot campfire, especially when he can fill out a pair of jeans."

"Watch out." He grinned at her. "I'm liable to start feeling like a sex object."

"I know how you would hate that—having me pester you constantly to strip down so I can worship your body."

"Yeah, that sounds awful. When does the pestering start?"

"If that steak didn't smell like heaven, it would start right away. But I don't want to interfere with this promising meal preparation."

"Tactical mistake on my part." He stood. "I should

have waited to put on the steak until after you'd come back to camp, in case you wanted an appetizer."

"I'll settle for a kiss."

He laid the fork on a rock and walked toward her. "Think we can stop with a kiss?"

"With that steak sizzling on the grill? You bet. Every cowboy and cowgirl knows it's a crime to burn a good steak."

He cupped her face in both hands. "I'll keep that in mind." Then he tilted her head back and brushed the corner of her mouth with his thumb. "Open up, Naomi. I'm coming in."

She moaned softly and met him halfway, parting her lips and welcoming the thrust of his tongue. He delved into her warm mouth with the urgency of a man who'd been denied for weeks, instead of mere hours. She tasted so damned good.

Vaguely he heard a popping sound but didn't realize it was the sound of his shirt being unbuttoned until she slid both hands up his bare chest and pinched his nipples. His cock swelled in response. He lifted his mouth a fraction. "You're not playing fair."

"I didn't say I would."

"Then neither will I." He slipped a hand under the back of her T-shirt and unhooked her bra. Then when he made a frontal assault with that same hand, he discovered that her nipples were as rigid as his.

She moaned deep in her throat.

"You're asking for it," he murmured against her mouth.

"Uh-huh. Make it fast."

Fire licked through his veins. He backed her toward the tent. "Get in there and take off your shorts." He released her, unbuckled his belt and unfastened his jeans.

By the time he crawled in after her, she was in the process of kicking away her shorts and panties. He felt under his sleeping bag, located a condom and knelt at the tent entrance while he quickly took care of that chore.

Then he was on her. With his booted feet sticking out of the tent, he took her with such enthusiasm that he lifted her bottom right off the floor of the tent. She squeaked, but that squeak soon became a whimper as he pumped rapidly.

She came fast, and he followed right after. Then she started laughing, and he did, too. It was crazy to be doing this when it might mean ruining their meal.

But apparently she didn't plan for him to do that. "Go." She kept laughing as she gave him a little push. "Check the meat."

"What if I want some cuddling?"

"I'll cuddle you later! Don't burn the steak."

Grinning like a fool, he backed out of the tent, disposed of the condom and zipped up. He glanced over at the steak, which looked about perfect. Still chuckling, he made a megaphone of his hands. "Dinner's ready!"

God, but she was fun. Yep, best day ever.

9

"THIS STEAK is fabulous." Naomi sat on a flat rock with a tin plate balanced in her lap and a bottle of beer at her feet. Good sex followed by good food was a combination she hadn't had that often, but she'd like to make it a habit.

"I'll bet you say that to all your camp cooks." Luke sat cross-legged on the ground near her. The campsite had one decent sitting rock and he'd insisted she take it.

"I do. You're the first one I've ever had. Are you sure you're okay on the ground? I can go get the camp stool. I didn't even think about seating arrangements. I'm so used to eating alone here."

"Next time we can bring the stool down." He looked up from the ear of corn he was eating. "Assuming I'll get invited back."

"The odds of that are very good."

"I can bring you fresh food each time. I know you're surviving on energy drinks and canned goods, but that must get old."

"I consider it part of the job," she said. "The main focus is the eagles, and I just need to stay reasonably fed and hydrated so I'll be able to keep climbing that ladder."

"Which reminds me. Next time we decide to have sex up there, we—"

"Liked that, did you?" She was amused at his eagerness to continue their adventure. Amused and flattered. Something about this setup had touched a chord, and she wasn't going to argue about that. She reaped the benefits.

"I can't imagine why I've never had sex outside before. Maybe it was the fear of getting caught. That platform gives us a measure of privacy that's not easy to find."

She laughed. "I'm sure that's something Jack and Emmett didn't envision."

"They didn't count on me."

"Neither did I. But I'm so glad you showed up, Luke."

He held her gaze. "Me, too."

Maybe this was her perfect moment. "I've been thinking about something."

"So you had the same idea? Pull up the ladder so we don't get surprised by an unexpected visitor?"

"No, I didn't think of that, but it's a good idea. Yes, it will look suspicious, but better that someone imagines something is going on than that they see it in living color."

"My thought exactly."

"But that wasn't what I was going to say."

"Okay, shoot." He picked up his beer and took a swallow.

She loved looking at him sitting there, his shirt unsnapped at her request, his posture relaxed, happy. He was a gorgeous man. Even watching him drink his beer was a treat.

"What?" He smiled at her.

"You're incredibly good-looking, Luke."

He actually blushed. "That's not what you were going to say."

"No, but it doesn't hurt to tell you."

"You're not afraid it'll go to my head?"

"Actually, no. You're brash, but you're not conceited."

"Thank you." He put down his empty plate. "But you still haven't told me this big revelation."

"Okay. We had a discussion about my potential plans for the future. They're different from yours."

"Yes, they are."

"Just so you know, I realize the difference. When you said this was possibly your best afternoon ever, you could say it because you'd already announced your plans to leave. It was possibly my best afternoon ever, but I was afraid to say so, in case you'd think I was trying to, I don't know…trap you into something."

His expression brightened. "It was possibly your best afternoon ever?"

"Yes. But that doesn't mean that I—"

"I'm glad. I'm really glad. As for being worried that you'd try to trap me, I'm not."

"That's good, but why not? We get along and we

have great sex. Why wouldn't I want to try and change your mind?"

"Because you believe in the principle of live and let live. You're watching those eagles from afar. You're not trying to capture them and band them."

She nodded. Good observation on his part. "So if I'm enthusiastic about something we're doing together, you won't worry that I'm building castles in the air?"

"No. I trust you. If I didn't, I wouldn't be here."

"Fair enough."

"Ready for dessert?"

"You brought dessert?"

"Of course. Hang on." He stood and walked over to his saddlebags. He pulled out a plastic container. "I put them in here so they wouldn't get crushed."

Popping the top on the container, he showed her two chocolate cupcakes.

"Yum."

"Even better, they have cream filling."

"I love that." She reached for one.

"You know what I wish?" He took the other cupcake and returned to his spot on the ground.

"What?"

"That we didn't have to worry about bears. Because if we didn't have to worry about bears, we'd be eating these in the tent."

"You mean like at a slumber party?" She wasn't sure where he was going with this story.

"An X-rated slumber party. Yours would be served on my abs, and mine would be served in your cleavage."

"Mmm." She glanced over at him. "Hold that thought. You can bring cupcakes to the next picnic on the platform."

"Damn. I didn't think of that. We could have—"

"We don't have to do everything at once. I'll be out here until the nestlings fly." *And you leave.*

"You're right. Maybe we should pace ourselves. But you've given me a challenge. It'll be fun to think of all the interesting ways we can have sex between now and then."

"I'll look forward to your boundless creativity." She'd just had another insight. By setting a limit on their time together, he'd ramped up the tension. Lovers faced with a ticking clock always cherished the moments more than those who thought they had forever.

She needed to remember that truism as she joined him on this roller coaster. He was an exciting lover, but he was also a bit of an adrenaline junkie. He didn't know how to relax into a relationship and live it day by day. So she would accept him for the thrill ride that he was and understand that when the ride was over, he'd be gone.

Luke wasn't worried that Naomi would let herself get attached to him, but it didn't hurt for her to say that she wouldn't. He let her go into the tent first and undress while he smothered the fire and made sure every trace of food was packed in airtight containers and stored in the sack she hung from a tree.

Someday he'd love to devour a cream-filled chocolate cupcake that was resting in the valley between her breasts, but he wasn't sure when that would be. Even if they met in town, she'd be staying with her parents. There would be no cupcake games under that roof.

But he wasn't about to complain. He stripped down outside the tent in deference to the cramped quarters. Then, holding the battery-operated lantern he'd used for the last stages of the cleanup operation, he crawled into the tent.

Entering a tent where a naked woman lay waiting was arousing enough. But when the light fell on her lounging like Cleopatra on her barge, he was immediately ready for action. His cock twitched with impatience as he zipped the tent closed.

He turned toward her and pretended shock. "My God! There's a stark-naked woman in this tent! What shall I do?"

She crooked a finger. "Come closer and let me whisper some suggestions in your ear."

"Excellent." He moved within range and set the lantern at the end of the tent before bending down to let her murmur sweet nothings. Except they weren't sweet. They were inventive and extremely specific. He proceeded to follow those suggestions, which involved Naomi rising to her hands and knees and Luke, once he'd rolled on a condom, taking her from behind.

Judging from her response, she liked that very much, so much that she climaxed in no time. He wasn't quite there yet, so he proposed the next phase, which involved lying on their sides facing each other with her leg hooked over his thigh. He stroked slowly as he caressed her warm breasts.

How he loved touching her. "I could do this all night."

"It wouldn't be a bad way to while away the hours."

"No, but let's take it up a notch." Reaching between her legs, he found her trigger point and began an easy massage as he continued to rock his hips back and forth.

She drew in a breath. "That's nice."

"I can tell." By the light of the lantern he could see her pupils dilate and her cherry-red lips part. His massage became more insistent. "Still nice?"

"You want me to come again."

"Bingo."

"I don't know if I...oh, Luke...*Luke.*" She bucked against him, and that was all he needed. He climaxed with a grateful moan of release. Good. So good.

They lay there breathing hard, gazing at each other.

Reaching over, he stroked her mouth with his forefinger. "Thank you for today."

She sighed. "My pleasure." Her eyes drifted closed.

"Mine, too." He could tell she was tired and ready to sleep. He managed to ease out of her arms without disturbing her. Once he'd dealt with the condom, he switched off the light. "Good night, Naomi."

She was already asleep.

He lay in the dark listening to her breathe. In the distance an owl hooted. A small night creature scurried through the bushes somewhere near the tent. He felt at one with the night and the natural world. His heart filled with gratitude that she'd allowed him to share it with her.

He woke up to hear birds chirping and pale sunlight glowing on the sides of the tent. Naomi was gone. In a sudden panic, he sat up and grabbed his briefs and jeans.

Wherever she'd gone, she'd zipped the tent after leaving it. He took a deep breath. She'd probably left to go to the bathroom or put on coffee. Still, he had a strong urge to know where she was.

He crawled out of the tent wearing only his jeans and his briefs. He thought about pulling on his boots, but that would only slow him down. He needed to see her, needed to know she was okay.

She wasn't within sight. The campfire was still cold. He called her name softly in case she was nearby. No answer. Maybe this was why he'd never gone camping with a woman. You could lose track of them.

Maybe she'd gone to check on the eagles. The soles of his feet weren't used to pine needles and sharp rocks, and he winced as he made his way down the path to the platform. Climbing quickly, he stuck his head over the edge. Nope, not there.

Only one more place to look. He really should have put on his boots, but it was a little late to think about that now. He took the other trail, the one leading to the stream. The rocks seemed even sharper there.

Swearing under his breath, he gingerly picked his way along until he was in sight of the bubbling water. Then he sighed in relief. His wood nymph sat in the middle of the stream, up to her nipples in cold water.

He couldn't imagine how she could tolerate it, but she looked blissful with her hair slicked back and the water swirling around her. He started forward and stepped on a particularly sharp rock. He yelped and she turned to face him.

"Luke! What are you doing walking without your boots?"

"You did it." He saw no evidence of her clothes or her hiking boots on the shore.

"I'm used to being barefoot. Most cowboys aren't."

"That's a fact." But he was nearly there now. "How's the water?"

"Icy when you get in, but you get used to it."

"Really?" He had his doubts.

"After all that sex, I wanted a dip in the stream."

There was a gauntlet thrown down if he'd ever seen one. He'd had as much sex as Naomi, which meant he could use a dip in the stream, too. Or he could eat breakfast with her in his current unwashed state, which didn't seem particularly polite, now that he thought about it.

Hobbling to the edge of the stream, he unbuttoned his jeans and pulled down his fly. "I'm coming in."

"It'll feel really good once you adjust to the temperature."

He wished like hell he believed that. Vaguely he remembered that women had a different tolerance for heat and cold than men. It had to do with some primitive conditioning because they were the ones who had babies, so they needed protective fat layers. Something like that.

But he'd committed himself to this, and backing down would look bad. The very second he put his foot in the water, he regretted his decision. He deeply re-gretted it. Some people thought the Polar Bear Club was a great idea. He was not one of those people.

"Come on, Luke. Seriously, it feels great once you get past the first few steps."

Damn it. If he turned and went back, she'd think he was a wimp. But if he continued into that water, he might never be able to get it up again in this lifetime. His cock would freeze solid, which would do irrepa-rable damage.

"You're not going to chicken out, are you?" Her laughter was the final straw.

"Absolutely not!" Gritting his teeth, he splashed to-ward her, and when he reached the spot where she sat chest-deep, he plopped right down. He thought he was going to have a heart attack. "Holy hell! This water's *freezing.*" He would have stood up again, but he wasn't sure his legs would support him now that they were shaking like a willow branch in the wind.

"Wait it out. It gets better."

"No, it doesn't. You're numb by now. You're proba-bly in shock. Can you feel your toes? I can't feel mine."

"You're such a baby. I do this every day."

His teeth started to chatter. "F-first thing in the m-morning?"

"Well, no. I usually wait until the middle of the day."

"Let's do that." He tried to get up, but the rocks were slippery and he was still pretty shaky. "Let's get out and try it again at noon."

She put a hand on his shoulder, so cold it felt like the clutch of death. "You won't be here at noon. Look, you're in the water now, so you might as well relax and enjoy it."

"You realize this could be the end of our sex life."

"How's that?"

"My cock is never going to be the same after this."

"Sure it will." She reached over and cupped his cheek. Her fingers were frigid. "Kiss me."

"The way my teeth are chattering, I might bite you instead."

"Try it."

He figured all was lost anyway, so he might as well go along with this kissing routine. Turning toward her, he tried not to quiver as their lips met. At first it was a chilly proposition, indeed, but then her warmth began to penetrate the frost.

The effect reminded him of a movie where the prince kissed the sleeping princess and she gradually turned from deathly white to pink and glowing. Only he was the deathly white prince and Naomi was the princess reviving him. The longer they kissed, the better he felt.

Soon he had so much feeling in his fingers that he remembered she was naked in this water and he could reach over and play with her breasts. So he did.

She drew away from his kiss. "See? You're starting to enjoy yourself."

"Some. Kiss me again."

"Sure." Sliding around to face him, she held his head and really began to kiss him with enthusiasm.

That helped enormously because now he could fondle both of her plump breasts at once, and as he toyed with her nipples, he felt the most incredible miracle happen. Even in water cold enough to chill a beer keg, his cock began to rise.

She nibbled on his lower lip. "I'm getting hot. How about you?"

"I wouldn't say I'm hot, but I'm hard."

"You are?" She reached under the water, swishing her hand around until she found him. "Oh, my goodness."

"They said it couldn't happen."

"Let's see what else might happen." She began to stroke him.

"Naomi, no." But he didn't pull away.

"Why not? Aren't men more potent in the morning? Let's take the edge off."

"I can't believe you're doing this." Still he didn't stop her. His balls tightened and his breathing grew shallow.

"You want me to. I can tell." Her tongue traced the curve of his lower lip as her hand moved faster. Then she caught his lip in her teeth and fondled the tip of his cock, squeezing, stroking....

He groaned. "Yes...ah...*yes*." He came, spurting into the cold water that no longer felt cold at all.

Her chuckle was rich with triumph. "Wasn't that great?"

He gasped, but not because he was cold. She'd taken care of that in fine fashion. "Great." He wondered if she was spoiling him for anyone else. Now, there was a truly scary thought.

10

NAOMI HAD ENJOYED her first week alone in the forest with the eagle family. But her second week had taught her more about herself than about the nesting habits of eagles. She'd spent her days studying and recording the raptors' behavior, but she'd spent her nights with Luke.

His arrival had depended on his duties. Sometimes he'd show up before sunset and they'd make love on her observation platform, surrounded by fiery hues and the twitter of birds settling in for the night. Other times he'd ride into her camp after dark, when she'd already built a fire in preparation for dinner.

On those nights, he'd swing down from the saddle and pull her into his arms with an impatient oath, as if he'd been gone for days instead of hours. The first time that had happened, he'd been so desperate that he'd backed her up against a tree. Thrilling though that encounter had been, she'd chosen to have a sleeping bag conveniently positioned by the fire the next time he'd arrived after dark.

Sharing her work space and her campsite with Luke was the closest she'd ever come to living with a man. Because she'd fared so well on her own, she'd always wondered how well she'd tolerate such an arrangement. She not only tolerated Luke's presence, she craved it.

With Luke she lost any lingering sexual inhibitions. Having sex with him every night had taught her how responsive she could be. She vowed not to lose that information after he was no longer inspiring her to enjoy her body to the fullest.

Luke had also raised the bar for any guy she would ever become involved with. Although she couldn't dream of a forever-after with Luke, she wouldn't settle for less than someone with his vibrancy. No more underdogs for her.

She was grateful that Luke Griffin had ridden under her tree nearly a week ago. As she swept the meadow with her binoculars around noon, she foolishly wished that he'd appear. He wouldn't, though, not for several hours.

She might have worried about her eagerness to see him, except that she could guarantee he was thinking of her at this very moment, too. Somehow he'd managed to perform his duties to Emmett's satisfaction, even though he'd told her that his thoughts were always on her. He'd described some of those thoughts, and they were all X-rated.

So were hers. Whenever she remembered all they'd shared this past week, she grew moist and achy. Sitting on the camp stool, she took off her hiking boots and socks, even though she knew for a fact he wouldn't be riding out into the clearing until the sun went down.

Standing barefoot on the platform, she still felt restricted by her clothing, so she stripped everything off. She'd love to walk around the platform naked, but after Jack's surprise visit, she wasn't comfortable doing that. She put her shorts and shirt back on, but going without underwear felt risky and fun. No doubt about it, Luke had changed her outlook.

Too bad he wouldn't be here for a sexy picnic. After checking the eagles and typing more notes, she snapped off a few shots with her digital camera. Then she grabbed an energy drink and paced the platform as she sipped it. She pictured what Luke might be doing right now.

He'd mentioned teaching roping tricks to the eight boys who were spending the summer at the ranch as part of Pete Beckett's youth program for troubled kids. Naomi smiled at the thought of Luke working with those boys. He had such an adventurous spirit that he probably had them eating out of his hand. He certainly had her eating out of it.

A movement on the far side of the clearing caught her attention. Quickly setting her energy drink on the folding table, she grabbed her binoculars and her pulse leaped. As if she'd willed him to be there, Luke was riding in her direction on Smudge. What a glorious sight.

Capping her energy drink, she gave in to what was probably a ridiculous impulse. She tugged on her hiking boots, leaving the socks off, climbed down the ladder and started across the meadow to meet him. He'd ridden this path so often that he'd worn a little trail she could follow through the ankle-high grass and wildflowers.

She knew the minute he'd spotted her, because he urged Smudge into a canter. Laughing, she started to run. She couldn't remember the last time she'd run without a bra, and her breasts jiggled under her shirt. This was crazy, but crazy was how he made her feel.

When they were about ten yards apart, she stopped running so she could catch her breath before they met. He slowed Smudge to a trot and then to a walk.

His grin lit up his entire face as he approached her. "I liked that."

"Which part?"

"You being so excited to see me that you had to race out here gave my ego a boost, and the fact that you're not wearing a bra made it even more fun to watch." He tipped back his hat with his thumb. "What's the occasion?"

"I felt like staying loose today."

"That sounds promising. Can I hope it was for my benefit?"

"Let's say it's for our benefit."

"Works for me." He drew alongside her. Sliding his booted foot out of the stirrup, he held out his hand. "Come on up."

"Is there room for me up there?"

"Plenty of room if you sit on my lap."

"Will Smudge be okay with that?"

"Smudge is so well trained you could do a lap dance and he wouldn't spook."

"Is that what you envision? Me doing a lap dance on horseback?"

"Nope. You don't have to do a thing except enjoy the ride." He wiggled his fingers. "Let's go."

She didn't need to be asked again. The sight of him cantering toward her, his body moving in rhythm with the horse, had aroused her beyond belief. She wanted to feel all that manly coordination up close and personal.

Placing her hand in his firm grip, she put her foot in the stirrup and swung up and over the horse's neck so she faced Luke. She marveled at the strength in his arm as he steadied her movements one-handed.

"Hold on to my shoulder."

He circled her waist with his free arm and cinched her in tight against his crotch. "There you go." He clucked his tongue and Smudge started walking down the trail. "How's that? Comfy?"

"You have no idea." She slipped her feet free of the stirrups and hooked her heels behind his knees so she could feel the hard ridge of his erection rocking against her as the horse moved. "I took off my panties, too."

He groaned. "You are rapidly becoming the sexiest woman I've ever had the good fortune to meet."

She wound her arms around his neck and lifted her face to his. "You've always been the sexiest man I've ever had the good fortune to meet."

"Then you won't be surprised if I put my hand up your shirt." He held the reins and focused on the trail ahead, but he slid his free hand under the hem of her shirt and cupped her breast. "I like this decision of yours to ditch the undies." Slowly he rolled her nipple between his thumb and forefinger. "I like it a lot."

Sensation zinged straight to the spot being massaged by the bulge in his jeans. "Mmm." She pressed against his fly and let the steady movement of the horse work its magic. "You can do that some more if you want."

He kept his attention on the trail. "You're trying to come, aren't you?"

"You told me to enjoy the ride."

He glanced down at her and his dark eyes glittered. "You realize what this means, right?"

"Yes." She sucked in a breath as she felt the first twinge. "I'm going to run out to meet you more often."

"It means that the minute we get off this horse, you and I will get very busy."

She moaned softly and rocked a little faster. "Doing what?"

"Take a guess. Now go for it, you loose woman." He pinched her nipple faster. "We're almost there."

"So am...I." When the spasms hit, she pressed her face against his shirt to muffle her cries. She didn't want to scare the horse. But, oh, this was fun. Before meeting Luke, she would never have dreamed of doing such a thing.

True to his word, Luke had her out of the saddle the minute they reached the shade of her pine tree. She was feeling pretty mellow, so she didn't mind when he laid her down on the pine-needle-and-leaf-strewn ground. His expression was so intense that she figured this would be an epic coupling.

He had her shorts off in a flash, but he wasted no time on his clothes. Hooking his hat on the saddle horn, he unbuckled his belt and wrenched down his zipper so he could free his cock and suit up. He didn't bother with foreplay, either. Moving over her, he spread her legs and drove in deep.

She expected him to pump fast and come quickly, but he surprised her. Once they were securely locked together, he propped himself up on his forearms and shifted so he could cradle her head in both hands. They stayed like that as he gazed down at her without moving. He seemed to be studying her.

Wrapping her arms around him, she looked into his eyes. They were still hot, but his expression had lost some of its desperation. "I thought you were in a hurry," she said.

"I was. To get here." Although he'd seemed to be up to the hilt, he managed to slide in a fraction more. "Right here."

"I thought I wouldn't see you until later."

"I switched afternoons with Shorty." He eased back and shoved home again. "I'll work for him tomorrow afternoon."

"Why?"

"I needed this." And he began a slow, steady rhythm as he held her gaze. "I needed...you."

The walls she'd carefully constructed around her heart began to weaken. He shouldn't say things like that. He didn't mean it the way another man might, but...how sweetly he was loving her. How easy to look into those warm brown eyes and imagine that some-thing more than lust had captured him.

"I'm glad you're here." She grasped his hips and lifted to meet him. "I needed you, too."

He smiled as he continued the lazy back-and-forth movement. "Guess so. Running around the place with-out underwear. What were you thinking?"

"This."

"Yeah? You wanted to have sex on the ground?"

"No. I just…wanted you inside me."

"That's nice to hear, but how about a side order of a nice juicy orgasm?" He leaned down and brushed his mouth over hers. "I know you've already indulged, but…"

"I'll take another, please."

"I thought you might. FYI, don't yell. Smudge is a calm horse, but let's not push it."

"I won't yell."

"You might want to." Nibbling on her lower lip, he increased the pace slightly. "How's that feel?"

Tension coiled within her. "Good."

He moved a little bit faster. "And that?"

She gasped. "Better."

"Wrap your legs around me. We're going for best."

Once she did, opening to him completely, he took command, his rapid thrusts bringing her quickly to the edge and hurling her over.

As sensations brilliant as diamonds cascaded through her, she started to cry out. He kissed her hard, capturing her cries as he continued to pump again and again. At last, wrenching his mouth from hers, he groaned and plunged once more.

His body shook and he gulped for air. "Hope I didn't...hurt your mouth."

Her words were forced out as she panted. "No... sorry...forgot the horse."

"I'll take that...as a compliment."

"Do."

"Ah, Naomi." He leaned his forehead against hers. "You're every man's fantasy."

"I like the sound of that."

"And I like the feel of you...under me, on top of me, riding in front of me on my saddle while you give yourself a climax...." He lifted his head and smiled down at her. "You know what we should do now?"

"I can't imagine, but whatever it is, I'm up for it."

"See, that's what I'm talking about. You're ready for whatever."

"I am, if I can do it with you."

"Then let's go skinny-dipping in the stream. I'm all sweaty after that little episode. You, of course, are perfect and only a bit moist, but—"

"Liar. My hair's plastered to the back of my neck. But I thought you didn't like cold water."

"I think I'd like it better in the heat of the day than first thing in the morning."

She laughed. "Luke, it's still cold in that water, even at this time of day."

"Not as cold, I'll bet, and I want to prove to you I'm not a wuss. Also, I want to talk to you about something."

"What?"

"Nothing earthshaking, or at least I hope it's not, but I want your opinion. Let's go get in the water and talk. Unless you need to check on the eagles."

"The webcam's babysitting the eagles and I changed the batteries this morning. We can skinny-dip."

"Great."

Twenty minutes later, Luke had staked Smudge to his grazing spot and they stood by the stream like Adam and Eve. Their clothes lay on the bank, along with Naomi's beach towel.

"I'm going first." Luke started down to the water. "To prove I'm a manly man."

"You don't have to prove that to me, cowboy." She drank in the sight of his tight buns, muscled back and strong thighs. Talk about a fantasy.

He stepped into the water and his breath hissed out.

"Want to change your mind?" Naomi couldn't help smiling. He was a baby about cold water. "We could put some water in a saucepan and let it warm in the sun. Then you could take a sponge bath."

"Nope. I'm doing this." Taking a deep breath, he plunged in, sending water splashing as he plowed over to the deepest part, which was still less than three feet. Then he sat down with another loud splash and a strangled groan.

"That was quite a production."

"It's cold as hell."

"I told you."

"Shouldn't it be warmer by now?"

"Did you happen to notice there's still snow on the mountains?"

"Yeah."

"That's where this water comes from. It's snow-melt."

"Oh." He glanced over at her. "You're coming in, right?"

"Of course. I do this every day." She stepped into the water.

"How come you're not shivering?"

"I have this mental trick. As I'm immersing myself in cold water, I visualize it being warm." She made her way over to him and sat down.

"You can do that?"

"Sure. So could you. Don't think about the water as being cold. Tell yourself it's like bathwater."

He gazed at her. "I'm going to visualize having sex with you, instead. That should heat me up really fast."

"If you keep looking at me like that, you'll heat me up, too. And then what?"

His slow smile hinted at watery pleasures. "We'll do something about it."

Despite what they'd already shared today, her body responded. "I thought you wanted to talk. But if you'd rather get friendly instead, you're headed in the right direction."

He sighed. "Right. I do want to talk. It's just that you're so beautiful. I can't seem to get enough of you."

"Then talk fast."

He chuckled. "Okay. It's about my dad."

11

"YOUR DAD?" Naomi stared at him, clearly startled.

He should have led up to it more gradually, but they'd become so close in the past week that he'd forgotten she didn't know anything about his parents. Yet why would she? He'd never told her. But now he needed a friend's advice. He would have gone to Nash, except Nash was involved in wedding and honeymoon plans. And besides, this was the sort of touchy-feely situation that he sensed Naomi would understand. He trusted her.

"Let me back up." He gazed down at the water and trailed his fingers through it. "It's been easier to focus on the fun you and I are having. I'm not into deep analysis of my past anyway."

"So what about your dad?"

Luke looked out across the water tumbling over rocks and gathered his thoughts. "He always claimed he wanted to travel and see the world, but because he married my mother, who hates travel, and he has the responsibilities of a home and his job, he's never gone anywhere."

"That's too bad."

He took a deep breath. "I talked to Emmett about it last week, and he started me thinking. My dad could travel, if he'd allow himself to. If my mom doesn't want to go, that's up to her. But I'm considering calling him and asking him to come out here, maybe even for the Fourth of July. He'd have a little time off then."

Luke had never done anything like this before, and he was surprised he hadn't. Maybe all that his dad needed was someone to say, "Hey, come on, let's go." On the other hand, if Luke invited him and he refused, that rejection would be tough to take. It might also mean his dad's spirit was truly crushed, assuming he'd ever really had a vagabond spirit in the first place.

"I think that sounds wonderful, Luke."

He looked over at her, drawing strength from the certainty in her blue eyes. "So I should do it?"

"Definitely. Where do your parents live?"

"New Jersey. He'd have to fly out, but he could. They have money. Hell, I'd pay for his flight if necessary."

She opened her mouth. Closed it again.

"If you have advice, please give it. That's why I asked you about this before I did anything. I want to make sure I'm not crazy to consider it."

"Okay. I wonder…maybe it would be better if you let him pay."

"You think so?" Luke thought about his mother,

who could raise an objection about the cost of a plane ticket, especially at the last minute.

"It would mean he's making more of a commitment to traveling, which you said he's always wanted to do."

Luke nodded. "You're right. But it could be pricey."

"It probably will be. But if he's been saying all his life that he wants to travel and he never has, then he's saved a lot of money by not traveling."

"That's a good point."

"The biggest thing is whether he can move that fast, but maybe choosing a last-minute vacation is better. Still, this is… My gosh, it's July 1 already, Luke. You should call him right away."

He knew that, too, and he'd wanted her support while he did that, but her location didn't help matters. "I don't know if my cell phone will work out here. It's an older one. Sometimes it gets a signal in this area and sometimes it doesn't."

"Did you bring it?"

"Yes." That was a huge admission because he never brought his phone, first of all because his reception was dicey and second of all because he didn't want to be interrupted when he was with her.

She stood. "We need to go back to camp so you can try to call."

He gave her a rueful smile. "You're right, but we just got here. I'm not sure we've dipped enough skinny."

That made her laugh. He loved it when she laughed, because she seemed to glow with happiness.

"The stream's not going anywhere," she said. "We'll have more chances. The phone call can't be postponed."

No, it couldn't, unless he abandoned the idea. But now that the concept had penetrated his thick skull, he wanted to act on it, especially if Naomi thought he should. He put a lot of faith in her opinion.

So they took turns using her beach towel to dry off. She dressed more quickly than he did now that she'd decided to dispense with underwear. He got such a kick out of that. She was turning out to be quite a seductive woman.

He figured that their week together had something to do with that. Oh, hell, *he* had something to do with that. Might as well admit that he'd coaxed her into becoming less inhibited.

And now what, genius? Will you go off and leave her, so that some other yahoo can reap the rewards? Or does that stick in your craw a little bit?

It did. But unless he planned to stay in Shoshone and make things permanent between them, which he didn't, then he had to live with the fact that she'd bestow her newly discovered sexuality on some other lucky slob. Better not to think about that.

Back in camp, wearing his jeans and boots with his shirt left unbuttoned, he pulled his cell phone out of his saddlebag and turned it on. As he'd feared, the signal was weak. It would be better in town or back at the ranch, but he didn't want to leave Naomi so he could make a damned phone call.

He turned his phone around to show her the bars, or lack of them. "I can call tomorrow."

"Or you can ride back."

"No." He didn't like that scenario at all. He'd always

been able to slip away from the ranch without attracting any notice, but if he went back to make a phone call, someone would see him, and leaving again would be problematic.

Besides, he wanted Naomi's moral support, and he couldn't very well take her back with him. If he had to call tomorrow without her, so be it, but he wasn't leaving her tonight to make that call, no matter what she said.

She slapped her forehead. "Luke, we should try your phone from the observation platform. That might make all the difference. The signal is stronger for my laptop, so it should be stronger for your phone, too."

"Sure, okay. We can climb up there. Let me get the cold fried chicken I brought."

"You brought *chicken?* Why haven't I heard about this before?"

"Sorry. I've been a little preoccupied."

"No kidding. I *love* fried chicken. If I'd known that you brought some, I would have—"

"Wanted that instead of sex? Then I'm glad I didn't mention it." He crouched down and pulled the plastic container out of his saddlebag. "Remind me never to make you choose between sex with me and fried chicken."

She gave him a saucy smile. "Why can't I have both?"

"Oh, you can. I'm just worried about how you order your priorities. I want to be at the top, but I have a feeling that when it comes to fried chicken, I'm not.

And I—oof!" He nearly fell over as she launched herself at him.

"Listen here, my friend." She wound her arms around his neck. "I don't know how many times I have to say this before it makes an impression, but sex with you is the best thing that's ever happened to me in my entire life. Yes, I love fried chicken. And beautiful sunsets and baby eagles and the sound of the wind through the pines. But I would forgo them all for an hour alone with a naked Luke Griffin."

He couldn't have wiped the grin off his face if someone had offered him a million dollars to do it. She'd laid it on pretty thick and he wasn't sure he could believe all of it, but he appreciated the effort more than she'd ever know.

He cleared his throat. "Thank you. I'll probably still be thinking about that speech when I'm a white-haired old geezer who can't get it up anymore."

"You actually think the day will come when you can't get it up anymore?"

He laughed. "No, I don't, but that sounded good, didn't it?"

"It sounded like you're still fishing for compliments about your awesome package." She patted his cheeks. "Bring your chicken and your cell phone and your package up to the platform, okay?"

"Yes, ma'am." Luke followed her down the path to the pine tree that supported her observation platform. He knew she'd been teasing him and acting sexy on purpose to take his mind off the impending conversation, assuming he could make the phone call from her platform.

That was exactly why he'd sought her out once he'd dreamed up this plan. She was the soft landing spot if he should fall and go splat, psychologically speaking. He stood below the ladder and concentrated on the pleasure of watching her climb it. By tilting his head, he could almost see up her shorts. Not quite, but he knew she wasn't wearing anything underneath and that was enough to fuel his imagination.

He wasn't sure if he wanted this phone call to go through or not. He had such mixed emotions about it. But at least, whatever happened, Naomi would be there at the end of it. And he could lose himself in her lush body…if she wasn't too absorbed with eating fried chicken.

NAOMI HAD SENSED all along that Luke's wandering soul had a soft, vulnerable spot somewhere within it. Maybe she'd been afraid to find out what that was because she already cared too much for the guy. Discovering his secret pain could tear down the walls around her heart completely, and those walls were already displaying stress fractures.

But he'd come to her, like a bird with a broken wing, and asked for help. She could no more deny that than she could toss an injured animal out into the elements. Her creed was to live and let live, but when that life hung in the balance, was she supposed to turn away?

She was no psychologist but even she could figure out that Luke had become a wanderer partly by nature but largely so that he could live the life his father had said he wanted. Maybe he'd hoped to please his father and maybe he'd wanted to compete. It didn't matter. He'd come to a crossroads, a place where he wanted to invite his father to share in his adventures.

Luke knew his dad's response to the invitation was important to both father and son. She didn't have to tell him that. Whether it was important to her was another question.

She could no longer deny that she was getting emotionally involved with this drifter who had wandered under her observation platform one bright, sunny day. She knew how much he'd come to mean in her life. She was less convinced how much she meant to him.

Yes, he needed her now, when he was about to make this difficult phone call to his father. But was she only a temporary crutch to get him through this critical time in his life? Or had they made a deeper connection?

She had no answers. But while he stood at a far corner of the deck and dialed the number for his parents' home, she laid out their picnic on the red checkered cloth he'd left there after their first meal on this platform. Regardless of how the call went, she would offer him solace.

If that cost her dearly in the long run because she ended up with a broken heart, she'd deal with that. He'd given her so much in this past week that she couldn't begrudge him whatever he needed. She mentally crossed her fingers and hoped that his father would understand the stakes when he heard Luke's invitation.

She didn't eavesdrop, but she knew when he'd made

a connection because the low murmur of his voice drifted over to her. Sitting beside the picnic tablecloth, she stayed very still, not wanting to disrupt his concentration in any way. This could be one of the most important conversations he'd ever have with his dad.

After what seemed like an eternity but was probably less than five minutes, Luke walked over and sat cross-legged on the far side of the checkered tablecloth. Glancing over at her, he shrugged. "He says he'll think about it and get back to me."

She wanted to scream. Stupid, stupid father! She tried to imagine her own father acting with such indifference. He never would. She thought of the Chance men, devoted fathers, every one of them.

She'd been in Florida when Jonathan Chance had died in a truck rollover, and she'd heard the rumor that he'd been upset with his son Jack at the time. Yes, that had been difficult for Jack to reconcile. But at least Jonathan had been a big part of Jack's life.

All of Jonathan's sons—Jack, Nick and Gabe—were passionately involved with their children. Nick wasn't biologically connected to Lester, the troubled boy he and Dominique had adopted after Lester had spent last summer at the ranch. But Nick was a committed parent.

Naomi searched for the right thing to say. "I'm sure you caught him by surprise. It's hard to make snap decisions."

His dark eyes were bleak. "No, it's not. You and I make them all the time. It's what you do when you're actually living life, instead of hanging on the fringes of it." Anger and disappointment rolled off him in waves.

"Don't give up."

"I won't. But the only way I'll get his call is if I'm up here."

"Then we'll stay up here."

He held her gaze. "Thank you. I…" He looked away and swallowed.

That's when she knew that he needed something more than fried chicken right now. Moving purposefully, she cleared all the food aside. He watched her without moving.

Then she sat on the tablecloth, right in front of him. Cupping his face in both hands, she kissed him as thoroughly as she knew how, putting all her caring, her longing and her passion into that kiss. At first he simply let her kiss him without responding.

That was a new experience for her, and one she didn't care for in the least. Luke had always been eager for her kisses. Once their lips met, he'd usually been the one who had pushed the kiss to the next level.

Not now, and for a brief moment her courage failed her. But she'd told him not to give up, and so she couldn't, either. She kissed his forehead, his eyes, his cheeks and once again his mouth.

With that the floodgates opened. With a groan, he pulled her into his lap. After that she didn't have to worry about how to kiss him. He took care of all the mouth-to-mouth contact, and the mouth-to-body contact, and every form of contact that followed.

Soon she lay sprawled naked on the tablecloth, and he'd covered every inch of her with his mouth and tongue. If she had been an ice-cream cone, she'd be long gone by now.

Standing, he gazed down at her as he took off his clothes with deliberate intent. "I'm going to have you six ways to Sunday," he said. "And then we'll start over and go through the whole damn week again."

"Okay." She watched him pull off his boots with angry motions and shuck his jeans and briefs. But after he'd located the condom in his pocket and put it on, she sat up and reached for his hand. "Lie down here. Lie down and let me love you for a change."

The fierceness left his expression as if a cloud had scudded away from the sun. Without a word, he knelt down and stretched out on the tablecloth. Her heart constricted with the surrender implicit in his reaction. This was what he wanted, what he needed—not to take her six ways to Sunday, but to be loved and cherished by someone who asked nothing in return.

What an easy assignment that was. Straddling him, she began with his beautiful face. She followed the curve of his cheekbones with her tongue and placed butterfly kisses on his eyelids. His mouth became a playground for her lips, his determined jaw a place to nibble and tease until she felt him slowly relax.

With a deep sigh he let his arms fall to his sides, and she traced each vein, each corded muscle in those arms with her fingertips. As his mighty chest rose and fell with his labored breaths, she toyed with his nipples and stroked the silky black hair covering that massive display of strength and power.

She followed the trail of dark hair to his navel, and

as she dipped her tongue into the shallow depression, he quivered. She stroked his cock and wished that nothing prevented her from feeling the velvet-on-steel wonder of it. But she could also fondle what lay beneath and watch as those heavy sacs drew up in tight readiness.

"Take me," he murmured. "Please take me."

She wondered if he'd ever begged a woman in his life. Maybe not. But she wouldn't make him do it more than once. Rising above him, she guided his taut cock into position and began a slow slide downward.

His breathing quickened as she descended, and when she'd taken all of him, he began to tremble. "Go slow," he said. "I don't want to come yet."

Leaning forward, she feathered a kiss over his lips and felt him sigh. Then she lifted her head to look into his eyes. "Tell me," she said softly. "Tell me what you need."

Passion burned in his gaze. His hands found her hips, bracketing them. "Easy strokes." His voice was strained. "Go easy. Let me... I want to wait."

She lifted up only a little and made her way gradually back down.

"Good." He held her gaze. "Again."

She repeated the motion.

He groaned. "So good. Again."

Once more she rose up and came slowly down.

He sucked in a breath. "Good Lord, I want you, Naomi. I want to come. But I don't want to end this."

She smiled. "We can do it again sometime."

A fire ignited in his eyes. He swallowed. "Then ride

me, lady." His words echoed their first time together. His fingers gripped her hips. "Ride me hard."

That was all she'd been waiting for. Yes, he needed the sweet loving, but more than that, he needed heat that would burn away grief, incinerate sadness. She brought the heat, pumping up and down with a frenzy that made her breasts dance and her bottom slap against his thighs.

His first cry was low and intense, his second louder and when he came, his shout of triumph sent the songbirds fluttering and squawking from the branches of the tree. He laughed at that, a breathless, happy sound that resonated in her heart.

She laughed with him, collapsing against his chest and panting from the effort she'd made.

He wrapped her tight in his arms. "Thank you, thank you, thank you. I know you didn't come."

"It doesn't matter."

"It does. I'll make it up to you." He rocked her in his arms. "I will make it up to you a dozen times over. But that…Naomi…that was exactly what I needed."

"I know."

"How did you know?"

"That's my secret." And it would remain her secret. If he ever guessed she was falling in love with him, he'd leave.

12

LUKE WASN'T SURE what he'd done to deserve someone like Naomi, but she was a lifesaver. As the sun went down, she insisted they should haul the sleeping bags up to the platform for the night. Even when he protested that his father was probably in bed by now and wouldn't call, she refused to consider going back down to the campsite, where the phone reception was bad.

"Just don't let me fall off in the middle of the night," she said, laughing.

The thought made his heart stutter and he stopped unrolling the sleeping bags. "Do you think you might? Are you a sleepwalker?"

"No. At least I don't think so."

"Let's forget this." He started bundling up his sleeping bag. "If there's the slightest chance that you'll wake up at night and start wandering around this platform half-asleep, it's not worth the risk."

"I won't. And we're staying." She crossed her arms and planted her feet. "I've always thought it would be fun to sleep up here, but I was a little worried about doing it by myself. This is perfect." She peered at him. "Unless *you're* a sleepwalker."

"Nope. Never been a problem for me." He crouched next to his sleeping bag, thinking. "So spending the night up here would be an adventure for you?"

"Yes. Absolutely."

"You're not just saying that because of the phone thing?"

"That's a good excuse to do it, but from the moment I first climbed onto the platform, I thought of spending the night, pretending I'm Tarzan. I've just been too chicken."

He smiled. "You wouldn't make a very good Tarzan."

"You'd be surprised." She took a deep breath and let out the most Tarzan-like yell he'd ever heard.

He laughed so hard he had to sit down.

"Wait, that wasn't as good as I can do. I'll try again." She sucked in more air.

"No, no, you're great!"

She looked at him. "Yeah?"

"Amazingly good. I wasn't laughing because you were lousy at it. I was laughing at that big Tarzan yell coming out of such a blonde cutie-pie. It's so unexpected."

"My college friends and I taught ourselves to do it. When we backpacked through Europe, we sometimes entertained people in pubs by doing our Tarzan yells. I'm better after a couple of beers."

"I'll bet." He chuckled. "I can just imagine that." He

also felt a pang of longing. Although he'd traveled with friends when he was younger, they'd all settled down with families. They still traveled, but now it involved taking spouses and kids, which was a whole other ball game. Not his deal.

He stood and surveyed the platform. "So if this is something you want to do for the adventure factor, but you're a little scared of falling off, we'll put your sleeping bag next to the tree and mine next to yours so I'm on the outside."

She nodded. "I like that. Thanks."

"You're welcome. It'll be fun." He knew that for sure because everything involving Naomi was fun. He couldn't remember the last time he'd laughed this much.

They ate cold sandwiches for dinner, watched a family of deer graze in the clearing and made love to the sound of wind in the trees. They slept spoon-fashion, with Luke on the outside. He figured if he kept a hand on her at all times, she wouldn't get away from him and risk falling.

That thought made him restless. And then there was the issue of a potential phone call. It didn't come until dawn, and it woke them both.

Luke scrambled to pick it up before the chime disturbed Naomi, but he was too late. She sat up, rubbing her eyes, as he put the phone to his ear.

"Luke, it's Dad."

Luke grimaced. "Hi, Dad." Who else would it be at this hour of the morning? His father had probably forgotten the time difference. Travelers usually thought about that when they made phone calls. Nontravelers, not so much.

"Listen, I thought about your invitation, and it won't work for me."

Luke had prepared himself for that answer, but even so, disappointment sliced through him. Apparently he'd placed more importance on this than he should have. "Okay."

"I checked flights, and it'll cost an arm and a leg."

"So it's the money?"

"Well, that, and your mother has a cookout planned with the Sullivans. She has her heart set on that cookout. You remember the Sullivans, don't you?"

"Yep." They were neighbors whose attitude toward travel was exactly like his mother's. They claimed everything they needed was right there, so why go anywhere else?

"Anyway, thanks for asking. Maybe next time."

"Sure, Dad. Have a nice Fourth. Talk to you later." Luke disconnected and laid down the phone.

"He's not coming."

Naomi put a hand on his shoulder. "Luke, I'm sorry. It was a great idea."

He shrugged. "I should have known better. He'll just keep watching documentaries about places he'll never see."

"His loss."

"I think so, too, but I can't make him get out there and see the world." He gazed at her. "I did think it would be cool, though. I've never been here for Fourth of July, but the town's really gearing up. Are you coming in or staying here?"

She smiled. "Are you inviting me to come and party with you?"

"Hell, yes! We'll have a blast. Although maybe the fireworks will look more spectacular from this platform, come to think of it. We could—"

"Hold on. Did you say *fireworks?*"

"Yeah. Everyone's all excited because Shoshone's never had fireworks before. What's the matter? Don't you like fireworks?"

"That depends. Are we talking about little stuff, close to the ground? Backyard fireworks?"

"Not from what I heard. This Clifford Mason guy, the one we saw having dinner with Pam Mulholland at the Spirits and Spurs, is arranging for a huge spectacular. Tyler Keller...you know Tyler?"

"Yes, she's Josie Chance's sister-in-law. She plans tourist-type events for the town. So she set this up?"

"I believe that's what Emmett said. And Pam's underwriting it. Everybody's happy about it except Emmett, who thinks Clifford's romancing Pam."

"Luke, this is a disaster. I have to stop it."

"I don't think it's our place to interfere in Pam's private life."

"Not that. The fireworks. I know people will be disappointed and I hate that, but we can't have fireworks."

"Why not?"

She gestured toward the eagles' nest. "It's too close. The parents might become terrified and abandon the nest. The babies would die."

"Town's not *that* close."

"I know it doesn't seem like it, because from the ranch road it's about ten miles. But we're out on a far corner of Last Chance land. When I hike in from my folks' place, it's only about five miles straight across. That's way too close to nesting eagles."

He sensed a train wreck coming. "Are you sure the eagles would abandon the nest?"

"Not a hundred percent sure. You can't ever be positive when you're trying to predict the behavior of wild creatures. But I'm sure enough that I don't want to take the risk."

"Okay, but I'm afraid you're going to have some tough sledding. Everyone in town is looking forward to this."

"I'm sure they are. If it weren't for the eagles, *I* would be looking forward to it. But we do have eagles, and fireworks are a bad idea. Tyler's a very compassionate person. When I explain the situation, I'm sure she'll cancel."

He wasn't so sure. "I don't want to be the prophet of doom, but there could be economic repercussions. The fireworks have been paid for and the merchants are expecting to cash in on all the excitement."

"But what about the other activities? They always have a ton of things going on. Won't that be enough?"

"I don't know. Maybe, maybe not. I think you'll get push back. That's all I'm saying."

"I know." Her blue eyes clouded with sadness. "I really hate that, and I hate having people disappointed.

But I can't let them light up the sky only five miles from a nest of eagles."

"No, you can't. I can see that." He picked up his phone and hit a speed-dial number.

"Who are you calling?"

"Reinforcements." He gave her a quick grin. "Hello, Emmett? Listen, I need to take the morning off, if there's any way you can arrange it."

"I probably can," Emmett said. "What's the problem?"

"You might want to take the morning off, too. Naomi needs to shut down the fireworks display and she could use backup. Fireworks are a danger to the eagles. The parents might spook and abandon the nest."

"Is that so?" Emmett sounded pleased. "Never did care much for fireworks, myself."

"Or the guy who sells them?"

"Don't much care for him, either."

"I was thinking we need to have a little chat with the folks involved, but I don't have everybody's numbers."

"I can arrange a meeting," Emmett said. "How soon can you both get to the diner?"

"Thirty minutes to get organized and an hour of travel time, maybe less if Smudge is feeling lively this morning."

"Good. I'll round up the parties involved and meet you both at the diner in an hour and a half."

"Sounds good."

"Thanks for the call, Luke. It made my day."

"I thought it might. See you soon, Emmett." Luke

disconnected the phone and glanced over at Naomi. "Does that work for you?"

Grabbing his face in both hands, she kissed him soundly before releasing him. "Yes, sir, it most certainly does."

RIDING DOUBLE ON a five-mile trip turned out to be an interesting experience. Neither of them thought it would be wise to try it with Naomi sitting on Luke's lap facing him. They couldn't handle the distraction.

So they chose for Luke to sit forward in the saddle, with Naomi perched behind him, hanging on to his waist. Once they were settled, she couldn't see where they were going, but she trusted Luke to get them there safely.

She was, however, concerned about his package. "Are you squished up there?"

He chuckled. "A little. Can't be helped."

"I don't want you to injure yourself."

"I'll be fine unless the conversation turns to sex. Any expansion could jeopardize this entire arrangement."

"Understood. Maybe we shouldn't talk at all."

"We should definitely talk. If we ride along in silence, with your luscious body pressed tight against mine, my imagination will get me into trouble in no time. So think of a topic. Just don't make it anything sexy."

"I know the perfect thing. Tell me about some of your favorite places."

"Well, your mouth, and your—"

"No! In the world!"

"Oh." He laughed. "My mistake."

"You knew what I meant."

"Yeah, I knew what you meant. But sometime, not now, I'll list my favorite places on Naomi Perkins."

"You're not helping your cause, Luke."

"You're right. Okay, favorite places in the world. Jackson Hole is one of them, believe it or not."

"I believe it." She rested her cheek against his broad back. "I've always felt lucky that my parents chose to live here. So, what else?"

He began to list the places he'd seen that had made the biggest impression on him. He'd traveled widely in the United States and had made it to several South American countries. He'd also seen most of Australia and New Zealand. He talked lovingly about his trips, leaving no doubt that being a wanderer was in his blood. It was a good thing he knew that about himself.

About halfway there, he switched the conversation to her and she listed all her favorite spots, although she didn't have nearly as many as Luke. Privately she admitted that his life had some appeal, but she still thought it sounded like a lonely existence.

Thanks to their conversation, the trip went by faster than she'd expected. She didn't stop to think about the message she and Luke would convey with this cozy riding position until they were almost there.

She'd enjoyed resting her cheek on his warm, strong back, but she'd be wise to stop doing that. "I wonder if I should get off here and walk in."

"Why would you—? Oh, I get it. Wagging tongues.

Do you want to walk in? You're the local girl, so you decide. I told Emmett that we'd ride in together, but he probably won't mention it to anyone."

"He won't have to. If we ride down Main Street like this, I can guarantee we'll be noticed. Comments will be made. I may be the local girl, but you'll probably be hit with some personal questions. Assumptions will be made."

"I figure that'll happen anyway if we spend Fourth of July in town together, so I'm okay with it. Your call, though."

She thought about how he'd jumped right in on her side of the argument regarding the eagles. He'd pulled Emmett in, too, which was a brilliant move and something she might not have thought of.

She hadn't been privy to the semicourtship between Emmett and Pam Mulholland, but Luke, having worked at the ranch for nearly a year, knew all about it. Emmett Sterling was respected in Shoshone. If he supported the eagles, that would go a long way toward helping their cause.

"You know what, Luke? If you don't mind having people assume we're a couple, I don't mind, either."

"Good. That makes life less complicated in some ways. But by saying *people,* are you including your parents?"

"Um…" Their opinion wasn't as easy to ignore as everyone else's. She hesitated.

"You're not so sure about them, are you?"

"No."

"Is your father a shotgun-totin' man?"

That made her laugh. "He owns guns, if that's what you're asking. Most people around here do."

"Yes, but would he use a gun to make sure a fellow did right by his daughter?"

"No, he wouldn't. That's an old-fashioned view and I can't believe he'd ever take that kind of stand. Besides, I'm an adult, and I've been on my own for quite a while. But I'd hate for either my mom or my dad to think poorly of you."

"So?"

"So I'll talk to them and explain the situation." She didn't look forward to that, because her parents were eager for her to find the right guy. If she seemed interested in Luke, they would be, too—as a potential son-in-law. She had to nip that concept in the bud.

"Do you want me there for that conversation?"

"Good heavens, no." But she appreciated the courage it took for him to make the offer. "Thanks for your willingness, but I'll handle it."

As they rode down the street toward her parents' diner, she noticed the festive bunting decorating each storefront. Most shops also proudly displayed a poster advertising Shoshone's Fourth of July celebration and the word *fireworks* took center stage on the poster. She felt a little like the Grinch.

But two vulnerable young eagles might die as a result of those fireworks, and she couldn't believe her friends and family would want those nestlings to pay the price for a human celebration they couldn't escape. If she'd known about this sooner, she might have

avoided a confrontation two days before the scheduled event.

She searched her memory. Had the information been
out there and she'd simply missed it? Maybe. For the
past month she'd been totally engrossed in the eagles,
and more recently she'd been focused on Luke, as well.
She hadn't needed to make trips to town, because he'd
come out every night laden with food. One midweek
trip would have told her what was coming down the
pike.

When she had hiked in more than a week ago, no
one had thought to inform her of the big plans because she hadn't been involved with them. She'd been
gone for so many years, first for college and later for
her job in Florida. She wasn't hooked into the rumor
mill anymore. After this episode, she'd be *fodder* for
the rumor mill.

A few businesses in Shoshone still had hitching
posts in front of them, and the Shoshone Diner was one
of those. It was at the far end of the curbside parking.

Logistics required Naomi to dismount first.

As Luke swung down to stand beside her, he
chuckled. "One disadvantage to riding double is that
I couldn't help you down from the saddle like a true
gentleman."

"People understand that."

"I hope so, because I'm already going to be in trouble with your folks. I don't want them to add a lack of
manners to my other sins."

"I won't let them blame you for anything."

He smiled. "Good luck. I expect they'll blame me

for everything. But don't worry. I can take it." Then he tied Smudge to the rail.

She supposed that he could take it. For his sake, that was a good thing. But in some ways, she wished that someone would finally pierce his coat of armor and touch the man underneath.

13

Before they walked into the diner, Luke took Naomi's laptop out of the saddlebag and handed it to her. "Ready?"

"I am. I wish I'd had time to get some of the pictures printed to pass around, but at least we have something to show."

He took her by the shoulders. "You'll do great." Then he gave her a quick kiss, because the way he saw it, he'd already been labeled as her boyfriend. Might as well take advantage of that label.

"Thanks, Luke." She smiled. "I'm glad you're here."

"Wouldn't miss it." He walked to the door and held it open for her. When they stepped into the crowded diner, all conversation stopped. Luke had never been in that situation before. Unfortunately the belligerent stares from people seated at the various tables eating breakfast weren't directed at him. He would have preferred that, but all the glares were focused on Naomi.

He gave her shoulder a squeeze before they started

over to the spot where two tables had been pushed together. Obviously this was the setting for the pow-wow. Emmett was already there, sitting on the far side on Pam Mulholland's right, and the dandified cowboy Clifford Mason had positioned himself on her left. Tyler Keller, a dark Italian beauty, had taken the opposite side of the table, flanked by Nick and Jack Chance.

Luke wasn't sure why the Chance boys had come, but then he remembered Nick was Pam's nephew. He might have come to give his aunt some moral support. As for Jack...well, Jack didn't like to miss out on anything. The mood at the table was decidedly tense.

A red-haired waitress bustled around the table filling coffee mugs, but nobody had food yet. Edgar Perkins, a tall man who wore glasses and was going bald, stood talking to Jack. His wife, Madge, wasn't in evidence.

Then she came out of the kitchen. A trim blonde with her hair in a ponytail and an apron tied over her jeans and Western shirt, she looked like Naomi probably would in twenty-five years. She walked straight over to her daughter and gave her a hug. "Whatever support you need from us," she said, "you've got it. We don't care about the fireworks." Then she flashed a look at Luke. "Thanks for bringing her in."

"You're welcome, Mrs. Perkins." He didn't read any friendliness in her expression. But he didn't see open hostility, either. She'd apparently decided to stay neutral for now. Luke thought that was eminently fair.

They continued to the table on the far side of the diner. Edgar ended his conversation with Jack and walked over to gather Naomi in his arms. "We're on your side, sweetheart," he murmured.

After he released her, he turned to Luke. "So." He stuck out his hand and Luke shook it. "I know we've met before, Luke, but I can't seem to remember where you're from."

"Most recently from Sacramento, Mr. Perkins. I worked with Nash Bledsoe over there."

"Oh, right. I did hear that." From behind his wire-rimmed glasses, Edgar continued to scrutinize Luke as if wanting to ask more personal questions but hesitating to start in, considering the circumstances. "We'll have to talk later," he said finally.

"I look forward to that." What a whopper that was. Luke doubted that a heart-to-heart with Naomi's dad would go well.

By the time Edgar headed back into the kitchen, Naomi had already taken one of the two remaining chairs, which were at opposite ends of the table. She'd chosen to sit with Emmett on one side of her and Nick Chance on the other.

Luke didn't blame her. He'd gladly take the other end and be the one closest to Clifford Mason, who was dressed in a bloodred shirt with silver piping.

Mason spoke first. "I know who you are, young lady, but I don't believe I know the person you came with. Or why he's here."

Luke's jaw tightened. He didn't care for the tone or the implication. The guy had better watch himself.

"Luke's my research assistant," Naomi said smoothly. "He's here on behalf of the eagles."

Clifford glanced over at Luke, and Luke gave a nod of acknowledgment. He *was* a research assistant…sort of.

Pam Mulholland leaned forward. "Naomi, Emmett has related some very disturbing news regarding our fireworks display. Could you clarify the situation?"

"Certainly." Naomi switched on her laptop. "These pictures were taken yesterday, so the nestlings haven't changed much in twenty-four hours. I wanted you all to see them." She handed the laptop to Emmett. "If you'll pass that around, everyone can get a look at what we need to protect."

Luke had seen the picture. Naomi hadn't had much time to choose one, but she'd found a charmer. The baby eagles looked bright-eyed but vulnerable while their mother perched on the edge of the gigantic nest and gazed down at them. Luke would have liked to say she gazed at them fondly, but an eagle couldn't look fond if it tried. She was imposing, though, and a preview of what those babies could become if allowed to grow up.

Everyone else's food arrived as the laptop circled the table, so there was some juggling involved. Luke didn't have food yet, so he was free to watch all the reactions to the picture.

Emmett chuckled and Pam's expression softened. Mason looked pissed—no surprise there. Jack grinned as if he were personally responsible for those nestlings looking so adorable. Tyler studied them closely, and she too seemed caught by the winsome image.

Nick studied them even more closely than Tyler. "They look healthy to me. Perfectly viable."

Then Luke realized that Nick might be here in his capacity as a vet more than for his aunt Pam. In practical terms, if the nestlings hadn't seemed healthy, then protecting them from fireworks wouldn't have made economic sense.

A waitress came for Naomi's order and she shook her head. Luke caught that and decided he wouldn't get any food, either. He probably couldn't stomach a meal right now anyway. They could eat a late breakfast at the campsite before he went back to work.

Once the laptop had made the rounds, Naomi described the proximity of the nest to the town. "A constant barrage of explosions at close range could easily scare away those parents, leaving the babies to starve. There have been documented cases of that happening, and I can supply that evidence before the end of the day, if you need it."

Mason leaned back in his chair. "Please do. We need a lot more evidence. I find this hard to believe, frankly. Aren't wild creatures supposed to defend their young fiercely? Why abandon them at the first hint of trouble?"

"Not all wild creatures respond the same to a perceived threat," Naomi said. "Some parents defend their young, and others abandon them. Eagles tend to leave."

"You say they *tend* to leave." Mason glared at her. "And you're proposing we cancel a major civic event, one that will bring much-needed revenue into this community, on the *supposition* that two little eagles *might* be harmed. That's a lot of variables. I don't buy the argument."

"I'll have statistics available later today," Naomi said. "Personally, I can't imagine going ahead with a fireworks display if there's even a slight chance that two of our valuable eagles will die as a result."

Mason sent Tyler a challenging glance. "How about you, Mrs. Keller? Are you ready to have all your hard work go down the drain on the slight chance it will cause harm to a couple of eagle chicks?"

"Naturally I would rather we go ahead as planned," Tyler said. "We've put in a lot of work. But this area is dedicated to honoring and protecting its wildlife. To ignore that doesn't feel right."

Jack cleared his throat. "Mr. Mason, have you considered the potential PR nightmare if word gets out that a fireworks display provided by your company caused the death of baby eagles?"

Luke was impressed. Maybe Jack deserved to be in charge of the world after all. The guy had come up with a killer argument.

"Most likely the eagles will be fine," Mason said. "Even if they're not, who will know?"

"Me," Naomi said. "And I will report my findings to Professor Scranton, who's funding this study."

Emmett leaned around Pam, obviously wanting more eye contact with Mason. "I can't say how a college professor might influence the situation, but I can guarantee the influence the Chance family will have. The Last Chance gave permission for the study, and we support Naomi's work. Right, Jack?"

"Yes." Jack's face was like granite. "We certainly do."

Emmett's blue eyes grew very cold. "Just some friendly advice, Mason. When in Jackson Hole, don't mess with the Chances."

Mason laughed. "What do we have here, a gunfight at the O.K. Corral? Give me a break. I have a contract that says I'm supplying fireworks to this event. Cancel the contract and I'll have you all in court."

Pam Mulholland turned to him. "That's enough, Clifford."

He blinked. "Pam? Surely you're not going to let some silly eagles' nest spoil the town's Fourth of July celebration. We're going to put Shoshone on the map, you and I. The townspeople won't be happy about this." He stood and addressed the rest of the diners. "Help me out here, folks. You want your fireworks, right?"

"My kids are counting on it," said one man.

"It'll be good for business," piped up a woman.

Naomi stood, too. "I'm sorry about the last-minute notification, but I've been out at the observation site and just found out about the fireworks. Yes, I'm sure kids will be disappointed, but we're preserving those eagles for their generation. I'll bet if you explained the situation to them, they'd understand. Kids have an affinity for baby creatures."

"So do I." Tyler stood and turned toward the group. "And had I known that fireworks could be a problem for those nesting eagles, I never would have accepted Mr. Mason's offer to provide them."

"I wouldn't have, either." Pam also rose from her

chair. "I own a business, and my guests may be disappointed initially, but not once I explain. Anyone who comes to Shoshone knows it's a haven for wildlife. That's one of the main reasons they visit. Not for fireworks."

Mason glanced at her. "You're missing the point, Pam. There's only a possibility that the eagles will be harmed. To cancel all our careful plans for the *potential* harm to a couple of eagles isn't good business. It's not smart."

Emmett unfolded his lean body from his chair. "Excuse me, Mason." His voice was dangerously low. "But I won't have you taking that tone with the woman I love."

Pam gasped. "Emmett!"

Mason's mouth twisted into a dismissive sneer. "This isn't any of your concern, Sterling. You had your chance. Now it's my turn. Pam and I have a business arrangement. Her emotional response to the eagles is understandable. She's a woman. But once she has a chance to think logically, she'll—"

"Shut up, Mason." Emmett moved Pam gently aside. "Sorry. I know how you hate to make a scene." Then he grabbed Mason by his gaudy red shirt. "I didn't like you when I first laid eyes on you, but I tolerated you because you were a guest in Pam's establishment. Now that you've insulted her by implying that her gender has affected her good judgment, I don't have to tolerate you any longer."

"Pam!" Mason's eyes bulged. "Are you going to let him talk this way?"

"Yes, Clifford, I am. Because you are a horse's ass."

Luke felt like applauding but decided that wasn't appropriate. He did note that both Nick and Jack were smiling.

Emmett continued to hold Mason by his shirtfront. "I'll tell you this once, and once only. Get out of our town. And leave my woman alone." He released his hold, and Mason had to scramble to keep from falling down.

Pam sighed. "Oh, Emmett."

"I'll leave, all right." Mason backed away from the table. "Because you're all *crazy*. Your little town is going to amount to *nothing*. I hope you all rot!" And he ran out of the diner.

Emmett stood there breathing hard, but he didn't seem to know what to do next. Luke considered whether or not to tell him. Emmett had asked him to offer suggestions regarding Pam at any time. This was a critical moment. Even Luke, who avoided entanglements at all costs, recognized it.

He leaned toward Emmett. "Propose, man," he said in an undertone. "Now's the time."

Emmett gulped. Then he squared his shoulders and turned to Pam. "I think you'd better marry me before some other damned fool comes along and thinks you're available, because you're not!"

Pam laughed and threw her arms around his neck. "Finally!" Then, still holding on to a very red Emmett, she glanced at the other customers. "I have witnesses, right? He asked me, and I accepted!"

"We'll back you up, Pam!" shouted someone in the far corner of the room.

"You waited long enough!" cried another.

"This is better than fireworks!" yelled a third person.

Pam gave Emmett a quick kiss before grabbing his hand. "Let's get out of here."

"Hell, yes. This is a nightmare." Blushing furiously, Emmett allowed himself to be led from the diner amid laughter and cheers.

Luke sought Naomi's gaze and they exchanged smiles of triumph. But he detected something else in her expression, an emotion that put him on alert. She seemed…wistful.

He shouldn't be surprised. She wanted a happily-ever-after someday, too. She'd admitted as much. So naturally, when she watched a man declare his love for a woman, she had to start thinking about when that might happen for her.

And here he was, enjoying all the privileges of a potential life mate, without any intention of filling that role. He felt like a poseur, a selfish bastard who was taking the place of someone who could promise to love and cherish her forever.

Then she looked away with an abruptness that made him wonder if she'd been able to guess his thoughts. They'd been together so much lately she might be capable of doing that. He didn't want to hurt her, but he had the horrible suspicion that he wouldn't be able to stop that from happening.

NAOMI TRIED TO talk Luke out of taking her back to the observation site, but he insisted. Arguing with him about it while everyone filed out of the diner wouldn't have been classy, especially because so many people stopped to thank her for protecting the eagles.

So she climbed on behind him as she had before, attracting more attention in the process. She ended up introducing Luke to several people who'd never met him, so getting out of Shoshone took some time.

Finally they reached the outskirts of town. "Thank you for being there," she said.

"I didn't do much. You handled everything beautifully."

"I didn't have to do much, either. Mostly I let Clifford Mason dig himself into a hole. I think if Emmett hadn't grabbed him by the shirt, someone else would have."

"Like one of the Chance brothers?"

"Or others sitting in the diner. Pam is well liked. She runs a quality bed-and-breakfast that's a credit to the town, and she's generous with her money. People don't forget things like someone buying new Christmas decorations for Main Street or having the Shoshone welcome sign repainted. Any man insulting her is creating a problem for himself."

Luke chuckled. "I think he figured that out. His talk about lawsuits faded fast."

"I spoke briefly with Jack, and they've had the guy investigated. He's a shady character, so I think the lawsuit was an empty threat. He might have thought he was dealing with a bunch of hicks who wouldn't know any better."

"Then he didn't do his research."

"Obviously not." She gave in to the temptation to lay her cheek against his back again. But she couldn't shake the nagging feeling that things had changed between them in some subtle way. Emmett's proposal had touched her, and then she'd made the mistake of gazing at Luke. He'd probably thought she was dreaming about the proposal she'd like to receive someday.

Well, she had been, but that didn't mean she expected Luke to do the honors. Luke had said something to Emmett before that proposal, though, and she was curious. "You made a comment to Emmett after Mason left. What was that all about?"

"I told Emmett to propose."

"I wondered. I could sort of read your lips, and then he turned around and did exactly that, as if he might be following orders."

"If he was ever gonna do it, that was the time."

"Oh, Luke." She allowed herself to hug him just a little bit. "Do you realize how long that proposal has been dangling between them, waiting to be said?"

"Awhile, I guess."

"My mother said it's been years. Pam desperately wanted him, but he couldn't get past her wealth, when he doesn't have a whole lot of money. Your nudge was a good thing, Luke."

"You talked to your mom? When?"

"As everyone was leaving, we grabbed a few minutes." She'd noticed Luke having a conversation with

Nick and Jack, so she'd ducked into the kitchen to say goodbye.

"How about your dad? Did you talk to him, too?"

She heard the note of anxiety. "Briefly. He's glad the eagles are safe." In reality, she hadn't invited a deeper discussion with either of her parents. Earlier today she'd thought that speaking to them about Luke was important. Now she wasn't sure.

Luke was pulling away. She couldn't explain how she knew, but she did. To confess everything to her parents made no sense if her special time with Luke was coming to an end soon.

"So you just talked about the eagles."

"Yes. If you're asking whether I explained our situation to them, the answer is no, I didn't."

"Okay." He didn't ask why, and that was telling.

She fell silent for a while and just soaked up being close to him as Smudge walked along the path with a slow and steady gait. She had the distinct feeling she wouldn't ride like this with him again, so she wanted to get all the pleasure from it that she could. He was such an enigma, this man she'd known so intimately yet in some ways knew not at all.

"Tell me something," she said at last. "If you're convinced that marriage ties a person down, why urge Emmett to propose? It seems as if you'd be the least likely one to do that."

"Because I think it would work for him. He's not a traveler. He likes it fine right here, and he's already tied to the ranch. Being tied to Pam, a woman he clearly loves, isn't adding much to his obligations. He was letting her money get in the way, which was only making both of them more miserable."

"I agree, but I'm still surprised you made the suggestion."

He laughed. "You mean because it's none of my business?"

"Well, yeah."

"The night we came home from the Spirits and Spurs, after he'd danced with Pam, he told me that if I ever had another bright idea about how to deal with her, to let him know. So I had a bright idea today, and I let him know."

Naomi smiled and hugged him again. "Then all I can say is well done. Pam looked as if she was lit from within. And I don't suppose she'll ever know that she has you to thank."

"She won't hear it from me, and unless Emmett's completely clueless, he won't tell her. She needs to believe it was Emmett's idea."

"Yes, she does. No woman wants to think a man had to get cues from the sidelines when he was proposing."

"He probably would have thought of it himself anyway."

"I don't know, Luke. He's been shilly-shallying around for a long time, according to my mother. I'm glad you gave him a push."

"Yeah, me, too. They'll be happy."

Luke was such a puzzle to her. He sat on the sidelines—matchmaking, babysitting other people's children, having brief affairs with women—but he never really got in the game. He saw amazing places, but he made no permanent connections with them. He truly was a drifter in the old-fashioned sense of the word.

And yet she felt the tug of strong emotion whenever they had... She couldn't even say they just had sex, because it was more than that. At least it was for her. In her biased opinion, they made love.

They might not be *in* love, but they made love. They cherished each other in a way that lifted the act above the simple joining of bodies for mutual satisfaction. At least she thought so.

But maybe he didn't think so. No, he did. She'd seen it in his eyes. And after watching that special tenderness in his expression while he loved her, she wondered if he'd be able to walk away without regret this time around.

"You're awfully quiet back there."

"It's peaceful riding along like this." She wasn't about to admit that she'd been wondering whether he would miss her when he left.

"So are you hungry?"

She lifted her head in surprise. "Yes, come to think of it, I am. I wasn't the least bit hungry when we were at the diner, but now I'm starving."

"Me, too. So here's my plan. When we get back to the campsite, we cook up some breakfast."

"I'd like that." She wanted to recapture the cozy atmosphere they'd created when it was just the two of them. He didn't seem threatened by that. But when they were in town, surrounded by people who had conventional expectations of what their relationship might become, that was when she felt him starting to leave her.

"You know what else we need?"

"What?" She hoped he was thinking the same thing she was.

"A victory romp."

"Is that what I think it is?"

"Well, you do it naked."

She hugged him tight. "Then it's exactly what I think it is. And yes, we need that." She had him back again. Maybe not for long, but for now.

14

In town Luke had begun to feel trapped, especially after seeing Naomi's reaction to Emmett's proposal, but the closer they came to Naomi's campsite, the more he relaxed. And the fact was, he loved being with her. It wasn't only the sex, which was fantastic. He just plain liked her.

He'd never met a woman who was so at one with nature that she could completely abandon makeup, skinny-dip in a cold stream and walk around a camp without underwear. He admired her devotion to the eagles and her ability to be alone for long periods of time without freaking out.

As if all that weren't enough, she could imitate Tarzan's yell perfectly. He almost asked her to do it again on the way home, because he had loved hearing it. But Smudge might not appreciate that, so he didn't ask.

Then he realized how he had just thought of the campsite: *home*. He had pictured where they were heading, and in his head he'd called it *home*. Oh, boy. That wasn't good.

Maybe leaving the campsite together and returning together had created that sense of coming home. If so, he wished he hadn't brought up the idea of going into town for the Fourth of July celebration. He'd invited her to the celebration, so he should escort her there, right? That would set up another leaving-and-coming-back scenario, as if they lived together.

He'd never lived with a woman, because he'd wanted to avoid that feeling of domesticity, which could lead to marriage, which could lead to the end of life as he knew it. Apparently he'd kidded himself that coming out to her campsite night after night was different from moving in with someone, because, hey, it was camping. She didn't exactly *live* here. Except she did.

And in a sense, so did he. He'd left his sleeping bag, a personal possession, with her. No, it wasn't the same as if he'd brought clothes and toiletries and his collection of DVDs. But it was more than he'd ever done with any woman.

He had a problem, but it wasn't too late to fix it. It wouldn't be too late until he was so firmly tied down that he didn't feel he could leave. He wasn't to that point yet, so he needed to start planning his exit strategy.

He couldn't leave now, with the Fourth of July celebration coming up, especially since he'd asked her to go with him. But afterward he might just as well go. Better to leave while she was still involved with the eagles so she'd have something to take her mind off him. Maybe she wouldn't miss him all that much, but he had a feeling she might.

He had a feeling he was going to miss her, too, and that was all the more reason to get out of town. Staying would only make things worse for both of them. And summer was a good time to travel and find another great place.

Riding into camp after making that decision was a bittersweet experience, because he really had grown to love spending his nights beside her campfire and in her little tent. He and Naomi had fallen into a routine that seemed to suit them both. That also should have been a warning to him. He was becoming entirely too comfortable here.

"I need to check the eagles before we eat," she said as she dismounted.

"You bet." He gave her a smile and swung down from the saddle. "I'll start the fire and get things going." Then he kissed her, because very soon he wouldn't be able to do that anymore. She tasted so damned good.

He forced himself to end the kiss, resisting the temptation to drag her into the tent for the activity he'd planned for after breakfast. He had to keep his eye on the time. Emmett had given him the morning off, not the whole day.

"Get going, lady." He turned her around and gave her a little push. "Before I forget the plan."

"Okay." She blew him a kiss and jogged down the path to the observation platform.

Fool that he was, he watched her go and felt a lump

form in his throat. Wow, he was in way more trouble than he'd thought if he could get choked up over this woman. Clearing his throat, he turned back to Smudge.

The paint stared at him with his warm brown eyes, and Luke realized he was also going to miss the horse, for God's sake. He'd let himself get attached there, too. For a guy who was supposed to have his head screwed on straight, he seemed to have it right up his own butt.

"Come on, Smudge." He led the paint over to his little plot of grass and dropped the reins to the ground. No point in unsaddling him when Luke would be leaving in an hour or so.

First he unzipped the tent flap and double-checked that there was a condom under his sleeping bag. Soon after that, he had the fire going, coffee brewing and bacon sizzling in a pan. That was the other thing. He'd done more cooking this week than he had in the previous six months. At the Last Chance bunkhouse, the cowhands took turns cooking breakfast and dinner. Lunch took place in the ranch house's big dining room, a tradition that allowed the Chances and their hands to mingle and exchange ranch-related information.

Luke had rotated through bunkhouse kitchen duty with the rest of the guys, but he hadn't put much thought into it. Nothing like the planning he'd done for breakfast and dinner with Naomi. He couldn't complain, though, because he'd enjoyed making meals the old-fashioned way, over a campfire. Naomi's gratitude didn't hurt the situation, either. She'd acted as if he were doing her some huge favor when in reality he was simply having fun.

By the time she returned to the campsite, he'd put the finishing touches on the scrambled eggs by adding a little salsa. Naomi liked them that way. He'd piled a few fresh blueberries on each of their tin plates because he knew she liked those, too.

She walked into camp carrying the stool. That had become part of the routine, too. Now he took the flat rock and she took the stool.

"This looks so good!" She gave him a quick kiss on the cheek as she accepted her full plate and a tin mug of coffee. "I was way too nervous to eat anything at the diner, but that's over and we won!"

"We did." He touched his coffee mug to hers. "Or rather, you did. Congratulations."

"No, *we* did. If you hadn't mentioned the fireworks, I hate to think what would have happened." She sat down on the stool.

"That was dumb luck. I didn't know it was important." He settled on the flat rock. "Jack mentioned the fireworks to me the day he came out with little Archie. I didn't have sense enough to realize you needed to know about them." He dug into his food, which tasted better this morning than it ever had, probably because he knew he might only have one more breakfast with her.

"You couldn't have known the fireworks were an issue unless you'd spent a lot of time studying eagles like I have. Clifford Mason is a jerk, but his attitude is common. Why would anyone assume eagles would abandon their young if they felt threatened?"

"I didn't. I had no idea how fragile the situation is.

They build this big-ass nest, and they're such fierce-looking birds. You'd think they'd hold their ground. Or their sticks."

"Well, they might." She gazed at him. "I screwed up part of the celebration without knowing for sure that they'd abandon the nest. I do feel sad about that."

"Don't." He looked into those blue eyes and wondered how in hell he was going to leave. "Mason wasn't exactly a crook, but he wasn't totally legit, either. No telling whether he would have substituted crummy fireworks for the ones he promised."

"True."

"And you gave Emmett a reason to object to the guy on grounds other than jealousy, which led to a proposal. I'll bet Pam is happy about the way things turned out, and knowing her, she'll figure out a way to make up for the lack of fireworks."

"You're right." She smiled at him. "I thought of something else, too. We know about this nest, but there could be others within range of those fireworks. More than two eagle babies might have been at risk."

"There you go." Luke polished off the last of his breakfast. "You might have saved a bunch of little eagles. The Shoshone eagle population may boom as a result of this day." He sipped his coffee and in the process managed to check out her plate to see if she'd finished her meal.

He'd thought he'd been sneaky about it, but her laughter told him different.

She stood and dumped her plate in the kettle of water they always had available for that purpose. Another routine. They'd created them so effortlessly together that he hadn't seen the net of routine and connection being woven until today.

"Yes, I'm finished," she said. "I take it you're ready to move on to our victory romp?"

"I'm more than ready." He got to his feet and dropped his dishes in the same kettle. He needed to hold her, yearned for it in a way that was also a warning. Sure, he was eager for the sex. But he wanted the closeness more.

She pulled her shirt over her head and tossed it on the stool. "Whoops. Hiking boots." She sat down to take them off.

"Let me." Crossing to her, he dropped to his knees.

"I can do it." She grabbed his hands. "Unlacing and removing hiking boots has got to be the least sexy part of undressing a woman."

"Unless it's me taking off your hiking boots." He shoved his hat back and looked at her. "Let me."

Her voice softened. "All right."

As he leaned over her and untied the laces, his hat kept bumping her knees. Finally he took it off and handed it to her. "Hold this a minute."

"I'll just wear it."

"Be my guest." He glanced up at her just to check it out. He was curious, nothing more. She'd never worn his hat and he wondered how she'd look in it.

Then he went very still. He couldn't explain why, but seeing her looking so cute while wearing his hat flooded his chest with warmth. He had a pretty good idea what that indicated, and it wasn't good news.

"Do I look bad?"

"No." He swallowed. "You look so good it hurts." He didn't know why he'd said that and wasn't even sure he knew what he'd meant by it.

But she seemed to. Cupping his face in both hands, she gazed into his eyes. "I know."

That blasted lump formed in his throat again and he broke eye contact. "Let's get these things off." He'd intended to do it slow and sexy, but that didn't matter anymore. He needed her too much to play seductive games.

Pulling the boots off, he tossed them aside. Then he scooped her up and carried her over to the tent as he kissed everywhere he could reach. They'd established another routine—taking off their clothes before they climbed into the small tent—but he ignored it. He didn't have time for that, either.

Their entrance into the tent wasn't elegant, but he got her in there without landing on top of her and squashing her flat. Then he continued kissing her as he worked her out of her bra, shorts and panties.

There. At last he had her the way he wanted her— all creamy, soft skin exposed; all fascinating dips and crevices, mounds and deliciously slippery places available to his hands, lips and tongue. He covered every last inch of her as she moaned and thrashed beneath him.

He made her come twice and would have gone for a third time, but she clutched his head and dragged him up her moist body until she could look into his eyes.

"You," she said, panting. *"Inside me. Now."*

He was still completely dressed, but a man didn't ignore a command like that. He got his pants pulled down and a condom on in less than twenty seconds. It was as close to "now" as he could manage.

He'd prepared his way quite well. One quick thrust and he was right where she'd asked him to be. Bracing himself above her, he looked into her blue eyes. "Like that?"

"Exactly like that." Breathing hard, she pulled at his shirt and the snaps gave way, popping wildly. "This was supposed to be a two-person victory romp, remember?" She stroked his damp chest.

He rocked forward, cinching them up even tighter. "I've been fully present."

She slid her hands upward and cupped his face again as she'd done before. Her gaze probed his as she drew in a ragged breath. "What's going on with you, Luke?"

He was afraid she saw too much, saw through him. "I just…needed to…touch you, kiss you…" He couldn't explain.

"You're leaving, aren't you?"

His pulse leaped. "I always said that I—"

"Yes, I know. But you're going soon. I can feel it."

No, he couldn't tell her like this. Not when he'd plunged into her warmth, when she'd opened herself to him with such trust. Agony sliced through him and he groaned. "Naomi."

"It's okay, Luke." She laid her finger over his lips. "Don't say anything. Just make love to me."

There was that damned lump again, blocking his throat. He couldn't have spoken if he'd wanted to. So he spoke with his body, instead. Holding her gaze, he began to move.

With deep, steady strokes he told her how much she meant to him. He told her that there would never be another woman like her in his life. She would hold a unique and precious place in his memory. And if he were a different sort of man, he would stay and fulfill all those dreams she kept close to her heart.

Her body responded, as it always had. He doubted she could help it, just as he couldn't. They communicated on a different level when they were locked together like this.

And so she arched beneath him as an orgasm claimed her, but this time she didn't cry out. Instead her eyes welled with tears.

The sight of those tears filled him with despair, but he was no less driven by the pulsing of their bodies than she was. He came because he had no choice. Her response demanded his. His surrender was not much of a gift, but it was all he had to offer.

When the shudders lessened, he lowered his head and kissed away her tears. He'd vowed that he wouldn't hurt her, and he'd failed to keep that vow. He might never forgive himself for that.

He left the tent quietly. She'd told him not to say anything—there wasn't anything he *could* say. He'd intended to stay long enough to be her date for the Fourth of July celebration, but he hadn't even been able to accomplish that. She'd guessed his decision, and he'd never lied to her. He wouldn't lie to her now.

Putting himself to rights didn't take very long. His

hat had fallen to the ground when he'd swept her up in his arms. He picked it up, dusted it off and put it on.

Sometime soon he'd give the hat away and get a new one. He'd never be able to wear it after today, transfixed as he'd been by the sight of her wearing his hat. He'd leave it for her, but she wouldn't want the thing, either. She'd have reminders enough without something like that hanging around.

Thank God he hadn't unsaddled Smudge. He climbed aboard the patient horse and rode away from the campsite. About ten minutes into the ride he remembered his sleeping bag, which was still in her tent. Screw it. He'd never be able to use that sleeping bag without thinking of her, either. She'd probably burn the damned thing, and he couldn't blame her if she did.

The ride back to the ranch seemed to take an eternity, and at every turn in the path, he asked himself if he should ride back and talk to her, comfort her in some way. But what good would that do? The only thing that would comfort her was if he stayed, if he changed his entire way of life and became what she needed.

He knew how that could turn out—attending cookouts with stodgy neighbors instead of heading off on adventures to parts unknown. Maybe his father had done him a favor by rejecting his invitation this morning. Luke had probably needed a reminder as to why he'd chosen this life.

When he reached the ranch at last, he felt as if he'd been traveling for days. The place looked familiar, but strange, too, as if he'd already left it in his mind. No one was around, and he realized they were all up at the main dining room for lunch.

Just as well. He gazed at the huge log house that the Chances had built. The grandfather, Archie, had started with a boxy two-story structure. Over the years, two-story wings had been added on either side, canted out like arms ready to welcome visitors.

Or ensnare them. This Chance family was about as tied to one place as anybody could be. Luke had found a few travelers on the fringes of the clan. Tyler Keller used to be an activities director for a cruise line. She and her husband, Alex, traveled quite a bit because Tyler loved doing that.

And to Luke's surprise, he'd found a couple of fellow travelers in Mary Lou Simms, the ranch cook, and her new husband, a ranch hand who went by the single name of Watkins. Gabe Chance competed in cutting-horse events, so he occasionally went out of state for that.

But other than those folks, nobody at the Last Chance had a burning desire to explore the world. They were content to enjoy what they had right here. Luke agreed it was beautiful, but for him it wouldn't be enough. There were too many other beautiful places, and he couldn't ignore the urge to see them.

Because of that, he'd quite likely broken Naomi's heart, and once Emmett and Jack found out, Luke wouldn't be welcome here anymore. With that concept in mind, he quickly took care of Smudge and turned the brown-and-white paint into the pasture. He didn't linger over the horse any more than he'd lingered in

Naomi's camp. Prolonging the moment of separation was never a good idea.

Packing up the belongings he'd stashed in the bunkhouse took no time at all. He had everything loaded in his old truck before the hands started trickling back from lunch. He accepted their good-natured ribbing about his absence this morning as he waited for Emmett to show up.

Eventually he realized Emmett wasn't coming. When he asked someone, he discovered that Jack had given Emmett the rest of the day off so that he could spend it with Pam. They had a wedding to plan.

That meant Luke would have to deal with Jack. Emmett might have been easier to break the news to, especially after Luke had helped the foreman out during the scene at the diner. However, as a result of that event, Emmett wasn't here.

With a resigned sigh, Luke headed up to the main house. He wasn't sure whether to hope that Jack was or wasn't in. If he was out, Luke could talk to Sarah, who held equal power with her sons in anything to do with the ranch.

But Jack had been the one who'd taken Nash's recommendation and hired Luke. If Emmett, Luke's immediate boss, wasn't available, then Jack was the next logical person to accept his resignation. He was also the one most likely to want to clean Luke's clock for hurting Naomi.

Luke mounted the porch steps. He had to admit the long porch, which stretched the entire front of the house, was a good feature. Rocking chairs lined the porch, but Luke had never sat in one. He supposed it would be a nice enough experience.

Sarah came to the door. Tall and silver-haired, with the regal bearing she'd inherited from her New York model mother, she commanded respect with a glance. "Hi, Luke." She opened the door with a friendly smile and stood back so he could walk in. "I'll bet Naomi's a happy lady now that Clifford Mason has left town and taken his fireworks with him."

"She's very glad about that." Luke could say that much without stretching the truth. "Is Jack around?"

"He's in the office. You know your way." She gestured to an open door on the far right side of the living room area. "Go on in. He's handling some paperwork, so he'll welcome an interruption."

"Thanks." Luke touched the brim of his hat before proceeding through the living room. The massive stone fireplace and leather furniture gave the room an air of permanence. No doubt about it, this house was an anchor—that could be seen as a plus or a minus, depending on a person's viewpoint.

Jack sat behind a battered wooden desk that Luke had heard once belonged to his dad. His hat rested brim up on the edge of the desk, and his hair looked as if he'd been running his fingers through it.

He glanced up when Luke came through the door. "Hi. Have a seat."

Luke decided it was best to do that, so he lowered himself into one of the wooden armchairs positioned in front of the desk. He'd sat in this same chair when he'd interviewed for the job last October.

Jack made some notes on a pad of paper before tossing down the pen. He studied Luke for a moment. "I heard what you said to Emmett at the diner. That was good. I appreciate you stepping in."

"He'd mentioned something a few days ago about being open to suggestions when it came to Pam. So I made one."

"We're all in your debt. The guy needed a push in the right direction. Thanks to Mason and you, he got it."

"I hope they'll be very happy."

"Oh, they will. My mom is one of Pam's best friends, and she'll see to it that everything goes smooth as silk." He leaned back in his chair. "But that's not what you came here to talk about, is it?"

"No." Luke cleared his throat. "I hate to do this on short notice, but—"

"Damn it. You're cutting out, aren't you?"

"Yeah. I'm sorry, Jack. I know you could use more notice than this, but it's time. If you don't want to give me a recommendation as a result, I understand."

"You're a good hand and you'll be missed, but we can manage until we find somebody. I'll give you a recommendation. But all that's beside the point. Does Naomi know you're leaving?"

"Yes."

"How's she taking it?"

Luke just looked at him. There was no good answer to that question.

Jack steepled his fingers. "I see."

"You and Emmett were right all along. I shouldn't

have… Well, she would have been better off if I'd left her alone. But I didn't, so the best I can do now is let her start forgetting about me."

"There's a lot of truth to that. If you're not sticking around, then you might as well leave." Jack stood and held out his hand. "When you get settled, send me your address and I'll mail that recommendation."

"Thanks, Jack." Luke shook his hand. "I thought you'd be ready to take me apart."

Jack's eyes glittered. "I haven't talked to Naomi yet. If she's a basket case, I reserve the right to do just that."

"Then maybe I won't send you my new address." Luke touched the brim of his hat. "Thanks for taking me on last year."

"Yeah, well, I'll say one thing for you."

"What's that?"

"You're one hell of a roper. Now get out of here and don't come back unless you have a ring in your pocket for our mutual friend."

"That's not going to happen. I'm not the marrying kind."

"Then I guess we won't be seeing you around these parts."

"No, you won't. Goodbye, Jack." Luke walked out of the office, through the living room and out to the porch. There he paused to catch his breath. Sometimes leaving a place was easy, and sometimes it was hard. Until now it hadn't been gut-wrenching.

But standing around wouldn't make it easier. Hurrying down the porch steps, he climbed into his truck, closed the door and started the engine. As he drove away, he glanced in the rearview mirror. Yep, that house was definitely an anchor.

15

Naomi had zero interest in hiking into town for the Fourth of July celebration, but she'd promised her folks she'd be there. Besides, if she hid out in the woods, everyone would assume that she was devastated by Luke's departure.

Jack had come out to check on her and had confirmed that Luke was gone. She'd put on a brave face then, and she'd do the same today. Even though she ached as she'd never ached before, she'd keep that fact to herself.

She'd hiked in very early so she'd be able to shower and change clothes at her parents' house before the parade. She walked in through the kitchen door, as she usually did, and came face-to-face with the one person in the world who could always see right through her.

Her mother stood in front of the stove frying up eggs and bacon, but she put down her spatula and turned when Naomi came in.

"Hi, Mom!" Naomi pasted on the biggest, fakest smile she could manage. "Did you make enough for me?"

"Of course." Her gaze met Naomi's.

And just like that, the charade was over. Naomi's resolve to be tough was no match for the warmth and understanding in her mother's blue eyes. Leaving the backpack by the kitchen table, Naomi went straight into those comforting arms.

"I'm so sorry." Madge Perkins was a small woman, but she had the biggest hug in the world. "I know you cared for him."

Naomi sniffed. "Yeah, I did. But he wasn't right for me."

"No, he wasn't."

"And I'm well rid of him." Naomi didn't believe that, but maybe saying it would start the healing process.

"You most certainly are. You can do much better than him."

"Right." Naomi gave her a quick squeeze and stepped back. "He's last week's news. We have a Fourth of July to celebrate."

Her mom's smile was filled with pride and encouragement. "That's my girl."

"Is everybody okay with not having fireworks?" That was the other reason Naomi hadn't been eager to show up today, in case some folks continued to be upset.

"Absolutely. Pam's subsidizing Lucy over at Lickity Split so Lucy can give away free ice cream all day."

"Oh, good." Some of the tension eased from her

shoulders. "Everyone will love that, and Lucy gets the revenue instead of that creep Mason. I—"

"Hey, has my favorite wildlife expert arrived?" Her father walked into the kitchen wearing a Western shirt with pinstripes of red, white and blue.

"Hey, Dad!" She gave him a hug. "Love the shirt. You're stylin'."

He glanced down at his shirt and smoothed the front pockets. "Just so I don't look too much like that Mason fellow."

"Not a chance. This is way too subtle to be in the Clifford Mason category."

"Well, good, because your mother bought it at some fancy-dancy store in Jackson and wouldn't tell me what she paid for it, which means it's probably the most expensive shirt I've ever owned."

Naomi gave him a thumbs-up. "It looks great on you."

"Thanks." He peered at her through his wire-rimmed glasses. "Are you okay?"

"I'm fine, Dad." It was a forgivable lie. She wasn't going to tell him how much she hurt, because there wasn't a damned thing he could do about it. "All set for the watermelon-eating contest?"

"You know it." He seemed relieved at the change of subject. The contest was the Shoshone Diner's traditional contribution to the festivities, and her father loved it. So did the participants. The Chance boys had multiple wins to their credit.

"I think you should enter this year," her father said.

"Nope." They'd had this discussion in years past,

so she was surprised he'd bring it up again. "Not when you're the judge. It would look bad if I won, and I might. I'm pretty good at eating watermelon."

"So I'll get somebody else to judge."

Both Naomi and her mother stared at him. He'd never offered to give up his cherished role as judge. Then Naomi figured out why he would now.

He wanted her to be so immersed in the activities that she forgot her broken heart. In his mind, a watermelon-eating contest served that purpose like no other. That was both touching and incredibly cute.

Resting her hands on his shoulders, she stood on tiptoes to kiss his cheek. "That's the sweetest thing you've ever offered to do for me. But I'm not robbing you of something you love so much."

"Seriously, I could get Ronald Hutchinson to judge. He'd do it. He knows my watermelon-eating contest is way more fun than his sack race."

"No, Dad." She patted his shoulder. "But if you want to partner up with me and reclaim our title in the sack race, I'm your girl."

"Hey, that sounds great." He grinned at her. "It's good to have you back, kiddo, at least for the summer."

"I love it here. It's my favorite place in the world." The words created an unwelcome reminder of Luke and their recent discussion about favorite places. As she thought about that discussion, her feelings toward him began to shift. Slowly, the deep sorrow that had threatened to drown her began to evaporate in the heat of her growing anger.

Two days ago Luke had claimed that the Jackson

Hole area ranked as one of his favorite places. Yet he'd left. Working at the Last Chance was a dream job for any cowboy, and through Nash, Luke had been lucky enough to land a position there. Yet he'd left.

More than once he'd said how much he enjoyed being with her. Even without the words, she'd known just by looking in his eyes. He had strong feelings for her, perhaps stronger than he'd had for any other woman. Yet he'd left.

Well, good riddance! If he couldn't appreciate that both she and this place were wonderful beyond belief, she was glad that he was gone. He was officially an idiot.

LUKE WAS A certified moron. He surveyed a panorama of snowy peaks, shadowed valleys and a denim-blue lake in the fading light of evening. He'd always wanted to visit Glacier National Park but had never made it. So here he was atop Apgar Mountain with a bucket list–worthy view of the park—its North Fork, to be more precise—but could he enjoy the splendor of the scenery? No, he could not. Oh, he'd tried. He'd told himself that this landscape was spectacular, that it rivaled the Grand Tetons. Even better, he was once more on his own, free to stay here until he grew tired of the place or until his money ran out, whichever came first.

He'd been in the park for three days, hoping that he'd snap out of the funk he was in and get back to his normal travel routine. He'd hiked the impressive trails, all the while congratulating himself on what a great life he had because he was so free of entanglements.

So far he hadn't been able to swallow a single line of that bullshit. In his heart, a place he'd avoided going for years, he knew why he wasn't having any fun. Naomi wasn't here.

And she needed to be here, damn it. There were critters *everywhere*. Deer, bears, raccoons, wolves, birds galore—specifically eagles. Oh, my God, she'd go nuts over the eagles.

Finally, here on this mountain, he faced facts. When he'd met Naomi Perkins, his life had changed forever, and it was never changing back. He'd only put about five hundred miles between them, but even five thousand wouldn't matter. He'd still feel that magnetic pull, still see her face in his dreams, still…love her.

Because he was a moron, he hadn't figured out that he loved her until now, after he'd broken her heart. He knew for a fact he'd smashed it to smithereens. He'd seen it in her eyes when she realized he'd moved up his departure by a couple of months.

He'd seen the misery he was inflicting and he'd left anyway. If he were in her shoes, he wouldn't take him back under any circumstances. A guy who could walk away from Naomi Perkins didn't deserve her.

That was the crux of his dilemma. He didn't deserve her, but if he couldn't have her, he was doomed. She'd shown him that being connected to someone didn't mean being tied down if she was the right someone.

Naomi was the right someone for him. So basically he had no choice but to head back to Shoshone and grovel. It might not work. But it was the only strategy that he'd come up with.

Shoshone was approximately eight hours away, which meant he could be there before dawn the next day. He decided to start driving and hope that a more imaginative approach to winning her back would come to him before he arrived. It didn't. After hours behind the wheel, he still saw groveling as his only option.

He couldn't expect her to respond to that right away, so he could be in for days, weeks, maybe even months of waiting her out and hoping she'd forgive him. That meant he needed his job back, but he'd have to grovel to get that, too. Jack was none too pleased with him.

Then he remembered Jack's final words. Luke wasn't supposed to show his face without a ring in his pocket. Okay, so he'd stop in Jackson and buy a ring. He pulled into town long before the shops opened, so he cruised around the square, located a jewelry store and parked his truck.

He must have dozed off, because the next thing he knew, the sun was out and the square was no longer silent. Shops were open, cars drove past and people walked along the sidewalk in front of him.

He got a better look at the jewelry store and decided it looked pricey. Well, okay. He had quite a bit of room on his credit card.

The brunette woman behind the counter gave him a friendly smile, but he didn't miss the quick once-over that told him he probably looked like hell. That made sense. He hadn't shaved since yesterday morning or changed his clothes—he wore rumpled jeans, hiking boots and a faded plaid shirt.

"May I help you with something?" she asked in a pleasant voice.

"I need a ring." Then he realized that wasn't specific enough. The glass cases glittered with what might be hundreds of rings. "An engagement ring."

Her gaze softened. "Are you interested in a diamond ring or something less traditional?"

"I don't know." He thought about it. "A diamond," he said finally. He figured he couldn't go wrong with a diamond, but if he ventured into that "something less traditional" area, he could get into trouble fast.

"That narrows it down a little. We have solitaires, of course, and then there are the clusters, with a central diamond in the center and smaller ones arranged around it."

"A solitaire. She's not a fussy woman. She'd appreciate simplicity."

"Then let me show you a few and see what you think she might like." The saleswoman laid a couple of trays on top of the case.

The diamonds sparkled under the high-intensity lamps and Luke blinked. He should have had a cup of coffee before coming in here. And maybe some food. He couldn't remember the last time he'd eaten.

"Do you think she'd prefer an emerald cut? Or perhaps a pear shape. Then we have—"

"That one." Luke pointed to a ring with a roundish stone that seemed to shoot fire. "She'd like that."

"You have very good taste." The woman plucked the ring from its slot and held it out.

Luke took the ring between his thumb and forefinger, and his heart began to pound. He was buying a diamond engagement ring. He also was buying it for someone who might never accept it. "Do you have a return policy?"

"Of course." She didn't hesitate. "The choice of a ring is so personal. Couples often come in together. After all, this is something she plans to wear for the rest of her life. You want her to love it."

Luke began to hyperventilate. Until now he'd only thought about getting back in Naomi's good graces. Jack had been the one who'd said a ring was necessary to the process.

"Do you want to think about this?" The woman sounded sympathetic.

"Just for a minute."

"Take your time."

Luke stared at the ring. Soft music played in the background. He hadn't been aware of it before now, but as he listened, he wondered what kind of tunes Naomi liked. Country-and-western probably, but what else?

Did she like to sing? He knew she could yell like Tarzan, but he didn't know if she could sing. Or whistle. He yearned to know every detail about her, big or small.

That would take a long time…years. A lifetime. And when he thought of growing old with Naomi, warmth filled him.

He cleared his throat. "I'll take it."

"All right."

He started to hand it back, and that was the moment he noticed the little white tag fluttering from the band.

He glanced at it and gasped. He'd had no idea. Not a clue. But why would he? He'd never shopped for a diamond ring before.

"Is there a problem?"

He took a shaky breath and handed over the ring. "No. This is the one I want." Reaching in his back pocket, he pulled out his wallet and extracted his credit card. He needed to get his old job back. Immediately.

NAOMI PULLED AN energy drink out of her cooler and unscrewed the cap. The eagle parents had finished feeding their growing nestlings, so she could take a lunch break. Moving the camp stool next to the tree trunk, she sat down and leaned back while she sipped her drink.

Moments like this were dangerous because it was way too easy to think about Luke. If she'd known he'd leave so abruptly, she might not have allowed him to invade her observation post, because now it was filled with vivid memories she couldn't seem to stamp out.

But she hadn't known, and to be fair, neither had he. He hadn't realized their relationship would get so hot so fast. She'd scared him to death, no doubt. She closed her eyes and gave in to the temptation to remember.

She replayed it all—the first day when she'd spilled this green drink all over him, the day when he'd galloped toward her like a Hollywood cowboy and all the days and nights after that. She thought about the way he'd complained about the cold water in the stream, and how much fun they'd had cooking meals together, and sharing the tent, and...

The sound of hoofbeats roused her. Damn. Both Jack and Emmett were worried about her. It would be just like one of them to come up with an excuse to ride out here and see how she was doing.

Sighing, she stood and walked over to the edge of the platform. And there, about a hundred yards away and riding toward her at a brisk trot, was none other than Luke Griffin. Setting down her energy drink, she rubbed her eyes and looked again.

Nope, still seemed like him. Same horse, same broad shoulders and narrow hips. Same tilt of the hat and casual grace in the saddle.

Her heart began to race, and she forced herself to take deep, calming breaths. If he thought he could come out here and make up with her, then leave again when he felt threatened by his feelings, he could forget that noise. She didn't plan to go through that ever again.

Frankly, she was disappointed in whoever had loaned him Smudge after the way he'd left everybody in the lurch, including her. Was he that charming? Could he really make them forget his past sins? Well, *she* wasn't going to forget.

She didn't care if he'd wangled his old job back and planned to spend a few more months here after all. He wouldn't get the time of day from her. She almost wished she had a shotgun so she could point it at him and tell him to back off. Bear spray wouldn't have the same dramatic effect; besides, she'd left it in her tent.

Because she didn't have a shotgun, and because she had no intention of letting him come up on this platform, she ran over to the ladder and pulled the whole thing up. Now she was protected from whatever scheme he had in mind.

Then she returned to the front of the platform and waited, arms crossed. She could tell when he spotted her there, because he slowed Smudge to a walk. About ten yards out, he stopped completely and gazed up at her.

She wished he didn't look so damned gorgeous with his manly physique and freshly shaven jaw. He always had looked like a fantasy and probably always would. That was what he did—traveled around making women salivate. He was very good at it.

She waited for him to speak first. He knew why he was here. She could only suspect, and what she suspected didn't bode well for him.

He rested his hands on the saddle horn. "You seem upset."

"I'm not upset. Just determined."

"About what?"

"That you aren't going to run me around the mulberry bush the way you did before. I've pulled up the ladder."

The irritating man actually laughed. "Good for you. I deserve that, and more."

"What are you doing here?"

"I came to see you."

"That's obvious. But if you came here expecting me to be the same willing wench you left, think again, cowboy."

"I came expecting exactly what I've found, a woman who's furious with me because I ran out on her."

She shrugged and tried for nonchalance. "Don't flatter yourself. I'm over you."

He sighed. "I can't say the same."

"Sweet-talk me all you want. It won't do you a damned bit of good."

Pushing his hat back with his thumb, he gazed up at her. "I haven't treated you the way you should be treated, Naomi, and I readily admit that. But have I ever lied to you?"

She thought about it. No, he hadn't lied. Instead he'd been brutally honest about his drifter lifestyle. She'd known he would leave. She just hadn't expected him to leave so soon.

"No," she said. "I suppose you haven't lied to me."

"In that case, you should be able to take me at my word."

She wasn't sure where this was leading. "I suppose."

"Then here's the deal. I've discovered that life without you is not much fun."

"What?" She stared at him, not comprehending.

"I came back because for the first time I can remember, I'd rather be with someone, with *you,* than be alone. After the way I've treated you, I don't deserve to be welcomed with open arms. But I...I'm planning to stick around and see if I can change that."

She had difficulty forming words. She wondered if this was some sort of hallucination brought about by too many days out here by herself. But the horse snorted and pawed the ground. Birds chirped in the trees, and not far away the stream gurgled over a bed of rocks.

Then a shadow passed overhead, and she looked up as the female eagle returned to the nest. This was real. She was standing on the platform and Luke had just claimed that he preferred being with her to traveling through life alone.

"She's returned to the nest," he said. "So you need to go back to work. I'll leave you to it. See you around." He wheeled Smudge around and started back the way he'd come.

"Wait! You can't make a speech like that and then leave!"

He turned Smudge to face her. "I figure you need time to think about what I've said. I don't want to push you."

Her breath caught. "Push me toward what?"

"Me," he said simply. "I've hurt you. I can't expect to come waltzing back into your life and have you believe that I want to stay."

"Do you?" She began to tremble.

"Yes. I do. Here in this place, but if you have to move for your job, then I'll go there. I want to be with you, Naomi."

As she held his gaze, Smudge walked steadily closer. She gulped in air. "What are you saying, Luke?"

"I love you."

She thought her heart would beat itself right out of her chest. "You...love me?"

"With all my heart. My wild, crazy heart."

"I'll let down the ladder." She whirled around but her foot caught something solid. In that moment she knew what it was. "Watch out!"

But it was too late.

"Aah, shit!" Luke sputtered and cursed.

"I'm coming down!" She dropped the ladder and scrambled to the bottom as fast as she could. By the time she rounded the tree, Luke had dismounted. He'd taken off his hat and was wiping his dripping face with his sleeve.

"I'm so sorry." She ran over to him. "I'm so, so—oof!" The breath left her lungs as he grabbed her and pulled her hard against his chest.

"Don't be sorry." He held her tight. "Just kiss me."

So she did, until both of them were so sticky that she wondered if they'd be glued together for eternity. And that was fine with her.

At last he got them unstuck so he could look into her eyes. "Naomi, I've been a complete fool, but I'll make it up to you, I swear."

She smiled. "You've made a good start."

"I have more than a start. I have a ring in my pocket. I know that was extremely optimistic of me, but I—"

"A *ring?*" She stared at him. "Who are you and what have you done with Luke Griffin?"

His dark eyes clouded. "You don't want it."

"I didn't say that. It's just…you're not the type—and you said…"

"I wasn't the type. But that's because I believed a bunch of junk that wasn't true, and I'd never met you. I'm probably doing this wrong, and I can't get the ring out now because I'm all sticky, but…will you marry me?"

She looked into his eyes and realized he actually

wasn't sure how she'd answer. That was touching. "I'd love to."

The air whooshed out of his lungs. "Oh, thank God. I thought this would take weeks."

"You were prepared to wait weeks for my answer?" She was stunned.

"I was prepared to wait for as long as I had to, but I was determined to make you love me."

"And here I've loved you all along. But I couldn't let you know until…"

"Until I stopped being a damned fool?"

She laughed. "Exactly." And she pulled him into another very sticky kiss. It was the sort of kiss that could last a long, long time…maybe even an eternity.

Epilogue

MICHAEL JAMES HARTFORD was screwed. Putting down his cell phone, he wandered to the window and stared out at the green swath of Central Park five stories below. As Western writer Jim Ford, he'd portrayed himself as a genuine, gold-plated cowboy. His readers believed it, his agent believed it and his editor believed it.

For some reason they'd never questioned why a real cowboy would choose to live in New York City. His books were so authentic that everyone had assumed he owned a secluded ranch where he spent a great deal of time. They'd assumed he could ride and rope and shoot.

He'd let them make those assumptions because the truth—that he belonged to a wealthy New York family and had never been on a horse in his life—wouldn't sell books. Although he didn't need the money from those sales, he needed the satisfaction of being read. He also needed the joy of living in the fantasy world he created every time he wrote a new story.

He'd been caught in a web of his own making. The

books had done so well that he'd become a minor ce-
lebrity, which had aroused the interest of his publisher's PR department. They wanted to push him to the
next level.

As part of that campaign, they'd scheduled a video
of Jim Ford doing all those cowboy things he wrote
about. All those things he couldn't do. And they wanted
to shoot the video at the end of the month.

Michael had to think of a solution, and he had to
think fast. He could fake an injury, but that seemed
like the cowardly way out. He'd always meant to visit
a dude ranch and learn some of those skills, but dead-
lines had kept him busy.

The dude ranch still seemed like a good solution,
but he'd become so well-known that he couldn't book
a week just anywhere and admit that he didn't know
how to ride. He required discretion. As he racked his
brain for people who might have a ranching connection, he remembered Bethany Grace.

He'd appeared with the motivational author on Opal
Knightly's talk show a few months ago, and while
they'd hung out in the greenroom, she'd mentioned
growing up in Jackson Hole, Wyoming. They'd hit it
off so well that they'd exchanged phone numbers. On
impulse he scrolled through his contact list and dialed
her number.

She answered on the second ring. "Jim! Wow, it's
lucky that you called! I'm going to deactivate this number next week."

"How come?" Last he'd heard, she was on the fast

track to becoming a permanent guest on Opal's show, which was a terrific career move.

"I'm getting married and moving to Jackson Hole."

"No kidding? Hey, congratulations. But what about—?"

"I know. Opal's show. I'm not cut out for that, and thanks to various circumstances, I've realized it. So what's up with you? Your books are doing great!"

"They are, and that's why I called you. My publisher wants a video of me being a cowboy, and my skills are…rusty." He winced at that whopper. "I wondered if you know anyone out in Wyoming who would help me on the QT."

"I sure do. I'd work with you myself, but between the televised wedding and leaving on a honeymoon afterward, I'm going crazy."

Michael chuckled. "Opal's making you get hitched on TV?"

"She is, but I can't begrudge her that after the gracious way she's let me out of my contractual obligations. Listen, call Jack Chance at the Last Chance Ranch. Tell him what you need and that I recommended him for the job."

"And he'll be discreet?"

"I guarantee it. The Chance family is a classy bunch. You'll love them all. Let me give you the number."

Michael grabbed a notepad and jotted down Jack Chance's contact info. "Thanks, Bethany. This could save my life—my writing life, at least."

"I just thought of something, though. Jack's mother, Sarah, is getting married soon. Call right away so you can sneak in there and get the job done before the festivities start."

"Don't worry. I'll call the minute I hang up. But back to your marriage. Who's the lucky guy?"

"Nash Bledsoe. He owns a ranch that borders the Last Chance."

Michael heard the love vibrating in her voice as she said that. "He must be special."

"He is."

"I wish you the best, Bethany. I'll admit I'm a little envious." Living a double life, he was caught between two realities—his family's glittery world of charity balls and gallery openings, and the writing community he loved but didn't allow himself to embrace. He didn't belong in either group, which meant he was sometimes lonely.

"You sound a little wistful, Jim. Is everything okay?"

"Sure. I'm fine."

"Well, the Last Chance will do you good. Take it from me, that place has a way of reordering your priorities."

"Right now my priority is getting comfortable on a horse."

Bethany laughed. "I thought I knew what I wanted when I went out there, too. And now look at me. My life is taking off in a totally different direction."

"I doubt that will happen. In fact, I don't want that to happen."

"If you say so. But let's keep in touch. I'm curious to know how this turns out."

"I'll fill you in when you get back from your honeymoon."

"You'd better, or I'll have to rely on Jack's version."

"Then I'll definitely be in touch. And congratulations." As Michael disconnected the call and keyed in Jack Chance's number, he remembered what she'd said about how the Jackson Hole area had affected her. But he didn't need his priorities rearranged. All he needed was riding lessons.

* * * * *

A sneaky peek at next month…

Blaze.

SCORCHING HOT, SEXY READS

My wish list for next month's titles…

In stores from 19th July 2013:

❏ Half-Hitched – Isabel Sharpe

& The Heart Won't Lie – Vicki Lewis Thompson

❏ From This Moment On – Debbi Rawlins

& Taking Him Down – Meg Maguire

Available at WHSmith, Tesco, Asda, Eason, Amazon and Apple

Just can't wait?

Special Offers

Every month we put together collections and longer reads written by your favourite authors.

Here are some of next month's highlights— and don't miss our fabulous discount online!

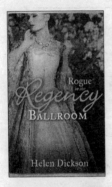

On sale 2nd August

On sale 2nd August

On sale 19th July

Save 20%
on all Special Releases

Find out more at
www.millsandboon.co.uk/specialreleases

Visit us Online

0813/ST/MB428

The World of Mills & Boon®

There's a Mills & Boon® series that's perfect for you. We publish ten series and, with new titles every month, you never have to wait long for your favourite to come along.

Blaze.®
Scorching hot, sexy reads
4 new stories every month

By Request
Relive the romance with the best of the best
9 new stories every month

Cherish™
Romance to melt the heart every time
12 new stories every month

Desire™
Passionate and dramatic love stories
8 new stories every month